WHERE IS SATHARIEL?

Jinnaoth took another step toward the child-devil, his gold eyes flashing with hunger as the old question left his lips, his heart beating with faint hope that he might yet receive an answer.

He is beyond you. Better to seek a cleaner death with me.
I will merely break you, but him, the angel, he shall devour you.

The devil's shoulders popped and shifted beneath a rubbery sheet of skin, tearing in places to reveal black scales and bony barbs, muscles rippling with a power that the illusion of the child could no longer contain.

Then bring him! Have him kill me, rip me apart, devour me,
but bring him to me!

Jinnaoth rushed forward and gripped the devil by the throat, hauling him into the air and slamming him against a fragile table covered in a bloodstained cloth, a meager altar to a devil-god.

Fool. The angel is merely a means to an end . . . the First Flensing
will come . . . no matter how you struggle against it.
And this wretched city will know that my lord is coming.

Asmodeus is coming.

ED GREENWOOD

PRESENTS

WATERDEEP

FORGOTTEN REALMS

ED GREENWOOD
PRESENTS
WATERDEEP

CIRCLE OF SKULLS

JAMES P. DAVIS

Ed Greenwood Presents Waterdeep

CIRCLE OF SKULLS

©2010 Wizards of the Coast LLC

Cover art by: Android Jones
First Printing: May 2010

9 8 7 6 5 4 3 2 1

ISBN: 978-0-7869-5485-8
620-25380000-001-EN

U.S., CANADA,
ASIA, PACIFIC, & LATIN AMERICA
Wizards of the Coast LLC
P.O. Box 707
Renton, WA 98057-0707
+1-800-324-6496

EUROPEAN HEADQUARTERS
Hasbro UK Ltd
Caswell Way
Newport, Gwent NP9 0YH
GREAT BRITAIN
Save this address for your records.

Visit our web site at www.wizards.com

DEDICATION

Once again, for my Megan.
Your love and your smile are the best parts of my every day.

ACKNOWLEDGMENTS

Many thanks to my editor Susan Morris for keeping me on
course as I walked through the streets of Sea Ward.

And to Ed Greenwood for the city that lives and breathes in his
imagination, for the startling detail, and for showing me the
cracks in the cobblestones, the shadows in the back alleys,
and the best ways to evade the Watch when one is in a hurry
and has a deadline to catch.

Welcome to Faerûn, a land of magic and intrigue, brutal violence and divine compassion, where gods have ascended and died, and mighty heroes have risen to fight terrifying monsters. Here, millennia of warfare and conquest have shaped dozens of unique cultures, raised and leveled shining kingdoms and tyrannical empires alike, and left long forgotten, horror-infested ruins in their wake.

A LAND OF MAGIC

When the goddess of magic was murdered, a magical plague of blue fire—the Spellplague—swept across the face of Faerûn, killing some, mutilating many, and imbuing a rare few with amazing supernatural abilities. The Spellplague forever changed the nature of magic itself, and seeded the land with hidden wonders and bloodcurdling monstrosities.

A LAND OF DARKNESS

The threats Faerûn faces are legion. Armies of undead mass in Thay under the brilliant but mad lich king Szass Tam. Treacherous dark elves plot in the Underdark in the service of their cruel and fickle goddess, Lolth. The Abolethic Sovereignty, a terrifying hive of inhuman slave masters, floats above the Sea of Fallen Stars, spreading chaos and destruction. And the Empire of Netheril, armed with magic of unimaginable power, prowls Faerûn in flying fortresses, sowing discord to their own incalculable ends.

A LAND OF HEROES

But Faerûn is not without hope. Heroes have emerged to fight the growing tide of darkness. Battle-scarred rangers bring their notched blades to bear against marauding hordes of orcs. Lowly street rats match wits with demons for the fate of cities. Inscrutable tiefling warlocks unite with fierce elf warriors to rain fire and steel upon monstrous enemies. And valiant servants of merciful gods forever struggle against the darkness.

A LAND OF
UNTOLD ADVENTURE

INTRODUCTION

Waterdeep is truly a city of a thousand tales. A thousand new ones each month, that is. Far more than even a room-full of new novels can hope to tell.

Some of them are small and sordid, some of them are airy and frivolous—and some of them *matter*.

Not to mention those that can send those proverbial chills up and down your spine.

Like this one, for instance.

Circle of Skulls is in some ways the darkest offering in this series of standalone novels set in post-Spellplague Waterdeep.

It reminds every reader that there are indeed dark things lurking down those dangerous-looking alleys, and even darker things behind the closed doors and elegantly draped windows of noble mansions and grand academies.

Not to mention that any crossroads trading city, Waterdeep included, will be home—if only temporarily—to all manner of monsters.

Monsters who have lives, too. That is, they don't just wait in a room for their chance to mindlessly gnaw on the first adventurer to blunder through its doors. They have dreams and goals . . . and revenges, too.

Revenges that can drive them on through several lifetimes, or one long and terrible one, to wind up in Waterdeep awaiting their chance to pounce.

Coming together, with all their quirks and grudges and hungers, in a confrontation that you can watch unfold.

"You are there" writing, folk used to call it. Peering over the shoulders and past the elbows of entities who'd tear you apart in a moment if you were really present, the magic of a very capable storyteller letting you float unseen in the heart of all the unfolding unpleasantness.

Oh, sorry. Please replace "unpleasantness" with the more palatable label "adventure."

That's what we've got here—a dark, terrible, splendid adventure.

From crooked lawkeepers and corrupt nobles to murderous predators who lurk among humans to feed upon them and worse.

Worse how? Oh, no, you have to read the adventure to find that out; the fun's in the journey, not the final, city-shaking destination.

Yes, there *is* a city-shaking confrontation at the end. Real "good-versus-evil, but is good still good after all these years of the hunt and the strife and the madness?" stuff. While some of Waterdeep cowers and trembles, and more of Waterdeep goes blithely about their business, never knowing the doom that threatens . . .

Ahem. Mustn't get ahead of myself, carried away by my own glee over this striking story, with its superb depictions of non-human—or no longer human—Waterdhavians and visitors.

So, now, refurling my cape and wrapping myself in a shred of dignity thereby, hear this: Earlier novels in this series have shown us several seamy sides of Waterdeep. And that's the beauty of a diverse handful of scribes and a broad, deeply detailed, *living* city; we can see the City of Splendors from many sides, all of them true and valid and yet very different, and every one of them entertaining. But *Circle of Skulls* shows us that there are shadows and dangers and then there are deeper, darker perils and glooms within them, that threaten everyone and everything from the highest spires and turrets to the lowest sewers and cellars.

I do believe it also shows us what true heroism is, and how hard even small triumphs can be to wrest from life.

If you're (wisely) reading this before plunging into the narrative itself, I envy you the first thrills of descending into the darkness.

I'll be settling in to re-read it a dozen times or more. On top of the half-dozen times I've already read it.

Yet don't take false comfort from that. When you're in the thick of it, alongside Jinnaoth, no one has your back.

Ed Greenwood
May 2010

PROLOGUE

Dason stood at the corner of Diamond Street, knees slightly bent, one arm held at his back, the other resting lightly upon the pommel of a well-notched rapier. He scanned the wide avenue, the very picture of a steady soldier at the forefront of danger. At length, he peered over his shoulder with a grin, raising a sly eyebrow to the young woman waiting several paces behind him. She returned his grin from over crossed arms.

A slight breeze sent snow swirling through the streets, gusting through the night's shadows and dancing in the yellow-orange glow of the street lamps. The days were getting colder, and many inhabitants of Sea Ward had already become scarce after sundown, leaving the chillier evenings to those with the hot blood of youth.

Clearing his throat, Dason straightened and waved the woman forward with a dramatic bow. He didn't have to see her face to know she would be smiling broadly and stifling a laugh at his heroic antics, placing a graceful hand over her mouth to hide the expression lest she encourage him to greater shows of bravado.

"Milady," he intoned deeply as she passed, unfolding his tall frame. "The way is clear."

"Indeed, young Master Dason," she replied with no small amount of humor as an older woman waddled toward them, burdened by a heavy sack thrown over her shoulder. "Clear as market at highsun, would you say?"

Dason smiled sheepishly as they turned up the street, making way for the old woman who seemed in a bit of a hurry, unlike him and Alma, who'd made the journey from North Ward last far longer than perhaps it should have. He brushed a few flakes of snow from his shoulder and fell into step beside Alma, straightening his back and attempting to appear more important next to his noble charge. Though he had dressed well for the evening, he was no match for the Lady Marson, a vision in silver-embroidered white, a soft cloak of fine fur resting across her shoulders and folded with her arms against the evening's chill.

"I daresay that I judged the way clear of *danger*, fair lady, not inhabitation," he said, smiling and nodding to the old woman as she passed, though his smile faded a bit at the manic look in the woman's eye, quick breaths steaming from beneath her piled-high scarf. Narrowing his eyes, he studied the lane a bit more closely, careful not to alarm Alma unnecessarily, but his jesting caution put aside for the moment.

"Ah, I see, Master Dason," she said and patted his hand gently, her touch nearly derailing his attempt to find what might have alarmed the old woman so. Little shocks traveled up his arm from where Alma's fingertips had brushed against his wrist. He nodded sagely, speechless as he focused and listened for any disturbance. Though Sea Ward was relatively quiet at night and usually well patrolled by the Watch, he hadn't seen a single patrol since they'd crossed into the ward three blocks back. Alma had attended a gathering at the Raventree Manor and Dason insisted she have an escort to and from her outings among the other nobles and wealthy families of Waterdeep. Even on nights she spent alone, he would engineer some excuse to come calling.

Alma never questioned his devotion to the task, enjoying the company of a childhood friend, though he was neither a noble nor wealthy by any stretch of the imagination. As they'd matured such differences rarely mattered, the fine line between friendship and something more blurring each time they were together. She had sought out his company more frequently in the past few tendays, the unexplained disappearance of her parents leaving her alone in a large home with naught but the remaining servants to see to her well-being.

"Shall we take the long way 'round again tonight?" Alma asked, breaking his concentration, but not before he spotted what appeared to be movement in the shadows of the next intersection, clinging close to the high walls.

"Not tonight, I'm afraid. I . . ." Dason paused, still not wishing to alarm her and unsure of his own growing sense of unease. "I must be awake early on the morrow. Your uncle has promised me a tour of the Westwall prior to my training with the Watch."

"Ah, it would be just like Allek to ruin a perfectly good evening," she replied.

"Mayhap, but he worries about you, as do I. Has there been any news of your parents?" Dason asked, spying glittering pinpoints of light among the trees near Ivory Street ahead. Swiftly he turned Alma's elbow to the western side of the street and cast a quick glance south, still hoping to catch sight of Watch lanterns approaching or passing through. Though he was handy with a blade, there was no reason to risk a confrontation if help were nearby.

"Allek doesn't say much really: 'They're doing all they can.' 'I'll be the first to know.' But I can't help wondering if he knows more, if perhaps he's protecting me from something?" Alma's voice lowered in thought. Dason knew the subject was difficult for her, but she'd not spoken at all the first few days after they'd gone missing, terrified of what might have happened.

Dason eyed the well-lit entrance to an alley along the south wall of the Saerfynn Manor and directed them toward it. The figures among the shadows of the east wall were unmoving but surely watching as he and Alma evaded them. He gripped his sword tightly, leading Alma ahead of him and wishing he had eyes in the back of his head.

"Rorden Allek is a keen-minded man. If anyone can find your parents, it's him," Dason replied and glanced back to see if they'd been followed. The alley closed around them and the evening's mist seemed thicker between one street lamp and the next. Dason held Alma's elbow a little tighter, drawing her close and no longer hiding his concern as he made out the shape of a figure leaning against a darkened wall.

"I know this place, Dason. I've heard stories—" Alma stopped, noticing the figure as well and gasping as it shuffled from its place and into a patch of light. Unwashed hair hung in thin strands around the man's unshaven face, wild, bright eyes peering at them from beneath a bushy brow. Dason angled them away from the wretch, the stench of the transient's torn, unwashed robes particularly sharp and pungent. One unsteady step set him leaning closer toward them, and Dason braced himself, drawing half a hand of his blade from its sheath.

"Move along, saer," he said forcefully, affecting his best version of the typical Watch order to such interlopers in the wealthier neighborhoods of the city.

The man straightened and paused, raising an eyebrow at the couple then wordlessly scanning the area with a confused expression. Dason noted a strange symbol, faded and worn, on the man's left sleeve.

"Aye, young master," the man replied in a whispering, wheezing voice with a feral smile of yellowed teeth, his pale eyes flashing dully as he bent forward in a graceful, mocking bow. "I cry your pardon."

Dason relaxed only when the strange man had continued on several paces behind them, though he kept a white-knuckled grip on his rapier as he recognized the alley. Its far end opened onto Flint Street and the House of Wonder, a place of wizards that few save other magic-users ever visited, and in alley along its side, beneath the house's looming towers, ghosts were said to dwell.

" 'Tis Pharra's Alley," Alma said breathlessly, her eyes wide with excitement.

"I am sorry," Dason said, "perhaps we should not have come this way."

"Nonsense," Alma replied, pulling him toward the House of Wonder with a mischievous grin. "No harm done and perhaps we shall spy a ghost or two."

"Forgive me if I'm not as eager to—" Dason cast one more look over his shoulder, just to be sure the transient had moved on, and his breath caught in his throat. A dozen similar figures stood at the alley's edge. He drew his sword and hurried Alma along.

"Dason! What is the matter?" she asked.

High above them the towers of the House of Wonder stood silent sentinel in the mist, dark windows eyeing them coldly as they hurried along. Past the tall, iron gates of the house courtyard, Dason could make out the glow of Flint Street.

"No time for ghosts," he said, pushing at her arm, though she resisted slightly and tried to turn around. She caught sight of the strangers and quickly fell in step with him. The figures had formed a line across the mouth of the alley, their glittering eyes visible through the mist and snow. "Mayhap they're harmless, but I'm of no mind to take a chance."

"Too late," Alma said quietly and stopped short.

"What—?" Dason began, but a shooting pain stabbed through his temples and silenced him, dropping him to one knee and leaving him gasping for air. Confused, eyes watering, he raised his head as an ethereal green glow rose from the cobbles. Deep, hollow voices chanted at the edges of a ghostly circle that grew brighter by the moment. The icy breeze grew colder still.

Alma dug her fingers into Dason's arm, trying desperately to lift him from the ground but unable to tear her eyes away from the circle of green mist as floating skulls, wreathed in emerald flames, coalesced in the mysterious vortex.

"Dason? Dason!" she repeated as the skulls rose to roughly the height of a man's shoulders, bobbing gently in the air and swaying as they chanted harsh syllables that droned and echoed through the alley. Dason could not answer her, could barely stand as the pain in his temples came again, increasing in intensity until he thought his head would burst. For half a breath, he thought he might wake up, sweating in the midst of some horrible nightmare, but the ground felt too real beneath his hands, his sword too cold in his fingers, Alma's fear reaching out to him like a tangible force.

Panicked, he tried to stand, stumbling against Alma as the nine hollow-eyed skulls regarded him blankly, grinning liplessly at his plight.

"Go!" he managed through clenched teeth. "Run!"

He turned away from the skulls, looking over Alma's shoulders to the line of figures blocking their path. His breath caught in his throat as another figure descended from above on graceful, black wings, trailing long wisps of smoky shadow. Black eyes that should have been hidden by the mist and distance stared him down with a soul-chilling power that turned his blood to ice.

"What's wrong with your eyes?" Alma cried, backing away from him.

Dason's legs trembled and he tore his gaze away from the winged figure, his mind reeling with pain as he saw the fear in Alma's eyes, saw his own eyes reflected in hers: twin orbs of glowing green flame. His arms spasmed and fresh pain flowered in his head as he raised his sword arm, unable to stop the ascent of his blade, as though it had become a sudden traitor to his will. Darkness gathered at the edges of his vision, and he felt as though he were falling. Hollow voices filled his thoughts, mumbling and muttering as exhaustion flooded his senses.

"Dason, what's wrong? What are you doing?" Alma asked, her voice barely reaching him through the pain and the dark. Steel flashed before his eyes and he fell into a deep peace, where he dreamed of skulls and the black eyes of a dark angel.

>———W———<

Rough hands shook Dason awake where he lay frozen on the damp cobbles of the alley. Blearily he opened his eyes and squinted into the green light of a Watch patrol lantern. Relief flooded through him at the sight of it, and he tried unsuccessfully to sit forward, but a strong hand held him down and rolled him onto his side.

Several figures were in the alley, slowly pacing and pointing at something he could not see. Dason blinked fiercely to make out details as the officers talked among themselves in hushed voices, glancing at him with hard looks, some shaking their heads.

A white shoe lay nearby, modestly heeled and embroidered in silver, a dark splash of rust staining the toe. Fear shot through him like a lightning bolt. Beyond the shoe a bare foot pointed up, a graceful leg covered in white cloth, also embroidered and also stained in splashes of reddish brown. A knot formed in his throat, painful and thick, choking off his breath as he tried to sit up. The effort afforded him only a brief glance of crimson and white, of sightless eyes turned toward the sky and a pale hand sliced from palm to wrist.

"Hold still, boy!" a voice said. Rough hands jerked his wrists behind him and tied them together with a short length of coarse rope.

"No," he croaked, his thoughts racing as more uniformed men approached. One held a bloody rapier in his gloved hand.

"Murder weapon here, sir," the man said, stepping past Dason with the blade.

"No," Dason said louder, his throat aching with the effort. His hands felt sticky, his breath tasted of blood and bile as he wheeled wild eyes from one officer to the next.

"Quiet, boy!" The rope around his wrists cinched tight. Hands grabbed his shoulders and pulled him to his feet. He struggled away from them, trying to see Alma, hoping to see some spark in her eye, some look telling him that all would be fine, that she would call upon him in the morning. He would forgo his visit with her uncle Allek to spend the day with her, Westwall be damned.

He saw naught in her gaze but death and more blood than any man should see upon the face of the woman he loved. The unseen hands pulled him away, shook him hard. Other hands grabbed his elbows, hauling him to his feet.

"No!"

ONE

J innaoth made slow progress through the noisy streets and crowded merchant stalls of Trades Ward. Myriad scents wafted from food-laden carts, open tavern doors, and alleys piled high with refuse. The smell of hundreds of souls, bartering, shouting, singing, and fighting, filled the air with an unmistakable aroma of city life, yet even among so many, Jinnaoth stood apart and watched. He kept his hood low and his eyes forward, a long greatcoat held tightly against the chill in the air.

Children ran through the streets, jostling their way through the crowds, playing and staring at newcomers in strange clothes or at mercenaries' swords with wide-eyed awe. Hands were slapped away from tantalizing merchandise as one group of children was scattered by a shouting merchant. A thin, dark-haired boy chanced a look over his shoulder, laughing at the red-faced man as he ran headlong into Jinnaoth. The boy stumbled backward and started to run the other way when he looked up and froze in Jinnaoth's gaze. He stammered something unintelligible and shook his head weakly, caught in the flashing glitter of two golden eyes.

Without a word, the boy ran off, pointing and whispering conspiratorially to his friends as they ducked into the opening of a nearby alley, poking their heads out to stare as Jinnaoth turned. He was accustomed to such reactions, earning far more than his fair share of curious onlookers whenever an errant breeze blew his hood back, exposing deep black hair and pale skin adorned with dark and sinuous patterns. Most mistook the symbols that crawled across his neck and left cheek as tattoos, symbolic markers of one faith or another.

He never bothered to correct them.

It had been some time since he'd braved the busy city streets during the day, preferring to conduct his business under cover of night. He squinted up at the pale disk of the sun and leaned into the corner of a large tavern hall, shielding himself against a cold breeze as he waited, watching the crowd for familiar faces. Most took no note of him at all, just another stranger on an avenue filled with strangers, but some paused to look his way, fixing him with dark stares before melting back into the press of bodies, sensing his otherworldly nature even as they hid their own behind masks and illusions. At one time he'd have felt duty-bound to expose and challenge such beasts in hiding, but times had changed—he had changed—and after several millennia, he had learned the wisdom of patience and the advantage of being discreet.

Bells struck the hour, their ringing echoing across the city, declaring it one bell past highsun, and as if on cue, he stood straight and spied Maranyuss making her way toward him, a splash of striking green upon the day's otherwise gray palette. Tall, with chestnut hair that she wore bound in a long braid, Mara's soft features and shapely hips garnered her many a lingering stare. Her green dress, of fine make and decorated in lacy gold, clung to her like a living thing as she passed men who would elbow their companions and nod approvingly, though few ever approached her. Fewer still were even able to ask her name or speak when they did work up the courage to face her dark eyes and withering stare.

Jinnaoth could not help but smile at such displays, wondering if there ever existed the man who might win her attention—and sorely pitying the poor soul if he did exist. Mara scowled disapprovingly at him as she crossed the street, as if reading his thoughts. He quickly hid his grin. He'd grown comfortable with Mara over the years, but he was ever cautious not to offend her too seriously, and he suspected she was already in foul mood enough for one bright day.

"I do not like this, Jinn," she said, little storms brewing in her eyes. "Too many people, too much light."

"It's just one day," he replied and stepped into the street, setting a steady pace toward the far end of the markets. "Let's make it a good one."

"And your source, she is reliable?" Mara asked as she stared down a small man hawking his wares. He nervously turned away, choosing instead to bother a well-armored dwarf.

"As much as any," Jinn answered and nodded toward a large dirt circle of gathered carts, scents of meat pies and livestock emanating from the area. "She was a servant girl, recently in the employ of the order. An employment that we played a part in ending, but enough gold can do wonders for hard feelings."

In truth the girl took some time in being convinced. Her fear of the Vigilant Order was paralyzing, but her growing fear of Jinnaoth swiftly overcame her hesitancy. She'd been drawn in by the order's wealth and promises, a typical tactic that made most forgo any idea of questioning the source of such assurances. Behind smiles, coin, and lavish mansions, they hid their ancient truths, tapping into the essence of the Hells themselves for the sake of a world made over in the dark vision of an ambitious god. One servant girl had stood quaking in Jinn's golden gaze, imagining the horrors she would endure for betraying her cruel masters and comparing it against an ancient rage that had forced the order into hiding.

Jinnaoth passed through the crowded circle, gesturing to a darkened alley just beyond the shouting and haggling. He and Mara slipped into the garbage-strewn alley, scattering rats before them, to find a plain wooden door. A small, crimson symbol had been painted in the top left-hand corner of the door, a mark for the number nine in an infernal language that few would recognize or even notice, a mark signifying a house devoted to Asmodeus.

"Shall we proceed as usual?" Mara asked, a crimson light flashing in her dark eyes.

"No, I'll go in first," he said, pulling back his hood.

"They will not tell you what you want to know," Mara said. "You know this?"

"I do," Jinn answered. "It doesn't change anything."

"It never does," she grumbled and kept watch as he opened the door and stepped into the dark hallway beyond it.

Jinn stood still for a moment, closing his eyes and breathing in the dusty, stale air of the old house. Mara's words echoed in his mind, as they always did when he faced the order, each time reminded of their devotion, of their willingness to die rather than betray their faith in Asmodeus. And each time Jinn gave them the chance, asking his questions even as they spit on his offers of mercy.

Sighing, he opened his eyes and strode down the hall, searching the first room to the left for a mildewed carpet, which he kicked aside, revealing a trapdoor with a rusted iron latch. As he opened the door and stared down the dark stairway beneath, Jinn felt his blood rise, an ancient sense of duty pounding in his heart as he slowly descended, following the flickering light of a candle from somewhere below.

Drifting through his thoughts were images of other temples, of high, stone columns and bloody altars, of marble floors and hellish statues. Each grander than the last, and all palaces compared to the kingdom of dust and rot beneath Trades Ward. The memories were fleeting and without context, like intricate paintings rather than anything he'd actually experienced, the legacy of a thousand lives swirling like dreams through his soul.

Voices echoed from the bottom of the stairs, leading him to a heavy curtain through which shafts of yellow light breached moth-eaten holes. Peering through the holes, he saw several figures on their knees in a circular chamber, each in dark robes, their left sleeves marked with the crimson symbol of nine. Before them, his head bowed in prayer, stood a small child, a boy of seven or eight years with orange-red hair and pale, freckled skin, also wearing the garb of the Vigilant Order. Such corruption of the young was not uncommon, especially among the faithful of Asmodeus, the devil-god bearing a particular taste for the souls of the innocent. The boy's head rose, his blue eyes bright as he seemed for a moment about to speak, then he gasped quietly as Jinn parted the curtains and stared down the small congregation.

The kneeling figures turned in confusion, looking nervously from Jinn to the child, most edging away from the intruder and eyeing the visible hilt of his sword. The boy merely tilted his head slightly, smirking beneath half-lidded, knowing eyes.

"Have you come seeking forgiveness, old one?" the child asked sweetly, raising his hands in an attempt to calm his fearful gathering.

Jinn ignored the boy, staring into the eyes of the robed figures, mostly human, men and women seeking some way out of their miserable lives and finding themselves in places darker than they'd ever imagined. They looked back into his golden eyes only briefly, seeing in them a sorrowful judgment that made them turn away, ashamed. Jinn pitied them, but only to a degree, knowing the precipice they stood upon all too well and fully aware of the choices that had brought them so low. None of them could truly know the nature, much less the name of the god they would serve, but there was an inkling, always a hint of darkness in the Vigilant Order, despite its beguiling promises.

He sensed no evil in them, no malice or cruelty, only selfishness and greed, smoldering desires stoked to flames by desperate, silver-tongued devils scraping the dregs of society to maintain their Vigilant Order.

He reached down, grasping the collar of a middle-aged man who cowered and raised his hands before his face, whimpering as Jinn leaned close.

"Leave this place and never return," he said loud enough for all to hear as he hurled the man through the curtain and stood aside as others slowly rose from their knees, unsure of what was happening. "Or stay and learn the full measure of the mistakes you have made."

The child-priest scowled angrily as the congregation rose and quickly shuffled through the curtains, none meeting Jinnaoth's gaze as they passed. A few cast aside their dirty robes, throwing them to the ground as they ran up the basement stairs. As the last footsteps faded away through the house above, Jinn faced the child and placed a hand upon his blade.

"They will return; they always do," the boy said, crossing his arms. "You accomplish nothing by coming here."

"Perhaps you are right," Jinn replied, lowering his eyes menacingly, "but they shall not find you again to mislead them."

"You would kill a child?" the boy asked. "Is this what you are reduced to?"

"No, I'll not stain my hands with the blood of a child," Jinn said, stepping forward and drawing blade enough to shine in the candlelight, casting the reflection upon the child's face. "However, this child I see before me I recall being fished from a well more than a tenday ago, quite dead if memory serves."

The boy's blue eyes darkened to smoky pools of deep black. His arms lowered slowly, fingers curling like claws as a very unchildlike growl escaped his snarling lips.

Jinn smiled at the display, always enjoying the illusion's fall, when the predator was exposed and the acts of innocence fell away. Even among the order's mortal priests, he had found the beasts hiding beneath their robes, their true faces, full of vitriol and cowardice. It was that alone he had come to see, the last vestige of the Vigilant Order, a small but integral cult in the worship of Asmodeus, laid bare in the last pitiful temple to which they could lay claim.

"You play with fire, half-blood," the boy said, his voice deep and thunderous. "You have no idea—"

"I know to whom I speak," Jinn said, kneeling down and matching the fiend's rage-filled stare, then adding, *Belsharoth.*"

The child-devil drew away, narrowing his eyes suspiciously at the sound of his name and looking intently into the golden gaze of Jinn.

"Irramael?" the boy asked hesitantly. "I watched you die."

"Aye, as have many others," Jinn said and stood, drawing his sword, an ancient blade stolen from the order years earlier. It pleased him to use the cult's tools against them. "And that name died over seven hundred years ago."

"Myth Drannor." Belsharoth smiled, small teeth protruding at odd angles as longer, sharper ones grew in to replace them. "Those were good days."

"And long behind you, it seems," Jinn added, gesturing to the cold, dusty chamber as he raised his blade threateningly. "Shall we continue?"

"I see little need," the devil said with a sigh, the skin along the right side of his face drooping, slowly sliding away. "You know I will not betray him."

"I must ask. Tradition demands it, especially now." Jinn took another step toward the devil, gold eyes flashing with hunger as the old question came to his lips, heart beating with faint hope that he might yet receive an answer. "Where is Sathariel?"

"He is beyond you. Better to seek a cleaner death with me," Belsharoth answered, his shoulders popping and shifting beneath a rubbery sheet of skin, tearing in places to reveal black scales and bony barbs, muscles rippling with a power that the illusion of the child could no longer contain. "I will merely break you, but him, the angel, he shall devour you."

Jinnaoth rushed forward and gripped the devil by the throat, hauling him into the air and slamming him against a fragile table covered in a bloodstained cloth, a meager altar to Asmodeus. Flesh squirmed and changed beneath his fingers as Belsharoth laughed, a hollow chuckle that shook his small frame.

"Then bring him!" Jinn shouted, struggling to hold the devil emerging from the child. "Have him kill me, rip me apart, devour me, but bring him to me!"

A small, freckled hand rose at Belsharoth's side, shaking and twisting unnaturally as if serpents coiled beneath his skin in place of muscle or bone. Daggerlike claws erupted from the fingertips, followed by a long, powerful arm that struck Jinn across the chest. He flew backward and slammed against the back wall of the chamber, though he swiftly rolled to a defensive crouch, ready for the devil to pounce.

"The Vigilant Order is fallen, Irramael," Belsharoth said, shaking his head in mock compassion, one black eye bulging from the child's face, a horned brow piercing through his hair. "It lost the favor of Asmodeus some time ago due to your efforts. Enjoy your victory and be pleased that your soul shall escape Sathariel's gut!"

The half-changed devil charged with a blinding speed, but Jinn was prepared, hurling a small vial from his belt that shattered on Belsharoth's broken face. Holy water steamed on the fiend's flesh, and he screamed, an unholy sound that sang in Jinn's blood like a trumpet of war.

Gods, he thought as age-old memories surfaced in the depths of his being. The trumpets, how I remember the trumpets!

Belsharoth turned away, momentarily blinded, but an inky darkness swirled into being behind him, and pale hands reached for him as he stumbled into a soft embrace. Mara appeared from the smoke, turning the thrashing devil around and whispering words of magic as she caressed the remaining thin wisps of orange-red hair atop his head. She smiled close to his pointed ear, her teeth yellowed and lionlike, her eyes burning like coals.

"Hush," she whispered as Jinn approached and tendrils of energy flowed from her fingertips, slowing Belsharoth's transformation and leaving him trapped between two awkward forms, neither recognizable. "Be still and parley with us."

The devil's spiny back arched as he attempted to resist her magic, mismatched eyes rolling ceaselessly, mouth working as he drew long breaths, trying to speak.

"Leave me be . . . traitorous hag," he wheezed, his voice also trapped, shifting between the thunderous tone of the devil and the sweet lilt of the young boy whose form he had stolen. "How much does he pay you? Allow me to make an offer . . ."

17

"He pays me in revenge," Mara said, smiling sweetly and licking her long incisors. "Do you propose there is commerce more appealing?"

"Enough," Jinnaoth said and knelt, leaning on the point of the stolen long sword, the silvered runes down its length glittering in the candlelight. Belsharoth squirmed a moment more then shuddered, falling into Maranyuss's grasp like a scolded child. Bloody tears welled in his horrible eyes and streamed across the two sides of his malformed face, an inexplicable sorrow twisting his features into a helpless look of pure hate.

"Kill me," the devil whispered through clenched fangs. "What you want . . . is not mine to give."

"Where is Sathariel?" Jinn pressed. "How do I find him? How do I summon him?"

"Fool," Belsharoth replied, a wave of renewed strength trembling beneath his flesh that caused Mara to hiss, straining to hold the fiend. "The angel is merely a means to an end . . . the First Flensing will come . . . no matter how you struggle against it."

"Flensing?" Jinn looked to Mara curiously, but her concentration was stolen by the effort of keeping the devil still, a battle she was quickly losing. "What is the Flensing?"

"None shall know when . . . or how . . . but it is near," the fiend replied, a barbed tail snaking out from his back, growing longer and lashing weakly.

Mara gasped, growling in frustration as the energy of her spell flickered like a dying lamp.

Belsharoth smiled, the symmetry of his face more distinct, red eyes glowing bright as he added, "And this wretched city will know that my lord is coming."

"Asmodeus," Jinnaoth whispered, wondering what horror he had stumbled upon.

"Jinn!" Mara cried as the devil broke free, his true form bursting forth: a hulking beast of scales and bone spurs with a beard of tentacles writhing beneath his fang-filled mouth.

Jinn rolled to the side, narrowly dodging the fiend's whipping tail, and rose to face the devil. Mara fell back against the wall, clutching her chest as she caught her breath. Jinn cursed and leaped at the devil, slashing madly to distract Belsharoth long enough for Maranyuss to regain her strength; he would likely need her magic. He twisted and turned through the devil's claws, dancing beneath its reach then lunging upward to open fresh wounds in its stomach.

Belsharoth's clumsy attacks grew more precise, the effects of Mara's spell wearing off, and Jinn made one lunge too many, leaving an opening for the fiend. A claw closed around his leg, squeezing tightly and lifting him into the air. As he spun he tried to keep his focus, to lash at the arm holding him, but the devil kept him off balance long enough to hurl him against the far wall.

The small chamber became a swift blur followed by a sudden stop. Stars streaked across his field of vision, and slow throbs of pain arced through his back. He blinked and fell forward on his hands and knees, barely aware that the devil had turned on Mara. Hellish shrieks filled the chamber as the pair tore at one another like animals. The scent of blood brought Jinn to his senses, and he found his sword.

A glimpse of crimson streaking across Mara's forearms in little rivers brought him to his feet, and he charged back into the fray. In a breath Mara fell back, dissolving into smoky mist and leaving Belsharoth to pound only at the wall, clouds of dust and splinters of rotted wood surrounding him as he turned. Jinn jumped over the barbed tail as it swung toward him, turning as he landed to slice an arm's length from its end. Belsharoth seemed unbothered by the wound as they circled one another, the face-off drawing Jinn back to another confrontation with the devil from another time, another life.

"You die again, half-blood," Belsharoth growled and pounced, claws outstretched, his hulking form enough to easily crush anything in its way, but Jinn saw his opportunity and rushed into the fiend.

He accepted the deep wounds in his shoulder as he rolled beneath the fiend's right claw, gaining position to use Belsharoth's momentum against him. The point of his blade slipped beneath the mass of bone that served as the devil's rib cage, sliding through thick skin and dense muscle, scraping along the spined backbone to emerge from Belsharoth's back.

"This isn't Myth Drannor," Jinn said as he twisted the blade and pulled, bracing his boot against the devil's right leg. The wound opened like a toothless grin, and Belsharoth roared, steaming blood pouring from his side. Before he could take breath to roar again or twist to dislodge the blade, blue fire arced through his chest, a bolt of lightning silencing his pain and throwing Jinn away from the thrashing fiend.

Jinnaoth's hands tingled and shook, numb as the devil rolled onto his back, reaching blindly and kicking before falling still, a smoking hole in his chest filling the chamber with the scent of charred flesh.

Mara knelt over the defeated fiend, tracing the edges of the wound with a deft hand, drawing little symbols in the air and smiling cruelly when the ritual was done. As Jinn sat forward, he watched her palm a small, red gem that she quickly placed in her purse.

"We should be quick," she said, flinging droplets of blood from her claws. "That last roar may have drawn the Watch."

"Right," Jinn replied and stood, pulling his sword from the devil's corpse before scanning the chamber, his eyes quickly falling on the stained tablecloth of the makeshift altar. He turned his head to the side, studying the shape of the dried blood in the cloth. "Flensing?" he asked.

Mara shrugged, tending to the wounds on her arms, her face once again as human and soft as it had been outside.

"Just one of their rituals, as far as I know," she answered, gesturing to Belsharoth. "Torture for those souls destined to serve as devils."

Jinn lifted the tablecloth, narrowing his eyes as a familiar shape appeared in its stains like a map. A long and winding wall, dark drips serving as watchtowers, the spread of blood through the thick weave almost like streets. The undeniable shape of Waterdeep had been splashed into the cloth.

"And as it might apply to a city?" he asked, raising the gruesome image for Mara's inspection.

"That would be . . . *ambitious*, to say the least," she said, pointing to the darkest splash on the cloth where all the others seemed to have flowed away from. "Something to do with Sea Ward perhaps?"

Jinn sighed and rolled the cloth up, stuffing it into his belt as they exited the chamber and sought an alternate route back to the streets. His mind raced with possibilities, wondering what he could have missed in all his years of battling the Vigilant Order. But for one talkative devil, he might have thought his task complete.

The memories brought back by Belsharoth were already fading, too vague and indistinct to hold on to, just another ripple in four thousand years of time's river. He disliked the term *half-blood*, though many with an idea of his true nature had used it to describe him. He had dreams occasionally of his second birth, ripped from the higher realms of the gods, forged into a body of blood and bone that he could never escape, to serve his lords in battle.

They had called him a deva, an angel made flesh.

Bright sunlight struck his face as Mara led him out the east side of the ramshackle home and down yet another street crowded with mortals ignorant of the wars that went on beneath their boots. Mara flashed him a smile as a patrol of Watchmen disappeared down the garbage-strewn alley. He eyed her warily, following her down twisting avenues back to her shop and the room he'd rented from her several years ago. She maintained her illusions of beauty among the citizens of Waterdeep, but he could see the face of the night hag she hid beneath her false green eyes, and he wondered if one day, despite their strange alliance, she would come to place his soul in one of her little red gems.

He wondered, with a soul that had survived a countless number of deaths, if such a thing were possible.

TWO

J inn stared down upon the hustle and bustle of Suldown Street, absently studying the faces of passersby and listening to the broadcriers hawking the latest scandals. Shadows lengthened as he stood, still as a statue in the window above Pages Curious, the bookstore owned by Maranyuss since she had been exiled to live among mortals. His room was small and uncluttered with the things many people took for granted, the various trappings and mementos of a long life lived. Only the window stood as a connection to the world outside. The furnishings consisted of a chair and small table for his meals and a simple bed for when he grew tired.

Though his rented room was nigh bare, his mind was a labyrinth of information and memories, cluttered and filled with the details of more than a hundred lifetimes. He was never privy to all his lifetimes of memories at once—just a recalled name here, a familiar place there—but even so, each life had made its mark on the next. Only the details of his current existence were fully open to him. He cursed his limited memory, wishing for some insight into the devil Belsharoth's warning.

Even in its apparent fall, the Vigilant Order vexed him.

Sighing, he stepped away from the window and leaned over the small table next to the view of the city, his eyes scanning the rough map on the bloody tablecloth for clues. He did not look up when Mara arrived at the top of the stairs, though he could feel her watching him. She could be as silent as the grave, but her presence exuded a dark aura that raised the hairs on the back of his neck.

"This business is not done yet," she said. "We'll find him."

The angel Sathariel, an agent of Asmodeus somehow bound to Waterdeep, was Jinn's only focus, his one reason for having hunted the Vigilant Order, for living in the city when he might have adventured across the length and breadth of Faerûn. Mara and he shared that focus, and it had bound them in purpose, though their reasons were vastly different.

He shook his head and rolled up the cloth, tired of staring at blood for answers that never came.

"I had hoped that he might find us," Jinn replied. "We've weakened his following, set spies in every ward of the city, and still he will not view us as a threat."

"Perhaps we aren't," Mara said. "Not yet anyway, not until we figure out why he's here."

Jinn's hand rested on the bloody tablecloth, the crimson map of the city burned in his memory, the dark splash of Sea Ward teasing him with mysteries. It was in that moment he considered the poor soul who had likely been sacrificed to scrawl the crude map, and he instinctively whispered a short prayer, though the gods of Mulhorand he had once served were long gone from the world.

A bell rang downstairs in the shop, and Mara turned to go, her cruel sense of business always ready to greet a customer with a smile.

"I'll pay a visit to Sea Ward after gateclose," he said to her as she descended.

"Waste of time," she called back.

"Better than wasting it here," he whispered. He had no mind to sleep despite his body's desire for rest. His head ached from the strain of trying to recall something useful, something that might point him in the right direction. He yearned to simply challenge the angel as his kind once had in older days, to bind it and strike it down, devote the victory to his ancient masters, but more compelling reasons than celestial blood spurred him on.

His kind were rare—at any given time, less than a handful existed within a day's dragon's flight of one another. It had been centuries since he recalled meeting another deva, but in Waterdeep, in his life as Jinnaoth, he had met one. The stolen blade, laid across his bed, shined, and he remembered her face. He blinked the image away.

"No," he whispered. "It is not a waste of time."

"Jinn!"

Mara's voice startled him from his vigil, and he turned to the stairs, looking over the railing to find her there, motioning him down with a curious light in her eyes. Though cautious, he decided not to belt on his sword and descended the stairs to find an officer of the Watch standing among the shelves and tomes of Mara's shop. He felt a moment of alarm, wondering if he and Mara had been spotted that morning, but the captain's mark on the officer's tabard—signifying his rank as a rorden of the Watch—settled his concerns. As the officer turned to meet him, Jinn recognized his old friend and smiled.

"Well met, Rorden Allek," Jinn said, though his smile faded at the unusually stern expression upon the rorden's face. "How can I be of service?"

"Jinnaoth, I—" Allek paused, clearing his throat nervously. "I cry your pardon, Goodwife Mara, but I should speak with Master Jinn alone."

"But of course, Rorden," Mara replied demurely, playing her part well and smiling sweetly as she gathered a small armload of books for cataloguing. "I shall attend to the shop, but please call if you should need anything."

"I shall. Many thanks for your understanding," Allek said, and he gestured to the cushioned chairs by the tall, arching window at the far end of the shop. Few of Mara's usual customers used the chairs, their pursuits far too secretive and Mara's selection too arcane for casual perusal, but the chairs gave the shop a comfortable and inviting atmosphere.

Jinn sat down guardedly, wondering at Allek's dark and secretive manner. The rorden sat at length, clearly troubled. He clasped his hands before him, knuckles white and dark circles beneath his eyes. His boots were strangely unpolished for Allek, and his uniform was rumpled. The visible evidence sparked Jinn's interest. Also the fact that Allek's current station was in Sea Ward.

"What's wrong, Allek?" Jinn finally asked, taking the rorden's attention away from the floor.

"Yes, right. I must apologize for my manner; it has been a long day," he said. "I'm still trying to get things straight."

"Not at all. Take your time," Jinn replied.

"What I am to tell you must be held in the strictest of confidence," Allek said, his eyes set upon Jinn's, one of the few humans who could endure the deva's golden gaze without flinching.

"You have it," Jinn said, growing more excited, his heart once again racing with hope, though he suspected whatever answers he sought had been bought at a great price.

Allek nodded and took a deep breath. "Over a month ago, and each night since, I and a handful of Watch patrols under my command began an investigation into several murders occurring in Sea Ward," Allek said, looking over his shoulder hesitantly as he spoke.

"I recall some news about it, though the broadsheets at the time were lacking in detail," Jinn replied.

"Aye, that they were." Allek nodded. "And not a word about them since, with good reason. The bodies . . . gods." He paused again, collecting himself. "Specific mutilations, identical in each case with varying degrees of defensive wounds, struggle, and so forth. The scenes left in full view, no attempts being made to hide the bodies. No witnesses or at least none willing to come forth. And I . . ." Allek's voice trailed off as he shook his head, speechless.

"Pardon my assumption," Jinn said, "but you have surely handled such cases before. Strange deaths in Waterdeep are nothing new."

"My niece," Allek said, his hard eyes dry but reddened with a sorrow Jinn hadn't noticed before. "My brother. His wife. All slain."

"Suspects?"

Allek smiled sadly. "There's a bright coin of a question," he answered. "We have almost as many bloodstained killers in custody as we do corpses."

"Gods," Jinn whispered, thoughts racing, trying to understand. "Why have you come to me with this?"

"We've known each other for a long time, Jinn. I trust you and I know you've dealt with these kinds of things before." Allek seemed tired, at the end of a long rope and exploring resources beyond the Watch. "I need your help."

"But surely there are others more qualified, wizards perhaps, the Watchful Order must—?"

"No wizards," Allek said swiftly. "Not yet at any rate. Magic, so far, has failed us in this."

At first Jinn wondered if Allek suspected a wizard was involved, but there was a general mistrust of arcane magic since the

Spellplague. He understood the rorden's hesitation to employ such spells, though distrust could hold for only so long before necessity demanded extra measures be taken.

"I am at your service," he said, adding, "Specific mutilations, you said?"

"I can show you."

"Tonight?"

"As you wish."

Feeling refreshed and ready to accompany Allek immediately, Jinn found himself walking a fine line between respect for the rorden's loss and his own fierce desire to view the bodies, to discover the source of the bloody river on the map upstairs. Instinct told him he was close, that Sathariel was near.

Mara appeared as if on cue as the two men approached the front entrance.

"I apologize for so brief a visit, dear Mara," Allek said, "but duty seems determined to keep me busy at every bell this day."

"No need, Allek," she replied, placing a hand lightly upon his arm, a motion that both amused and at the same time sickened Jinn as he imagined the gnarled, clawed fingers hiding behind her delicate skin. "Visit when you're able and worry not between."

"At evenpeal, then?" Jinn said.

"Aye, Pharra's Alley," the rorden answered, adding, as he stepped out into the street, "Fair evening, gods will it."

The doorbell sang as he left, and Jinn stood pondering why they should meet at Pharra's Alley, so close to the House of Wonder's wizards. At length he caught Mara staring him down, one eyebrow cocked. Jinn cursed the hag's impatience, knowing she'd been listening the entire time.

"Pharra's Alley?" she said, turning back to her books. "Interesting."

"Indeed?"

"They say it's haunted," she replied ominously with a little grin. "Well, those that survive say so, at any rate."

Jinn's furrowed brow at that news did not leave him as he ascended the stairs, picking apart the rorden's tale, turning it over, looking for something to match all that had gone before. He took his place by the window again, watching the world go by as he pondered and waited for sundown and answers.

It was not quite evenpeal. A cold wind whistled through the streets, bringing with it scents of snow. Layered against the chill, Jinn strolled beneath the blurry light of a half-moon. He appeared neither wealthy nor informal but bore enough of both to walk where he liked in whatever company.

His step was smooth and sure; he knew the city by heart. Shops were closed and quiet, and the taverns were growing louder. He was more comfortable with his off-human appearance at night. His pale face and skin sigils tended to make those who hunted the dark think twice before confronting his golden gaze.

Somewhere, somehow, a life would soon end, the chill and night's shadows told him as much. The chill wanted a better cloak or coat, warmer boots, and a warm meal. Shadow gave that want a place to hide a knife.

"Need a guide, saer?"

Jinn turned, startled from his thoughts by a child's voice.

"Find your way through the city, I can!"

A glance at the boy, out at night and alone, told him much that the boy's thin clothes and thinner health had not already declared, though the child's bright eyes held a wisdom beyond his young years.

"You know these streets well?" Jinn asked.

"Well as any man o' the Watch, saer!" the boy answered excitedly.

"What is your name, young master?" Jinn asked, kneeling down and receiving the usual shocked stare as the boy looked into his eyes in wonder.

"Tombil," he said, taking half a step backward nervously.

"Well, young Master Tombil, I am Jinnaoth, and I have no need of a guide this night." He stood but swiftly produced a large, platinum coin, called a sun, and let it shine before Tombil's eyes before adding, "But should we cross paths again, I may have need of your mastery of the streets." He pressed the coin into Tombil's hand and grinned, letting the boy get a good look at him. "Remember me well."

"Aye, saer. I will, saer!"

Tombil ran off, clutching the coin tightly. Jinn watched after him a moment, always fascinated with children of all races, as he had never been a child and could not fathom the games and rituals of childhood and growing up. Several of the shadows in Tombil's wake, along the walls of closed shops and noble mansions, shifted slightly, huddled figures sidling away from his sight.

It wasn't long before he arrived at the outer walls of the Saerfynn Manor. As he entered Pharra's Alley, he studied what details could be made out along the walls, on the cobbles, already assuming the place to have been the scene of one of Allek's mysterious murders. The alley was wide and clean, as was most of Sea Ward, the wealthiest in Waterdeep. It was decently lit save for the middle and the end, the latter of which bore the gates of the House of Wonder. A Watch patrol made its way by at the far end, one man separating from the group and offering Jinn a wave.

Jinn paused close to the wall across from the Saerfynn grounds, finding a spot that had been missed when the scene was cleared. A thin splash of rust lay in a short, straight line on the stone at shoulder height. He studied the angle and direction of the stain as Allek approached, reading a piece of the tale of what had occurred there.

"Jinn, well met," the rorden said.

"This was recent?" Jinn asked, pointing to the stain and noting the look of surprise on Allek's face.

"Yes," he answered. "Last evening, roughly four bells before sunrise."

"It was a long blade," Jinn said, tracing the arc of the splatter with a gloved finger. "A shallow cut, imprecise and unpracticed. Possibly a defensive injury, not a killing wound by any measure."

"Gods, Jinn," Allek whispered and turned away from the wall, shaking his head. "I need those eyes on my payroll."

Jinn looked away from the stain. "I'm sorry," he said. "Old blood tends to tell stories of how and sometimes when, but very rarely who. You have my deepest sympathies for your loss. I didn't realize—"

"No, forgive me," the rorden said. "It has been difficult separating duty from family. I honor them more by working to find out what curse has befallen us."

"Why this place?" Jinn asked, putting the moment behind them.

"Right," Allek said, an officer of the Watch once more. "Here we received the first and only evidence we've gotten from this whole mess." The rorden led Jinn to the House of Wonder's gates. "Are you familiar with the circle of skulls?"

"No."

"An old wives' tale, according to some. Others call them ghosts, bogeymen, or spellhaunts, believing them to be magical remnants of the Spellplague. But tales of the skulls go back much farther than the Spellplague." Allek's gaze drifted to the stones of the alley with a haunted, faraway look. "I saw them once, when I was a child.

Glowing with green flames, spitting fire at anyone that came near. Then they just faded away. Always in this spot."

Jinn circled the area, studying what appeared to be a normal patch of ground, nothing out of the ordinary that he could see.

"How does this connect with . . . ?" Jinn asked.

"The killer, a young man named Dason Hallsahf, before he lost his ability to reason, spoke of skulls, of green fire. Rambled on and on about them." Allek's voice grew tight, angry, barely held in check.

"What else did he say? Anything?"

"There was something about being trapped and 'dirty men,' " Allek answered, then added, "He said he saw an angel."

Hands curled into fists, Jinn attempted to calmly nod, still pretending to study the ground where ghostly skulls were said to rise, though his heart pounded and his breath quickened. Reflexively, he glanced at the sky, expecting dark wings to descend at any moment and fiercely willing them to do so.

━━W━━

The corridors of the Westwall were of cold stone as Jinn followed Rorden Allek down quiet hallways, through empty rooms, and into chambers well guarded from the public eye. Beyond the guards and heavy doors was a series of small rooms pervaded by a strange, sterile smell. Jinn's skin tingled with energy, sensing magic. Allek nodded to an officer with a gray goatee and a well-worn saber at his side. The old man, introduced as Officer Yarrow, produced a ring of keys and led them down to the last door on the left.

"Don't use the quiet rooms much anymore," Yarrow said as he fumbled for the right key. "Had 'em down here more than a century or so now, just collectin' dust mostly."

"These chambers cease the body's process of decay," Allek explained. "Useful in somewhat rare cases like this."

"Eastwall used to have somethin' similar, until the Spellplague came through and ruined it," Yarrow mumbled. Then he smiled as he found the right key. "Rooms on that side started workin' too well, bringin' folk back to life . . . well, not *life* mind ye, but—"

"I think I understand," Jinn said as the door opened, lanternlight spilling across the stained white dress of a young woman, lying atop a rune-inscribed slab of stone. Allek turned away but did not leave. He dismissed Officer Yarrow as Jinn examined the body of Allek's niece, Alma Marson.

Her wounds, as Jinn had surmised from the alley, were mostly small and superficial, painful but not deadly, save for a small puncture in the left side of her chest. The cut was just wide enough to allow a thin blade to pass between the ribs and find the heart—one precise, fatal stab, amid a flurry of wild blows. Jinn took the wounds in, committing them to memory, though his eyes were fixed upon the line of injuries running from the base of her neck to her navel. Each was thin and deliberately shaped: an alphabet of some sort that he had never chanced upon before, possibly arcane and utterly mysterious.

"Alma was the most recent," Allek said as Jinn quickly sketched the characters carved into the girl's skin. Her dress had been cut down the center of her chest, exposing a scarred ribbon of pale flesh. Little blood seemed to have flowed from the precise wounds, possibly a sign of magic or that the cutting had been done with little struggle. "We did not keep the other bodies, cremating the remains until such time as we can safely inform the families."

"Their wounds were the same?" Jinn asked, examining the girl's left hand where the ring finger had been neatly removed.

"Yes," the rorden answered. "On all save Dessa Marson, my brother's wife. Her . . . throat had been cut, a single wound."

"She got in the way," Jinn muttered, replacing the small chapbook of sketches in his coat.

"That was my suspicion," Allek said.

"Which suggests the victims were specific targets."

Jinn stepped back from the body and nodded to Allek, who waved Yarrow back to reseal the quiet chamber. The rorden's face seemed older, expressionless as they walked back to the end of the corridor.

"Have you had a priest or wizard examine any of the bodies?" Jinn asked. "Perhaps one could attempt to speak with the spirit."

"We made one attempt with a priest," Allek answered, "and he has yet to recover. Some kind of . . . backlash is the best I can describe it. It threw the man across the room, left him burned and senseless. For their safety we've kept those few among the Watchful Order that know of the murders away from the bodies themselves. As I said before, magic is serving us very little as of yet."

With the suspicion of wizardry in Waterdeep of late, Jinn could understand why Allek was hesitant to involve spellhurlers, but he couldn't abide not exploiting whatever resources might prove useful. As they ascended to the more common hallways of the Westwall, Jinn stopped Allek before they were in earshot of the other officers.

"We will need a wizard," Jinn said, knowing that Allek, despite his distrust, had to agree with the next most logical avenue of finding answers.

The rorden merely nodded, crossing his arms, clearly troubled by the prospect of involving anyone else in the mystery.

"I have some contacts," Jinn added. "I'll be discreet."

"Do what you need to," Allek said. "I'll meet you back in the alley at gateclose tomorrow."

"Get some sleep," Jinn said before taking his leave of the rorden, though Allek did not answer. Jinn did not envy the man the long night he faced, trying to rest, keep his composure, and see to his duty as a Watchman amid the loss of his only family.

Outside the wall, Jinn raised his collar against the cold and set out toward the House of Wonder, one last thing to do before succumbing to his own exhaustion. The Watchful Order, while capable wizards, could not be trusted with the discretion he required, and though Mara was quite skilled with spells and rituals, her resources and contacts within Sea Ward were limited. Jinn suspected one person in particular could prove invaluable, both due to the nature of the crimes and in knowledge of the ward in general. He sighed, however, dreading the task and having his own reasons for avoiding certain magic-users.

THREE

Steam swirled above the greenish sludge in the labyrinth of Waterdeep's sewers. Rats huddled along the bordering catwalks, gathering for warmth, fighting and cannibalizing the weak when hunger demanded a sacrifice. Moonlight glimmered ghostlike down through a hidden entrance in Torch Lane above, twinkling in Essirel's eyes as he drew his dirty cloak tighter against the cold. His breath came slow and even, almost mechanical, his heartbeat much the same.

Thought and even the memory of emotion was rare and fleeting, serving more to confuse him than to offer hope, though he struggled to hang on to those moments. He could not help but fail, so lost was the soul that had driven his ambitions and desires. Only the moon and the rats kept him company as he waited, filled with dread—the only real feeling he had been allowed to keep—for the beating of its wings, the call of his master's voice.

Others shifted closer, their once-fine robes almost unidentifiable, covered in the filth of miles of sewers. Dull eyes led them to share in Essirel's moonlight, to watch for the shadow across the moon, to listen for the thunder of the angel Sathariel. They crawled closer on hands and knees, pressing close at Essirel's shoulder, the stink they brought swallowed by the pervading scents of the sewer. He swayed as they crowded around him, blank faces upturned to the glow.

A terrible will was gathering them, bringing them to clean streets and wealthy homes with the promise of redemption. Essirel gasped at the thought but was left slack jawed a breath later, drool stringing slowly down his chin. There had been a moment, seemingly eons ago, when he'd seen the bright spark of himself, watched it glow, tethered to him by ephemeral strands of being before it had been ripped away. Every moment since, every breath had been the same, lost in the moonlight, moving to the will of some distant mind, shuffling through the streets to that place, far from the dark altars of the Vigilant Order.

Heavy ripples flowed through the sewage, and Essirel's eyes widened, his gut twisting in pain as a quiet rumble of thunder resonated through the tunnels. In that breath he felt his soul shudder in its prison, writhing in the guts of his lord's servant, the devouring angel sent to punish him and his brethren. The bodies around him stirred and began to rise, reaching up with filth-encrusted hands, ready to serve if only for the chance at forgiveness. The clarity held for a moment, and Essirel resisted the call, drawing breath to scream and clutching at his chest where he'd last seen the spark of his existence torn from him, but the scream never came.

His hands fell to the damp stone beneath him, and he pushed himself to his feet, reaching for the rusted rungs of an old ladder, and pulled. Soulless and directionless, he followed the rumbling voice of an angel, determined to serve, called to hide among the cold streets until the time of the Flensing when he might glimpse the terrible face of his god.

And the time was near.

Jinn paused before the gates of the House of Wonder, studying the symbols on the wrought iron and steeling himself for what lay within. The sketches of Alma's body seemed to burn a hole in his pocket, teasing him. Like found gold, he clutched them close on the walk from Westwall, certain he was close to his quarry and half expecting Sathariel to come for him any moment. He was tired of the constant questions and cryptic answers. He had no care for the blood spilled in Sea Ward and had quietly promised whatever Power might be listening that he would walk away from the strange killings happily if he might do so with Sathariel's angelic blood on his blade.

Sighing, he resigned himself to the slow hunt and raised his hand to the house's gate.

"Are you a wizard, saer?"

Jinn spun around, hand on his sword, only to find an officer of the Watch at his back, a lean man with a sharp, wolflike face, half-lidded eyes, and a thin smile set on his wide mouth. A pair of crossed, diagonal slashes on the officer's tabard declared his rank. At the officer's back, a patrol of seven men had paused, glancing toward the pair at the gates, but talking low among themselves. Jinn let his hand fall away from his sword.

"Not at all, Swordcaptain," Jinn answered. "Merely visiting, Officer . . . ?"

"Dregg," the man replied. "It's a bit late for a visit, isn't it? Streets can be dangerous after dark. Lots of *undesirables* hanging about lately."

Jinn narrowed his eyes at Dregg's ignorant comments. There were some in Sea Ward who referred to any race other than human as *undesirable,* sneering at the so-called lesser races as unworthy upstarts, usurpers of human wealth and safety. At each meeting with an elf or dwarf in the streets, they scowled, considering the high walls of Waterdeep a failure for allowing such trash to contaminate their communities.

"You speak true, Swordcaptain," Jinn said with a threatening smile, gold eyes flashing. "One would do well to avoid such confrontations, wouldn't one?"

Dregg's smile faded, but he did not avert his gaze. He took a step forward, looking Jinn up and down with a cold sneer.

"Jinnaoth," Dregg said as if spitting the name. "You are Rorden Allek's pet, are you not?"

"Allek is an old friend," Jinn replied, sensing something other than mere racism in Dregg's demeanor—something personal, though he had never met the man before.

"The rorden thinks you may be of use somehow, though I cannot imagine why." Dregg stared down his nose at the deva. "Perhaps he is more desperate than I thought."

Jinn clenched his fists and half turned back to the gate, determined not to fall prey to the man's baiting. Should he strike an officer under Allek's command in full view of a Watch patrol, he would find his task in Sea Ward doubly difficult to accomplish. Collecting himself, he raised his hand again to the gate, assuming their conversation to be at an end.

"Careful," Dregg said. "They'll not just let any stray from off the street darken their doorstep."

"Indeed," Jinn replied and quickly traced a sigil over the gate latch, the iron glowing softly where he touched it before producing an audible click. As the gate swung inward, Jinn stepped inside, turning to close it behind him and adding, "I trust I'll not see you within, Swordcaptain Dregg."

He left the human glowering at his back as he calmly made his way through the wizards' well-tended courtyard, measuring his stride beneath the tall towers of the House of Wonder. Dregg joined his patrol at length and disappeared down the street. Jinn stared after him, composing himself before entering the house and wondering when he might encounter the swordcaptain again.

He had a feeling that no matter when it occurred, it would be far too soon.

The tall, ornate doors of the House of Wonder opened with a welcoming rush of warm air but left Jinn standing alone in the shadowed entrance hall. Though it was late, enchanted candles still flickered in sconces along the walls, scents of jasmine and sandalwood drifted on the air, and voices echoed softly nearby in whispered conversation. The distinct hiss of turning pages drew his eye to an archway at the far end of the hall, the main library, where he might begin his search for the origins of the sigils that had been carved on Alma's stomach, but he stood still, not venturing beyond the dark, patterned carpet within the front doors. The House of Wonder was not without its guardians.

In moments the air before him thickened, wavering as a misty shape coalesced an arm's length away. White eyes stared at him from a nearly featureless face, though he could see, through the specter's haze, the fading details of a once-proud wizard in long, flowing robes. An unnatural chill surrounded the ghostly figure as it regarded him blankly.

He repeated the sigil he had traced on the gates, drawing it in the air.

The specter nodded and faded away. As it did, the whole of the hallway shimmered, an illusion giving way to reality. The arching doorways changed places on the walls, and the length of the hallway doubled, revealing yet more doors and a tall, winding staircase at the end. Jinn smiled at the old magic, putting his meeting with Swordcaptain Dregg to the back of his mind, and made his way to the library's familiar arch, on the opposite wall from where it had appeared earlier and more brightly lit than before.

Several figures sat huddled over old tomes, their faces lit by the house's seemingly endless supply of enchanted candles. No one looked up at his arrival, too engrossed in their studies or quiet conversations to bother themselves with guests. He turned to the tall windows in the southern wall. Where one might have expected to find a view of the surrounding gardens, the high wall, and the city skyline beyond, the windows showed only rolling fields of waving grass beneath a brilliant, moonlit sky full of stars. A familiar figure in simple, dark blue robes stood before the easternmost window, twisting a long braid of dark red hair through her fingers as she gazed upon the false stars, her moon elf skin almost glowing in the illusory light.

Jinn took a deep breath, and though he approached her quietly, she turned almost as if she were expecting him. Her pale blue eyes regarded him without the least bit of surprise.

"I had not thought to see you so soon, Jinnaoth," she said, "though the stars have, of late, told me otherwise."

"Quessahn," Jinn said quietly. "I am sorry to disturb you, but—"

"No, you are not," she said sharply with a tight smile. "You are a single-minded bastard with little thought for anyone or anything that gets in your way."

Jinn noticed several nearby students look up, eyeing the pair before returning to their studies. He bit back a curse and wondered if he had made a mistake. It would not be the first time where Quessahn was involved.

"Then I pray you forgive my futile attempt at formality," he replied.

"No, it suits you, despite all." Quessahn turned and motioned him toward the hallway where they could speak without disturbing the others. "What brings you here?"

"Murder," he said, measuring his words and seeing no need to mention Sathariel or the Vigilant Order just yet. "A series of them."

"All in the last month or so," she added. "Yes, the Watch keeps many secrets at times, but this is one they've been hard pressed to maintain."

"How many others know?" Jinn asked, already imagining doubled Watch patrols, curfews, wealthy families abandoning their manors for other homes while adventurous sightseers sneaked through the streets hoping to glimpse the murderer, all the things that might make his job that much more difficult.

"Know? Only myself that I'm aware of," Quessahn answered, leading him farther down the hallway, where a smaller extension of the library lay empty. "But rumors spread, about missing people—kidnappings, ambitious sons and daughters unwilling to wait for inheritances, and the like."

"And how do you know they are anything more than just rumor?" he asked.

"I saw," she said plainly. "Three of the bodies, recently, but only at a distance. The Watch had already arrived with dark sheets and sawdust to clean the blood. It seemed as though they had things under control, so I never bothered to ask. I doubt they would have wanted my help anyway."

Relief trickled into his thoughts, though he had suspected the wizards had known about the murders all along, as he had almost hoped they knew of Sathariel. He paced to the window, plotting how he might catch a killer that could be anyone—and wondering if the effort would only be a waste of time. There was no assurance the angel or the order were involved at all.

"I expect that if you are here, there is more than just blood on the ground," Quessahn said, pulling him from his thoughts. The unspoken question sparkled in her eyes, but there was also accusation in their sky blue depths. She'd worn a similar expression before, shortly after they'd met a few years earlier, but Jinn was never sure where her suspicion had come from nor her strange familiarity with him. She spoke to him as if she'd known him all his life. He never asked why, and she never offered explanations.

He pulled the sketches from his coat and handed them to her wordlessly, unwilling to lie but not yet ready to divulge the full truth. She turned the pages slowly with a troubled expression, tracing the symbols.

"They are old," she said. "Older than me. Arcane to be sure, but something else taints the way they are rendered, markings where there should be none, almost like two languages overlapped."

"Also, what do you know of a circle of skulls?" he asked.

"What?" she said. "The skulls?"

"Quessahn."

Jinn turned, finding a bearded man in dark robes standing in the doorway, dark eyes glowering at the elf under bushy, black eyebrows. A young man stood at the wizard's back, sneering over his shoulder at the startled pair.

"Archmage Tallus," Quessahn replied as she turned, hiding the sketches behind her back.

Tallus strode into the room, calmly looking Jinn up and down as he tapped a gnarled wooden staff on the floor with each step. Turning to Quessahn, he stopped, glancing between her and the deva.

"It is not your place to entertain guests here at your whim, Quessahn," he said, eyes sparkling in the candlelight. "I suggest if you wish to continue your studies, that you escort this fellow—"

"I am not the guest of Quessahn, Archmage," Jinn said, taking a half step between the two. "I have been given, some time ago, a standing invitation from Master Bastun Nesraan of Rashemen, currently in Shadowdale, I believe."

"Master Bastun," Tallus muttered. "Why am I not surprised, with his soft spot for adventurers and trouble-makers. He would open our doors to all manner of . . . *guests,* if he had his way, I imagine. However, Bastun is not here, it is late, and our students cannot be interrupted—"

"I'm afraid my invitation is not dependent upon the kind master's presence." Jinn stepped forward. "And I doubt your peers would look favorably upon your ousting the invited guest of a colleague, even in his absence."

Tallus adjusted his staff before him, its dull tap on the floor more firm than before. "Indeed," he replied, a slight growl hiding behind the word. "And what business brings you here to disturb dear Quessahn so late? What, might I ask, could not wait until morning?"

"My business must remain my own, Archmage," Jinn answered carefully, detecting a knowing smirk behind the wizard's beard. "And it has no hour upon which it is dependent, though when it calls, I answer with haste."

Tallus stood quietly a moment longer, as though considering the answer and still sizing up the deva with his dark eyes. Jinn noted the man's white-knuckled grip on the gnarled staff, the detail belying the wizard's otherwise perfect calm.

"I see," the archmage said, slowly turning to leave. "Then may your stay be pleasant and your business conducted swiftly, saer Jinnaoth."

"I do not recall introducing myself," Jinn said to the wizard's back.

"You did not," Tallus replied. "Give my regards to Rorden Marson."

Jinn stood stone still as the wizard left, though his eyes burned into the archmage's back, questioning his instincts and finding suspicion seemingly at every turn. He preferred dealing with devils and monsters; any beast that wore its intentions honestly was better than the petty secrets and half-hidden prejudices of mortals.

"Well, I see you're still making friends as easily as ever," Quessahn said, "though in your defense I doubt that Tallus has any friends at all."

"Can you decipher the symbols?" Jinn asked, more sharply than he'd intended.

"I will try," she answered. "And afterwards I will also assist you and the rorden."

"No. That will not be necessary—," he began; then he caught the stern look in her eye and cursed the eladrin's stubbornness.

"It is most certainly necessary," she said. "I don't know what your true business is here, but I have some knowledge of your technique in matters like this. These are murders, Jinn, not casualties. I intend to make sure that is not forgotten."

A part of him knew she was right, a part that seemed to speak up less and less in his thoughts as centuries and lives rolled by. He found compassion to be a difficult trait to maintain, one that every evil in the world took pleasure in exploiting.

"Fine," he answered and strode toward the door. "Gateclose tomorrow, in the alley."

He didn't wait for her reply, shoving the house's doors open. He missed the glimmering memory of ancient wars, the simplicity of facing an enemy across a shining field of battle, the trumpets of challenge and victory, but most of all he missed the memory of her,

Variel, the deva he'd found after four millennia in the unlikely city of Waterdeep—the companion he'd lost to Sathariel.

By the time he'd reached Mara's shop, his fury had faded somewhat, replaced by exhaustion. Bodies, sigils, rumors, and ghostly skulls haunted him up the stairs, mysteries for which he had little stomach or patience, but for Variel, he would answer the call of his ancient spirit, with all eternity laid out before him to make right what he had once let slip away.

Tallus stood at his chamber window, looking down as Jinnaoth disappeared in the dark of Pharra's Alley. He ground the base of his gnarled staff into the floor angrily, drumming his fingertips on the windowsill and contemplating the winding, well-lit streets of Sea Ward from the heights of the House of Wonder.

"Gorrick," he called, causing a sharp intake of breath from the doorway.

His apprentice rushed into the room, robes swishing on the floor. "Yes, Archmage?" Gorrick said, and Tallus could imagine the fear in the ambitious young man's eyes. He would have smiled, enjoying the boy's discomfort, if not for the fact he knew Gorrick's fear did not lie entirely with the archmage.

"Return to the libraries. Keep a watchful eye upon Quessahn," he commanded. Though he doubted the eladrin warlock would discover anything useful in the common books available to students of the house, he did not want to take any chances. "Be discreet."

"Yes, Archmage," Gorrick said and swiftly left to obey, closing the chamber door behind himself.

Tallus was not overly fond of his apprentice, but he and Gorrick were two of a kind in the city, held under the same thumb and both threatened by the arrival of Jinnaoth. Gorrick was unaware of the threat the deva represented, but Tallus would not underestimate Jinnaoth as his brothers once had—he would deal with the problem quickly and efficiently.

"You are a fool," a hollow voice thundered, sending chills down his spine. Shadows lengthened through the room, encroaching along the walls and ceiling, crackling like dead leaves. The darkness pressed against him, edging him closer to the pane of glass. Tallus imagined he could hear distant wails and screams, the thousand or more souls trapped within the innards of the angel, imprisoned by foul and ancient magic.

"Sathariel," Tallus managed. "You should not come to this place. You risk too much."

"Your wizards do not care." Sathariel chuckled, the sound rumbling in Tallus's mind, scattering his thoughts. "They have their studies and spells, desperate for what magic they can grasp in their greedy minds. The world will have been long burning before they think to research rituals of water."

Despite himself, Tallus nodded in agreement, suspecting few of the idiots downstairs could see far beyond their own noses, but he knew there were a few who watched and listened, who still imagined themselves a part of the world beyond the walls of the house. Quessahn was a threat. Willful and often disobedient, she sought magic not for herself, but for others, wasting her talents on those who would never accept her, never trust her.

"Beware the deva, Tallus," the angel whispered in his ear, the words stinking of decay. "Leave him and the moon elf be."

Shapes fluttered at the edge of the crawling dark, brushing against the walls like long, black feathers. Motes of disturbed dust drifted down from the ceiling. Tallus pushed back from the window slowly, forcing himself to stand against the inexplicable heaviness of the angel's presence.

"They will get in the way and slow the process down," he said. "I cannot risk their interference."

"Alas, it is your pride you fear to risk," Sathariel replied, chuckling again close to the back of Tallus's neck without breath or humor. "Pardon my amusement; I have some appreciation for the vices of mortals."

"My pride shall be satisfied by following the correct course of action," Tallus shot back angrily. "The deva must be removed. As for his allies . . . well, all in due course."

"I shall leave you to it, then," the angel said softly. "But do not neglect your obligations to me, wizard. Let the nine skulls of the circle be an example to you. Should you fail me, you will not be as fortunate as they."

The shadows receded, the sound of blown leaves being withdrawn as the angel's wings disappeared into nothingness. A forgotten candle guttered back to its false light, leaving Tallus to watch as shambling figures wound their way down Pharra's Alley, scattering themselves throughout the ward. He shuddered at their miserable fates and absently rubbed at the crimson tattoo on his left arm beneath his robes.

The Vigilant Order might rise again or fall to the depths of the Nine Hells, all on his success or failure in the next few days. His gaze rested at last upon the innocuous cobbles before the gates of the House of Wonder. He placed thoughts of the angel at the back of his mind and focused instead on the circle of skulls, preparing himself for their service.

As he did so, he smiled, a plan forming that would end his concerns about the deva and leave him to finish his great work in peace. Breath shortening, he coughed, a stab of pain rushing through his chest. He gasped as his heart seized and fluttered. He stumbled backward, leaning against the edge of his desk, breathless and wide eyed, gritting his teeth until the pain passed. The recurring attacks had grown more persistent, leaving him weak and clutching at his chest for what seemed an eternity. Recovering slowly, he breathed deeply and looked forward to the moment when such debilitating ailments were no longer his to worry about.

FOUR

Sunset did not last long, dark clouds rolling in to steal the sky's red-orange, replacing it with deep blacks and undulating purples. Pharra's Alley was thinning out, the usual crowd of merchants and hopeful students meandering away from the wizards' gate, revealing the bare stones where the skulls were said to appear. Rorden Allek arrived, disturbing Jinn from his study of the rumored spot. He was not entirely convinced the circle existed at all.

"Master Jinn," Allek said, seeming more rested that the previous night but no less weary.

Jinn opened his mouth to respond then spied Quessahn approaching from behind the rorden. She handed him back his sketches, causing Allek to regard Jinn with a glowering, curious stare.

"Forgive me, Rorden Allek, this is Quessahn Uthraebor," Jinn said swiftly before either of them could speak. "I have asked her to assist us."

Allek glanced at the moon elf briefly before gesturing toward the end of the alley. He led them north through the ward as lamplighters gathered at street corners, long, iron hooks slung over their shoulders for the oil-pot lanterns that lit the city by night. Small, portable merchant carts rolled by, their wares folded away until the following morning's business. Horse-drawn carriages, well shined for the appearances of their wealthy occupants, set out from walled mansions, heedless of those foolish enough to get in their way.

"You call this discreet?" Allek said at length, eyes forward and in step beside the deva.

"She already knew about the killings," Jinn responded quietly, "and I suspect we'll need her insight."

"Insight?" Allek asked. Then he sighed, shaking his head. "A wizard . . ."

"Warlock," Quessahn corrected.

The rorden paused, turning to face the pair with a defeated expression. Jinn had gone against Allek's wishes, but they had both known the exclusion of arcane insight could not have lasted long.

"Well met, then, Mistress Uthraebor," the rorden said, though he glared at Jinn. "Let us be swift before the whole of Waterdeep knows our troubles. Then we'll be up to our eyeballs in wizards and the gods know who else."

Across the street from the corner of Stormstar's Ride and the Street of Glances, Allek stopped, gesturing to the tavern on the northwest corner.

"The Storm's Front," he said, "a popular gathering place for the young and wealthy. Many of the most recent victims were last seen here. The Watch has staked it out before with no success, but I'm hoping that between the two of us—"

"Three," Quessahn added quickly, studying the two-story stone and wood tavern as a well-dressed couple slipped inside. Scents of roasted meats wafted from the open doorway, and Jinn noted several patrons already seated, getting an early start on the evening's revelry.

"Three, yes," the rorden said. "I was hoping we might spy something of note, something the average officer might not notice."

"Is this all?" Quessahn asked. "After a month, this tavern is all you have?"

"I've added an extra man to each patrol and an extra patrol after evenpeal," Allek said angrily, keeping his voice low. "Beyond keeping our eyes, ears, and feet busy, I've little else to go on at this point."

"Fair enough," Jinn said, glaring at Quessahn as Allek made his way across the street ahead of them. Jinn caught Quessahn's elbow, holding her back a moment. "Any luck with the sigils?"

"Some but nothing very helpful," she answered. "Likely more than the Watch has uncovered yet. If they'd just trust a wizard long enough to—"

"We'll talk later," he replied and followed the rorden. "Until then try to keep in mind that the last victim was Allek's niece and that you're not the only one who cares that people are dying."

Jinn did not look back to see her reaction, though he felt the effect of his words in her ensuing silence. He was not fond of the general distrust of magic some people held, but by the same token, he despised the knee-jerk reactions of magic-users who suspected prejudice at every turn—an effective circle of ignorance begetting yet more ignorance.

Laughter and bright lanterns greeted him as he entered the Storm's Front, a large, curved main floor contoured to the shape of the street, the opposite end bearing a double stairway to a second floor and more private gathering rooms. The interior was well decorated with polished wood tables and chairs, candles at every seating, and an elaborate bar serving cold drinks and hot meals. It seemed to reflect what Jinn suspected to be a wealthy clientele, but it was also less than what he had been expecting. That he and Quessahn had entered without being stopped at the door was evidence of an inclusiveness that some finer establishments of the ward lacked.

Several weapons of an ocean-themed nature hung on the walls and a wooden plaque over the bar bore a storm-cloud design over a crude wave of water. The tavern had an air of false roughness, alluding to a true sailors' tavern, though Jinn imagined that the only sailors who had ever entered the place were either long retired or owned small ships that they occasionally visited.

Jinn felt eyes upon him and the eladrin as they crossed the common room, joining Allek at a table that afforded a view of the entire bar and seating area. He caught more than a few sneering looks from the growing crowd and paid them no mind, sitting back and letting his gaze wander from one person to the next, trying to appear casual. He studied clothing, visible weapons, those who were quiet and watchful, and those who laughed and caroused. His eyes were drawn to the roughness or smoothness of exposed palms and took note of their footwear, marking filth and cleanliness, loud heels compared to smooth, quiet soles.

Altogether, he could piece together one suspect from among several familiar traits, though could not attribute any particular crime to the amalgam. No one presented themselves as anything other than what they seemed, and with Allek's admission that several unconnected murderers had already been placed in the Watch's custody, Jinn began to realize the difficulty of the task the Watch had undertaken.

"Rorden Allek!" a young woman at the door called out, extracting herself from a small group of admirers and sauntering over to their table. She was a short, curvy woman festooned with lace and jewels, a tight-fitting crimson dress leaving little to the imagination as she leaned against their table with a conspiratorial wink at the rorden. "How is my favorite niece of yours, Rorden? I haven't seen Alma in ages!"

Jinn noticed a brief shadow cross Allek's features, and Quessahn looked away uncomfortably. However, the rorden composed himself quickly, his voice bearing not the slightest hint of what he truly felt.

"Mistress Lhaerra," he said, "I fear that Alma has taken ill of late—"

"The poor dear!" Lhaerra exclaimed, an exaggerated look of concern on her face disappearing quickly as a round of laughter from the bar caught her attention. "Give dear Alma my best, will you?"

She was gone before Allek could respond, lost in a crowd of smiling suitors and jealous rivals. The rorden merely sat in silence, eyes seeming to burn a hole in the tabletop for a moment before returning to his perusal of the common room. No one else approached the trio for some time, and for that, Jinn was grateful.

As the evening wore on closer to evenpeal, he sipped at a glass of water, earning scornful looks from the barkeep. Jinn fought the urge to suggest leaving, seeing little in the vapid decadence of those gathered that reminded him of the Vigilant Order.

He saw them more as prey than predators. The more they drank, the more closely he watched, waiting for signs of an approaching threat that might sniff and prowl at the weaknesses of those with too much coin and too little sense.

"Are we entertaining criminals in taverns rather than the jails now?" a young man at the bar called out to the amusement of his snickering companions. Only a few among them tried to shush the tall, lithe young man in black trousers and doublet, a fine-stitched storm cloak thrown over his shoulder to reveal a jeweled rapier at his side.

"Callak Saerfynn and his toadies," Allek said, nodding to the bar with a half-lidded gaze that turned more than a few heads back to their drinks. "Coins too shiny for the commoners and nary a kind word to the servants that tolerate them."

"Wits as dull as their gilded blades," Jinn muttered as Quessahn stood, tight lipped and with fists clenched. Jinn was prepared to intervene should the eladrin attempt to confront the group, but he relaxed when she turned away.

"I'll have a look around," she said almost calmly. "I need to stretch my legs."

Over the laughter and dull roar of conversation, Jinn heard the bells announcing evenpeal outside, the last bells of the night. The sound was comforting to him, more acquainted as he was with the later hours, and he renewed his scrutiny of the tavern's guests. Most of those in the city with foul intentions did their work under night's cover.

Allek shook his head and rubbed his eyes. "I feel a fool here already," he said, pushing away from the table. "I'll have a quick look upstairs, and we can leave soon."

"Take your time," Jinn replied, narrowing his gold eyes and sensing an unmistakable hush hiding among the tavern's crowd, a familiar calm that raised the hairs on the back of his neck. He absently tapped at the pommel of his sword, searching for what had caught his interest, some movement among the crowd that stood out from the rest. He added quietly, "And be careful."

It slid among the young and perfumed, the wealthy and foppish. A shock of dark blue traced with lightning-white lace. With bright hazel eyes, she watched him demurely over the shoulder of one oblivious patron then another as if she moved apart from them, commanding space for herself by presence alone. Long, blonde hair, strands of it framing her soft face, fell down her back as she approached, appearing between two shocked young men like a ghost.

Dark crimson lips smiled, and her eyes wandered to the patterns on Jinn's cheek, down his neck where they branched between his shoulder and collarbone.

Despite her beauty, or perhaps because of it, Jinn held still, waiting for a knife to appear in her delicate hand or horns to sprout from her forehead. The woman, in one way or another, was the predator he had expected to find. She sat across from him wordlessly, her body curving in practiced motions to accentuate its many attributes.

"You are Jinnaoth," she said matter-of-factly, leaning forward with a grin.

"And you are the third stranger in the last day claiming to know of me," he replied, sensing a game in her sparkling eyes, a game he was determined not to play. "I grow tired of being marked before being introduced."

"Rilyana," she said. "Rilyana Saerfynn."

"You'll be the sister, then," he said, glancing to the disapproving glare of Callak by the bar, her brother red faced with drink and on the verge of what was likely an unseemly display of violence for the likes of the Storm's Front.

"Unfortunately," she said, following his gaze to Callak casually. "I hope you'll not judge me too harshly by his example."

"It seems I am forced to think just the opposite, wondering how the brother is related to the sister at all," Jinn said, narrowing his eyes suspiciously. "The sister that knows my name. I must also wonder what else she knows about me?"

"I have my sources. Despite its size, Sea Ward is actually quite small," she answered, staring deep into his golden eyes, though whether her stare was challenging or an attempt at seduction, he could not be sure. "You don't want to be here, do you?"

It seemed an innocent question, but Jinn felt the depth of it, even if such was unintended. A flash of the brilliant light from his dreams passed through his thoughts, the celestial glow of an ancient home abandoned. Though he tried to banish the image, it was strangely persistent, and he felt a slight pressure in his chest. Alarmed, he felt eyes upon him, glowering at him beneath a bushy brow from the doorway, the faint tap of Archmage Tallus's gnarled staff putting him on guard. A twist of pain wrenched his stomach, and he winced, reaching for his sword and comforted by the coolness of its grip as he glared at the wizard.

"What sources, pray tell?" he said as Tallus was covered by the crowd, lost to him near the tavern's door. A needling sensation pricked at his palms and worked slowly up toward his wrist and forearm.

"Pardon?" Rilyana asked innocently.

"Who told you about me?" he asked directly, standing as the pressure in his chest seemed to spread through his body. His mind raced, wondering what spell had hold of him. Instinct told him to draw his weapon and present it, but he resisted, confused by the sudden urge.

"Ask me nicely," Rilyana said coyly, ignoring his discomfort and flashing gold eyes.

"What?" he managed to ask as a scream echoed from upstairs, silencing the tavern's patrons. Smoke curled along the ceiling, and raised voices warned of fire as the crowd began to swiftly disperse. The ceiling shook with some unseen struggle, and a small explosion turned the crowd's dispersal into a desperate press. Rilyana disappeared among them, and Jinn stumbled forward, searching for Tallus when he caught sight of a growing shadow on the far wall.

Heartbeat thrumming in his ears, his sword fairly leaped into his hand, some remembered battle cry teasing at his tongue, waiting for the trumpets of war. Massive, black-feathered wings took shape, hovering over the heads of the crowd and sprouting from armored shoulders. A wavering, blank visage watched him with coal black eyes that danced with the sparkling light of a thousand souls. Jinn was pulled forward, each step his own but compelled by a greater force, dragged like a lodestone to the north. A feral grin spread across his lips as the angel regarded him coolly.

He forgot the murders, ignored the smoke and the screams, had no care for the fear of those driven before spreading flames. Sathariel had come and all the world's troubles were but trifles compared to Jinn's desire for the angel's pain. He jumped onto the bar, prepared to charge and end his years-long quest.

"Jinn!"

A faint voice cried out from somewhere amid the smoke, giving him a moment's pause, but he strode forward, stolen blade rising in his hand almost of its own accord, brandishing itself like a holy symbol to rebuke the unholy. He kicked half-empty glasses out of his way, striding toward his foe, but Sathariel's shadows began to dissipate, the wings slowly withdrawing.

"No! Gods damn you, come back!" he cried as the black eyes faded.

"Jinn!"

He blinked, fury clouding his vision until the angel was gone. The pressure in his chest faded, the needling on his skin disappearing in a breath. Turning, he found Quessahn at the bar, frantic eyes pleading for him to hear her, though he'd abandoned his last care for anything else at the sight of the angel.

"Allek is up there!" she pointed to the stairs and the cloud of smoke drifting from the second floor like misty snakes crawling along the walls. He gasped, cursing as the peculiar bloodlust left him, the stolen blade in his hand lowering as he realized he had forgotten his friend.

Jumping down from the bar, he raced for the stairs. At the bottom step, he caught a blur of motion above him, a dark shape hurled against the upper wall like a rag doll. Wood splintered beneath Allek's body as the rorden fell limp on the stairs, arms splayed over his head, his uniform's tabard torn away. Blood trickled down from the carved wounds upon his chest, already pooling in the hollow of his neck, dripping like a crimson necklace to the stairs. His friend's blank eyes stared at him almost accusingly beneath the wavering, smoky figure that stood at the top of the stairs.

Shadowy curls of black mist obscured the figure's features from head to toe, only the fiery glow of two flaming green eyes was visible within the insubstantial cloak. Allek's blade gleamed with red in the figure's hand.

Sigils, Jinn thought. Green flames. The killer.

He took the stairs two at a time as the figure turned away, billowing shadow stuff trailing behind the murderer in wispy ribbons. Jinn skirted the edges of a roaring flame, his boots crunching on the shards of a broken lantern as he made the last step. A private feast hall lay in ruins, the long table and chairs thrown aside, blood streaked across the floor. The killer stood at the broken window, eyes tilted curiously as Jinn approached.

"We do not recall you, deva," it said in a hollow, split-toned voice that growled and rolled through the room well after the words had been spoken.

"After a day of being recognized by strangers, I find that refreshing," Jinn replied and charged forward, but the figure had already slipped through the broken window and had begun to climb.

Jinn followed, pulling himself out onto a small balcony and jumping for the edge of the low roof. Shouting voices filled the streets, and fire bells had been rung, summoning water lines to douse the flames inside. He struggled at the damp edge of the roof, fingers chilled by bits of forming ice as he pulled himself up into a crouch. At the top of the cornered rooftop, the killer stood watching, eyes still tilted quizzically at his efforts.

He bounded up nimbly, navigating the rows of roof tiles. Swords raised, the pair met in a flurry of flashing blades. In three quick, hand-numbing clashes, their blades locked and the killer leaned in close, studying Jinn's face casually as the deva struggled against its unnatural strength. Winter wind whipped at his cloak and blew thin the wreath of smoke around his opponent, revealing a human figure if little else beneath the obscuring mist.

"Why have you come here?" it asked. A warm stench like burning flesh wafted across Jinn's face. "What do you wish of us?"

Blood, Allek's blood, slid down the killer's sword, dripping cold over Jinn's hands. He squinted in the ghostly light of the green eyes. The wetted blade pushed closer to his throat, and he strained, finding strength enough to hold it back.

"The angel," he managed to answer.

"Ah," the killer replied, pulling back. His blade twisted in a smooth motion, sliding down with a hellish screech until the pommel rested on Jinn's shoulder. The push seemed effortless, though it threw Jinn back as if he weighed nothing. He rolled down the roof, knocking tiles free as he scrambled to halt his descent, stopping only at the edge, his boots braced just at the drop. The killer never moved. "We smell vengeance in your blood, deva."

A chorus of discordant chuckles growled at Jinn as the killer tossed aside his bloody weapon, letting it fall to the street as he walked the apex of the roof, standing at its edge carelessly.

"It seems we know of you after all," the figure continued, letting one foot dangle over the drop. "We shall speak again, killer of angels."

In a whoosh of smoke, the figure fell, disappearing as Jinn crawled to his feet and ran to where the killer had disappeared. Though the alley behind the Storm's Front was still dark, he could see the dying light of the flaming green eyes as shreds of shadow dissipated and flew away from the broken body below.

Quickly he lowered himself over the side, climbing down from one windowsill to the next lower until he could jump to the ground. As he approached the body, the smoke was all but gone, the emerald light leaving behind pale, glazed-over eyes.

The body of a young woman, one of several who'd been in the tavern barely hours earlier, drinking and laughing, lay dead in the alley. Jinn shook his head, sheathing his sword and kneeling to study the girl in confusion.

"Possession?" he muttered quietly, feeling the chill of the girl's skin on arms as fragile as a child's, nowhere near capable of the strength he'd encountered above. Allek had spoken of multiple suspects, of madness and frantic claims of innocence. The fallen rorden's words began to fall into place, answering questions and at the same time creating new ones. Jinn stood back from the body, recalling more of what he'd been told. "Green flames . . . and skulls."

Iron clattered to the cobbles at the other end of the alley, a long, metal hook left in the wake of a frightened lamplighter. The boy glanced back once, enough to provide the Watch with an accurate description of what and who he had seen. A flickering glow of firelight illuminated the dead girl as shouts for water echoed from the front of the building. Jinn sank back into the shadows, his stomach turning as he caught his breath and contemplated his options.

"What lows to which you have stooped, deva," called a voice rumbling with power. A night black figure with wide wings, dark and feathered, crouched on the roof above. It half unfolded its wings with the hissing and crackling noise of dead leaves. "Presiding over the deaths of innocents? What a cold and unfeeling thing you have become, Jinnaoth."

Jinn stared up into the midnight dark of the angel's glistening, black eyes, hand drifting to his stolen blade, overcome by a familiar sensation of unnatural bloodlust.

"Sathariel," he whispered through clenched teeth, cold steel tingling beneath his fingertips as he faced his enemy.

FIVE

Quessahn flinched as flames licked above her head, cinders popping around her as she knelt over the rorden's body. She traced the sigils carved in his chest one by one, noting the depth and preciseness of the cuts. She fought her natural instinct to look away, to flee the encroaching fire, her breaths coming short and quick as she tried to ignore the blood on her hands and the pale bone showing just beneath the edges of Allek's wounds. Lost in the puzzle of arcane runes and trying to remain calm, she almost missed the rorden's hand.

It had fallen across the human's stomach, seemingly normal, until she noted the dark spot of one knuckle. Leaning closer, she found the left ring finger neatly severed and wondered at the mutilation, some obscure bit of her studies attempting to surface in her thoughts. At a loud crack, she abandoned the body and her curiosity as a section of the ceiling fell onto the stairs. She threw herself backward, landing awkwardly near the bottom of the steps and scrambling back on her hands to escape the flames, which glittered in the fallen human's blank eyes.

She shuddered and ran for the common room, ducking low instinctively as sections of the ceiling bowed, slivers of orange light shining through the cracks. A lungful of smoke set her to coughing as she fell through the front door, landing on her hands and knees.

Strong arms pulled her away from the burning tavern. Buckets of water sloshed by as she rubbed the redness from her eyes, steam hissing as several volunteers attempted to douse the flames.

Pushing her way through the crowd of gawkers that had gathered to witness the spectacle, she pulled a small, bound book from her belt and quickly began to draw what she had seen before memory had any chance to fail her. Smudges of blood and ash accompanied each drawing, her hands shivering in the cold as she fought to reproduce the intricate patterns of the symbols. She slipped to the back of the crowd, observing her work and nodding in satisfaction.

Must compare these to the others, she thought.

"More water!"

Quessahn flinched at the shout, recognizing the voice of Swordcaptain Dregg and drawing back farther from the crowd, pulling up her hood to conceal her elf features. She'd dealt with Dregg on more than one occasion and had no desire to encounter the foul man again. Studying figures outlined by the flames, she noticed quite a few of the Watch surrounding the tavern, not the least of which was Dregg himself, pacing with his fists planted on his hips, a swagger in his self-important step that made Quessahn want to vomit.

She angled herself closer, watching for Jinn to come stumbling out of the smoke, but after several breaths, the flames just grew higher, defying her hopes and the buckets of water being splashed through the windows. A young officer approached Dregg with a worried expression, and Quessahn leaned forward, trying to listen.

"Swordcaptain, several in the crowd say that Rorden Allek Marson was inside and has not escaped," the Watchman reported. "Maybe we should attempt to take one last look—"

"Nonsense," Dregg cut him off. "We've already sent one man in; the good rorden is dead. However, we do have reports of a suspect, the rorden's companion, a man by the name of Jinnaoth."

Quessahn's eyes widened at his words. She'd seen no one else inside, though the smoke had admittedly been thick, and she reasoned it would make Dregg only too happy if Jinn had murdered Rorden Allek. The swordcaptain would take great pleasure in hunting down an "undesirable" through the city streets.

"Find a runner," Dregg continued. "Have him inform the other patrols of the deva; consider him well-armed and hostile."

"Yes, Swordcaptain," the officer replied, turning to go. He was stopped by Dregg's hand on his arm.

"Acting Rorden, Officer, at least until Lord Neverember makes it official," he said with a slight grin. "This investigation is mine now."

The young officer seemed confused for a moment but nodded and left to follow Dregg's orders. Quessahn cursed and slipped away from the light of the fire. The Watch had protocols and procedures for rank promotions, procedures that should have weeded out dangerous men such as Lucian Dregg, but if Lord Neverember had paved Dregg's path through the ranks . . . Allek's investigation had been in secret. Dregg could maintain total control for several days before the Watch commanders could reassess the situation.

Plenty of time for much damage to be done, she thought. I've got to find Jinn, and quick.

She studied the burning tavern, her eyes settling upon the edge of the angled roof and following it around, past the crowd, to a darkened alley. A woman stood at the edge of the alley, eyeing the Watch and the crowd but suspiciously ignoring the burning tavern. Quessahn skirted behind the gathering, trying to appear casual as she studied the dark-haired woman and the unlit alley.

Common spells slid comfortably to the forefront of her thoughts, arranging themselves like familiar constellations in her mind. Others, darker spells that slithered comfortably in the recesses of her memory, she held in reserve, just in case. The dark-haired woman casually stepped into the alley, disappearing in the shadows.

Taking a deep breath, Quessahn followed.

Jinn pulled his hand away from the stolen blade, a breath of clarity leaving him a bit dazed as he stared up into the black eyes of Sathariel. He sensed some hitherto unknown enchantment in the weapon, something trying to force his hand when he had his own pool of hatred to draw from when dealing with the angel. Study of the sword could wait. He couldn't reach Sathariel, not fast enough at any rate, and refused to amuse his enemy by attempting to do so.

"You're lost in this, deva," Sathariel said, scanning his black eyes across the city. "Out of your depth, a relic of wars long over and meaningless."

"I found you," Jinn replied. "And the wars never ended."

"Mulhorand's gods are lost. They left you here, stuck in that mortal body," the angel said. "And here you are, scrambling for purpose, fighting for fleeting glories in mortal causes that serve only to feed your arrogance. Variel was right about you . . ."

Jinn's fists clenched at the sound of her name from the beast that had taken her away from him. For a breath he considered the height of the nearest wall, the street lantern hook above, the window ledge above that, but fought the impulse down. He was certain he would battle the angel on even terms soon enough and would not be goaded into making himself vulnerable.

"She said you would never quit, never stop long enough to see the lives you might have spent together. She knew that my destruction would mean nothing," Sathariel said, rising and spreading wide his black wings. "You cannot stop what is to come, Jinnaoth. You should have left this city when Variel asked you to."

Cold wind gusted through the alley as Sathariel ascended into the night, one shadow among many in the rolling clouds, leaving Jinn to stare for what seemed forever, hand once again on the blade stolen from the Vigilant Order. He recalled the scent of Variel's hair resting on his shoulder, the look in her silver eyes as she'd pleaded for him to abandon Waterdeep, a city not yet named when they had been already quite old. He wondered, as he always did, if he would have answered her differently if he had the chance to do it all over again.

"One of yours?"

Mara's voice pulled him away from reverie, and he turned to the body of the young woman in the alley. Mara knelt over the girl, sniffing the air and tracing the twisting angle of a lifeless arm.

"No," he answered as the hag whispered harshly over the corpse, eyes burning red as she cupped her hands close to the girl's lips. "She was possessed by something."

"Useless!" Mara growled, recoiling from the body and shaking the red dust of a crushed gem from her hands. "The soul is like ash, burned away to nothing."

"Jinn!" Quessahn arrived, circling round the scowling Mara, hands almost glowing with arcane threat. "The Watch is looking for you; Dregg is in charge."

"That didn't take long," he muttered, placing a calming hand on her shoulder and nodding to Mara. "We'll need to be quick, then. Distraction?"

"How far?" Mara asked, old strategies already in motion.

"Slow down! Who is this?" Quessahn asked, shoving his hand

away and eyeing the body between them. "What in the Abyss is happening here?"

"Pharra's Alley," Jinn replied, ignoring the eladrin's confusion. "And take Quessahn with you."

"If you insist," Mara said, staring her up and down disapprovingly.

"Jinn, what's going on?" Quessahn pressed, narrowing her eyes.

"No time," he said. "Just follow Mara's lead. We'll meet up later."

He didn't wait for her response, turning the east corner. He half hoped she might just leave her findings about the sigils with Maranyuss and abandon him for her studies at the House of Wonder, but he knew her stubbornness would keep her around a while longer.

Sliding along the wall, he peered around the corner at a slowly dispersing crowd bathed in orange light. The Watchmen present seemed focused on maintaining a perimeter as the bucket line did what it could to quench the fire. A handful of the Watchful Order had arrived, producing spells of water to douse the hottest of the flames.

Taking advantage of the distraction, Jinn sprinted across the street, keeping to the shadows of back alleys and smaller roads. He didn't know what he might find at Pharra's Alley, but he needed a chance to look closer, to find the circle of skulls.

Halfway to Ivory Street, he paused, seeing the bobbing light of a Watch patrol coming toward him. Cursing, he turned back, entering a winding series of alleys behind the shops and homes of the Street of Glances. The dark was more pervasive there, with lanterns spaced at wider intervals. In any other part of the city, it might have been considered a place to avoid after evenpeal. As it was, in Sea Ward, the dangers were less random and brutal than specific and well planned. Good coin was spent to keep certain elements out of the ward, and for the most part, the Watch was quite successful.

Shadows shifted in Jinn's wake, shuffling footsteps barely heard over the low whistle of wind that carried through the alleys. No one approached or made himself known, but Jinn slowed down all the same, walking the center of the alley like a tightrope, blade low and ready at his side. Stalkers at one's back usually indicated an attack from the front as a chosen mark was herded toward a place where brigands could conduct their business undisturbed. As Jinn made out the dim silhouettes of bodies pressed against walls and hiding in doorways ahead of him, he prepared to give whomever it was more of a disturbance than they were likely expecting.

First one then two shuffled into view, figures covered in cloaks and tattered robes. Scraggly hair haloed darkened faces in the lantern light. Jinn stopped, glancing sidelong at the stretch of alley behind him as more figures gathered in front of him. Curiously they stood in the light, fully visible, their eyes fixed on him, their faces expressionless. It was as though a gang of the homeless and destitute threatened him, a stale smell like dried sewage drifting toward him on the wind. Edging forward, he squinted, picking out details that raised the hairs on his neck and further deepened the mystery he found himself in.

Several bore faded red symbols on the left sleeves of once priestly robes, and many produced short, curved daggers, always wielded in the left hand. Their faces were unfamiliar—he'd rarely taken note of those who ran from his sword—but their allegiance to the Vigilant Order and Asmodeus was unmistakable. Their bright eyes regarded him without emotion, slack jawed and drooling into their tangled beards as they shuffled toward him, only the barest hint of life still shining in what was left of their minds.

"Ahimazzi," Jinn muttered, recognizing those punished by Asmodeus, their souls taken until they could make amends for failing in the devil-god's service. More than a dozen of them stood out from the shadows, lurching toward him, and by what he could hear, at least that many approached from behind. "No time for this."

He bolted forward, blade drawn and angling toward their left flank. The ahimazzi managed little more than faint moans as they slashed their rusted blades at him. He parried their clumsy stabs and thrusts, steel ringing loudly in the alley as he sought to slip through their numbers. He winced at the sound, fearful of drawing a Watch patrol to the alley. A dirty hand gripped his cloak, and he spun, kicking an unarmed woman out of his path as he swung his potential captor off balance. Once free, he blocked another dagger to the cobbles and tumbled into three of the stinking men, tripping one and punching another, though the third opened a burning cut on his arm.

On instinct he angled his sword to thrust through the man's chest but twisted the force of the strike into the blade's pommel, driving it into the ahimazzi's face. Teeth clattered to the ground as Jinn escaped to the end of the alley, casting a glance over his shoulder at the shocking number of the soulless who had gathered to spill his blood.

"So many," he whispered in astonishment. "All here in one place."

They shuffled after him, their eerie silence making it seem as though a graveyard had given up its dead to roam the streets of Waterdeep. A faint green glow reflected off of shop windows down Ivory Street, signaling the arrival of yet another Watch patrol. Swearing, he looked between the two groups and carefully plucked a small pouch from his belt. The smell of the ahimazzi grew closer as he watched the patrol make its way toward him from the east, judging the distance and muttering a swift prayer as he timed his strike.

As the soulless neared, within a few strides and wheezing, Jinn charged into the street, hurling the pouch into the Watchman's lantern. It burst into a puff of acrid, black powder, killing the light as surprised shouts echoed at his back. He dived into the shadows of a garden outside the walls of a large mansion, ducking alongside bushes as he ran from tree to tree. The Watch quickly lost interest in him as the ahimazzi stumbled into the street. Jinn pressed on as the two groups met, the officers' signal horns calling for reinforcements as he slipped across Flint Street and approached Pharra's Alley from the north.

Catching his breath, he entered the alley from its middle, at the edge of a street lantern's light, and noted the unlit lantern near the House of Wonder. He reckoned spreading rumors had kept the lamplighters from their duty in the supposedly haunted alley and was grateful for the dark, though he could see little of the famed place where the skulls were said to appear. Panting, he knelt down, feeling foolish as he tended to the stinging wound on his arm. The cobbles were cold and lifeless, as they'd been before, though each small clue seemed to draw him back to the place.

"Bogeymen," he whispered, wincing as he tried to clean the wound without water and fearing infection. "What in all the Hells did I expect to find?"

He leaned to his right, his hand, still sticky with Allek's blood, pressed to the cold ground. The brief contact jolted his arm, ripples of pain radiating up to his shoulder as the ground trembled beneath him. He fell back against the wall, sword half drawn and eyes wide as a nimbus of green energy swirled through the alley. It rose from the ground, spinning and flaring with flashes of emerald light. The smell of burning blood stung his nose, his rust-colored handprint sizzling where he had touched the ground.

Nine small spheres distinguished themselves in the circle,

forming swiftly, their shapes unmistakable as the circle's flames fragmented, gathering around the skulls in fiery auras. He had seen flameskulls before, undead creatures created as guardians, covered in runes carved into them by their makers, but the nine skulls that turned to face him were smooth and unmarked as if newly torn from their missing bodies.

It appeared as though the circle of skulls had no maker.

"The deva is persistent," one said, its deep, gravelly voice radiating with a power that caused Jinn's head to ache.

"Good," another replied. "He is useless to us otherwise."

Jinn backed away, slowly drawing his sword, wide eyed and waiting for some ancient memory, an insight from his old soul to come rushing forth and advise him as to what he should do. There was something there, hiding in his mind—a sense of familiarity that resisted his attempts at recollection, like a whispered rumor from his soul. The skulls floated closer, though they did not stray far from the gates of the House of Wonder.

"We cannot trust him," yet another spoke, a high, shrieking voice that set Jinn's nerves on edge. "We must kill him now!"

Their green flames roared higher as they turned on one another, arguing in a harsh language that crawled across Jinn's flesh like ants, but in the midst of it all, he heard them plainly. The sound of their arguing, nine voices shouting in unison, flames of green energy flaring from their eyes and between their teeth.

"The killers," he whispered. "These are Allek's murderers."

"You see!" The high-pitched one turned on him, shrieking. "He knows too much already! Kill him now!"

The skull's grinning mouth opened wide, issuing forth jets of emerald flame.

Quessahn eyed Mara suspiciously as they exited the alley opposite the direction Jinn had taken. She cursed the deva's mystery despite realizing his need to escape the Watch and exit the scene of the grisly crime. Plumes of smoke rose in twisting towers above the tavern, the flames under control, though the Storm's Front was certainly lost. The smoke gathered in dark clouds, joining those already blocking the stars from her view. She felt cut off from the sky, lost and flailing from one puzzle into another without the stars to guide her. And without that comfort, she pressed outward, seeking stability beyond the celestial veils in darker places of power. Something in that dark realm sparked her senses, focusing her attention on Mara as the strange woman stepped out into the orange light of the roaring flames.

Though Quessahn turned away from the burning tavern and the Watch, Mara went toward them, calmly approaching the nearest officer of the Watch. Quessahn swore, a spell coming to her lips, certain that Mara intended to betray Jinn at her first chance. She held back the dark magic, surrounded by too many witnesses, and reached for her dagger instead. If necessary, cold steel would cause less of a stir than hostile spells.

"Officer!" Mara called out, suddenly appearing frightened and fragile as the Watchman turned. "It's terrible! Murder in the alley! You must see!"

She pointed daintily, her face a perfect mask of distress as the officer pressed by her dutifully. Quessahn gripped her dagger so tightly, her hands hurt, but as the officer turned into the alley, Mara's expression hardened to a grim smile. She winked at Quessahn as she followed the man.

"Careful there, girl," she whispered, gesturing to the dagger hidden beneath the eladrin's cloak. "You'll cut yourself."

Quessahn narrowed her eyes and loosened her grip on the knife but did not release it. The Watchman paused as he neared the young woman's broken body, swearing as he turned and reaching for the signal horn at his belt, but Mara stood in his path. She hissed a stream of arcane words, waving her hand in a sweeping gesture that sparkled like glitter. The officer flinched as if struck, his eyes glazing over as the glittering light of Mara's spell swirled in his widened pupils. He stumbled forward, catching himself for a breath before slumping to the ground, snoring soundly.

"You might have warned me," Quessahn muttered as Mara knelt over the man's body.

"I might have, yes," Mara said as she stole the officer's signal horn. "But I don't know you, and I don't trust you. I think that puts us on even ground, does it not?"

"Fair enough," Quessahn replied as they exited the alley away from the tavern, hoods kept close as a Watch patrol passed them by and still more gawkers stopped to watch the last of the tavern's embers hiss with steam. They followed the wide street north, keeping to what shadows were available on the fairly well-lit street, avoiding taverns where curious patrons had gathered outside, staring down toward the glowing light of the Storm's Front.

Mara turned left into the narrower streets of Morningstar Way, and Quessahn let her lead, not wanting to let the wizard out of her sight. Most of the windows they passed were dark, curtains and shutters drawn against the chill, night air, but a few remained lit, usually near servants' entrances where there was still work to be done for their wealthy employers.

"How do you know Jinn?" Mara asked, breaking the silence between them.

"I-I helped him once, a few years ago," she answered, stammering, surprised by the question and stumbling over the half lie ungracefully. Mara seemed not to notice as they angled north again, darker alleys flanking them and stinking with refuse. "Something to do with an underground cult he'd been pursuing for some time."

They entered a longer stretch of shadows and dark windows, and Mara paused, pulling forth the signal horn from beneath her cloak. She raised it to her lips then paused, lowering it and smiling at Quessahn knowingly.

"I understand that you've helped him," she said and leaned closer, winking conspiratorially. "But you did not answer my question."

Mara blew several strident notes on the horn, employing a common Watch signal used to call reinforcements, before Quessahn could respond. The echoing blasts would reach most of Sea Ward, drawing the Watch away from Jinnaoth and keeping them busy while he attended to his suspicions. Quessahn let Mara's statement be, turning as several windows lit with fresh, flickering light.

"Where to now?" she asked, imagining patrols converging on them already.

"Now we shall go to meet Jinn," Mara answered, replacing the horn in her cloak, still smiling with a mischievous look in her dark eyes.

Quessahn averted her gaze, trying to appear concerned, though the Watch would not be looking for two women. They walked swiftly east, silent and stealthy, Quessahn's heart racing as she fought to banish the memories stirred by Mara's question.

SIX

Roaring flames rolled over Jinn's back as he jumped out of their path and tumbled into an awkward crouch, his swiftly drawn sword at odds with his instinct to retreat. He wasn't sure if he was even able to harm the skulls, much less battle them all at once. And though he had discovered the source of Sea Ward's sudden rise in mortality rate, he did not yet know the reason, and, most importantly, he did not know how Sathariel was involved.

As the circle devolved into chaos, arguing with one another over his fate, he fell back, observing them from a safer distance and wincing as their ghostly voices pierced his skull. Pressing a palm to his forehead, he noticed that the stain of Allek's blood had been burned away during the skulls' manifestation.

"Be still!" One voice rose above the others with a note of authority, silencing the circle's bickering. The speaker drifted to the circle's edge to face the deva as it addressed the others. "He doesn't care about us. He wants the angel, correct?"

Jinn remained silent as the other skulls turned toward him, hissing in impatience, their green flames diminished as they regarded him. He returned their cold scrutiny, the pits of their glowing eyes mirroring the emptiness he felt in his gut as he considered the accusation. Yet he could not deny the statement.

"Yes," he answered at length, tucking his quiet shame away for more peaceful times when he could look back and afford the luxury of regret.

A sibilant sigh passed through the skulls as he took a tentative step into their flickering, emerald light. They arranged themselves into the even circle they'd appeared in, their flames barely more than candlelight in the dark alley.

"Know this, deva," the skulls' apparent leader continued, "you have earned Sathariel's attention of late."

"The fall of the Vigilant Order," Jinn muttered, though he wondered how true that fall had been. The soulless ahimazzi were bound to the pleasure of Asmodeus, seeking redemption in suffering and service. Their numbers in Sea Ward suggested that his work—and theirs—was not yet complete.

"The angel's time here in Waterdeep is ending, and his purpose becomes more fragile with each day that passes," the skull added. "You shall soon have your reckoning."

"And what does this have to do with you?" Jinn asked, his jaw clenching as he fought the celestial blood in his veins, urging him to attack, to mete out justice and have done with questions and mysteries. "What does the blood you spill mean to him?"

"That is our business, deva," the skull growled. "Take care to bend the crusading mercy of your morals upon Sathariel, and we shall both have what we desire."

"And you take care not to presume what I desire," Jinn said threateningly, gold eyes flashing and stolen blade rising in hatred at the skull's condescending tone. The circle chuckled in unison, the sound of it rattling in his head like boulders.

"Agreed, deva," the lead skull said finally. "We wish you happy hunting."

The green flames flickered and began to fade as the circle spun slowly in an emerald fog that stank of dry rot and decay.

"No!" Jinn cried, slashing his sword through the dissipating mist. "Why is he here? What does he want? Tell me or I'll—!"

But the skulls were gone, only the lingering scent of their passing, of char and rot, hanging on the air. Jinn swore, slashing his sword across the ground with a shower of sparks before sheathing the weapon and calming himself. He paced in a circle where the skulls had appeared, staring at the cobbles and willing the undead things to reappear. One night had brought him closer to his desires than he'd ever been, and despite the slow-burning fires of his patience, another day of waiting, so close to his quarry, seemed more than he could suffer.

He stared into the middle distance, slowing his racing heart and breathing deeply for long moments before setting off toward North Ward and Mara's shop. Mysteries raced through his thoughts, but he felt certain that the key to finding Sathariel lay within the secrets of the circle of skulls.

The scent of smoke fit well on the breeze of winter's first night. Mingling with that of grand fireplaces throughout Sea Ward, the smell of charred flesh was obscured but did not go unnoticed. Tallus skulked in the shadows across the street from the dying fire, glowering at the blackened, smoldering remains of the Storm's Front. He spun his gnarled wooden staff slowly, grinding it between the cobbles absently as Rorden Dregg swaggered and handed out orders as if they were gold. Dregg disgusted him but Tallus knew it had been time for a change in the local Watch's leadership. Dregg's connections, however ill gotten, had proven a timely convenience.

Allek Marson's time had gone on for far too long, and there was no ward rotation scheduled for another month or two. Tallus's days were numbered, with too much to do and too little time, and his work could not go unnoticed for much longer.

Better that it be Dregg, he thought, fool that the man is.

Tallus fumed, having watched the deva easily escape, assisted by the meddling Quessahn and another woman whom he had not recognized. That there would likely be a bounty on their heads did not comfort the archmage in the least. He needed Jinnaoth dead, needed anyone with a chance of uncovering his secrets removed as quickly as possible. Marson's Watch, ironically, might have been well suited to the task of tracking down the deva, while Dregg would be lucky to find a decent place to drink while his men did all the work.

A section of the tavern's roof collapsed, sending showers of sparks dancing over the heads of those left to witness the destruction as if it were the evening's entertainment. Tallus scowled. Rumors would spread more quickly, prompting some, those wealthy enough, to move on to secondary homes within the city. Still others would remain as they were, willing pawns to his devices, their hidden altars burning nightly with offered sacrifices. Even to the wealthy and powerful, perhaps especially, promises of yet more wealth and power had driven many to debase themselves before dark and hidden lords. Many of those even reveled in the bloodletting, an extravagance beyond common parties and social status.

Tallus grinned at the thought. Though fallen, his order's reach had not been completely lost.

"I warned you, wizard," Sathariel's voice wrapped around him like a shroud, holding him in a sudden grip of terror, the trembling shadows of the angel's presence fluttering at the peripherals of his sight. His heart jumped wildly, and he coughed, fighting for breath as the fit overcame him. He found specks of blood on his hand when it had passed. "The deva is a trifle, a minor inconvenience unless you antagonize him."

"I . . . was trying to kill him!" Tallus replied, his throat sore between ragged, bone-chilling breaths.

"Then I expect he is sufficiently antagonized," Sathariel growled close to the archmage's ear. "Tell me, what have you gained for your efforts?"

"For one, another Marson is dead, the last of them," Tallus answered, regaining his composure and taking pride in the one small victory of the evening. "One step closer to the end of this business."

"There is that, I suppose," the angel said. "But you have also introduced Jinnaoth to the circle of skulls."

"Nonsense," the wizard retorted, searching for Sathariel's dark eyes in disbelief. "Impossible."

"He has already spoken with them." The words pressed upon Tallus's chest like a load of rocks. The familiar tickle itched in the back of his throat, but he breathed deeply, fighting the urge to cough. "I'm beginning to suspect the deva may be a more suitable ally to my purposes than you. His agenda is pure, if a bit distasteful, and his betrayals are more direct and predictable."

Tallus turned away from Sathariel's ebon visage, ignoring the angel's goading and already devising how to sever the deva's presence from his work. The Art was stable enough after the Spellplague, more so with the assistance of older magic, yet his task was not easy and, thanks to the mysterious skulls, not yet fully understood to him. Claiming his prize would be that much more difficult with the deva to contend with. As he pondered the problem, his gaze lingered over the dispersing crowd in front of the tavern, drawn easily to the sight of crimson lips and fair locks in a night blue dress as Rilyana Saerfynn followed some distance behind her drunkard brother. The soft, undulating curve between her breast and hip derailed his thoughts for a moment; the thought of her flirting with the deva derailed them further.

"Jinnaoth also knows how to place duty before lust." The angel chuckled, a hellish sound that conveyed an insatiable hunger for mortal failings.

"Fear not," Tallus replied, collecting himself though he could not help but keep a possessive eye upon Rilyana until she had strolled out of sight. "I will not fail you."

"As you wish, Archmage, but I truly do not have the capacity for fear or worry," Sathariel said. "Should you fail, your soul is forfeit, your order is dead, and my master shall have the prize I was sent for in the first place. You are merely a means to an end, but you are not the only means by any stretch of the imagination."

"An end," Tallus repeated wistfully. "The First Flensing."

"Do your work. Give to the skulls the power they need for all the bloodletting they require." The angel's oppressive voice grew fainter as the shadows receded. "And perhaps you and yours shall be forgiven."

A light snow began to fall as the angel departed, leaving Tallus both momentarily relieved and full of dread as he turned back toward the House of Wonder under a cloud of dark thoughts. Some distance away he could make out faint shouts and at least two signal horns echoing through the ward. He cursed Dregg and shook his head, already lamenting the regrettable loss of Rorden Marson's subtle yet effective leadership of the Watch.

"Dregg will wake all Waterdeep with his floundering," he muttered, turning in to a darkened block of narrow streets and widely spaced lanterns. Here and there among the shadows and short alleys, he could see them, blank eyes staring back, too dull to even carry a glitter of hope at his passing. Their stench stung his nose, and he covered it with a perfumed sleeve, trying not to imagine himself wandering among their pitiful numbers.

He sighed in frustration, contemplating more direct means of eliminating the deva without disturbing the delicate details of his work. He no longer required the stealth of the past month, but secrecy was paramount lest he fail as famously as those who had gone before him—or worse. Mere thought of the circle of skulls sickened him, their desperate hunger and practical impotence a fate worse than death, though he suspected his own fate, should he falter, would be legendary, delivered not by a prince among devils, but by a god.

"Mere days," he whispered hoarsely, banishing the imagined terrors. "Then I shall breathe easier, should I require breath at all."

Quessahn sat in the dark, keeping silent as Mara made her way from one arched window of Pages Curious to the next, tracing the edge of each drawn curtain with whispered incantations. Gold needlework in the cloth flared at the woman's touch then faded as she passed, warding the interior of the shop against intruders or eavesdroppers. From the front of the shop to the back, Quessahn marveled at the collection of old magic, pre-Spellplague items of effortless function, the nearness of their energy feeling like the presence of an old friend.

Her circuit completed, Mara settled over a wide table of books and scrolls in the back corner and blew to life an enchanted candle. Quessahn edged close to the table, her eyes drawn to the candlelight and in particular the ornate candleholder it sat in. She narrowed her eyes at the worked silver, noting the alarmingly familiar design of a sword within an archway, encircled by a stylized shield.

"You are a thief as well?" she asked, gesturing to the candleholder and crossing her arms, recognizing the mark of one of the House of Wonder's masters. "Where did you get that?"

Mara looked up from the scrolls, her eyes flashing with anger as she slid the candle closer to herself and out of the eladrin's reach.

"It was a gift," Mara answered sharply. "One of very few that—" She stopped, sighed angrily, and turned back to her work upon the table. "I am no thief. Well, no common thief at least."

Even in the candle's light, it seemed that shadows deepened in Mara's presence, the effect lingering in places where she had been for long moments. The strange woman appeared and acted human, but there was a timeless spark in Mara's gaze that gave Quessahn pause. She kept her guard up, ritual dagger at hand and spells on the tip of her tongue, as they waited in silence for Jinn's arrival.

A click at the back door sent a cold chill down Quessahn's spine. She spun around, a spell on her lips, before finding the deva's gold eyes in the dark. She relaxed as he closed and locked the door, sliding a kissed finger over the bolt that caused it to snap tight with a flash of light.

"Any trouble?" Mara asked.

"No more than usual," he replied, throwing his greatcoat over a cushioned chair. "Any news?"

"A little more than usual," Mara answered. She pulled a large tome close to the candle's glow. "It seems these murders have happened before."

Quessahn's frustration at being ignored by the pair faded as interest in the book took over. She edged closer to the table, trying to read as Jinn perused the page, a look of confusion crossing his smooth features. He glanced at her once, as if noticing her for the first time, then returned to the book.

"How is this possible?" he asked. "The broadsheets would have been selling out toes to heels at news like this."

"And they might well have been," Mara said and flipped the book closed, pointing to the cover. "Around three hundred years ago."

"Toes to heels?" Quessahn muttered as she leaned close, the book's leather cover showing the date *The Year of Sinking Sails, 1180 Dale Reckoning.*

"From the poor to the rich," Jinn answered absently, running his fingers over the date as his golden eyes darkened. "When did the circle of skulls first appear?"

"Sometime thereabouts," Quessahn said, "if I'm not mistaken."

Jinn and Mara looked at her in unison, still bearing the same expression of having been interrupted, as if she'd disrupted a well-practiced routine. She saw in that look the years they had worked together, both committed to some task that seemed to have consumed them, isolating them from the normal lives of others. The look concerned her and made her fear for the possible victims they might find in the coming days. She wondered if Jinn still had the capacity to care for the lives of others in the midst of the war he fought.

"What about the sigils?" Jinn asked, breaking her troubled line of thought.

"Difficult, but the signs are striking," she answered, laying her sketches on the table beside Jinn's chapbook. "These are a kind of spell, a ritual, but they're incomplete. However, the patterns, the . . . *context* of their proximity makes some sense."

"I see," Mara said, turning the sketches around and tracing them lightly with a painted fingernail. "Almost like a cipher."

"What's the connection?" Jinn asked.

"It is a spell of a sort, only it's still being cast," Quessahn said. "These are just random sets of runes, from one body to the next, sort of like reading a book, but only reading every tenth word at a time."

"But the Watch has destroyed many of the bodies," Jinn said thoughtfully. "Would that not break the spell?"

"The sigils have already been cast," Mara answered. "Their place in the overall pattern is taken and they"—she twirled her hand as if searching for the right word—"*exist,* until the spell is completed or until it fails."

Jinnaoth stood perfectly still, head bowed, as though frozen in thought. Quessahn fought the urge to place a hand on his arm, shocked by the impulse and stepping away from the deva lest she forget herself. Her gaze lingered on the way he kept one finger on the middle of his chin, just at the terminus of a swirling design that rose from beneath his collar. She smiled, but stopped when she caught Mara staring at her.

"So I suppose all that remains is the question of the day," Jinn said at length, leaning on the table. "What kind of spell?"

"Impossible to say," Quessahn said, pulling her eyes away from the knowing gaze of Mara. "Though, considering the method of casting, I'm not sure I'd want to find out."

"We must find out." Jinn turned to Mara, once again seeming to lock Quessahn out of some private understanding. He tapped a finger on the sketched sigils. "This is what we were looking for; this is what will lead us."

Quessahn was troubled by the strange light in Jinn's eyes, the cruel smile on Mara's lips. They turned to the books, ignoring her as she observed them, fuming with disbelief and feeling betrayed by the dim hope that Jinn had truly changed since she'd last seen him. She recalled the face of a murdered child, the body she'd last seen being taken away by the Watch, and rounded on the pair.

"Why didn't you mention the fingers?" she asked, stealing Jinn's attention though Mara only glanced at her with a knowing smile before returning to her study. "What does it mean?"

"The left hand is a symbol," Jinn said after some consideration. "Many religions hold some significance for it, primarily because most people are dominantly right-handed. In this case it is a symbol of divine will, the hand bound to the purpose of a god's law . . . the law of Asmodeus."

"Asmodeus?" Quessahn uttered the name in a whisper, a hundred different depictions of Hells and devils rising to the forefront of her mind, classical images of both speculation and arcane fact.

"The left hand of Asmodeus represents the forceful nature of domination, fierce loyalty, and wrath," he continued, holding up his hand and bending the ring finger forward. "The ring finger symbolizes the covenant made and the bound soul."

"And when severed?" she asked.

"The soul is claimed, and the body is forfeit, either abandoned or controlled," Mara said, not looking up from her book. "Not that the how of the matter is truly important, but the symbolism of the act—"

"Suggests followers of Asmodeus," Quessahn finished quietly, staring off into the shadows and seeing the murders in a new and frightening light.

"And that is why we agreed to help Rorden Marson," Jinn said.

"What do you mean?" she asked, searching the seriousness in his gold eyes and fearing his answer even as she allowed herself to reluctantly accept the inevitability of what he would say.

"Asmodeus has some stake in these killings," he answered. "One of his servants, an angel known as Sathariel, has been drawn to Sea Ward because of them—"

"And you've come to stop the murders," she said. "To stop whatever this cult is up to and—"

"No," Jinn said and her hope faded, seeing in him what she had not wanted to see, what she had always seen and tried to deny. "We've come for the angel."

"I should have known," she replied. Fury filled her as she pulled her cloak tight and stormed toward the door, shaking her head and cursing herself for a fool. She glanced back, her hand on the door, and saw a familiar glimmer in his gaze that pained her. There was hope, she decided, somewhere between his celestial sense of duty and the mortal heart that had been forced upon him, but she couldn't rely on it to do the right thing when it mattered. "I'll be back," she said. "There's something I need to do."

Then she charged out into the winter night before she could change her mind. She didn't need another chance to search him for what was no longer there, the ghost hiding in every gesture and stare. Snow swirled between the buildings as she walked the circle of crowded buildings around Pages Curious, the cold bracing her and keeping her alert.

The stars were caught behind a net of white clouds, and she let herself be further drawn into the darker places of her magic, letting the stark truths of half-formed, chaotic realms direct her thoughts.

"Better that it be the dark now," she whispered bitterly, a scent of smoke still clinging to her cloak, specks of dried blood caught in the creases of her hands. "Better that I be more prepared."

"I can see it, you know." Mara's voice stopped her cold, and she spun to find the dark-haired woman walking out of the shadows.

Quessahn slid a suspicious hand toward her dagger, magic tingling at her fingertips as Mara approached, the same knowing smile upon her face as before. "You love him, don't you?"

The statement pierced her like a knife, sharp and direct, flaying any attempt she might have made to deny the accusation and leaving the truth laid bare on her startled face. Wide eyed, she looked away, shaking her head in disbelief at being caught so unawares. She forgot her prepared spell and released her dagger.

"Not exactly," she replied, anger warming her. Mara spoke as though Quessahn's privacy were a mere puzzle for someone to figure out. But in that moment, her senses still freshly heightened by her magic, she caught another glimpse of the dark aura that hung around Mara, a shroud that squirmed with a life of its own. "You're not human."

"Not remotely," Mara said, still smiling.

They stood facing each other down for long moments. Quessahn's thoughts raced, wondering if Mara would tell Jinn, wondering if the next day would bring questions she didn't want to answer. Again she cursed herself for getting involved. For all of her indignant posturing with Jinn, she'd agreed to help for selfish reasons no less questionable than his.

"Well," she said at length and turned away. "We both have secrets, then."

"No," Mara said, a scratching tone in her voice that lifted gooseflesh on Quessahn's arms. She turned to find a tall, dark figure standing where Mara had been. Tattered, black robes hung thick across sharp shoulders, the cloth fluttering as shadows crept from crevices toward Mara. Thin wisps of stringy, black hair escaped the darkened hood where two pinpoints of coal red light glittered to life above a lionlike smile of sharp teeth. Skin the color of a dark bruise covered the hand that rose from Mara's robes, pointing at Quessahn almost teasingly as she said, *"You* are the one with a secret."

Quessahn backed away slowly and readied spells upon her tongue, dagger once again comfortable in her grip. But Mara merely turned away, her form melting bit by bit back into the illusion of a dark-haired woman, leaving Quessahn alone in the snow. She shivered as the shadows returned to their places. The hag returned to her shop and her strange alliance with the deva.

Finding her feet, Quessahn turned them back toward the House of Wonder, walking in a daze as she pondered what affect the years had had upon Jinnaoth—and the man she'd once known.

SEVEN

Several blocks of cold streets passed in an unremarkable blur, Quessahn's mind elsewhere, her eyes only mechanically watching her surroundings. The gates of the House of Wonder opened noiselessly, the cold iron numbing her fingers until the warmth of the House's corridors brought the feeling back in comfortable waves. Melting snow on the back of her neck sent chills down her spine as she passed the spectral guardian and made her way to the tall stairs at the far end of the house.

The scratching of quills on parchment was the only indication she was not alone as she took the first step, grinding her teeth and steeling herself to deal with the insufferable Archmage Tallus. She'd always rolled her eyes when others mentioned the patience of long-lived elves and eladrin, for she had no patience for the archmage, but she suspected he could be of help to her. Some of the books in his library were whispered about among other students of the Art, and having had only fleeting glimpses at the tomes, Quessahn knew that at least half of the rumors were true.

If anyone possessed the knowledge to unravel the spell being cast in spilled blood, it would be Tallus. The other masters she did not know as well and was not sure who among them she could trust, but with the archmage at least she knew where she stood. It would have to be enough.

The hallway at the top of the stairs stretched several strides to the south, far longer than any exterior view of the building might have led the casual observer to believe, just one of the many wonders in the old house. Her lip curled in disgust, expecting any moment to be accosted by Gorrick, Tallus's lapdog apprentice and as intolerable as his master. But halfway to the archmage's door, Gorrick never appeared, nor did there seem to be any light shining beneath the door at an hour the archmage was usually up and about.

She listened at the door, hearing nothing, and tentatively knocked just loud enough to be heard by anyone awake. There was no answer. She laid a hand on the handle, heart hammering in her chest, and the door opened easily, unlocked and barely shut. Pushing it open fully, she gasped in wonder, wide eyed at the bare walls, faint outlines of bright paint where shelves had once stood, impressions in old dust where a large desk had sat. Naught remained but a square of light from the window and the burned-out nub of a candle on the ledge.

Tallus was gone.

"Bloody Mystra," she swore, her mind racing at the possible implications, thoughts coming back around to what had brought her to the room in the first place. "If anyone possessed the knowledge," she muttered and closed the door behind herself, swiftly crossing the mystical hallway as if it, too, would disappear and leave her stranded somewhere between reality and nothing.

Nightal 21, the Year of Deep Water Drifting (1480 DR)

The afternoon sun painted the winter sky pink and violet as Jinn strolled slowly through Pharra's Alley, searching the faces of a dispersing crowd. Hopeful students gathered daily before the gates of the House of Wonder, some performing minor tricks for passersby. Illusions danced at their feet and flew through the air, their makers' chants accompanied by the occasional clink of a coin dropped into tin cups at their feet. Jinn saw no familiar faces among the crowd, but he hadn't truly expected to. He was passing by the House only on the remote chance of spotting Archmage Tallus.

Quessahn, after informing them of the archmage's disappearance, had remained strangely quiet, she and Mara regarding one another with a chilled silence he hadn't yet deciphered. He ignored their discomfort. Having last seen Tallus at the Storm's Front, just before Allek had been killed, he was more than eager to question the wizard.

As the bells of gateclose sounded, pealing through the streets, one crowd's dispersal seemed to cue the slow appearance of another. Jinn smiled slyly as they passed by the alley's mouth in small groups. Formal costumes of black and white, chased in silver and gold, were the favored looks for the evening as early celebrants gathered in the failing light. Painted masks leered as they drifted by, some simple with subtle designs, a few others garishly designed with feathers and fanged mouths. A pair of coaches sped toward one or another of several celebrations, false faces blurred within the confines of thin glass as they turned left up the street.

Jinn had no particular love of the revived Winterfirst celebrations, an archaic and mystical ceremony reduced to an excuse for expense and pomp among the wealthy. But he could not deny its usefulness. He adjusted the plain white mask over his features and pulled his hood low, nodding respectfully to a passing patrol of the Watch. For one night at least, he could conduct his business without too much complication.

"We can't just knock and expect to be invited in as guests," Quessahn said as they made their way up Flint Street. "Tallus is not entirely fond of either of us to begin with. If he's involved in these killings . . ."

"We'll only observe," Jinn replied. "At first."

"Then we'll knock," Mara added, smiling from behind her thin-handled mask. "I am infinitely curious to peruse his library."

They passed the hollowed remains of the Storm's Front, the windows not yet boarded up and the area still smelling of smoke. Jinn turned toward a district of tall towers and large homes, putting the tavern to his back, his stride quickening at the thought of Allek left to burn inside. He whispered a prayer for his friend's forgiveness just as he caught sight of a swaggering figure near the end of the street.

"Dregg," he said and slowed, sliding casually into the shadows of closed shops on the north side of the street. Though well out of sight, he soon realized he needn't have bothered. The former swordcaptain's swagger seemed well enhanced by early drinking. His uniform still dirty from the previous evening, his boots still grayed with ash, the acting rorden seemed comfortable in his new role—until, Jinn reasoned, the Watch superiors caught up to him.

Fortunately for Lucian Dregg, much of the Watch's attention was focused elsewhere; a gang war stretching from Mistshore into Downshadow had left the relatively peaceful Sea Ward under Rorden Allek's supervision for some time. Dregg would have time to enjoy his usurped title.

"Jinn," Mara whispered, pointing at the human. "The dagger."

Jinn narrowed his eyes, noting the glint of silver at Dregg's belt, an ornate dagger standing out on the unkempt rorden like a lit candle in a dark room. He balled his fists, eyeing the number of people in the streets with a curse.

Too many witnesses, he thought.

"What is it?" Quessahn asked.

"The dagger belonged to Allek," Jinn explained. "I gave it to him when he became rorden."

"Gods," she replied. "He stole it from Allek's body."

"No he didn't," Mara said, lowering her handled mask. "Allek never wore the dagger."

Mara's eyes remained fixed on the rorden as Jinn turned, seeing something in her face he'd glimpsed only a few times. She had been friendly with Allek Marson out of habit, a part of her disguise, but she had been among mortals for longer than even he knew. He would never see tears in her eyes, never remorse or regret, but the hag knew revenge, that he could count upon.

"Stay here," he told Mara. "Keep an eye on Dregg. See what he gets up to."

"Where are we going?" Quessahn asked, laying a firm hand on Jinn's arm and forcing him to face her, adding, "Do not even think you'll leave me here as well."

"No, I'll need your help," he answered and turned back the way they'd come. "We're going to Allek's home first. We'll catch up to Tallus later."

They rushed back down Flint Street to the southern end of the ward, hiding themselves in groups of party-goers, ducking down side streets to avoid Watch patrols. He had no fear of being recognized by Dregg, but he expected the men under his command to be more competent. They would begin questioning random citizens, ask for masks to be removed before moving on—all the trademarks of a well-trained force. It was Allek's legacy in uniform, and Jinn worked to avoid each patrol, not wanting to have cause to harm that legacy.

After several turns and a long, winding path through the southern part of the ward, they approached the modest home of Allek Marson warily, hiding in the shadows of early evening between the houses. Few in that area of Sea Ward would be attending any of the night's festivities, unless they were hired to cook or serve.

Satisfied that no one was around, Jinn and Quessahn ascended the short steps and tested the front door. The lock was smashed, the brass doorknob still lying on the ground, smudged by dark prints. Jinn entered the house, noting the ashy boot prints just inside and feeling his blood boil at the thought of Dregg violating the privacy of his friend's home. The office had been ransacked, though to Allek's credit, there was little to destroy save a small desk, a comfortable chair, and a low table covered in various broadsheets from across the city.

Quessahn lit a lantern, and Jinn's gaze immediately turned to the fireplace on the opposite side of the room. An empty knife stand remained on the mantle where Allek had kept the gifted dagger stolen by Dregg. A fine painting, one of Allek's few valuable possessions, lay on the floor, sliced to shreds.

"Should we be looking for anything specific?" Quessahn asked.

"No," Jinn answered. "But I expect we'll know it when we see it. We know how Allek was killed; now we need to know why."

He took a deep breath and closed his eyes. He opened them slowly, taking in the details of the room. Aside from the general mess, Jinn saw little out of order save for the dark smudges of heeled boot prints throughout the room. He followed them as Quessahn raised the lantern high, tracking them to the base of a narrow stairway just outside a small kitchen. He took the stairs and Quessahn followed. The eerie silence set his nerves on edge, and he kept a hand on his sword, wondering if they were truly alone.

Allek's bedroom was just as sparse as his office: a simple bed, a chest of drawers, and a small desk by the single window. Nothing appeared disturbed and the shadows created by the lantern revealed no hidden assassins. Just the same, Jinn did not let down his guard, sensing something beyond the mere ghost and memories of a murdered friend.

"How long before Dregg is replaced, do you think?" Quessahn asked as she set the lantern down and laid out a scroll on the bed, her rune-covered dagger in hand.

"Long enough," he replied and sat down at the desk, opening drawers. "It is not unknown for some officers to take private donations—sharpening the blade, I believe they call it. If someone in particular wants Dregg in charge for some reason, then it can be afforded."

"Long enough, then," she said as Jinn pulled forth a bundle of letters from the desk's bottom drawer, each of them smelling of fine perfume. He leaned closer to the lantern, making out the name Rilyana Saerfynn on each of the missives. Quessahn cleared her throat, waving her dagger over the scroll and whispering arcane words, each followed by a spark of glowing light from the parchment as the writing burned itself away.

Jinn tucked the letters into his coat and sat quietly as the eladrin performed the ritual, a working of sight from what he could recognize among the recited passages. Her eyelids fluttered as the magic took shape, tiny arcs of energy rippling across her face, her voice reaching a quiet crescendo, leaving her breathless and shaking. Her bright blue eyes pooled with clouds of swirling black as visions of the recent past rushed into them.

"Lucian Dregg," she muttered, cocking her head as if listening to a quiet conversation. "He was here, drunk and swearing at . . . something . . . at someone?"

"Who else?" Jinn pressed, and she spun around, blinking fiercely and squinting. She stood at the top of the stairs, her ear against the wall, eyes rolling.

"Archmage Tallus," she answered and squeezed her eyes shut, covering her ears. "They're shouting, fighting about something!"

Jinn stood and grabbed her elbow as she swayed forward over the stairway, reeling in the grip of the magic. She grabbed his hand, sinking to her knees, trembling and trying to catch her breath.

"What are they saying?" he asked quietly, careful not to startle her.

"Too many voices," she managed. "Hundreds . . . screaming." She inhaled, arching her back torturously and shouting, her voice hellish as she dismissed the spell and collapsed in Jinn's arms, breathing heavily. She got to her feet unsteadily, black eyes clearing to blue, like the sky revealed by a passing storm. "Something was with them. Something old and powerful. I couldn't see through it, couldn't hear. It was like a hole hanging in the air on black wings . . ."

"Sathariel," Jinn whispered, thoughts racing as he tried to fathom what business had been conducted in Allek's home, scarce hours after the rorden had been slain.

"Bloody Mystra," Quessahn swore, regaining her balance. Then she froze as a whimpering groan, guttural and plaintive, echoed from somewhere downstairs.

Jinn drew his sword, his instincts proving honest on at least one undeniable fact.

They were not alone.

Harsh-worded rhymes drifted in the air as Tallus chanted, slowly turning a short length of ash wood between his fists. Standing in the dark at the back door of Allek's home, he strained to pull the magic into shape, smiling in triumph at each victory, each curve or bend that formed to his will. The energy swirled around him tentatively, like an animal fearing a trap. He had read accounts of magic use before the Spellplague and pitied those who had drawn upon the well-ordered threads of the old Weave, as if magic were an instrument waiting for simple breath to give it life. They hadn't suffered for the Art, hadn't wrestled the raw energy of magic into a usable shape with mere words and willpower. He saw achievement of the Art as a crucible and many of those who had once been long lived upon the magic of the past were long dead due to the storm of magic that he had learned to command.

With a final phrase, the first spell was complete, and he stepped back, grinning as an oily sheen crawled over the windows and doors of the Marson house, sealing it such that his next spell would eliminate the loose threads Rorden Allek had invited into Sea Ward.

You're wasting time, Archmage, the angel said in his mind. Tallus sneered.

"The skulls are well tended," he replied, returning his attention to the spell at hand. "And I shall gain from them all I need soon after midnight."

Truly? Sathariel said. The winter air grew colder, numbing Tallus's hands. The angel's shadow fell upon the house, wings outstretched, his face like a smooth, black mask haloed by an ebony flame. *I wonder, who is betraying whom?*

"What do you care? We shall both have what we want!" Tallus spit back, growing tired of the angel's meddling and thinking he would have rather dealt with Asmodeus directly.

Take care, Archmage, that the skulls do not get what they want. The angel descended, his black eyes hovering inches from Tallus's face. *Or you shall share in their punishment.*

"You flatter me," Tallus said. "I would not dare attempt to fool a god as they once did."

Mind your tongue! Sathariel's voice tore through his mind like lightning, ripping through his confidence and racking his body with pain. He fell to his knees, breathless and clutching at his chest. *Have some respect or the only immortality you shall receive will be in the burning pits of Nessus. Now finish this petty business, and do not try my patience further!*

Cold wind rushed around Tallus, whipping at his robes as Sathariel left him gasping and shaking. Grunting with effort, he raised the ash wood, turned it once more between his fists, and chanted the last of his ritual. As the wood rotted and crumbled in his grasp, he threw it against the back door and fell forward, cursing as the pain faded from his chest and limbs. Rising slowly on his hands and knees, he spied the pale, wide-eyed face of his apprentice watching him from the bushes along the side of the house.

"Quit cowering, Gorrick," he said, clearing his throat and regaining his voice. He brushed the rotted wood from his hands and nodded in satisfaction, done with the deva and the eladrin. Leaning on his staff, he scowled as Gorrick fell into step at his side and prepared himself for the rest of the evening's work and for dealing with the circle of skulls. Though they had been weakened by the Spellplague, he knew his acting could not fool them for long. If he gave the circle of skulls cause to sense his duplicity, all would be lost. "Tell the others to ready themselves; then return to my tower. I have important work for you."

"Yes, Archmage," Gorrick said, grinning and placing a Winterfirst mask over his face before setting out to begin the last rites.

Tallus watched him go then limped slowly out to the street, heading home and taking a peculiar interest in his own weaknesses, his aching joints and untrustworthy pulse, forging a memory of them that would make his victory all the sweeter.

"Important work indeed," he muttered.

Quessahn flinched at the sound of a chair sliding across the wood floor. She stared down into the inky dark of the stairway, her moon elf eyes strangely unable to penetrate shadows that ebbed and flowed like water. Jinn stood still as a statue, sword drawn and listening intently, his gold eyes narrowed to tiny glints of light in the faint glow of the lantern. Closing her eyes, she pressed her palms to her head, shutting out the echoing sounds and sights from her previous ritual, the screams of a thousand souls in torment attempting to shatter the calm she would need in the next few moments.

The spells slowly overtook the visions, their singsong rhymes setting her at ease as she whispered their ancient names, calling upon the mystical sources that fueled her magic. A hand fell on her arm, and she looked up, her flesh tingling at the contact as she saw the question in Jinn's eyes. She nodded, waving her hand to signal that she was fine as she crept back into the bedroom and pulled back the curtains from the window. Her reflection stared back at her, illuminated by the weak lantern light. The glass was cold and clammy, black as fresh tar, and though the latch was unlocked, it resisted her attempts to open it. Desperate, she smashed the pommel of her dagger into the window, cursing as the spiderweb of cracks slowed and reversed itself, repairing the damage.

"We're trapped," she whispered.

"And something is down there," he added.

"Not some*one*?" she asked.

"No," he answered as a chill breeze blew up the stairs, bringing with it a stench of decay that burned her nose and made her stomach turn. The smell seemed to seep through the wood, hissing through the walls as an unintelligible murmur came from the bottom of the stairs.

"What is it?" she managed, covering her mouth in an unsuccessful attempt to block the smell.

"It's here," he said.

In the shadows at the base of the stairway, the shape of a figure coalesced in the dark, a black silhouette in the shadow so faint that Quessahn suspected she could have imagined it. The mere sight of it chilled her skin, and her breath came in steamy puffs as the figure half crawled up the bottom steps in nervous twitches. She stepped back as Jinn raised his sword, a spell on her lips as she brandished her ritual dagger and noticed movement to her right.

The lantern's light shrunk as a patch of shadow on the bedroom wall darkened, spreading like a mold stain and slowly taking shape. A masklike face of deepest black pressed through the wall with crude gouges for eyes and a pitlike mouth twisted in quiet suffering. A thin, emaciated arm stretched through the plaster, reaching for her as the thing's hollow eyes found her.

A shock wave of icy energy gripped her chest, and she fell back, her heart thumping painfully as the thing's torso flowed through the wall. Its ghostly face drooped, a theater mask of sorrow, as it moaned in hunger. Her hands seemed unnaturally pale as she raised them, turning her dagger in a graceful curve as the rhyme of the spell poured from her cold lips, pulling raw magic to her fingertips and shaping it into a searing light that blazed across the room.

The thing hissed in pain as the light crashed into its chest. It writhed and beat at the walls, the light spreading across its body, its flesh rippling as it pulled back into the wood and plaster.

Turning back to the stairs, she saw the dull flash of Jinn's blade as it severed the grasping fingers of another of the creatures, the wriggling digits hitting the ground like shadowy clay, dissipating in moments. He followed the slash with another, receiving little for his efforts besides voiceless hissing as the thing reached for his legs.

As Quessahn called upon another spell, the walls in the stairway rippled, wavering as more of the dark stains appeared, two then three, each slowly forming into crude, pained faces. Hungry moans escaped their toothless mouths as painful chills needled through Quessahn's flesh, her arcane rhymes growing stronger as she allowed the pain to push her, reaching into the dark places between the stars and calling forth the favors of the slumbering things that lived beyond the world's painful light.

The magic stirred through her body as Jinn's blade spun and slashed, surrounded, his gold eyes lost to her as she fought to keep them both alive for a while longer—long enough to reach him, to hold him, to let him know that in another place, in another life, she had loved him and had watched him die.

EIGHT

J inn kicked out, sending another of the undead creatures tumbling down the stairs as he slashed at hands grasping from the walls. Wood and plaster popped and split as the things pressed in upon him. Severed hands and shadowy limbs thumped around his boots, melting into stinking clouds of mist as they made slow progress down the stairs.

Shafts of screeching light splashed against the ceiling from Quessahn's hands, burning all that they touched and briefly illuminating simple faces set in silent screams. Her voice chanted unceasingly, deep with the harsh language of magic. The ebony hands raised against her burning light he cut away, the bodies they protected he cut down. Their flesh split like soggy, rotted wood beneath the edge of his blade. He spun at the sound of raspy moans close to his ear, his sword slicing through a stomach made of naught but ghostly hate, bleeding only a stink of death.

At the bottom of the stairway, a hand caught his left arm, black fingers digging coldly through his skin, burning his soul. Memories flashed through his mind as he struggled to free himself, stabbing the tip of his blade into the wall, causing the thing within to thrash and club at the corporeal barrier. He knew their crude faces. The hand melted away from his arm, and he reversed his stab into yet another of the things. He had seen them once before somewhere.

An eager hand closed on his ankle and pulled, dropping him to one leg, off balance.

The memory lost strength as he struggled to stand, hacking at the sinewy wrist near his leg, kicking at the wide-open maw of the thing's groaning face. He fell back as the wrist gave way, his arm and leg numb from the contact as he hit the wall. A silhouette manifested in the dark, tall and thin among the scattered broadsheets near Allek's chair. The pitlike eyes caught him in a bone-chilling embrace, and the memory crawled sluggishly from the thick mire of his ancient soul, whispering a single word.

"Bodak," he gasped as the dark eyes seemed to grow, curving wide like horrible mouths and drawing him further into their depths, though he could feel his body weaken. The void he found in the bodak's gaze howled in his mind, a familiar sound that caused him to shiver as he fought to resist its pull. "This is death," he whispered and felt his pulse grow faint, thumping slower and slower in his ears as he looked into the limitless dark as if visiting an old, abandoned home. "I died there once."

The realization sent a surge of strength into his limbs, and he shoved himself from the wall, charging at the bodak and closing his eyes. He knew blindness could not protect him from the undead thing's gaze, but instinct guided his sword in the dark far better than his ill-equipped eyes. He slashed at the cold and smiled when he found resistance. He stabbed into the nearing groans, feeling their hate and letting it fuel his renewed pulse. The sword play of several millennia spun his feet and flowed through his quick hands as the undead came for him.

But for all his skill, their claws still found him, their eyes still bit at his cold flesh, and their undead bodies refused to fall until only their indomitable will had been extinguished. He imagined himself like the feeble lantern upstairs, diminished and guttering until little but dying sparks remained.

"Too many," he muttered, opening his eyes and trying to regain feeling in his hands, his footing less sure with each feint and charge.

The room shook as Quessahn thundered down the stairs, her litany of arcane rhymes unending, light dancing in waves around her as she spun with spell and dagger, cutting a path through the undead. Jinn used the light, his steel flashing like fire, trailing a misty edge of black flesh just beyond the circle of magic that Quessahn wove with horrible words. For a moment he caught sight of her blackened eyes and pale skin and felt a twinge of regret that he could not place, as if he had somehow driven her to such dark rites.

"To me!" she shouted amid the chanting, holding out her hand.

A bodak materialized between them, and he raised his blade in a powerful stroke, slicing through its torso and letting the stinking chill of its body fall apart around him as he took the eladrin's hand. Energy surged through his arm painfully as she shouted, a circle of undead forming around them, hesitantly reaching through the glow of her ritual dagger.

The circle closed, their black eyes flickering as the air rippled. Quessahn's arm shook violently, and Jinn squeezed her hand, feeling light-headed, the bodaks and the house becoming blurry and indistinct. A collective wail rose among the bodaks as their drooping faces distended further in exaggerated sorrow. Then Jinn lost sight of them all.

Reality blinked out. His gut turned. Arcane phrases slithered like smooth fingers over his body, lifting him into a tenuous, unstable space. It pressed the breath from his lungs, holding him in a brief freefall before letting him go, falling into a green-hued glow.

The night grew colder as Lucian Dregg ambled through Sea Ward, a stench of wine in each steaming breath and a particular delight in the nervous fear he caused in passersby. Maranyuss was unbothered by the cold, keeping within sight of the ward's new and seemingly unwanted rorden, her step quiet and sure as she puzzled at his importance in the seemingly random murders. She eyed the lit windows of grand mansions as she slipped by them unnoticed. Each lilting bit of laughter she heard within could be cut off, silenced forever as far as she was concerned, so long as at the end of it all, she and Jinn found Sathariel.

She smiled at the thought, and it kept her going, though her interest in Dregg waned until evening turned lengthening shadows into pervading dark, a gloom that hid her well from the alert eyes of Dregg's fellow Watchmen. As the lamplighters made their rounds, the rorden's swaggering step seemed to find more purpose, a sudden shrewd sobriety infecting his mannerisms as he turned his boots south in confidence. She wondered at her initial impression of the man as he began to show a certain skill at directing his earlier pleasure toward the cold edge of something approximating duty. He saluted passing patrols, leaving them on their courses without stopping to dress them down and exercise his newfound authority.

His route was direct and sure, and Mara shook her head as he slowed at roughly halfway down Flint Street, stopping to glare at the high walls and lofty towers of the House of Wonder. Mara slid into the shadow of a shade tree north of the house, watching as Dregg paced, his eyes never leaving the wizards' school as if his vision alone might burn the walls to ash. Only the sharp tapping of a walking stick turned him away as a robed figure leaning on a gnarled staff approached from the south. Mara's keen eyes could make out the dark beard and bushy brow beneath the hood, the piercing, glittering eyes of a wizard descending on the waiting Dregg, who swiftly shouted orders to his men, sending them around the block as he awaited the mage.

"Archmage Tallus, I presume?" she whispered softly as the men met, their hushed conversation buzzing incoherently, though she did not expect to glean much. Dregg was a tool to be led along, used, and discarded as the wizard saw fit. Mara doubted Tallus would impart any details. As she waited for their meeting to end, a strange scent crossed her path, faint and enticing.

Sucking in a shuddering breath, she found herself transfixed on the alley at Dregg's back, the darkness calling to her fey blood with a smell as ancient as all of creation.

With a quiet glare, Dregg and Tallus parted, neither seeming pleased with the other. The archmage continued his path north as the rorden turned south, quickly meeting with yet another patrol of the Watch, a group of figures that caught Mara's eye despite her desire to reach the alley. The men did not salute as Dregg approached, their uniforms were ill fitting and unwashed, their weapons less than standard, and their wineskins unheard of among the city's officers.

"Thugs," she muttered quietly, sinking further into the garden's shadows and narrowing her eyes at Dregg's hired men. She suspected whatever was to occur would be coming soon, for even with Dregg in charge, such irregular Watchmen would be easily ousted if not jailed within a day or two. Tallus she eyed more carefully as he passed within several strides of her, his staff digging at the cobbles, his knuckles white on the gnarled wood as he made his hasty way toward Ivory Street. "No," she whispered. "The scheme is not yours either, dear Archmage. This smells of something far older than a limping, nervous wizard and his cruel, half-drunk blade-for-hire."

After both men had gone, she slipped from the shadows, prowling toward Pharra's Alley like a predator sensing prey hiding in the brush. She kept a wary, glancing eye on the House of Wonder as she neared, its wizards and their students toiling within without sense or care of the business going on at their gate. She smirked at their high-minded oblivion, quietly reciting a line from an ancient poem as she eyed the darkness within the alley.

> *Look down! Look down!*
> *Your towers are much too high!*
> *'Ware the fall from your tower wall.*
> *The sky will not protect you.*
> *Turn your eye to the world below,*
> *Else the ground will come up to claim you!*

In the dark she studied the cold cobbles, sniffing the air and noting the unlit lantern, creaking on its hook in the winter wind. The ground seemed to hum with power, the area filled with an unmistakable scent though she could not pinpoint its exact source. She turned a wide circle before the house's gates, smiling curiously at the place wizards had dubbed a spellhaunt, a play of tenacious magic that had resisted all attempts to explain or dispel it.

"They dismissed you as an interesting trifle, didn't they?" she said to the ground, almost willing the skulls to appear. "What are you up to, I wonder? And how did you do it?"

The scent was intoxicating, overtaking her with a greed she hadn't felt in decades, an avarice that any night hag worth her own word in the Feywild would gladly betray powerful archfey to satisfy. She breathed deeply, tasting that which she could not yet lay her hands upon.

Souls.

They were a treasure she suspected that all the pitiful creatures shambling in the City of the Dead could only dryly wish for. She studied the haunted ground a moment longer then made swift progress in the path of Archmage Tallus. As she passed homes, towers, taverns, and celebrants, Mara wondered how many might survive the conflict to come, eager to see what end Sea Ward might earn for itself. And though she desired to foil whatever plot Asmodeus had in mind . . .

The scent of unclaimed souls whetted her appetite for the endgame.

"Naught for now but to listen for the screams," she said under her breath, grinning and wondering if the screams would stop at all.

Jinn blinked, his eyes still adjusting to the half light he found himself in. Damp stone pressed against his cheek, the air stinking of urine, vermin, mold, and things he didn't wish to consider. A soft glow nearby illuminated a wide, stone tunnel, manmade though time and neglect had held reign far longer than any man. Arched and caked with a thick layer of brown and green sludge, the walls glistened. Thin light from distant cracks in the ceiling danced as it reflected off the surface of a thick, rippling mat of steaming liquid too discolored to be called water.

A hand shook Jinn's shoulder as he stirred and sat up, finding Quessahn at his side, the shining ritual dagger in her hand. Her eyes had returned to the pale sky blue he was accustomed to, the ones in which he saw some long-forgotten sense of regret reflecting back at him.

"Are you all right?" she asked, and he nodded in response, the spinning in his head still slowing down from her spell.

"No need to ask where we are, I take it," he said.

"I took a chance in getting us down here," she replied. "But if the house is sealed as tight as I expect, we won't be followed any time soon."

"Better to take a chance on the sewers than be dead," he muttered, rubbing feeling back into his arms where the bodaks had struck him, their claw marks angry, red lines on his near-white skin. After a moment he noticed Quessahn staring, her eyes fixed on the swirling black symbols that decorated his arms from wrist to elbow. He quickly pulled his sleeves down, covering the markings and startling the eladrin.

"W-we'll rest here for a bit," she stammered and stood, raising her dagger and peering into the dark in both directions. "I just need to get our bearings."

Jinn was about to reply when he recalled the bundle of letters in his coat. Leaving Quessahn to her nervous pacing, he pulled the letters out and unfolded the first of them, narrowing his eyes at the precise yet flowing script of Rilyana Saerfynn.

> *My dearest Allek,*
>
> *It has been some time since we last spoke, and I regret each day that passes that I do not call upon you, but it seems I am forced to break that silence and humbly ask for your help. Callak grows more protective of me and more violent every day, as though the bottle he drowns his life in replaces that life with something else, something sinister that frightens me. I fear angering him at home, yet in public it is the attentions of your swordcaptain, Lucian Dregg, that I must fend away lest Callak become enraged . . .*

Jinn finished the letter swiftly and turned to the next, scanning their contents and shaking his head in disbelief as the secret tryst between Allek Marson and Rilyana Saerfynn unfolded before his eyes. He couldn't understand why Allek had never mentioned the young woman or her troubles with her brother or Lucian Dregg. Passages concerning Callak Saerfynn he began to study more closely.

> *Callak disappears without explanation almost every night. Though he returns home smelling of ale and wine, or worse, there is something in his eyes, the way he dismisses his behavior, that disturbs me. More and more he is visited by Archmage Tallus and that simpering toad of an apprentice, Gorrick. I am kept away from their secret meetings, however each time Tallus looks at me I feel the need to scour his lust from my skin with boiling water . . .*

Jinn noted the date of the last letter as being within the previous month. Folding the letters again and tucking them back in his coat, he leaned back, the names and events described tumbling through his thoughts as he wondered at the game he had been drawn into.

"This is madness," he whispered, though his words were amplified by the acoustics of the sewer tunnel.

"Pardon?" Quessahn asked.

"What do you know of the Saerfynn family?" he said, standing and eager to be on the move again.

"I suppose it depends on the day and the rumor," she answered, nervously glancing to the northwest passage as she spoke. "The siblings are alone on their estate, sole heirs to their family's fortune. Callak is an arrogant drunk, and Rilyana seems to have a different man—or woman—on her arm at every outing, though many seem to think this is only to anger her jealous brother."

"Jealous?" Jinn pressed.

"It is rumored that she and Callak are far more than just brother and sister," she replied quietly, as if the statement alone might conjure an image of the implied perversity. "Why do you ask?"

"Most peculiar," Jinn muttered, ignoring her question. "Come. We still have another house to visit before dawn."

"No, not yet," she said, stopping him. "There is someone we should speak to first."

"We have no time. Tallus is already—"

"Under the impression that we are dead," she said, sharply finishing his words and fixing him with an almost accusing stare. "And we still have no idea what he is planning."

"And you know someone who might?"

"Perhaps," she said, turning away. "But we'll need to go deeper."

Jinn stood still, watching her navigate the narrow ledge alongside the dark green muck that flowed through the sewer. The letters weighed heavily in his pocket, another name added to his list of possible conspirators, and he wondered if any of the names would matter at all in the end. He had not come to chase murdered bodies of the upper classes and the more he learned of those who might be involved the more he felt drawn away from his true task. He eyed the bobbing light of Quessahn's dagger suspiciously as she pressed deeper into the sewers beneath Sea Ward.

"This 'someone,' " he called out to her. "They live in a sewer?"

She paused and turned, approaching close enough that he could see the determination on her face, her earlier nervousness, the hesitation he sensed, gone.

"I have seen Mara's true form," she said coldly. "How is it a night hag comes to an alliance with a deva?"

He matched her cold stare for several breaths, crossing his arms defensively as the spark of an old shame flared to life. He had made his peace with the decision long past, justifying any means he felt were necessary to hunt Sathariel, but in Quessahn's eyes he briefly recalled his view of the world as it had been before he had made such a dark pact. It was both encouraging and saddening that there were still those who might judge his choice.

"We share a common enemy," he finally answered.

"Sathariel? The angel?" she asked.

"Asmodeus," he replied, a grim silence falling between them at the uttering of the devil-god's name, but he broke it easily, holding no reverence or superstition for the names of even the darkest of gods and needing no unspoken secret to protect him from Quessahn's judgment. "Maranyuss hurt him somehow, and he cursed her, took from her all she had earned, and forced her to live among mortals, cut off and abandoned by her kind."

Quessahn stepped closer, nodding quietly in understanding, though a hard look remained in her eyes.

"I'm not judging you—not entirely—but do not think you are the only one with less-than-scrupulous allies," she said and turned back on her path, her dagger growing brighter. "Tallus can wait, as can your angel, but I need to know more about the murders and how to stop them if I am to be of any help to you."

"And how do you propose to find this out?" he asked, reluctantly following her, the stench of the sewer fading with every breath he took.

"By speaking to someone who was here three hundred years ago when the murders first started," she answered as their footsteps echoed through the winding tunnels.

Gorrick stood in the shadows of a well-tended garden, fantastical topiaries populating the inner walls of the estate as he watched silhouettes dance and laugh within tall, decorative windows. Casually he straightened his robes and fixed his short, golden hair, smiling as he pictured the effect his presence would have on the lady of the house, his arrival meaning nothing less than a direct order from Archmage Tallus.

He strode along the garden path confidently, nodding knowingly at nervous guards as he approached the grand double doors. Few of the older families had survived the Spellplague, but the one that resided there was one, old name and wealth stretching back centuries, waiting upon his call. It was a bloodline prepared at his word to lay down gold and status to answer the summons he bore.

The doors opened without a sound, a doorman averting his gaze as Gorrick entered the front hallway lined with ancient paintings of ancestors above a white marble floor. The house seneschal arrived to conduct the affairs of the family and see to the initial needs and comfort of their expected guests. At sight of Gorrick, the tall, thin man sneered, stopping in his tracks and folding his white-gloved hands before turning to summon the lady of the house.

Gorrick returned the sneer, though only to the arrogant seneschal's back. He had no time for rebuking the staff; Tallus's business took precedent over such petty concerns. A side door opened, and a burst of music and conversation rushed into the entrance hall. Lady Lhaerra Loethe swept through the door, her voluptuous curves wrapped in crimson, lace, and jewels, a Winterfirst mask dangling casually from her hand as she turned, smiling, to meet her guest.

The door closed behind her, and her smile faded, her jubilant demeanor and self-importance slipping away at the sight of the apprentice wizard. Gorrick smiled at her discomfort.

"It is too early," she said sharply, regarding him with a half-lidded gaze.

Gorrick scowled in disappointment. "Things are moving swiftly, Lhaerra," he said, eyeing her finery in disgust. "The archmage has little time to spare for your . . . *festivities*."

Lhaerra drew closer, the powerful scent of her perfume burning his nose as she gracefully crossed her arms, gesturing to the secret door that hid behind a large painting on the southern wall. Gorrick imagined he could smell the blood and sweat emanating from the secret chamber if not for Lhaerra's overzealous attempt to smell like an entire rose garden.

"Tell your master that all is prepared for the rite," she said, "and that we shall be ready within a bell."

"I shall," Gorrick replied. He turned to leave. "Make sure to have the *entire* family present for the ritual."

"Truly?" Lhaerra asked, a sudden lilt of hope in her voice.

"As I said, things are moving swiftly."

"And the other families?" she pressed, laying a soft-gloved hand on his shoulder.

"The other families have their parts to play as well," he replied, glancing sidelong at her and enjoying the desperate excitement in her eyes. "And at least one shall have their final rewards."

He removed her hand and left her speechless on the doorstep, striding confidently through the garden on his way back to Tallus's tower. His errands finished, he quietly wished good hunting to the circle of skulls and looked forward to a long and bloody night.

NINE

What little sense of direction Jinn had, he quickly lost as Quessahn wound their path through the sewers of Waterdeep, a dank and cold road that stretched for miles beneath the city's wards. They kept quiet and wary, though Quessahn occasionally whispered curses when a path seemed unsuitable for one reason or another, making their trek ever more labyrinthine. Several times Jinn eyed patches of light where hidden accesses to the surface called for him to abandon the eladrin's wild chase, but every time, he passed them by, holding on a bit longer.

He had heard rumors of the things that slithered in the lower tunnels, had seen one or two in the final days of his hunting of the Vigilant Order, but Quessahn seemed to know what signs to look for. Most often she took the faintly glowing paths of the muckers, those people considered among the lowest castes of society, sifting through the refuse of the sewers for lost treasures; trinkets; old clothing; or, for the worst off, food. They held crude candles in broken pots or mugs, continually hunched over the edges of the sewage flow, raking the muck with their bare hands, searching for the glint of something worth keeping. The muckers would barely glance at Quessahn and him as they passed, their blank, deathly stares beyond caring who visited the city's stinking underworld.

At one time Jinn would not have thought such an existence possible, a torment more fit for the Nine Hells or the Abyss, but enough time among mortals had shown him otherwise. Any degradation imaginable existed somewhere in the world, staining all else that might have seemed brighter to him, like the barest shadow on a blooming flower. Considering the plight of the muckers only made his impatience grow and the oft-seen exits shining down side tunnels more inviting.

At length Quessahn's step slowed, and a soft rumble echoed through the tunnels like crashing thunder. The walls vibrated with the noise, and he drew his sword. The eladrin turned at the sound, her eyes shining in the glow of her dagger.

"It's the ocean," she explained in a whisper. "Still far away but the sound of the tide reaches through to these tunnels."

Jinn relaxed only slightly, something else teasing at his senses that had naught to do with tides. The realization that something stank in the sewers struck him as odd, but a new scent slowly began to change the aroma to which he had grown accustomed. Death wafted toward them on the air and clung to their skin as it rode with the steamy mist. Quessahn raised a hand behind her, the light of her dagger fading to less than a candle's worth of glow as she stopped and crouched, resting a moment and placing a finger to her lips.

Though Jinn said nothing, something else spoke, a sibilant, echoing sound that sent chills down his spine.

It came and went like the distant sighing of the tide, an unintelligible whispering that seemed to border on true speech, the sounds approaching something like words before disappearing again. He caught Quessahn's eye, gesturing to his sword questioningly, curious as to whether or not a threat lingered nearby. She gently pressed his blade down, shaking her head even as the whispers grew louder.

There is a place without truth, where the bodies lie . . .

Jinn stiffened at the ghostly voice's words, searching for their source and finding nothing. Despite the eladrin's protestations, he kept his sword on guard as the spectral susurrus surrounded them, washing through the tunnel with biting cold, speaking nonsense in womanly voices.

Hold the blade firmly, else the bone may not break . . .

The mask he wears is for the children, and your laughter shall make them sicker . . .

Nine times folded upon nine is the sum, for the path is long and treacherous . . .

Jinn spun in slow circles, staring into the dark as the whispers rose in a crescendo of crowded words then descended into the barest hint of distant voices, joining the deep background noise of the ceaseless tide.

"The whisperers of Seawind Alley," Quessahn said at length and pointed to the ceiling. "A more recent haunt than the circle of skulls, but no less mysterious."

"What does it mean?" Jinn asked, turning the last few phrases over in his mind but finding no specific relevance in them.

"Usually nothing," she answered as a shuffling sound reached them from the far end of the tunnel. "But this time it means that we've arrived."

The faint scent of death rose, and a dry sliding noise, like bare feet on a sandy floor, turned them both toward a glimmer of tiny lights. They appeared in pairs, moving little but seeming fixed on the glow of Quessahn's dagger. Jinn eased forward, trying to make out details of the watchers, but the eladrin laid a hand on his arm and leaned close to his ear.

"Say nothing," she whispered. "Sheathe your sword and walk very slowly."

Jinn eyed her warily, hesitating. For all the sound he could hear in the tunnel, it was the lack of a sound, of breathing, that concerned him the most. Reluctantly he complied, sliding the stolen blade in its scabbard as he followed at Quessahn's side. The dim glow of her dagger reached the nearest pairs of eyes lining the side of the tunnel, illuminating slack-jawed faces eaten away with damp rot and the ravages of death. Old scars marked skin stretched taut over bones and compacted flesh. Strange tissue damage affected their arms and legs, indicating precise, clean slices as if cuts of flesh had been excised after their deaths.

Roughly a dozen of the standing corpses lined either side of the passage, their dull eyes registering nothing as he and Quessahn walked between them. A faint shaft of light revealed yet another surface exit, but the undead stood well away from the light.

"Why aren't they attacking?" Jinn asked quietly.

All at once the zombies twitched to life, shuffling toward him with blind, grim purpose. Sharp bones protruded from the thin, clawlike hands that reached for him as he drew his sword, cursing and pressing his back to that of the eladrin.

"I told you to be quiet!" she growled at him, her dagger brightening like a shard of starlight. "Briar!"

Her voice echoed but still the undead came, shuffling to within a sword's reach. Jinn raised his blade, ready to sever the hands that sought his throat, when the zombies suddenly stopped. Their heads shook, tilting as if confused, before they each turned away, returning to their places along the wall as if nothing had happened.

Quess? Is that you I hear?

A voice quite unlike the whisperers spoke in Jinn's mind, the words resonating deeply and thrumming with power. Something squished through the darkness to Jinn's left, and Quessahn strode toward it, her dagger dimming again as tiny, candlelike lights flared to life in a semicircle at the tunnel's end. Beyond them, in an archway of darkness, he caught a glimpse of yellow, membranous flesh glistening in the light, a form little more than a silhouette twisting beyond the orange glow of a dry chamber. Through the archway came a yellow, multifaceted eye, turning slowly on a pale ochre stalk like a tentacle. It regarded them for a breath before retreating, the twisting figure collapsing in on itself and becoming lost in the shadows.

"I apologize, my dear," the voice said, changed and out of Jinn's mind, followed by the appearance of a bald, tottering old man with spotted hands clasped before him. Wide, almost manic eyes blinked in the light above a curving, white-toothed smile. "The whisperers were quite loud just then. Did you hear? Very interesting indeed! I feel I am close to discovering some sort of pattern in their—why, dear Quess! You look absolutely horrid! And who is your friend here?"

"Jinnaoth, this is Briar—," she began, but the old man raised a quick, long finger.

"Mister," he prompted.

"*Mister* Briarbones," she finished, but Jinn held back, suspicious, sword still in the hand he might have offered to shake in any other circumstance, but the old man did not offer either, a detail Jinn dismissed as his mind was still torn between the well-lit chamber and the undead sentinels in the dark at his back. "When I felt there was no more I could learn from the masters at the House of Wonder, I found old Briar here. He has been . . . *supplementing* . . . my studies for a few years now."

"Indeed, and an astute student she has been," Briarbones said with a wink as he turned to a tall cabinet and brew pot by the west wall.

"This is all very well and good," Jinn said, uncertain as to where to keep the point of his blade and still unsure if it shouldn't be kept on Quessahn. "But we are in a bit of—"

"Care for tea?" Briarbones said, ignoring him. "I, for one, can only barely tolerate the stuff, but for guests I do make exceptions."

"I am no guest," Jinn said, his patience drawing to an end as he glared at Quessahn. "And this is no time for idle chatter or cups of tea!"

"Jinn, please, we should make some time—," Quessahn replied but was cut off by the old man.

"Very well," Briarbones said. His voice changed again, becoming stronger, deeper, and far younger. His eyes danced with a strange light, shining slightly as he continued. "Jinnaoth Ir'Gadohn, an odd surname, not of this world and, unless my studies are mistaken, not of any natural world known, but of places between worlds, realms closer to that of raw creation than those of rock and water. But you keep the name anyway. Through each life and death, those gold eyes, the symbols on your skin, and that strange last name never change, do they? Yes, deva, I know of you." Briarbones edged closer, the veins in his eyes squirming beneath the clear, soft layer of lens over his light gray irises. "Now have I proven that I may be worth your time and patience? That is, should I choose to assist you at all."

"Briar, I'm sorry," Quessahn said, shooting Jinn an angry glance. "I've come about the recent murders that we spoke of some time ago, but Jinn has come for—"

"Sathariel," Briarbones finished, still staring at the deva. "The Devourer, the Winged Pit, the Hunger of Asmodeus, oh yes, the deva's vendetta is known to me, as are those of his previous incarnations. The whispering souls you hear in the angel's presence, deva?

Some of them are your vengeful predecessors, a few of them having wielded the very same blade you choose to rudely bare in my home."

Jinn gave no indication of his interest in the old man's words, though his heart raced at the mention of Sathariel. He maintained the stare for several breaths, still as a stone and wondering what other secrets lay buried in the mind of Quessahn's strange friend. At length, he lowered his golden eyes and the point of his sword.

"I have misjudged the value of your time, sir," he said, sheathing his blade reluctantly. "I am sorry for my impatience."

"No need. In my experience, patience is often the first victim of passion, and it is nothing to apologize for, though it can make one very sorry in the end," the old man said, his voice returning to what one might expect from the frail frame and wizened eyes. "Now let us begin again. Would you care for some tea?"

Though the night had turned bitterly cold, Karras's blood was warm with wine and stronger spirits, such that he protested only a little as Lhaerra and her house guards had abruptly ended the Winterfirst celebration at Loethe Manor. He'd had his fill of drink and pursued much softer distractions to fill out the evening's remainder.

Rilyana's hips swayed rhythmically ahead of him, her elbow in the firm grip of her brother, Callak. She managed to keep an eye on Karras, a seductive, half-lidded gaze that forced him to keep a careful step lest his boots walk out from under him and leave him slumbering in the street until dawn. Her lascivious smile made promises that kept him all the warmer, though Callak's cold glare sought to extinguish the dim light of hope that kept Karras moving in the siblings' wake, a drunken promise to see them home.

Despite Callak's protective posturing, even he could not take away the stolen moments in Karras's mind. He still felt Rilyana's lips brushing next to his ear, her panting hot breath on his neck. His hands bore a memory of her body that her brother, his childhood friend, could never erase.

He rounded a corner, and the high walls of the Saerfynn Manor came into view, the mansion itself surrounded by a dark garden only barely held in check. Karras frowned at the sight of it, fearing Callak would have his way and keep him from Rilyana's attentions. He eyed the large mansion, the tall windows of more rooms than seemed necessary for two people, but he supposed wealth in Sea Ward was meant for little else than shows of grand excess.

At the gates the trio stopped, Karras stumbling forward then swaying back before righting himself, his eyes immediately meeting Callak's.

"We'll take our leave of you now, Karras," Callak growled, a strained smile on his square-jawed face as he pulled Rilyana behind him. "I'll see you tomorrow perhaps?"

"Of course, my friend!" Karras replied, dipping into a comic, sweeping bow. "I bid you the best of evenings!" He clapped Callak's broad shoulder but swiftly swept his other hand around to grasp Rilyana's delicate, gloved hand, planting a gentle kiss upon it. "An excellent evening to you and your fair sister."

Karras had time to see his breath steam upon Rilyana's jeweled bracelet and catch a last, lustful smile to send him home to bed before Callak opened the gate and pulled his sister along after him toward the mansion. Guards stood waiting to open the front doors, and the siblings disappeared inside. Karras leaned against the gate, drowsy and for the first time considering his long walk home. Squeezing the cold iron, he steeled himself to begin the journey as a window inside the Saerfynn house was lit by candlelight.

The silhouette of Rilyana came into view, and Karras lingered, admiring her curves, but was distracted as the shouting voice of Callak reached him from within the house. He could not make out the words, though he guessed it was none other than the eldest Saerfynn's usual tirade over his sister's wantonness. The argument did not last long, however, and soon Callak joined Rilyana at the window, leaning close to her, their silhouettes merging in an embrace that seemed beyond that of siblings. Karras's smile faded, his eyes narrowing as hands slid from shoulders to hips, faces pressed close together, turning in the window and obscuring the details that Karras could only imagine.

He pushed away from the gate, sliding toward the wall, wide eyed and suddenly feeling the effects of his long night of drinking. His breath caught in his throat, stomach turning at what he'd seen pass between brother and sister. The fine foods and wines that the Lady Lhaerra had provided for her guests quickly became a steaming stain at Karras's boots, his stomach emptying until he was left wheezing and teary eyed. Old rumors about the pair came back to him, haunting him as he stumbled away from the estate, shaking his head in disbelief and disgust.

He fell into the dark of a wide alley on the southern end of the manor wall, pulling himself around the corner as he attempted to still his spinning head and put his thoughts in order. He half sat, pressed against the wall, shivering as even the warmth of wine began to fade from his blood, and he recalled his private moments with Rilyana in a new light. His gut threatened to empty itself again as a soft green light flickered nearby and he straightened, expecting to find the glaring lanterns of a Watch patrol.

To his right an ethereal glow spun in slow circles along the ground near the gates of the House of Wonder, flashes of ghostly fire sparking as the emerald mist grew faster.

"What's this?" he muttered and slipped, falling to awkwardly sit and stare in awe at the eerie spectacle. Tales of the haunted alley swirled in his thoughts, childhood ghost stories to which he had lent neither belief nor fear, having nearly forgotten them.

Voices, deep and hollow, chanted softly at first within the glow but grew louder as the light grew brighter, spinning faster until nine turning objects could be seen in the circle. Karras pushed himself up to his knees frantically, a sudden sobriety making him quicker and more sure footed than he'd expected to be.

He didn't make it past his knees, a searing pain tearing through his head and spreading across his body in burning waves. He gasped, clutching the sides of his head and falling forward, unable to scream for the pain crawling through his skull. The voices shouted in his mind, a harsh language that filled him with fear. The ground, less than a hand's breadth from his nose, glowed as green flames erupted from his eyes.

His vision narrowed, becoming two points of glowing emerald light before disappearing altogether. The voices seemed to drag him away from himself, stuffing his will into a limitless dark where he drifted, blind and senseless, his body no longer his own. He flailed phantom limbs in the dark of his mind, tumbling as nine ghostly skulls took up residence in his soul and commandeered his flesh.

Jinn sat quietly, studying Briarbones as Quessahn explained what they had learned about the murders thus far. The old man nodded as she spoke, his movements forced as though he were mimicking something he'd seen but not understood. Jinn had met many of the things that hid behind smiling faces in Waterdeep, some of them pursuing honest goals—most of them not—but few chose to live in a sewer with undead guards. As Quessahn's tale reached mention of the circle of skulls and the older killings from centuries ago, Briarbones became animated, listening intently, his hands fidgeting.

"I recall the time well," he said, stroking his chin. "I had just arrived in Waterdeep a decade before. There were nine families involved in the killings as I recall. Though their names escape me, this one you mentioned, Marson, I believe? This sounds familiar."

"What about Saerfynn?" Jinn asked, leaning forward.

"No, not at all," Briar answered distractedly. "Much more recent, the Saerfynn name, last century or so."

Jinn nodded, still puzzling over Allek's apparent affair with Rilyana and wondering if she or her brother were somehow involved in the murders—or if they were possible targets.

"Nine families," Quessahn said, glancing at Jinn. "Nine skulls."

"Correct . . . but why?" Briar sketched swift notes on a foldout table by the wall.

"I cannot concern myself with why, only how and what," Jinn said, standing and straightening his coat, feeling as if the whole of the night might slip away in fanciful speculation over details while Sathariel continued to put pieces in play, complicating the game so that no one would discover what he was working toward until it was too late. "*How* are the skulls connected to Sathariel? And *what* is it about the murders that interests him?"

"And how can you use the deaths of these people to get to the angel?" Quessahn added, drawing a curious glance from Briarbones. "That's what you were thinking."

"I'll make no secret of that," Jinn replied. "I believe a few dozen dead is better than a few hundred."

"Perhaps," Briar said. "But more murders will get you no closer to the angel unless you know why these families are in danger. You must concede that Sathariel knew you would follow him and, therefore, has planned for your presence. It is very likely he is just using you and unless you look beyond the edge of that sword—that sword in particular, my friend—you won't realize how you're being used until it's too late."

"I'm only being used if I do what he wants me to do," he replied, turning toward the tunnel, intent on getting back up to street level and finding Archmage Tallus.

"Aren't you?" Quessahn asked, following him.

"He expects me to care. He wants me trying to save people," he said, looking up at the small, dim shafts of light from above and not wanting to see the look in the eladrin's eyes, the one he'd seen in the mirror in private, more honest moments. "But you don't win a war by trying to save lives. Usually it's the other way around."

"People are dying!" Quessahn said in disbelief. "More every day!"

Jinn took a deep breath and faced her, searching her eyes for some understanding.

"Death is merely a symptom of all this, a side effect," he said calmly but coldly, giving her the facts as he saw them, as he'd seen them for some time. "I know Sathariel. He doesn't just kill people for no reason. He is not a glorified assassin. He has a goal. These deaths and whatever spell they contribute to is just part of the show, a distraction to keep us chasing bodies in the dark."

"And what if they're not?" she asked.

"Keep working on it," he said. "I'm going to find Tallus. I'll be back later if I find anything out. Tell Mister Briar to keep an eye on this exit in case I need any help."

"You will," she said, turning away angrily. "Just go."

He glared at her back before taking the rungs of the ladder and climbing to the surface, his fury well fueled for an encounter with the wizard.

TEN

G et what you wanted, did you?"

Briarbones looked sidelong at her before returning to his note taking, working things out on paper in his furiously quick shorthand. Quessahn didn't answer as she slumped to the dry floor of his meeting chamber, flinching as the surface exit's cover slid into place behind Jinnaoth. She squeezed her hands into tight fists, contemplating punching the floor before calming herself with deep breaths.

"Well, you couldn't have hoped for much better when you tracked him down in the first place," Briar said. "That was a feat in and of itself. How long had it been?"

"One hundred and fifty years," she answered, closing her eyes and leaning her head against the wall, "seven months, and five days." Though the eladrin were a long-lived race and the turning of several decades could mean little in their experience, it seemed as though the weight of every day sat heavily on her shoulders. "It doesn't matter anymore; we have more important things to see to."

"Indeed," he replied, shuddering slightly as the skin on his face warped and slid toward his quivering neck, revealing a puckered mass of shifting, visceral flesh that erupted and grew by the breath.

She watched as she always did, fascinated by the transformation. Briarbones was an avolakia, a shapechanging, unnatural creature prone to magical curiosity and—she glanced toward his zombie sentinels outside the chamber—bizarre appetites.

"Do you have any theories about what we're up against?" she asked.

Theories certainly, he replied, his voice changing easily from that of the old man to the inescapable words that appeared in her mind. His body became a tall, smooth trunk of rippling pale yellow flesh, six suckered tentacles sprouting from its base, each tipped with a multifaceted eye. His arms were replaced by eight insectlike limbs that sprouted from thick ridges halfway up his frame, each ending with nimble-fingered claws. Where his head had been was a series of three hooked mandibles around a circular, barbed mouth. *But I believe I would be remiss if I shared any early suspicions just yet, lest I spoil our research with any false preconceptions.*

"Of course," she said, setting aside lingering thoughts of Jinnaoth as Briar selected several tomes from a hidden shelf within the darkened chamber where he, she assumed, slept. She'd grown used to his natural state over the years, actually preferring it to the puppetlike image of the old man he favored when in human form. "I've been hasty enough the last few days; no need for early conclusions."

Quietly she cursed her own traitorous tongue as Briar returned with the books, laying them gently on the table. One of his eye stalks turned toward her, and she cursed under her breath again.

It is understandable, Briar said, his deft, little hands already turning pages in two books, his other eyes trained on the pages intently. *There are few mated pairs among your kind that get the chance to reunite with dead lovers. Well, not without necromancy anyway.*

Quessahn took a deep breath, hoping to squelch Briar's barrage of questions and advice before they truly began.

"I had unrealistic hopes. The man I knew—most of him—is

dead. Jinnaoth, however similar, is a different person. Let's just leave it at that," she said matter-of-factly, though a pang of pain still coursed through her at the sound of her own words.

Of course, of course, I just— Ah, here is something, he said, interrupting himself excitedly, one hand tracing a line of text as another scribbled a note. *Interesting, yes. But what I wonder is, will you be able to leave it at that? Are you willing to watch him, what's left of him, die again?*

She considered the question quietly, her thoughts drifting dangerously close to memories that had seen too much revisiting since she'd seen Jinn at the House of Wonder. Absently she ran a finger down the spines of Briarbones's books, scanning the titles the avolakia had chosen for something to focus on besides the deva. One title caught her eye, and she stopped, pulling the tome free in confusion.

"This book," she said, turning the dusty tome over. "This isn't about history or spells." Her fingers slid over the raised image of a fiendish face in the old leather. "This is a treatise on prophecies of the Nine Hells."

Oh yes, the avolakia replied, his eyes and hands doing twice the research of several learned scholars as he spoke. *I have reason to suspect that the Watch, while well intentioned, may be far out if its depth.*

"Fools," Jinn muttered.

Curious eyes watched him from balconies overlooking Seawind Alley. He returned their furtive stares, seeing himself reflected in their scholarly spectacles as they fussed over strange instruments that spun and clicked, measuring the wind and tracking the stars. He wondered briefly if they knew of their counterpart, the old man—the thing—living beneath the alley itself, as close to its mystical phenomenon as they were.

They focused so intently on the cryptic whispers of what may be that they were blind to the world around them. He'd heard it said that devils resided in the details, as if tightly wound in the threads of a tapestry, and he agreed with the idea. The details so captivated the imagination that the overall design was often forgotten.

"A willful ignorance," he said under his breath, exiting the alley and heading east, angrily tossing aside the Winterfirst mask he had considered wearing to conceal himself in the streets. He cursed Quessahn's misplaced compassion as much as he respected her ability to maintain such conviction, and he cursed himself for being unable—or perhaps unwilling—to indulge in the same luxury himself.

He strode down the center of empty avenues, spotting only the occasional servant at back doors or swift-footed lamplighter returning home after the evening's work was done. Though he glared at any who crossed his path, yearning to draw his sword, he kept to back alleys and shadowed streets. He saw none of the order's soulless ahimazzi, and Watch patrols seemed more focused on main streets and wealthier blocks, where many of the murders had taken place. The ward was quiet, as if the streets themselves were holding their breath, waiting for something to happen.

Rounding a corner, barely two blocks away from where Tallus was said to reside, Jinn received his quiet wish.

"Hold there, deva!"

Jinn grinned at the sound of Dregg's voice and paused as four men in Watch uniforms stepped into the lamplight ahead. Five more approached him from behind, keeping their distance. Even so, Jinn could see the Watchmen's disheveled and dirty tabards. They wore scuffed swash-cuffed boots more suitable for dock work than Watch duty, and the weapons they had drawn were mismatched and nonstandard. There were nine of them, the increased patrol number set by Allek Marson before his death, but the men Jinn faced had never known the honorable rorden. He doubted they had any particular knowledge of the Watch at all save the dimensions of old prison cells.

"You couldn't hide for long, Jinnaoth," Dregg said, pacing behind the four men at the far end of the avenue, a depressing sight, seeing Allek's secrecy perverted and used to bring in hired thugs for Lucian Dregg.

"I'm not hiding at all, Dregg. Have you been looking for me?" Jinn replied, raising his arms and spreading his coat wide, sword clearly visible in its scabbard.

"You are a murderer, or haven't you heard? I imagine they'll make me a commander for bringing you in." Dregg smiled over the shoulders of his thugs.

"You're delusional, Lucian," Jinn said, though his thoughts drifted, old battles and duels flashing through his mind, the memories flooding through his flesh as they stitched his present to bits of his bloody past.

Rorden Dregg laughed, a deep, confident chuckle that lasted a breath too long, a note of uncertainty ringing in Jinn's ears as it faded.

"You'd be surprised at what a little coin and a good story can accomplish," Dregg replied.

"No, not that," Jinn said, lowering his arms and sweeping his coat over the hilt of his stolen blade. "I meant about you bringing me in."

Dregg ceased his pacing and glared at the deva. "Take him," he growled. "No need to be gentle."

Jinn drew his sword as the nine men approached, some forgotten instinct making him wave the blade's tip over the ground in a circular motion, an archaic duelist's ritual whose meaning had been lost centuries ago. Dregg's patrol of false officers swaggered as they neared, knowing smiles spread on their unshaven faces. They formed a crude circle around Jinn, their steps out of sync with one another as they revealed their inexperience in anything approaching a group strategy.

"No discipline," he muttered, keeping still and wondering which among them would break the circle first.

"Aye, there'll be discipline all right, bright-eyes," said their largest, a hulking man with a shorn scalp wielding a thick, jagged-edged blade. "First lesson, we teach you how to bleed."

The large man rushed in, sure on his feet and wielding the heavy blade with some skill as he anticipated Jinn's deft, quick slash and blocked it. Drawing the blade back to strike again as his grinning companions watched, the big man did not, however, anticipate the position of Jinn's feet. Jinn ducked low under the powerful stroke, his outstretched leg slipping between his opponent's and hooking one knee as he twisted toward the large man's back.

Unbalanced, the big man stumbled forward and caught a kick to the back of the head that sent him smashing facefirst into the cobbles. Using their surprise at the swift maneuver, Jinn spun into the others with deadly precision. Steel screamed as he struck forward, defended backward, and walked an invisible line where the thugs' circle should have been positioned, a careful offensive step that kept them on the move, stumbling over one another to reach him.

Three fell, clutching their stomachs, in Jinn's first pass. Two more fell as the other five attempted to join the fray, their swords tearing at only his cloak and glancing off of his leather armor, the luckiest strikes drawing thin, shallow cuts but little else. He attempted to return the wounds in kind, but ironically, as the number of his opponents diminished, their tactics grew stronger.

The remaining three thugs surrounded him more carefully, avoiding the groaning men on the ground and making use of the space they had available. Jinn glanced toward the rorden as the thugs studied him and each other. Dregg had slipped away, a disappointment that the deva hoped to rectify before morning.

His left arm and shoulder bled freely from the clumsy cuts that had reached through his defense. Wincing, he stretched his shoulder painfully as a wild-eyed, thin man snarled at him over the edge of a bloodied saber. Jinn nodded at the man in mocking approval and dashed forward, bending low as the sword on his left whistled over his head. The flat of the thrusting blade on his right he blocked barehanded, cold steel sliding across the numb flesh of his palm.

He came up between them, sword vertical as the thin man parried. At the ring of steel on steel, Jinn spun against the man's right shoulder, knocking the thin man off balance as the deva brought his stolen blade around. The swift, wide arc of his sword stopped only when it struck bone. The thin man's head lolled to the side, his neck gaping like a toothless mouth as he slumped forward, freeing Jinn's blade with a twitching jerk.

The other two men stared quietly at the third, their swords wavering as they stepped back a pace.

"Dregg's coin isn't enough for this," one said as he turned to run, his companion close behind.

Jinn breathed deeply, his lust for battle lessened but not sated. Frightened shadows hovered in the corners of several windows above the scene, but no one cried out for the Watch, too scared to call attention to themselves. Jinn sighed and resisted the urge to bow in a mocking salute to the voyeuristic eyes that took such a sickening enjoyment in the blood sport. At the sound of a pained groan, he turned. A large man rose from the ground to spit blood and teeth on the cobbles.

The big man surveyed the area, his eyes roaming from one body to the next as he wiped the thick crimson stain from his lips and met the deva's cold stare. He grinned and pointed.

"They cut your arm up pretty good," he said, resting the heavy sword against his shoulder.

"That they did," Jinn replied, narrowing his gold eyes and clasping the wound tightly. "It appears I already knew how to bleed. Is there to be a second lesson?"

The large man raised a thoughtful eyebrow and looked once again at the others. "Second lesson . . . is know when to quit," he answered and turned away, pulling the Watch tabard over his head and throwing it aside.

Jinn knelt to wipe the blood from his blade and paused, listening as screams echoed from the direction of the seaward wall. Annoyed, he stared down the avenue then glanced east, just a short run from the tower of Archmage Tallus.

The screams grew louder.

Cursing quietly, he followed the direction of his instincts, a slave to the celestial blood of his forced immortality. Despite himself and all argument to the contrary, he headed west, toward the screams.

The wailing screams had died down as Jinn arrived. He hid across the street from a modestly large mansion as servants and guests crowded outside an open iron gate. They huddled together for warmth, a few openly weeping as Watchmen entered and exited the home, speaking to one another in hushed voices and reporting each in turn to Lucian Dregg. The rorden seemed neither surprised nor concerned, pacing angrily outside the gates and glaring at those gathered before them. He crossed his arms as the first body was removed, covered by a stained sheet, and loaded onto an open cart. Eight more quickly joined the first, the crimson marks on each sheet suggesting a similar pattern of wounds suffered.

Jinn shook his head, troubled. There was no detailed observation of the scene, no interest in concealing the bodies or questioning anyone who might have witnessed the killings. He expected no better from Dregg. He did, however, think there might have been a show of some kind, an act to keep at least an air of professionalism. The scene was surreal, unfolding within the wealthiest ward of the city without care or procedure.

"And parading it all in front of the servants," he whispered, "from whom word will spread house to house like wildfire."

"I thought I might find you here."

Jinn turned slowly at the sound of Mara's voice as he bound a tight strip of cloth over the cut on his arm.

"Did you?" he replied. "Because I was wondering where *you* were about six dead men ago."

Mara slinked through the shadows, looking over his injured shoulder and shrugging. He eyed her suspiciously, curious as to what had pulled her away from following Rorden Dregg; the night hag was not prone to whimsy.

"Dregg is the little man in all this. When do we visit the archmage?" she said, smirking, a barely imperceptible note of hunger in her voice that only increased Jinn's suspicion.

"You sound eager enough," he said flatly, catching her eye.

"I found a familiar scent earlier. I'm looking forward to tracking it down," she answered. "That's strange."

She nodded toward the mansion gate, and Jinn tore his gaze

away from the hag, searching through the crowd until he caught sight of Dregg again. A woman stood at his side, her arm around his waist, her face buried in his shoulder as if in sorrow. When she lifted her eyes, turning to rest her head on the rorden's chest, Jinn's breath caught in his throat.

"Rilyana Saerfynn?" he muttered, absently placing a hand over the letters in his coat, written in her hand and full of her alleged dislike of Lucian Dregg. He leaned back against the wall, staring at the ground, puzzled once again.

"Are we going?" Mara asked, apparently having gotten her fill of the crime scene. Jinn stared at her a moment in a daze then blinked, seeing in the night hag the focus he was on the edge of losing. Too many mysteries, little details threatened to overcome his sense of duty to the bigger picture. He shook free of his bewilderment, glancing back only once as Dregg shouted orders to his men, who began ushering the crowd away from the mansion.

"Let's be quick and unseen," he said, heading east again. "Dregg is enforcing a curfew, and I expect there will be chaos tomorrow morning."

>———W———<

Pushing away from a desk overladen with reports, inventories, and old broadsheets, Commander Tavian yawned, stretching his lean frame in a plain, wooden chair made less for comfort than function. Less than a year ago, he'd not needed a chair of any kind save those offered to him occasionally by his superiors. Offices in the East Wall of Waterdeep's North Ward were places he had dreaded visiting, and he'd had his boots repaired or replaced more often than many of his own officers. Tavian glared at the little room, at the nearly bare shelves, the cobwebs swaying gently in a corner, and rued the days when he'd worked so hard for promotion.

He stood away from the parchment-crowded desk and took his heavy cloak, needing no window to time the end of shift, feeling in his gut the late evening slip toward very early morning. A long sword jangled at his hip, its blade clean and unblemished by wear or rust as he rounded the desk, satisfied with a good day's work, but less so than if he'd walked a patrol.

Reaching for the door, he paused at the sound of booted feet approaching down the hallway—four men, he reckoned, two of them restrained judging by the whispered curses echoing off the smooth, stone walls. A knock at his door swiftly followed, and he shook his head, whispering his own curse as he took the handle and faced what appeared to be four officers, two of them familiar and two of them in restraints.

"Commander," the officer on the left, known as Aeril, spoke first and gestured to the men in restraints. "A pair of unusual officers here to see you, sir."

"So you say?" Tavian replied, eyeing their dirty, ill-fitting tabards, worn dock boots, and matching black eyes, courtesy, no doubt, of the officers flanking them. "I don't believe I've had the dishonor of meeting these recruits on any of the regular patrols."

"Sir, we caught these two putting some quick heels to the cobbles just outside of Sea Ward on Shield Street," the officer on the right, called Naaris, explained. "We tried to question them, but they seemed more interested in resisting."

"No surprises there," Tavian replied, smiling and crossing his arms. "I imagine Rorden Allek didn't take kindly to impersonators of the Watch on his shift, eh?"

"They say they were hired on by Rorden Dregg last night," Aeril said, a strange seriousness in his gaze that caused Tavian's smile to falter, sensing something far graver than mere stolen uniforms.

"Rorden Dregg? *Lucian* Dregg?" he asked, incredulous.

"Aye, sir," Naaris answered.

"Dregg couldn't find his arse with both hands, and I doubt he'd have the work ethic to carry out the task in the first place," Tavian said and stepped back toward his desk, motioning for the officers and their charges to enter. "I'll never understand how he became swordcaptain, much less rorden. Who in their right mind would promote him?"

"Someone discreet, I'd wager, and quick," Aeril said, lowering his gaze and adding. "It seems Rorden Allek was killed in the line of duty last evening, during a fire at the Storm's Front."

"What?" Tavian said. It had to be a mistake. Allek Marson had sponsored his training, had put him in charge of his first patrol. "How do we know this?"

"A friend of mine patrols in Sea Ward, sir," Aeril answered. "He said things have been strange for some time now, but he was loyal to Rorden Allek, keeping things quiet to avoid a panic. When Dregg stepped into Marson's position . . ."

"He spoke up," Tavian finished, nodding absently as he stared at the floor and leaned against the desk, trying to absorb what he'd been told and formulate a suitable course of action. "A good man knows a bad officer."

"Aye, sir."

Tavian drummed his fingers thoughtfully, his eyes glancing over the scattered, mundane reports cluttering his office. He glared at the two men in stolen tabards.

"So Dregg steps up, a swift promotion under unusual circumstances, no doubt somehow funded by favors or coin. It'll ride for a day or so," he said at length. "If Allek wanted secrecy, we'll respect that until we know why. Keep in touch with your friend, Aeril. Put together a small patrol, and meet me here at midmorn tomorrow. Throw these two in a cell until further notice. Understood?"

"Yes, sir," both men replied and saluted before turning to go.

"And practice not doing that," Tavian said, stopping the men in midstride. "No salutes and no tabards tomorrow, this will be a quiet patrol. Eyes and ears only."

The men nodded and dragged the impersonators out, closing the door behind them and leaving Tavian alone. He sat still for a long time, trying to convince himself that Allek would turn up alive and well. As several broadsheets slipped to the floor, bearing stories of murder, conspiracy, and danger across the city, he had a fair idea of what he could truly expect to find.

"More of the same," he muttered, though he was eager to get his boots on real streets and deal with the situation on terms that felt more natural than sitting behind a desk.

ELEVEN

Jinn crouched in the shadows of a small park just outside the squat, modest tower of Archmage Tallus. Situated in the center of a large block of businesses and servant homes, the tower sat in darkness, an iron fence around its perimeter, a rusted gate left open and creaking in the winter breeze. Black windows at its base revealed naught but the reflections of weak streetlamps and the bare branches of thin trees. Decorative crenellations at its top were worn and cracked with age and exposure. Water stains crept down the sides like the tracks of tears down an old man's face collected at the bottom by dried-out vines of ivy clinging to the stone.

Had Quessahn's directions been any less accurate, Jinn would have thought the tower abandoned for years.

"No guards, no lights," he whispered. "Perhaps he's not in."

Maranyuss stepped closer to the park's edge, leaning on the bark of a winter-shorn tree as she lifted her nose to the air and closed her eyes.

"I smell blood," she said. "He's in there . . . and we are not alone."

She turned as a figure approached them, cloak and hood pulled tight against the cold. Jinn relaxed as the hood fell away, revealing the troubled stare of Quessahn. She met his gaze only briefly as she neared, averting her eyes to look upon the archmage's unkempt tower.

"Tallus is not in there," she said. "Technically Tallus does not exist."

"What did you and Briarbones discover?" Jinn asked, more eager to confront the wizard than argue with Quessahn over whether or not he should.

"Before he came to the House of Wonder, Tallus was known as Ashmidai," she said. "An aspiring, ambitious, and secretive wizard for the Vigilant Order of Asmodeus. This alone would not have barred him from becoming a master at the House of Wonder, but he kept it hidden anyway."

"Well," Jinn replied, "that's one puzzle piece that fits."

Shadows shifted near the encircling buildings, hunched figures drawing nearer. They were not close enough for Jinn to accurately identify them as ahimazzi, but instinct told him what his eyes could not. They were only a few, but their numbers could quickly swell. Mara hissed quietly at the sight of them. Her senses being far greater than Jinn's, she could smell their hollowed presence, their empty husks bearing no value to one dealing in souls.

"Let's get inside," she said, exiting the sparse tree line of the park. "I grow tired of pretending stealth will hide us from the wizard."

"Wait!" Quessahn said, glancing at Jinn in disbelief as she chased after the hag. "You can't just walk in through the front—"

"The door is open," Mara said sharply, staring down the eladrin and pointing at the tower, its wide double doors a dark hole beyond the iron gate. "If we're not going in now, we might as well abandon this little hunt altogether."

"Agreed," Jinn replied, already on his feet and following Mara through the gate. He paused briefly to glance at Quessahn, feeling as though some unknown confession were hanging between them, but he could not find the words to express the strange idea. She said nothing, appearing indecisive at the gate, her blue eyes glittering as they finally turned to him, something in their depths causing him a momentary pang of inexplicable sorrow. "We could use your help," he said at last. "Perhaps we'll find more about how to stop the killings."

"That's not what you're looking for," she said.

"I can think of few instances in the past tenday when I've ever found what I was looking for," he replied with a grin. "Perhaps this time we'll be lucky."

"I don't believe in luck," she said and passed through the gate to stand on the tower's doorstep a moment before entering the dark beyond.

"Me neither," he muttered, eyeing her suspiciously, certain that she knew far more than she'd been letting on.

The tower's interior stood in stark contrast to its humble exterior. A tall, circular chamber dominated the entrance, the ceiling lost in the shadows above. The floor was of a highly polished, dark marble and a wide set of fine, wood stairs spiraled up toward a second-level loft, the bases of several shelves just visible through the chamber's gloom. The whole of the room bore little decoration, all of it centered dramatically upon a massive statue set before the circle of windows.

Light filtering in through the windows seemed magnified, illuminating the tower and gleaming on the smooth contours of the statue's perfectly sculpted musculature. Carved from black stone, it stood three times as tall as Jinn surrounded by a circular pool of clear water. Jinn approached slowly, glaring into the blank eyes of the statue, its visage shaped into the likeness of a handsome young man, smiling with its head lowered, small horns curving gracefully from its brow. It held one hand, its left, palm up in a frozen gesture of dubious welcome.

"Asmodeus," he whispered.

"I'm guessing Tallus doesn't entertain much," Mara said as she explored the perimeter of the room, gently feeling her way along the walls. She added quietly as she neared the stairs, "The scent of blood is strongest here."

"We should search his books before he finds us," Quessahn said and took the first step, but Mara swiftly caught her arm.

"Not those," the hag said, crimson eyes smoldering through her illusory disguise as she scanned the stairway. "Anything in plain view is, at best, very plain. There is power here. Step back."

Quessahn backed away from the stairs as Jinn tore his gaze away from the statue of Asmodeus, half expecting the devil-god's likeness to awaken somehow. He left it feeling almost disappointed it had not moved to address or attack him. Unlike most, Jinn wanted the god's attention. Vague memories of having walked and battled alongside gods stirred strongly within him, but among all of his emotions he bore no fear of divinity. He had seen gods bleed, cry out in pain, and die on the field of battle, their dissipating essences wafting through the dissolving order of armies left in chaos. His pulse quickened at the thought of it, holding the memory of the act itself as an affront to the seeming power of Asmodeus.

Mara waved her hands slowly over the bottom steps of the stairway, her form wavering as she abandoned the illusions that disguised her true appearance. Bruise-colored skin spread across her arms and face as small, gnarled horns curved back from her brow. She spit harsh words through her lionlike fangs, wisps of gathering energy trailing from her black claws. Eventually her chanting ceased and the stairway rippled, several steps disappearing to reveal a second stairway leading down.

Led by flickering lights, they descended into the shadows beneath the tower, Mara hungrily taking the lead. Jinn drew his sword, nerves on edge, wondering if they might find Tallus and hoping they would encounter Sathariel. Sight of the statue above had excited his bloodlust, and he prayed that his hunt would soon be over.

A second circular chamber greeted them below, ringed on all sides by arcane torches that gave off no heat or smoke. Indeed, there were several old books lining shelves along the walls, some sat open upon pedestals, but it was the rune-covered circle in the center of the chamber that drew their full attention. Stinking of blood and fear, wide splatters of crimson radiated outward from the mangled corpse on the floor, its form only vaguely resembling something once human. Shredded bits of dark robes still clung to the severed and broken limbs, the body's torso barely clothed and still attached to a crushed lump that Jinn suspected had once been the wizard's head. Nearby a gnarled, wooden staff had been shattered into splintered stumps.

"I think Tallus has already had visitors," Quessahn said, keeping her boots at the edge of the mutilation but seeming unable to look away from the grim scene. Jinn stared as well, his eyes narrowed, seeing less the body than the questions it raised.

"But his books," Mara said. "By all the souls in suffering . . ."

Her deep voice was full of awe as she approached the first pedestal, heedless of the ruined flesh and blood beneath her, swearing quietly as she gently caressed the old tome's yellowed pages.

"What is it?" Jinn asked.

"Notes," Mara muttered, perusing the handwritten text. "Bits of an ancient spell, old magic, and here . . . the nine families . . . nine bloodlines . . ."

"Nine," Jinn whispered as Quessahn tore her eyes away from the body and strode through the blood to see what Maranyuss had found. They conferred in hushed whispers over the book, pointing at and debating the archmage's notes. Jinn didn't listen, his attention taken by a strange vibration in the floor. The walls shook, sending dust raining down from the ceiling. Cracks spread quietly out from the corners of the room, as if the tower itself were awakening and stirring into life. He backed toward the stairs, watching the ceiling closely as the cracks grew larger. "Let's be swift, ladies . . ."

"The Loethes!" Quessahn proclaimed, turning wide eyed as Mara took the book from the pedestal. "Their family is next!"

"The spell must not be completed, Jinn," Mara said, eyeing the walls as more dust drifted down in clouds. "Or we may never catch up to Sathariel."

A sound like stone grinding against stone groaned menacingly from upstairs, cracking and grating like the birth pangs of a mountain. A section of the ceiling buckled violently, covering the wizard's mangled body in dust and plaster. Chunks of masonry crashed from above as they dashed to the stairway, narrowly dodging being crushed. Mara and Quessahn fell into the wall behind the deva, panting and cursing, their robes and boots stained by the wizard's blood.

"The spell, Jinn . . . ," Mara said breathlessly, shaking her head as the ceiling buckled again. The enchanted torches were knocked from their sconces and buried, leaving the chamber in darkness.

Despite all, Jinn was most startled by the sense of urgency in Mara's voice, the earnestness in her ember red eyes. The night hag, in the end, was a selfish creature, devoted solely to her own interests and survival. The barest edge of fear in Mara was enough to put his boots in motion far faster than the threat of a tower falling on his head.

"Let's escape with our own lives first," he said as he bounded up the stairs two at a time. "Then we'll see to those of the Loethe family."

Stairs split beneath their heels as they ran for the surface floor, blinded and choking on dust, thunderous crashes booming from above.

>———W———<

Darvehsa strode slowly and deliberately through the ballroom, her gaze critical as she inspected every inch of every surface. Several times she clucked her tongue in disapproval, finding a smudge here, a patch of forgotten dust there. Even a casual glance at the long, velvet curtains revealed that they hadn't been beaten in days, covered in specks of lint and the occasional strand of hair. She picked at them meticulously, collecting the unwanted bits in a deep pocket of her apron, careful not to drop them on the finely woven carpet Lady Lhaerra had received from an old suitor in Calimport. As often was the case, Lhaerra had kept the carpet but done away with the man.

After inspecting the chamber to her satisfaction, Darvehsa sighed in satisfaction, folding her hands over her apron and looking proudly over the ballroom that had been filled but a few scant bells ago. She was grateful the Winterfirst party had been cut short, needing no more of the guests' messes to clean up, wincing at every spilled crumb or stray drop of hastily consumed wine. She shuddered at the thought of it and, with a silken handkerchief, took the double door handles and quietly closed them behind her.

Or course her arrival in the entrance hall meant no less of a daunting task, though her skills at maintaining the Loethe household were prodigious. The gleaming marble floor was rarely gleaming enough. The polished frames of old paintings often needed more polishing and occasional repair, the canvases themselves requiring almost yearly restoration to maintain the vivid colors of the family's patriarchs. Clucking her tongue again, she shook her head and imagined the eagerness of the younger staff to escape their duties and partake of their own celebrations. She didn't fault them entirely; however, she would have none of their excuses on the morrow. Double-checking the locked doors, she took down a list of mental notes as she walked through the room, her heels tapping on the marble loudly in the shadowy gloom of late evening.

She paused as the resounding click of the bolts faded from the chamber, listening as a faint noise like panting reached the edges of her keen sense of hearing. Turning slowly, she spied a door at the far end of the chamber standing slightly ajar, enough to let escape the dim, flickering glow of a torch or candle. She approached it carefully as a pained gasp stretched into an almost longing moan from the shadows beyond the door.

Hesitantly she pushed the door open wider, gazing down a spiral stairway that wound around a highly detailed column of stone. Hollowed faces in the column, carved into a myriad of ghoulish visages, held small pots of glowing embers and candles that dripped thick from the frowning corners of stone mouths. Wax coated the tips of her fingers as she quietly descended the first few steps, straining to hear more, her breath held in little gulps of air lest they obscure the approach of something hideous from below.

Murmuring voices rose and fell in a harsh language that flowed rough on the air, grating in her ears even though their melody seemed to call her farther down. Deep and sonorous, the chanting was joined by heaving breaths; contented sighs; and short, desperate wheezes.

On a wide, stone wall, the glow of unseen torches brightened, casting dark silhouettes that danced and wavered on a field of flickering orange. A crowd of figures in shadow intermingled on the wall, their forms merging with one another in lustful and furious configurations. Hands were offered to gently stroke a curving cheek or raised to smash violently down on something wet and indiscernible. Whispered pleas could be heard among the throng and a scent of heavy perfume, incense, sweat, and blood filled Darvehsa's nose as she turned to swiftly ascend the spiral stairs, stepping lightly toward the entrance hall above.

The door had opened wider behind her, a shaft of pale light illuminating the door handle. Turning back, she clucked her tongue as she reached the top step. Annoyed by her discovery, she pulled a clean square of cloth from her apron and wetted it on her tongue. Pressing down tight, she scrubbed a finger-long streak of crimson from above the brass door handle, cursing as the dried, rusty edges of the stain challenged her fastidious determination. At length she leaned back, studying the door before exiting the stairway and pulling the door closed.

Its edges matched the wall perfectly, the handle disguised as a candle sconce. Wiping her hands off on her apron, she tested the door's edge once more to be sure it was sealed before calmly glancing once more upon the entrance hall. Satisfied and deciding to use the dusty chamber as an example to her staff in the morning, she set off for Loethe Manor's kitchens, prepared to harass the staff there into working faster if they wished to rest at all before sunrise.

Books and loose pages fluttered down from the upper floor of the tower as Jinn cautiously ascended the hidden staircase. Freestanding shelves had fallen from above, smashing to splinters on the dark marble floor as he, Mara, and Quessahn rose from the archmage's secret library and into a sudden silence. Bits of debris still rained down, bouncing and skipping among shattered boards and broken artifacts. Dim shafts of light illuminated the dusty mist through the tall windows across the west and south walls.

A flash of alarm stopped Jinn in his tracks, noting a peculiar lack of shadow on the northern wall as loose rocks splashed into the circular reflecting pool to the south—the pool where the massive statue of Asmodeus had once stood.

"Move!" he yelled, pulling Quessahn behind him as he dashed toward the windows, trusting Mara to take care of herself. Something crashed into the marble where they'd been, the impact splitting the floor, spidery cracks racing alongside them. Cut off from the front doors, Jinn searched for a swift escape and made for the windows. Thinking quickly, he grabbed a chunk of fallen stone and hurled it at the glass.

As the stone bounced harmlessly away, Jinn cursed, having caused no more than a smudge of dust on the warded glass. He spun around, heart racing, eyes searching the clouded room for movement. Stone ground against stone in the dark and something large appeared in the gloom, flying toward them through the cloud of dust.

"Down!" he cried, ducking low as a section of shelving flew over their heads and crashed against the windows. Splinters and chunks of wood clattered all around them as he and Quessahn cautiously raised their heads and stood. Mara appeared at his side, her red eyes fixed on something in the dark.

"The statue, I presume?" Jinn asked.

"Yes and no," Mara answered. "An eidolon. The statue of a god, blessed by a god. Sometimes they think they are gods."

Heavy footsteps prowled slowly near the back of the chamber, a violet glow piercing the dust as a metallic smell wafted through the room.

"And we're stuck in here with it," Quessahn added with a cough. "Guess Tallus didn't want to be buried alone."

The violet glow intensified, becoming more distinct as the footsteps drew closer. The ebony statue's smooth surface had changed, a dense pattern of arcane and divine symbols shining across its massive frame. Purple light and mist issued from its eyes and smiling mouth, curling around the graceful horns sprouting from its brow. Jinn narrowed his eyes at the statue, caught by the pulsing sigils on the eidolon's brow as it approached. He was struck by the familiarity of the construct, though he was unable to place where or when he'd encountered such a monstrosity before.

"Spread out," he whispered to the others.

No sooner had the words left his mouth than the eidolon charged, its long, lumbering stride covering the distance between them swiftly. Mara slipped into the shadows, cloaking herself in darkness, as Quessahn drew her ritual dagger, chanting softly and backing away. Jinn held his ground, holding the construct's focus long enough for the others to prepare their magic, their rhythmic voices lost as the floor and walls shook. A massive fist, trailing wisps of purple mist, came crashing down as Jinn rolled backward, flying shards of marble stinging his skin.

Rising in a crouch, he swung his blade, the steel ringing off the eidolon's rocky arm harmlessly, though he noted a tiny crack of bleeding light where he'd struck. The second fist came soon behind the first, and he leaped forward, hacking at the statue's face. Sparks flew from the edge of his sword, leaving a miniscule fracture in its wake. The construct loosed a deafening roar as an acrid liquid seeped from the tiny wound, burning Jinn's wrist as he attempted to escape the eidolon's reach. A mere step away from clear ground, the thing's swiping claws caught his shoulder and sent him tumbling into rubble.

Pain seared through his arm, his recent wounds burning as the acidic blood of the eidolon mingled with his own. He rolled onto his back as the construct knelt over him, an artificial sneer on its face as it pinned his legs. His sword lost in the debris, he stared into the thing's hellish eyes, helpless. A spark in the fiery twin pits caught Jinn's attention, dragging him back to the first battles of his physical existence, back to the days when eidolons were yet young to the world. As the construct's other arm rose to crush him, he knew some minute part of Asmodeus was aware of his monstrous servant, and Jinn morbidly wanted, more than anything, to capture the attention of the god.

Shrieking voices heralded several bolts of scintillating light that arced through the eidolon's body, causing it to twist and writhe enough for Jinn to escape its grip. He crawled through the rubble, snatching up his lost sword and ducking low as Mara strode toward him, her hands spread in a fan of blue flames that charged the air with arcane energy. As swiftly as she appeared, Mara dissolved into the shadows as the eidolon thrashed toward her, its fist smashing the floor where she'd stood. Seizing the moment, Jinn's arm shot out, stabbing the ancient sword into a burning rune on the construct's side. As the steel grated against stone, the statue lurched violently to its side, pulling Jinn to his feet as he fought to hang on, his sword caught in the burning sigil.

From the corner of his eye, he saw the brief blur of a dark shape rushing toward him just before the world went black. Stars danced before his eyes, and a peculiar weightlessness held him for what seemed like an eternity. Yellowed parchment fluttered around him amid clouds of swirling dust as he fought to regain his sight, shaking his head slowly and finding himself in a sitting position against the far wall. The floor shook beneath him, and flashing lights filled the tower as Mara and Quessahn hurled spell after spell at the eidolon, none of their magic injuring the thing to any lasting effect.

A glimmer of shining steel protruded from the construct's ribs, just beneath its right arm. Jinn focused on the metal splinter and forced himself to stand. He winced as the right side of his body pulsed painfully as if it were made of a single bruise. He pushed the sensation to the back of his mind. He took up a length of fallen chain, a chunk of broken rafter dangling from its end as he charged at the eidolon's back. Mara slipped away into shadow as he passed, cold fragments of darkness clinging to his cheeks as he hurled the chain at the statue's head.

He missed and rolled beneath the swiping fist of stone that quickly followed. Muttering a curse as splinters dug into his side, he caught a brief glimpse of Quessahn in front of the eidolon, tendrils of darkness spewing from her palms. The spell briefly dimmed the molten energy of the construct, causing it to shriek, a sound like hail striking a tin roof, but the magic could not hold. The fist that had sought to smash Jinn reversed its course and struck the eladrin solidly. Jinn gasped as Quessahn's body flew through the air and crashed against the wall like a corn-husk doll.

The sickening thump of her body on the floor ripped through his gut, the sight of her senseless and bleeding awakening something within him. An image of her flashed through his mind, her smiling face looking up at him, a sea of waving green behind her. Her lips moved in the image, but he could not hear her words over his racing pulse, thrumming through his ears as he stood. Pangs of guilt and loss joined his bloodlust, though both gave way to a rage that burned from the depths of his pounding heart. Swinging the chain once around his fist, he dashed forward as the eidolon turned to present its curving horns. He hurled the chain again, wrapping it neatly around the statue's neck.

It whipped its upper body backward, roaring a sound almost like laughter as Jinn was pulled into the air, swinging at the chain's end. Black claws reached for him, but he swung his legs forward, pulling tightly on the chain as the room spun around him. The burning eyes followed him, hellish energy and caustic blood seeping from them as he turned through the air, whipping tight as the chain caught on the statue's left shoulder. The bright edge of his stolen blade glowed in the eidolon's side, the sword stuck, a thrust away from the statue's immortal energy.

The essence of a god, he thought. A shard of divinity.

Arms burning with the strain, he pulled the chain taut again and raised his legs, whispering a prayer as the hilt of his lodged sword came into sight. With a single thrust, he kicked the blade deep, sparks flying as the steel stabbed home into the fiery heart of the eidolon, shattering the god-forged splinter that had given the statue life. Power surged from the wound, washing violently through Jinn's body as the construct shuddered, purple mist steaming through the cracks and symbols across its stony skin.

The chain slipped from Jinn's fist, and he fell away, sliding across the marble floor as the burst of divine power wracked his flesh with pain. The eidolon's body quaked, falling apart in lifeless chunks through the chamber bathed in hellish light. Jinn gasped, a brief moment of pure clarity overcoming him. All the threads of his many lives were joined, fusing together like a winding road of long years, at their end the blazing light of the Astral Sea. The path of his soul from flesh to flesh, bound in blood for millennia, burned through his thoughts, every memory as fresh as when it was first crafted, the darkness of every death just as haunting.

He saw meaning and destiny in the whole of the pattern, his eyes torn away from the minute details of the individual lives he'd lived, and an unsettling calm overcame him. Somewhere in the long and winding maze of his soul, his fate had been written, and he was loath to look upon its conclusion . . .

In a heartbeat the vision was gone, leaving him trembling and struggling to breathe, his skull aching as the memories faded, and he felt empty and drained. He coughed and groaned, eyes burning as they adjusted to the dim light of the chamber.

Straining to right himself, he squinted through the dust and found Quessahn's hand nearby, her eyes closed and veiled in blood.

TWELVE

Q uess."

Jinn whispered her name, gently cradling her neck and stemming the flow of blood from a cut on her forehead. Her skin was soft in his hands, pale and familiar like a recurring dream. The sight of one limp hand sliding to the floor nauseated him, the smell of her blood stinging in his nose like the scent of a fresh nightmare. He leaned close, her breath on his cheek and her pulse beneath his fingertips calming him as Mara stepped out of her clinging shadows, baring her fangs at the pile of smoking stone nearby.

"Is she dead?" Mara asked as she carefully inspected the book she'd taken from downstairs, gently turning the pages as if they would fall apart at any touch.

"No," Jinn answered. "But she'll need some time to—"

"Time we don't have," Mara cut in sharply, her crimson eyes scanning page after page in quick succession. "This spell Tallus was working on puts us all in danger, one dead eladrin is a small price to pay if need be—"

"She is alive," Jinn insisted. "We're not leaving her."

"This isn't like you, Jinn," Mara replied, closing the book slowly. "You'd risk all the work we've done for one woman?"

"All the work I've done started with one woman," he answered quietly, brushing Quessahn's cheek as she stirred, though he imagined for a moment that it was a different face he looked upon, silver-eyed and cursed with immortality like himself. He'd abandoned her to fight the ancient war of his lost gods and he'd lost her, his Variel.

"Kehran?" Quessahn mumbled, coughing. "Is that you—?"

Her eyes fluttered open, squinting through the gloom until they found Jinn. At the sight of him, her face twisted slightly, a mixture of sorrow and disappointment that stabbed him far deeper than he'd expected.

"It's me, Quess, Jinnaoth," he answered. "Who is Kehran?"

"It's nothing . . . no one," she managed, rising on her elbows and wincing in pain. "Forget I said it. I'll be fine."

"The Loethe family is next," Mara said, her arms crossed as she stared at the deva, ignoring Quessahn. "We need to go to them. Now."

"She's right. Go," Quess said, wiping blood from her lip. "At the corner of Ivory Street and Gorl. Be quick . . ."

"Right," Jinn muttered, standing as the eladrin sat up, her left arm already darkening with early bruises. Looking from her to Mara, he turned on his heel and retrieved his blade from the steaming remains of the eidolon. "Stay here with Quessahn. I'll tend to the Loethes."

"I am not a nursemaid," Mara growled. "And you have no idea what you're running into—"

"I understand," he said, fixing her with his golden stare. "Do your best. And find out what you can from that book. I expect we'll need to know exactly what we're up against, yes?"

Her red eyes flared bright, a fury boiling behind them that Jinn was glad to see, a fresh reminder that his ally could become his enemy after all was said and done. Given half a chance, with her vengeance against Asmodeus complete, she would sell Jinn's soul to the highest bidder without a flicker of regret; of that he was certain.

"I'll find out what I can," she replied coldly, "but only until the eladrin can walk. I'll not stand around any longer while you blunder into the unknown."

"Fair enough," Jinn replied and headed for the door, the winter wind driving flurries of snow into the tower as he left her staring daggers at his back. Pulling his cloak tightly, he jogged out of the closed circle of buildings and held back in the shadows for a breath. Seeing no Watch patrols or shambling figures of the ahimazzi, he dashed down the street, keeping his eyes fixed on the sky as if the low, gray clouds would sprout black wings were he to look away.

Warm blood coursed through the body of a young man, sliding through muscle, turning along the curve of a strong bone, winding between tight lengths of tendon, and branching like a forest of crimson and blue trees rooted in a field of flesh. Each nuance of the city, the feel of stone beneath his hands and snow on his face, was a marvel to those housed within his mind.

The nine skulls ran him fiercely, leaping from one rooftop to the next, enraptured by their time back in a place of physical being, of pulsing hearts and base desires. Somewhere behind the burning green eyes and the shadowy shroud of the chosen body, the circle of skulls—once known simply as the circle of nine—still bickered and argued over details and trivialities, but in purpose they were of one mind and unified goal.

They followed a prayer-filled river of power, growing stronger with each step, fed by those who would assist them. One of them pressed forward, smiling with the young man's lips—and still able to taste the lust of Rilyana Saerfynn upon them—as they came within sight of the House of Loèthe. Blood stained their borrowed hands, the earlier killing merely an appetizer for the meal to come.

They crawled slowly over an adjacent rooftop, tiles abrading the soft skin they wore. Pain was a novel experience, one nearly forgotten in the long years since being cursed to live as mere skulls of enchanted bone. Cuts and scratches burned on the skin, growing numb in the cold, which caused its own sort of pain, the dull ache of exposure. Each sensation they sipped at like fine wine, tasting and savoring the experience, and each anxious to claim their own bodies once again.

A familiar scent gave them pause, and their stolen throat loosed an uneasy growl. They searched the sky, looking for the black wings of the angel, Asmodeus's pet. The devil-god would not soon forget those who had betrayed him so long ago.

"He shall not win," they muttered, nine voices in concert. "Sea Ward shall become a graveyard long before he can think to make it his Hell."

Smiling, they slithered down the slope of the roof, sniffing the air and smelling blood, the taste of it on their tongue sending chills down their spine. Murmuring incoherently, the nine skulls each attempted to use the voice of the young man, absently arguing over the wisdom of their plan as they'd done for centuries. Several distrusted Archmage Tallus, others doubted his talent, and still others could not see anything beyond reversing the monumental failure of three centuries ago, at any cost.

"The angel will find us, usurp all that we have worked for!"

"Nonsense! Sathariel is as blind as his master. He has no power save that which he can steal, and we have hidden ours well enough for centuries."

"Tallus will fail. He hasn't the discipline to—!"

"He has the desire, the greed for our power. That will serve him and us."

"Too much greed. We have given him the last of our secrets."

"Then we shall be swift!"

The argument ended abruptly as their body leaped from the roof, landing nimbly in the Loethes' garden. Blood and salt and lust drew them to a servants' entrance, the scents of older times when magic was a full cup from which they drank deeply. They had served Mystra once, the goddess passing little judgment on her followers' morals and choices, no matter how dubious, yet they imagined even she had paled when she discovered their intent, despite their failure.

There was no goddess to stop them anymore, and only a vengeful devil of a deity was left to try, but he was young to his power. Time was on their side, but only if they struck soon and only if they gambled on an eternity of suffering.

A muffled chanting reached their ears from somewhere within the house, thrumming through the walls and caressing their body with promises of power.

"Delicious fools," they whispered. "They think they are honoring Asmodeus, calling upon him to visit their wealthy coven with dark blessings." Chuckling, they placed a smoke-shrouded hand against a hidden door and pushed. "No doubt they shall find themselves with Asmodeus in good time."

Jinn prowled the edge of an iron-and-stone wall cautiously, studying the darkened windows and quiet gardens of the Loethe family home. He knew nothing of them save for his brief encounter with the Lady Lhaerra at the Storm's Front tavern, yet the size of their estate suggested room enough for a large family. He paced quietly, trying to decide if he should enter immediately or wait for something to happen, not wishing to call attention to himself unless he had to. Mara had barely glanced at Tallus's notes; he could not deny the possibility that she had been wrong. Despite that, something about the high, stone walls and the garden's eerie silence felt right, tugging at him like the insistent pain of an aching tooth.

He stopped cold, a squeaking sound sending a chill down the back of his neck. It squelched for a breath then stopped, like the sound of a damp hand being dragged across a pane of glass. He searched the windows along the upper floor, squinting through the snow for the source of the noise. There were eight gabled windows, all in a row and all of them identical save for the last one on the western end. A streak of crimson blurred the otherwise spotless glass, the shape of little fingers easily made out above the red smear. The curtains waved, revealing a sliver of darkness and the unmistakable glow of burning green eyes.

He leaped the fence and sprinted through the garden, spying no guards to slow him as he approached the front door. In a brief moment of hope, he tried the handle, but the door was solidly locked. Abandoning convention, he dashed to the rounded eastern corner where tall windows outlined a large side room. He tried to peer inside but whirled around as footsteps crunched on frost behind him. A haggard, bent woman in torn robes stepped out from the shadow of a large tree, her dull, soulless eyes regarding him blankly. She raised the curved dagger in her left hand high as she shambled toward him, a stumbling half run that gave him little time for caution.

He drew his sword and smashed the window with its pommel, grateful as the glass shattered, unwarded by magic as Tallus's had been. He deflected the ahimazzi's clumsy slash and kicked her back before jumping through the window, briefly engulfed by thick curtains as his boots crunched on broken glass. The soulless woman recovered, and others of her kind appeared in the garden but would not approach the house, wandering back to their cold shadows.

Holding still behind the curtains for several breaths, Jinn waited for the inevitable rush of guards or the screams of frightened servants. Greeted by only the strangely quiet house and a meticulously clean ballroom, he crossed the tall room to a sweeping staircase on the southern wall. At the top of the stairs, still he found no signs of life—no lit lanterns or sounds of snoring from the long hallway on his right, no source of heat to keep away the night's chill as the family slept. His breath steamed in the half light of curtained windows in room after room, their doors left open. Empty bedrooms bore straightened, unused sheets. A small library's hearth held no glowing embers of a forgotten fire.

It was as though no one had lived in the house for years, and if not for the lack of dust, Jinn would have sworn that to be the case. Finally, at the end of the hallway, he pushed open a cracked door, a single room to suggest the house had been occupied at all. Several wooden toys were arranged neatly on low shelves, causing him to momentarily wonder at the lives of children, what it must have been like to have a mother and a father.

After several breaths he let his eyes wander to the streak of blood on the window, following its course down to the small body on the floor. Though partially covered in a stained sheet, the inflicted wounds needed no close inspection to identify. A scent of fear still hung on the air. He didn't turn to look at the other small bed against the west wall; he didn't have to.

Back in the hallway, before he could consider rushing downstairs, he found the ghostly glow of emerald flames flickering from within a shroud of shadow at the top of the steps. An unholy growl escaped the tortured throat of the skulls' stolen body as it disappeared down the stairs. Jinn gave chase, leaping over the banister and taking the stairs several at a time, though the skulls had already crossed the ballroom in a dark blur, wisps of shadow dissipating in their wake.

Cursing, he held back, crossing the ballroom slowly, feeling less on the heels of a mystical killer and more a rogue's mark being led into a trap. Silhouettes passed the windows outside, lit by streetlamps and wandering in the garden, surrounding the house with their dead eyes and curved knives.

Too late, he thought.

Peering around the corner, he found the green gaze of the skulls, waiting for him within a doorway. A deep, droning chant echoed from the dark as the skulls crept backward, descending into a hidden stairwell as if beckoning the deva to follow. Jinn hesitated, weighing his options as the chant grew louder, punctuated by throaty gasps and moans. The voices slid on the air as if wet and clinging, like the silvered trail of a slug given sound. Despite all, he could not resist his nature, pulled forward by the chant as easily as if they were trumpets calling him to war.

Stone faces, filled with the glowing light of guttering candles, were set in the stairway's single column as Jinn cautiously took the steps. He followed the edge of his blade inexorably down, imagining that the Abyss itself awaited him below. The night's chill was replaced by the cloying, damp heat of bodies pressed to exertion. Scents of blood and sweat grew stronger, more sour, as they mingled with the none-too-subtle smells of sex and death. It called to mind many such gatherings he had witnessed in recent years, the same stench embedded in the threads of the bloody cloth map he'd found a few days before.

He did not flinch or recoil from the scene that awaited him below, having grown sickeningly accustomed to the extremes that foolish people embraced to alleviate the daily routine of their lives. For the poor it was the hope of a richer life, for the empty a plea for a life worth more than the nothing they felt. For the wealthy, more often than not, simple boredom ensnared them in pits of perversion.

A wide, shallow basin of marble dominated the room, sloshing with oils and blood. Bodies slid and grasped at one another in the basin with toothy smiles and wild eyes, their limbs tangled and stained so much that the meeting of one body and the next was lost in the press. Each already bore a series of symbols, neatly carved down the center of the chest, though they remained alive and seemingly oblivious to the pain of their wounds. The chant came from those surrounding the basin, in dark blue, stained robes. The blue-robed people exulted in a chaotic song of magic, voices upraised, almost pious, as though in prayer.

Blood dripped over the bodies from a curved blade held in the skulls' possessed hand at the far end of the basin. Ephemeral tendrils of energy flowed from the cavorting congregation and into the flickering shadows of the skulls' body, their darkness rising and licking the air like black flame. They regarded Jinn casually, beckoning him with the stained blade.

"Come, deva," they said, their voices booming in the small room, sending ripples through the bare flesh before them. "We would have words with you."

Jinn heard them speak but did not register what they'd said for several breaths, blinking and seeing the chamber as if for the first time, a sudden silence falling over the repulsive spectacle. A stinking miasma of evil overcame him, assaulting his senses and summoning a righteous rage that burned in his gut. Several half-lidded gazes fell on him at once as his golden eyes flashed in anger, looking down on the victims for whose lives Quessahn had argued, defending their right to live, to be represented rather than ignored.

"Innocents," he spat. He raised his stolen blade and charged.

Quessahn leaned to her left with a held breath, placing weight on the leg and half expecting it to collapse beneath her. It didn't, though she winced at the dull pain that throbbed through the limb. As the last streaks of stars left her vision, she stood straight, determined to at least appear strong. Mara sat, her legs crossed, as she pored over the contents of the archmage's notes. The hag's glowing gaze illuminated each page in a dark shade of red that sent chills down Quessahn's spine.

The sight of the night hag, so engrossed in powerful, arcane secrets—old magic rewritten for a spellplagued world—alarmed her more than if Tallus himself had appeared to reclaim them. Keeping an eye on Mara, Quessahn located her ritual dagger and retrieved it, stifling a gasp of pain as she knelt. Slipping the blade beneath her cloak, she approached the night hag warily.

"We should go," she said but received no response. Mara continued turning pages, one clawed finger tracing line after line of handwritten text. "Mara?"

"Are you certain?" the hag asked, not looking up. "Or should I betray you and Jinn now and save myself the trouble of worrying over how to stab you in the back later?"

She closed the book loudly before Quessahn could respond and stood like an apparition in her dark, tattered robes, the archmage's book disappearing in their many folds. She fixed her pinpoint red eyes on the eladrin.

"Save us both the trouble," Quessahn replied. "I'm tired of keeping one eye over my shoulder, wondering when you'll turn on Jinn."

"But you should, my dear," Mara said, twisting a sparkling jade ring. Her form melted and shifted, returning to the guise of a human woman, the unassuming proprietor of an unassuming bookshop. "Just as I keep an eye on him, wondering when he'll be morally struck by the dark bargains he has made over the last few years and decide to start making amends for his misdeeds . . . on the point of a blade."

"Fair enough, then," Quessahn said. She limped toward the doors. "He'll need our help now."

"Yes, I'm sure he will," Mara said, but she did not follow, instead drawing several items from within her cloak. "So I think we shouldn't bother with limping through the streets. If I read correctly, he'll need our assistance directly."

"What does the book say?" Quessahn asked as she scanned through Mara's spell components.

"You're not being fair to him," Mara replied, ignoring the question as she drew a circle on the floor in blue chalk.

"W-what—?"

"You have something that he has never known: direct knowledge of one of his past incarnations," Mara said. "You look at his face and see another. You say his name, but it sounds unnatural and forced. And you seem to expect him to be the better man you once knew him to be, despite the fact that he, I believe you called him *Kehran*, is long dead."

"Do you read minds now as well?" Quessahn asked coldly.

"I didn't have to," Mara answered, completing the chalk circle and holding out her hand for the eladrin. "You wear your every emotion plainly. Jinn may not see it—or may not want to—but I do. Putting the pieces together was not too difficult."

"Why do you care?" she asked, hesitating before taking the hag's hand and entering the circle. "If your alliance with him is just a convenience, what do you care if I hide things from him?"

"I do not," Mara replied casually. "I merely point out that betrayals take many forms. While mine, if and when it comes, will be direct and likely bloody, it will be just another in a long line of righteous battles for the deva, but you . . . you have a grip on his heart, something intangible and lasting that could follow him through every life he lives until the end of creation itself."

"I-I didn't mean . . . ," Quessahn stammered, taken off guard and stunned by the statement.

"It's all right," Mara said with a cruel, victorious grin. "Jinnaoth has little luck when it comes to matters of the heart. Do not think yours will be the first scar he has worn."

Mara whispered an arcane phrase, igniting the chalk circle to a bright, flaring blue that filled the rubble-strewn tower. Energy gathered around them, swirling faster and faster, and Quessahn's thoughts spun with the magical vortex. Blinking through the light of the ritual, she caught Mara's eye and tried to set aside her fear.

"What did you see in Tallus's book?" she asked absently as the hag watched the turning streams of blue with a practiced eye, waiting for the right moment to complete the spell.

"More than I expected," Mara answered. "And enough that I fear Jinn will find the Loethe family less than appreciative of his efforts to help them."

Her voice trailed off into a murmuring chant, one hand pressing into the swirl around them with precise gestures, directing the shape and flow as her words grew louder and more demanding. Quessahn felt the floor give way beneath her feet, but in the breath she might have clung tighter to Mara for support, the tower, and everything else, disappeared in a flash of blue.

THIRTEEN

Bloodstained hands clawed at the air as Jinn leaped over the hissing congregation, his blade curving a wide arc toward the shadowy neck of the green-eyed skulls. They reacted swiftly, deflecting his steel with their own, spatters of blood splashing Jinn's face at the brief contact of the blades. They traded blows, a blur of shining metal flashing between them as the dark ritual of the Loethes fell into chaos. Naked bodies slid across the marble, grasping for Jinn's boots as he maneuvered away from them, furiously slashing at the glowing gaze of the nine skulls, hidden behind the eyes of a stranger.

Nine distinct voices shouted curses from one mouth, each interrupting the last, spewing incomprehensible venom at the deva. Their vitriol washed over him comfortably, feeling right and whole as he opposed an ancient evil on his own terms. He winced as a quick cut slipped through his defense, the warm ache of the cut feeding his bloodlust.

"Idiot!" the skulls cried out. "You'll feed us all to the angel! Where will you find your vengeance then?"

Jinn did not respond, pressing his attack faster and faster, though he was intrigued by their fear of not him, but Sathariel. He turned in slow circles round the splashing thralls crawling out of the marble basin. Given time, he would slay them all, clean the ward's filthy slate, and track down the angel again. If Sathariel would not face him, he would destroy all that the angel worked for.

His sword pierced something solid within the skulls' wavering shadows, and his blade was wet when he drew back to strike again, but the skulls were ready. They spun, a swift kick catching Jinn in the chest and sending him tumbling to the back wall as they bounded through the shallow pool of blood, still cursing as they beat a hasty retreat.

"No!" he shouted.

A hand clasped onto his boot, holding him back. He barely recognized the crazed visage of the Lady Lhaerra, her body smeared with blood. Snarling at her in disgust, he kicked her away, presenting his sword to those gathered, the pitiful remains of what he presumed was the Loethe family, as he followed the skulls. Though he was loath to admit it, he knew he had likely saved their lives, protected their souls from the grasp of the circle of skulls, and the very idea of it propelled him ever faster after their possessed body.

The marble floor of the entrance hall was streaked with blood, boot prints tracked across its once-gleaming surface. A small crowd had gathered in the chamber, in servants' clothes with kitchen knives and fireplace pokers, led by a stern-faced woman of advancing years who looked from the floor to Jinn, madness in her eyes.

"What have you done?" she shrieked, raising a shining cleaver in her hand as she rushed him. "What have you—?"

With a quick swipe, Jinn knocked the blade from her hand, sending it spinning across the room as he reversed his blow and smashed her nose with the pommel of his sword. The crunch of bone echoed in the room as the woman slumped to the ground, clutching her face, dazed and bleeding. The other servants backed away from the deva, shying from his golden glare as he followed the bloody prints out of the room and back up the stairs. Wailing screams erupted behind him, and he paused on the stairs as if in the throes of a nightmare.

Movement caught his eye, shadows rushing by the windows and bobbing, green lights gathering out in the garden. The soulless ahimazzi were gone, shambling away from the house and quickly replaced by shouting officers of the Watch. He watched them gather in disbelief, wondering when the world had turned upside down, knowing the officers had come for him and not the depraved members and staff of the household.

"Chaos," he muttered as he ran up the stairs. "The world has gone mad."

In a rush of spinning black and blue energy, Quessahn felt solid ground beneath her feet as the weight of her body returned. She wavered a moment but maintained her balance despite the arcs of pain shooting up her left leg. Such instantaneous travel was not entirely uncommon for wizards, but Mara's use of the power over such a distance was extraordinary. As her eyes adjusted to the half light of a tall, marble-floored chamber, she reassessed her respect for the hag's magic—and renewed her concern over Mara's possible betrayal.

Shrieking voices echoed from a deep chamber to her right, and she eyed the dark doorway from which they emanated. The floor was covered in dark streaks of blood, most of it fresh and slick. Wet noises that reminded her of a butcher's shop came from the shadows of the doorway, each accompanied by a sharp intake of breath or a shuddering groan.

"Gods," she whispered and ran for the dark, descending the

stained steps beyond and praying that she hadn't waited too long, hoping that Jinn was still alive.

She stopped at the bottom step. Her breath caught in her throat and she blinked in the flickering light of candles and torches. Only bits of the scene came to her at first, flashes of horrible detail that she struggled to understand. They fell upon one another, some with long, curved daggers, others with their bare hands. Bared teeth grinned and gnashed, dark with flesh. Hair slapped against bare backs, wet and sticky as they arched in pain and pleasure. Pale limbs, limp and lifeless, suggested more bodies beneath the press, likely forgotten or ignored for their lack of feeling.

Quessahn backed away. She had known dark rites, had performed her own in years long past. She had explored avenues of magic many wizards and even warlocks had no stomach for, all in a manic attempt to find her lost Kehran or, at the very least, find some explanation for the death that had ruined her life. No spell had been too dark, no ritual too dangerous, but the indulgent self-slaughter she witnessed in the Loethes' basement was beyond her, anathema to all she had studied.

A loud bang from upstairs shocked her into movement, and she returned to the entrance hall, attempting to calm the aching tremble in her left hand. Swinging, green lights flashed through the narrow windows on either side of the front doors. Shadows approached, accompanied by shouted orders as Mara pressed her hands against the portal's frame, whispering words of magic and digging her fingernails into the wood, tiny sigils on her claws flaring to life.

"The Watch," Quessahn said, shaking her head and already imagining Dregg's smug face as he ordered his men into the house. The bodies, the blood, all of it he would blame on the *undesirables* his men found inside.

"Yes, the Watch," Mara replied, still tracing the frame with arcane symbols as she sealed the doors. The officers pounded on the door, demanding entry. "But the servants are of more immediate concern."

A side door had opened, revealing a glimmer of steel and several figures beyond, each with maddened eyes and raised weapons. Quessahn cursed, instinctively raising her hand as a swift incantation slid across her tongue like a sliver of ice. The magic swirled at her fingertips, dancing just beyond her will as she squeezed her fingers into a fist and forced the energy into Art.

A vortex of frigid flames leaped from her hand, engulfing the servants of the house and licking their skin with a burning cold. Screams erupted from the group, joining those from the basement as the family of the house slew each other.

"This will not hold long if they're determined," Mara said, the frame of the double doors glowing with indistinct runes all along its edge. They flickered as the officers struck the doors with something heavy, muffled curses accompanying the effort.

"I imagine they'll be more concerned with keeping us inside," Quessahn replied, drawing her ritual dagger as the shadows of robed figures appeared within the orange glow of the basement stairway, a droning chant preceding their inevitable arrival, their business downstairs finished.

Footsteps and crazed shouts announced the regrouping of the servants, their numbers split between the left and right exits from the hall. In the midst of the chanting, shouting, and powerful thuds against the sealed doors, Quessahn caught the faint ring of steel striking steel from somewhere upstairs.

Roping tentacles of indigo gushed from Mara's palms at the door atop the stairs, taking the first of the robed figures as he ascended into the room. The man's skin paled instantly as the tentacles wrapped around his body, dissipating as he slumped against the wall, weakly gasping for air.

Aching and finding her breath, Quessahn raised her dagger, found a wriggling spark of magic, and began to wring it into shape, chanting as the servants found their courage and entered the room.

A neat line of clean cuts sent the heads of a row of orchids tumbling from their stems as Jinn's blade swept toward the neck of the skulls' body. Winter-blooming flowers spilled from their pots, coating the floor of a domed greenhouse with dark soil and colorful petals. His sword scraped along the edge of a curved dagger, drawing sparks that died among damp flowerbeds. Jinn slid to one knee, ducking low as the dagger cut through the air, missing his ear by the breadth of a finger. With a powerful kick, he pulled their legs out from beneath them, his sword already rising as they tumbled through shattered clay pots and trampled rare specimens of seasonal blooms.

The shadow-cloaked body rolled as it landed, leaving Jinn's blade to strike point down, a breath too slow, in the stone floor. The skulls righted themselves and jumped backward. Rafters shook as the dark-flamed body landed upon a suspended walkway beneath the steel grid of a glass dome atop the Loethe mansion. More pots crashed to the floor as Jinn rose, meeting the burning, hate-filled gaze of the skulls.

"You're pathetic, deva!" they shrieked in unison, the glass above them vibrating with each word. "You honor oaths made to dead gods! You fight a war that means nothing!"

"It means everything!" he shouted back, tired of their whining curses and spying a narrow, spiral stairway at the end of the walkway.

"What? Defeating evil?" they replied, leaning on the railing and chuckling, a sound like bones rattling in a coffin. "It is a joke,

Jinnaoth, a maze to keep you busy while the real players direct the game," they said, voices calming somewhat to a more devious tone. "It is us or Sathariel. You cannot have us both."

"So you say?" he replied, taking the first few steps on the rickety stairway.

"We do indeed," they replied. "You must choose, us or the angel, or lose everything."

Jinn climbed the stairs carefully, never taking his eyes away from the skulls and tapping the point of his sword along the wired banister as he went.

"I've made too many dark deals," he said.

"Which is precisely why we thought you had potential, the ability to rise above petty morality," they said, several of the voices hissing in disappointment. "Your kind falls prey too easily to the hopes of one battle, one conflict. We offer you the chance to fight a real war."

"No more compromises," he replied sternly, but he paused at the first step, listening.

"So says the doomed champion at the gates of the Hells," they said, sighing in resignation even as others among the nine growled impatiently, the shadowy shroud around their possessed body wavering. "Sathariel smiles at your efforts. He uses you. Even now, with your righteousness and pomp, we see only him. And you will be left, raving at your dead gods amid smoking ruins and death."

"Smoking ruins?" Jinn asked, advancing, sword poised to strike. "What ruins?"

"Ah, he wants answers now, eh?" they responded, a rumbling, sardonic laughter infecting their voices. "No more sword first, ask questions later?"

Their emerald eyes blurred as they moved suddenly, a dark wave of shadow rushing across the walkway. Jinn narrowly deflected the first slash and parried the second, his hand aching from the strain as what strength they had left bore down upon him. The walkway swung precariously, a thunder of clay pots smashing on the floor below as their blades locked. An oppressive heat wafted over Jinn's face as the skulls pressed close, as if their body were burning from the inside out.

"You *are* being used, deva," they growled. "Ever since your first battle against the Vigilant Order, ever since you lost your dear Variel."

Jinn gasped at the mention of her name, pushing back on the curved blade, though he could feel the trembling walkway become less steady beneath him.

"Oh yes, we know of her and what you did. We know of your every step, your long road to Waterdeep, and of your arrival in this ward, with *that* sword to wield against one specific angel. Never doubt the schemes and vision of a god."

"You . . . lie!" he managed, straining against their strength. "To save yourselves!"

"We are in the endgame, deva," they replied, twisting backward and kicking him back into a tangle of loosened wires. "We have no reason to lie."

Jinn freed himself easily, but the shadowy figure leaped higher, landing on the narrow ledge around the dome of glass, dark hands pressed against the frosted pane.

"Nine silvered tongues. Nine families," Jinn provoked, hoping to anger them. "I've learned some. I will discover the rest."

"Perhaps." They chuckled again but weaker, more faint. "But for now you are mistaken. There are *ten* bloodlines to fall, not nine."

Their laughter rose, each voice taking an equal part, reaching a fevered, manic pitch as they smashed the glass barehanded. Blood rained down from the obscured flesh of their forearms, shards of glass jutting out at sharp angles through the clinging, smoky mist. Even as they jumped from the mansion's roof, the shadows dissipated, leaving the bloodied body of a young man with just time enough to scream, plummeting to the iron-spiked fence below.

Jinn flinched as the scream abruptly ended. He stood still in the quiet, eyes fixed on the clouds overhead, wondering what to believe and what to discount. With a measured step, he eventually descended the spiral stairway, boots crunching on clay shards and crushing dying flowers.

"Ten bloodlines," he muttered thoughtfully, listening as renewed shouts of the Watch echoed from outside. He did not sheathe his sword, a quiet fury still burning in his gut, shaking in his clenched fists, determined to have answers before sunrise.

"The Loethes are dead."

Mara stood at the bottom of the steps in the ballroom, looking up as Jinn descended the stairs slowly, one at a time, eyeing the shadows outside. Blood covered Mara's hands, dripping on the once-pristine marble floor, though no stains marred the illusory perfection of her dress. Despite the illusion, it seemed as though her eyes glowed with a quiet hunger.

"Your work?" he asked suspiciously.

"No," she answered with a sly wink. "They finished themselves. However, Quessahn and I did take care of the servants."

"She is here," he stated, his step quickening. "Good. I assume the Watch is ready to claim the bodies?"

"It sounds as though Dregg certainly is," Mara said, falling into step with him. "His men are at the door, but I do not think their hearts are in it."

"Dregg . . . ," he muttered, the name drifting into a low, guttural growl in the back of his throat, an anger within him demanding satisfaction as he peered out the narrow windows flanking the double doors. Watchmen had gathered in a group just outside, no longer attempting to beat down the doors as they conferred with the rorden near the gates. "Can you make a path?"

"I believe so," Mara replied, a quick wring of her hands removing the blood from them. "And it appears I shall have to. Do we want them dead or—?"

"Not dead," Quessahn interrupted weakly from the back of the room. She approached them steadily enough, but Jinn could see the exhaustion in her half-lidded gaze, the pain of her injuries taking their toll, though she seemed determined to put on a brave show. "There's been enough killing for one night, and the Watch isn't our enemy."

"No doubt," Jinn replied, turning back to the window. "But I did not have killing in mind . . . not exactly."

"We can't go back to the shop," Mara said, taking a place at the other window as she absently tapped the glass, counting the number of officers outside. "They'll come looking for us there, or rather, *he* will come looking for us there."

"We'll just have to make it safe, then," he replied. "Make ready your magic; leave Dregg untouched." He placed a hand on Quessahn's shoulder carefully, wincing at the brief flash of pain in her eyes and hating himself for what he must ask of her but having little recourse. "Can you send a message for me?"

———w———

"Why aren't we inside?" Dregg shouted at the officers, impatiently pacing.

Lamenting the loss of his hired swords and disgusted by the

Watchmen he had inherited from Allek Marson, he glared at his men. His gaze fell on the new swordcaptain in particular, an obstinate young man called Lutz.

"Their witch has sealed the doors—," Lutz began, his tone maddeningly calm.

"Then break the windows!" Dregg spit, putting himself nose to nose with the swordcaptain. "Get in there and drag that deva and his witch out into the street, or I will have you mucking the sewers for pickpockets!"

"We have them trapped, sir. We should just wait until more patrols can—"

"Break the damn windows!" Dregg shouted, exasperated.

After a breath, Lutz turned and waved his men after, pointing to either side of the house in as tight a formation as the two patrols could manage. The rorden shook his head, cursing quietly as they put his orders into action.

Despite the night's cold, he'd broken out in a sweat, desperate to get inside and make sure the deed had been done. He continued pacing as Lutz shouted orders, muttering to himself and keeping a fearful eye out for the archmage. He'd met with Tallus one too many times in the past tenday and wanted nothing more than for his business with the wizard to be done. He had his new title and would soon have the riches to be done with the Watch altogether. Smirking at the thought, he looked forward to being alone again with Rilyana—and even more, he looked forward to being alone with all her gold.

A cracking sound caught his attention, but as he turned to witness the shattering of the windows, already gloating over the deva's capture, his smile faded. Stone fractured around the double doors of the mansion, splitting and crumbling as his men drew their weapons and shined their lanterns on the front of the house. The doors buckled, in and out as though the mansion had come alive, breathing out clouds of dust like steam in the winter air.

"What in all of the Hells—?" Dregg muttered, drawing his own sword and backing up a step as a muffled chant rumbled from within the house.

With a final groan of pressure, the doors exploded outward in a shower of splinters. A dust cloud hung for several breaths as his men edged closer to the destruction, closing their ranks. Dregg held back, unwilling to sacrifice himself.

In the haze of dispersing dust, a figure appeared in the house's gaping wound, striding forward smoothly, almost gliding onto the front steps. Tall and gaunt, it wore long and tattered, black and brown robes that fluttered like wings in the wind. Like a splash of shadow, it spread its arms wide, coal red eyes burning in a deep hood, lionlike teeth gleaming in the light of the Watch lanterns as a foul chant escaped its lips.

"Halt!"

The shout rose from among the gathered officers, a weak, impotent command compared to the shrieking scratch of the figure's voice. Long-fingered hands tipped with black claws waved over their heads, silencing the others, turning their attempted shouts into slurred murmurs. Swords thumped into the grass as men stumbled to their knees, overcome by an invisible wave that shuddered through their circle. Hands lifted as though they might lean on one another for support, but one by one they fell, bodies sprawling in the garden until none were left to struggle against the magic.

The rorden cursed as the chanting stopped, leaving him alone as the robed figure slumped over, drawing its dark hands close together and stepping aside. Standing in the dark beyond, gold eyes glittering in the lantern light, the deva stood with sword drawn, his gaze fixed on the human. Dregg hesitated a moment, his instinct telling him to escape, though he wanted nothing more than to see the deva bleeding at the end of his sword. He considered gathering Jinn's finger, a present for the archmage, perhaps enough to see himself and Rilyana well away from Waterdeep long before the next evening. The thought of losing all he'd worked for to the heroics of a nonhuman mutt made him sick, and he spit, curling his lip in fury as Jinn descended the front steps and entered the garden with long strides.

Dregg backed away from the gates with his arms spread in a challenge, turning his sword in slow circles as if impatient for the fight to come. He stood in the light of a street lamp, snowflakes tumbling within its glow as he casually baited the deva to the center of the intersection. He glanced down each empty street, swearing quietly, though he suspected he would not have long to wait for reinforcements; Rorden Marson had seen to that.

Raising his blade with a practiced flourish, a cruel smile stretched across his lips, Dregg reached back and pulled the signal horn from his belt.

FOURTEEN

Anticipating the human's cowardice, Jinn sprinted through the garden gate with a sudden burst of speed, his eye trained on the false rorden's left arm as it rose, signal horn in hand. Though Dregg's blade was well poised to strike, Jinn ignored the practiced guard and twisted dangerously within its reach, forcing the human to face him. Teeth clenched, he accepted the gash in his side, shoving Dregg's right shoulder and hammering his blade at the signal horn.

Barely touching the rorden's lip, the horn split in two, cracked and useless as it fell from Dregg's hand and skittered across the street. The human stumbled backward, spitting and cursing, red faced and roaring as he struck back, his blade far quicker and more skillful than Jinn had expected. The deva slipped into a graceful defense, keeping Dregg on the move as he ducked and wove with the flashing sword of the human, infuriating his opponent even more.

With a broad flourish of his cloak, he hid his blade for the blink of an eye, spinning toward the trailing edge of the black cloth, thrusting into Dregg's attack and pushing the human back on his heels. He struck high and low, alternating swiftly between the two as he continued to prowl in and out of the rorden's reach, the pain of the cut in his side warm and familiar, keeping his senses sharp. After several ringing exchanges, he saw a quiet desperation blooming in Dregg's eyes, sweat pouring down the human's forehead as his arm slowed by degrees, his blade seeming heavier by the breath.

Several times Dregg's defense was laid wide open, and Jinn had time to stare longingly at the small gap in the rorden's leather armor, just below his arm and a cut away from his heart. Batting the human's blade away again, he would take a sliding step as the man tried to recover and slide the flat of his sword across Dregg's back, just above his belt. He pictured the wounds, imagined the gasps of pain, and dissected his opponent dozens of times in a myriad of ways but managed to hold back the rage that threatened to press the edge a little harder with each slash and thrust.

Despite all, he wanted Lucian Dregg alive.

At length, Dregg backed away, panting through clenched teeth as Jinn allowed him space and lowered his sword, tapping its point once on the ground. The human spat at the insult, muttering an unintelligible curse but keeping his distance.

"Run," Jinn said, forcing the word out through a bloodlust that urged him to cut the rorden's throat rather than let the human escape.

Dregg hesitated, only a misplaced pride keeping him from bolting at the first chance he was given, but Jinn suspected he had seen enough of the human to know he wouldn't give up the chance at survival. Alone and outfought, Dregg was far beyond his comfort zone, and Jinn wondered why the human had stayed to fight at all, curious as to what Tallus had promised him for covering up and assisting the skulls' killing spree throughout the ward. The questions burned brightly in his thoughts, and with effort he made sure his patience outshone even his desire for immediate answers.

With a frustrated, almost animal growl, Dregg turned and ran, heading west along the garden wall. Mara appeared at the gate, her crimson gaze fixed on the rorden's back as snow melted on her dark robes. She bared her fangs as the human turned at the end of the wall.

"You know where to go?" Jinn asked her, clutching the wound in his side as he sheathed his sword, blood trickling between his fingers. Mara nodded, lowering the short, knotted horns that curled from beneath her stringy black hair. "Keep close to him. I'll be along shortly."

With an arcane whisper, Mara loped forward, disappearing in a wave of shadow even as soft footsteps drew Jinn's attention back to the garden gate and the tired eyes of Quessahn. He was taken aback by the look on her face, struck by the familiar intimacy in her cold stare.

"Go," she said. "I'll be fine."

It seemed as though she had repeated the words a hundred times before, each time more draining than the last, her eyes exposing the lie on her tongue. He stared at her for several breaths, a glimmer of truth reaching out to him from some forgotten life like a deeply buried splinter, rising to the skin's surface and screaming to be pulled free. Each moment he had spent with her since she had found him replayed itself in his mind within a single beat of his heart—and each one he saw in a new light that shook him to his core.

In half a breath he left her, running as fast as his wound would allow, tracing the path of Lucian Dregg. Moments before, he had felt once again in control, turning his confusion since entering Sea Ward into a focused purpose, making the hunter the hunted, but with four words, Quessahn had shaken that certainty.

In nearly four thousand long years of forgotten names and buried memories, every lover he might have had was left—either mourning or rejoicing over stone tombs or shallow graves—in his past, a fragment of his soul lost to recollection and time . . . except for one.

He ran faster at the thought of it.

Dregg fell back against a cold, damp wall, panting and cursing as snowmelt dripped down the back of his neck, soaking through his tunic. He shivered and hung his head low, eyes darting at every shadow, hands trembling as he pulled his cloak tighter. In the silence between breaths, he listened for the incessant *tap-tapping* of Tallus's staff to come chasing him through the shadows. Upon each rooftop and against every patch of dark gray sky, he imagined flaming green eyes, watching him from a plume of smoke or standing in the darkness of curtained windows. He paled at the thought of running afoul of the nine skulls, having seen their handiwork firsthand.

His heart thumped a fearful cadence as he waited for the phantoms to become real and deliver his punishment. But the windows remained darkened, the streets empty, and most doors well barred for the evening.

"No more killing tonight," he whispered. "Not that a locked door could stop the circle."

Managing his fears, he stood straight and pulled his collar high to cover his face as he wandered the shadows, taking stock and determining which direction to turn his boots. Cautious, he stayed out of the burning lamplight, a decision more comforting than practical as the circle of skulls needed no light to see him. Though Tallus would discard him as a failure, Dregg doubted the Nine would be so forgiving. He had seen them once, in their circle, and overheard their dealings with the archmage. What they had begun, what they had planned, sent a shiver down his spine, a spark of urgency that quickened his step to escape Waterdeep at all costs.

Rounding a corner down a narrow avenue that would carry him out of Sea Ward and see him out of the city by sunrise, he paused, squinting as his vision blurred. Shadows quivered and shook then jumped from one side of the street to the next. He backed away, his eyes widening as a whispering murmur crawled toward him, creeping across his skin with harsh syllables that chilled him to the bone. They dug into his ears painfully, screeching through his thoughts and numbing his senses. He glimpsed a robed figure within the leaping shreds of darkness and fell to the cobbles in surprise, quickly scrambling to his feet as he clumsily drew his sword.

The murmuring stopped and the shadows stilled.

"Tallus . . . ?" he called out quietly, thoughts racing to excuse his failure, to save his own skin, but no answer came. Tentatively he stepped forward with a glimmer of hope, calling again, "Rilyana?"

A dull ache throbbed in his temples as the cobbles ahead rippled like water and began to swirl. He shook his head, blinking fiercely. A sound like ripping parchment filled the spaces between the buildings, and a fanged pit of utter darkness opened in the center of the unnatural tempest. It snapped and growled, blocking his path and edging closer.

He fell back, sweat beading on his forehead as he turned away, running headlong into the alley beyond. The air thickened as he ran, clinging to his skin like ice. Walls shivered as he passed, pulsing like flesh and growing ragged mouths that whispered his name through jagged, malformed teeth. Streets and alleys once familiar became the winding paths of a nightmare, leading him to strange and hellish places. The sky grew closer, pressing down upon the rooftops, clouds rolling almost within reach as the city threatened to crush him. He struck the reaching tendrils of living walls, drawing lines of foul blood that pooled into rivers at his feet.

The pain in his head, in his mind, intensified, and he fell to his knees, pounding his fists into the cobbles, each blow lessening the ache somewhat. The path ahead of him was swallowed by a wall of wriggling, red things and the alley at his back was gone, just a dark patch of gibbering nothing. From somewhere distant, he felt madness gently lay an unbalancing hand upon his shoulder, and in the brief contact, at the moment when he thought his mind would fracture, he spoke.

"Enough," he rasped, and everything stopped.

Snowflakes caught on his skin and melted as a mild breeze whistled down a stretch of alley. The sky had returned to its place, a flat, gray expanse of clouds above the cold cobbles and smoking chimneys. Up ahead a dark figure stood as though waiting for him. Dregg tried to catch his breath, cursing the circle of skulls even as he wondered how he might betray them and escape.

"This is Tallus's doing. He will betray you," he muttered as the figure approached, a silhouette that did not flicker with shadows or burn him with flaming eyes of emerald. A shining length of enchanted sword flashed in a weakening lamplight. Black hair whipped across cloaked shoulders, and chilling, golden eyes regarded him with hatred and pity.

"What do you know of the nine skulls?" the deva asked.

Taken aback, a burst of nervous laughter escaped Dregg, and he rocked backward, studying the strange alley as he leaned on the point of his sword.

"I surrender, deva. You win," he said, chuckling sheepishly as he reached for a pouch on his belt. "Now how much was Marson paying you?"

"What does Archmage Tallus have planned?" Jinn growled in response.

"I will double your pay," Dregg said, ignoring the question as he worked the bindings on his coin pouch. "And all you have to do is—"

"Where is Sathariel?" the deva asked, voice rising.

"Gold!" Dregg shouted in disbelief, stumbling to his feet and shaking the pouch in one hand, his sword in the other. "A small fortune here and more when we're out of Sea Ward! Understand? Your kind can't afford to turn down hard coin—"

The cold came again as shadows gathered at the periphery of his sight. He struck at them, swinging wildly and stumbling as though drunk, but his blade found nothing to cut.

"Enough sorcery, deva!" he shouted, finding his balance and throwing his coin pouch to the ground. "Save your breath and face me like a man."

Jinn did not move, standing as still as stone. Dregg chuckled wryly as something touched his boot, slithering over its top and wrapping around his ankle. He glanced down at the veined length of a yellow-gray tentacle, crawling out of a thin crack in the street. He pursed his lips in annoyance as he looked to the deva.

"More tricks, is it, then—?" he began but felt a strong tug at his leg.

Dregg slipped to one knee, staring in disbelief as the crack in the street widened and the tentacle wrapped further around his lower leg. More squirmed from beneath the cobbles, grabbing his other leg and reaching for his arms. His attempts to stand were futile, and he panicked, pulling at the rubbery growths even as others took his wrists, disarmed him, and pulled him forcefully toward the slit of darkness.

"No!" he rasped, hearing his sword clatter against a distant stone floor as he fought to remain above ground. A thick length of flesh encircled his head, filling his mouth with the foul taste of mold and decay, stifling his efforts to scream.

"Yes," Jinn replied, kneeling nearby.

The wind strengthened in the long alley as the rorden's legs were pulled into the dark, the frozen air carrying a sudden rush of sound, like a whimpering tide full of rushing, breathy voices. He felt his boots being peeled off, and he curled his toes as if he might stop them, kicking against nothing in a void full of tentacles and thin hands. The whispers grew louder, crashing around him in incoherent waves. He gripped the edge of the street, knuckles white with the strain of holding on as one feminine voice among thousands made itself clear, as if right beside him.

In the mountain's shadow, a king of bones shall hear their confessions.

Dregg puzzled over the words, feeling faint as his strength waned, desperate for meaning as the lamplight grew dim and his chest tightened. He felt divided from himself, a calm observer in a storm of mystery and aching. A sharp, distant pain traveled up his arm as one hand slipped and was jerked into the dark. The other quickly followed, and he strained to hear more of the whispering secrets as he lost the light and was borne down into the black.

Cold flesh shivered as weakened walls shook. Dust fell in gray, cloudy sheets, resting on a congealed surface of tiny, red lakes, their shores dried and blackened. The season kept flies away, though in time, rats appeared, edging furtively from disturbed homes to sniff at the bounty left for them. They scurried forth, snatching pieces away from the whole and returning to their secret places. The walls came alive with scratching and squeaks, some shrill as others stole their juicy prizes in greedy paws and yellowed teeth.

A figure overlooked the proceedings, perched upon an empty pedestal. His wings fluttered with interest as his cold eyes feasted upon the intricacies of the scene, devouring the aesthetics of a curled hand, somehow at odds with a length of glistening bone. Islands of red and blue, dried by exposure, lay scattered in the light of nearby candles. The ragged edges of once-fine cloth were soaked and sticky, wrapped around limbs that no longer required warmth or modesty.

Shadowy feathers in Sathariel's wings shook, briefly distinguishing themselves before dissolving again into the whole. He considered the nuances of the broken wizard's body, ever curious to witness the many stages of mortal death and wondering at the strange finality of the act.

"This all belonged to them once," a voice spoke from the top of the stairs, but the angel did not move, as still as stone, fascinated by the hungry chewing of a brave rodent.

"Yes," he replied. "I came here once over two hundred years ago, looking for the circle of skulls. And here I am again."

Dust and pebbles skittered down the stairs, followed by the *tap-tapping* of a gnarled, hardwood staff. Sathariel continued his study of the corpse, needing no eyes to smell the arrogant presence of the archmage. He felt as though he were joined by something less than a human and more like a smug smile that had grown a body and legs.

"They crafted genius here," Tallus said, leaning on his staff.

"And you sift through the scraps from their table," Sathariel added and turned his blank visage to the wizard, gratified to see him flinch. Sathariel did not bemoan Tallus his sense of greed or ambition, but the wizard had yet to learn any respect for the angel or Asmodeus, without whose consent he would gain precious little in the days to come. "And this poor soul, did he go willingly to his final rest, serving you until the bitter end?"

"Gorrick was . . . *surprised,* to say the least," Tallus answered, barely glancing at the unrecognizable body of his former apprentice. "Before he died he claimed he would see me in the Nine Hells, and he choked while attempting to laugh, but he was the last of my bloodline, a misplaced nephew I had some trouble in tracking down. I do not think I shall miss him much."

"Careful, Archmage. The circle of nine once boasted of slaying their entire bloodlines three hundred years ago and ended up little more than fleshless, floating heads in an alley of no consequence . . . Also, your enemies have captured Lucian Dregg; I wonder what he shall tell them of you?"

"More annoyances now than enemies; they are much too late," the archmage replied. "Tomorrow evening the spell will be complete, and I shall be far beyond their righteous reach."

"But the skulls' last secret?" Sathariel responded, his wings shivering in anticipation. "You have it?"

"No, though when I begin the ritual's ending, they will be forced to tell me," the wizard said with a sly smile that made Sathariel's claws itch. "If they do not, they will have failed again."

"You should not gamble on *ifs*, wizard," the angel said, the walls shaking with each word. "The consequences for failure . . ."

"Would be dire for us both," Tallus said, meeting Sathariel's cold eyes for a breath longer than the angel had expected, a feat few mortals were capable of. "I have all that I need to complete the skulls' ritual. I have fulfilled my duty to Asmodeus. Can you claim as much?"

Sathariel shook with rage, his wings eclipsing the last of the room's light. The wizard's audacity was almost fragrant, like so many challenges Sathariel had accepted in the throne rooms of dark gods without question, but despite all, he remained patient.

He felt threads upon threads tightening into a weave he had worked to orchestrate over centuries, and he would not let the arrogance of one human deny him the fires he so desired to set in Waterdeep.

"Let us not assume too much," he answered at length, drawing close to the averted gaze of the wizard. "The prophecy of the First Flensing was written centuries ago, divinely inspired by our master. You should have more faith."

"Faith in what, pray tell?" Tallus asked.

"That you are superfluous to our requirements, less than a footnote in Asmodeus's great plans," Sathariel replied, enjoying the twitch in the archmage's eye. "You were merely convenient and far less than ideal. We applaud your duplicity and eagerness to be of service, but do not estimate your worth as too much higher than the drying remains of young Gorrick. Be grateful you have lived this long."

Tallus turned and limped back up the stairs. Sathariel found the scent of the human's fury delightful and ascended in his wake, amused also at the scent of blood on Tallus's hands. There was blood and something else, something sweet—perfume. The angel chuckled, the susurrus of his laughter hissing through the remains of the archmage's tower.

"Find something amusing?" the wizard asked from the doorway.

"Indeed. It is a riddle, one that I look forward to being answered," he replied, rising into the tower, the *whoosh* of his wings stirring up the dust into tiny whirlwinds.

"Where are you going?"

"Worry not, human," Sathariel said, his voice booming through the tower as he rose toward the shattered roof. "We have not placed all of our faith upon you, and I have others to visit this night."

He broke through the remains of rotted rafters, winging into the night and leaving the aging wizard to stare after him, confused and mystified.

Good, he thought.

He banked south over Sea Ward, gazing upon the whole of Waterdeep, his appointed place to watch over and cultivate for his master. As the mortals below shivered in their beds and awoke to the horrendous murders of morning, they would scramble for meaning and search for the guilty. Sathariel almost pitied their ignorance, their fascination with the insignificant details of a crime that served only to trap their attention.

"All is well," he whispered, and he began a slow descent, to one last meeting before dawn.

FIFTEEN

J inn sat quietly in the pale light filtering through the cracks of the hidden sewer entrance. The stone floor was cold but thankfully dry, one of the few spots free of the city's sludge, if not its stench. He stared at his hands as if he'd never seen them before, their pale, ivory skin and the deep black whorls that reached across his wrist from beneath the sleeves of his coat. His palms bore few of the creases he had witnessed in others, only a few prominent lines crossing from finger to thumb, the marks of a short life in a body forged by mystic forces he might never understand. The prints of his fingertips were like none he'd seen—save one—and seemed too false, a manufactured show—a god's estimate of flesh that had no understanding of mortality or suffering or the scars of a long life.

Night black hair, the match of his skin's designs, fell into his golden eyes as he pondered the hands that had worked so hard for so long to do what was right.

He blinked, not turning as a pained gasp echoed through the tunnel behind him. Tight, leather straps creaked in the shadows as muscles flexed, knotting as an old man applied the gentle pressure of the torturous art to the flesh of Lucian Dregg. Something wet slapped to the floor, near the edge of the thick sewage, cast aside as Briarbones worked. Dregg whimpered.

Jinn stared into the dark at the indiscernible lump of meat, the shape of it providing no clues as to its origins or purpose, though its future was certain. The deva could hear rats gathering to the south, drawn to the scent of blood. Tiny wisps of steam rose from the flesh, cooling as the work behind Jinn continued.

"Who am I?" he said under his breath, studying his hands and trying to see the immortal spirit beneath them, the celestial soul he had stained while working for the greater good.

"You are yourself, I assume," Briarbones replied absently, muttering as he worked. Dregg was eerily quiet. "I have heard of devas driven mad, unable to recollect the details of a current incarnation and lost in a veritable eternity of identities, all only half remembered. But such cases, I do believe, are rare. You appear to be quite lucid, so I doubt you are so afflicted."

"And are you aware of devas who have lost their way? Turned to evil?" Jinn asked, knowing the answer in his blood but needing to hear it said out loud, confirmed by someone other than the doubting voice in the back of his mind.

"Demons. Rakshasas. Foul spirits, trapped in infinite existences and cut off from whatever wellspring of power kept them in the world. Damned," Briar replied, and Jinn nodded, exhaling as the words were spoken and letting them echo in his thoughts, something to remember as he walked the fine line between light and dark, something to remind him of his lost Variel. "I believe he is ready to speak now. I must admit, he resisted far more than I had predicted."

"Hate and ignorance can make a man strong," Jinn said as he stood. "But only for a short time."

He approached the human, strapped to a wooden table, bleeding slowly, a testament to the precise skill of Briarbones. Each breath came as a desperate gulp. Dregg was a murderer and a conspirator to murders, the very antithesis of everything Allek Marson stood for, yet Jinn found he could not help but pity the man—and in that moment, he valued his pity. Leaning close, he kept the wide eyes of Dregg focused on him.

"Tell me about the archmage," he said, an edge in his voice suggesting he would not hesitate to punish the human for lying.

"Tallus . . . g-gives them power. The circle of skulls," Dregg stammered, his pained gaze fierce and unwavering. "He helps them to kill . . . only certain families. Like the Marsons."

"Why did you help him?" Jinn asked.

"He promised me power . . . and wealth," the human spat. "I was to assist Rorden Marson, keep the killings quiet, until Allek grew nervous, started looking for answers in the wrong places."

"So they removed him, making way for you," Jinn supplied, careful to keep his hands at his sides, lest he choke the human. "What else? Tell me what I want to hear, and your pain will end."

"My pain will end?" Dregg asked, incredulous, chuckling and coughing on his own blood, flecks of it spattering on his chin. "Say what you mean, deva. You will kill me."

Jinn stood back, narrowing his eyes. "All right," he said at length. "I will kill you, but before you die, tell me who you would like to join you? Who failed you such that you have fallen to this place?"

Dregg's breathing slowed as he was taken aback by the question.

"Tallus," he said quickly. "He used me, lied to me. And he uses her . . ."

"Who?" Jinn asked, leaning close again, though he suspected the answer.

"Rilyana—Rilyana Saerfynn," the human answered, sighing in between heaving breaths. "He lusts after her, though he knows she is mine, and he forces her to choose. She chooses those to be taken by the skulls, marks them for possession. If she had refused, Tallus would have slain her brother. All I could do was make sure she was never investigated, but then Rorden Marson started to get too close . . ."

Jinn removed the bound letters from his coat, the discourse between Rilyana and Allek that stood in stark contrast to all he had witnessed. He wondered how close Dregg and Rilyana had been, wondered if the man's desire had crafted a relationship that didn't truly exist except within his own arrogance—but then, Jinn had seen them together. It seemed that if Rilyana had been too frightened to resist, she might have sought help from Allek, and if they had somehow fallen in love . . .

"You requested Allek's death, didn't you?" Jinn asked.

"Marson had gone too far," Dregg growled, his eyes rolling back. "He spoke against my promotion countless times, said I was too angry to lead. I enjoyed watching him squirm, looking for killers that had never really existed, but then he wanted Rilyana. Never!"

Dregg's tirade devolved into a choking cough, his chest rising and falling violently, little streams of blood becoming rivers from his wounds as he thrashed against his bonds. Jinn waited for him to spend his strength, stood by as the convulsions slowed before continuing.

"Who else is helping Tallus?" he asked.

"I don't know. He never told me," the human answered weakly. "But Rilyana's brother, Callak, was never in any danger. He and the wizard had some kind of an agreement."

Dregg's voice trailed off, his head lolled from side to side, delirious and either dying from his wounds or driven to madness by the pain of them. Jinn grabbed his shoulders and shook him roughly.

"The angel, Dregg!" he shouted. "What about the angel!"

"Voices . . . wings . . . he kept asking for the souls . . . ," the human slurred and muttered, falling deeper into a feverish dementia. "A circle of souls . . . Tallus betrays them all for loose fingers, hidden souls, and immortality. Kill me, deva. Go and let them use you too, so I can see you soon . . ."

"Gods have mercy," Quessahn whispered, standing in the doorway and staring at the rorden as he managed a weak laugh, rusty stains between his teeth as he began to bleed out, his life pouring onto the floor of Briarbones's chamber. The eladrin turned away, pushing past Mara as the hag entered the room and regarded the dying human.

"I was wondering when you would get your hands dirty," Mara remarked with a sly grin. She pulled forth a small, red gem from beneath her cloak. She approached the rorden with a hungry gleam in her eye. "No sense letting him to go to waste."

"No," Jinn said, grabbing her wrist and meeting the crimson glare that flashed beneath her illusory eyes. He ignored her anger, disgusted by her greed for souls and by himself for tolerating it for so long. "Let this one go."

"You overstep your bounds, deva. We have an agreement," she snarled, ivory teeth wavering, revealing the lioness fangs hidden behind her human lips. "What makes this soul special? Why protect it?"

"Because I haven't yet lost my own," he replied, forcing her hand away as gently as possible. His gold eyes gleamed in the candlelight. "I believe there will be dark souls aplenty for your gems in the days to come, do you not agree?"

"Very well," Mara answered curtly, putting the ruby away. "I suppose we all need something every now and then to help us sleep at night, eh?" She gestured at the rorden's broken body. "I trust your tender mercies did not keep you from questioning the poor dear?"

"Do you have the book?" he asked, ignoring her taunts.

"Of course," she answered, a suspicious glint in her eye as she stepped away from him, one hand hidden beneath her cloak. "It is quite fascinating so far, though parts are difficult to decipher—"

"Draconic?" Briar supplied, edging closer, his hands fidgeting. "Elvish? Infernal, Abyssal, Primordial, Deep Speech, or perhaps—?"

"Gibberish, in fact," Mara said, producing the tome, though she kept it far from Briarbones's reach. "The archmage's handwriting is atrocious, rambling, and excited, but all that the skulls had to tell him, he did indeed put to paper."

"Good," Jinn said abruptly. "Figure it out. Look for references to souls, special ones. Sathariel is after them, and I want them first."

"And in the meantime, you will be . . . ?" Mara asked.

"The skulls have more allies," Jinn replied. "Tallus is dead, the Loethes are dead, so someone else is helping them, giving them the power to possess."

"Any leads?" Mara asked, gesturing at Dregg with a raised eyebrow and a vicious smile.

"Callak Saerfynn," he said. "He may know enough to finish the spell, if nothing else." He paused, a thought occurring to him mid-stride. "How do we know the ritual isn't already finished?"

"We are still alive," Mara answered absently, pages turning in her deft hands. "The completed spell will not be an event one would wish to witness, unless Tallus's descriptions of widespread destruction are wrong."

Her words, cold and humorless, took hold in Jinn's thoughts, evoking images of burning homes, bodies in the streets, and a city's mourning, all over the ambitions of a greedy few. The idea of continued murders sounded almost appealing compared to the alternative.

"Are you ever going to rest?" Quessahn asked, sitting in the dark just beyond the pale light from above. Jinn did not move, fearful of seeing her face again, fearful of the memories she might arouse within him.

"I've grown accustomed to long nights over the years," he answered. "It makes things easier. I find that people tend to be more honest in the dark."

"I'm curious, then. What would you have done, had you slain Sathariel two nights ago?" she asked. "Would you still be here?"

"I don't know," he said. "It never crossed my mind."

"What did he do? What did he take from you?"

Jinn sighed under his breath, attempting to cool the sudden anger that raced in his heart, but he could not deny it its due course, just as he could no longer accept Quessahn's deliberate avoidance of what they both knew.

"Another of my kind. A deva," he replied. He turned to her, narrowing his gold eyes to fine points as he found hers in shadow. "A woman I loved."

She remained still as he studied her, watching for some reaction, seeking some quiet admission of guilt from the eladrin.

"He—he killed her?" she asked at length, a barely perceptible catch in her voice.

"No," he answered. "He corrupted her, confused her, and made her soul as black as his own. In the end, she took her own life."

Though he said the words, he found that he no longer felt them, unmoved by the gruesome truth of Variel's death, despite the hate that had taken root within him. Of all his time with her, the peace he'd once known, he had spent far longer tracking down the angel. He realized that the place in his heart where he'd once kept her memory had been filled by his hunt for Sathariel . . . and the attention of Asmodeus.

"Now he corrupts you," Quessahn muttered, just loud enough for him to hear.

Jinn looked up to the surface, tiny shafts of light beckoning him to leave the eladrin in the dark with her righteousness. He smiled, a forced grin.

"What about you?" he asked. "Was my death not closure enough? Did my grave, assuming I had one, not suffice your mourning so much that you felt inspired to bring your grief to this city? To find me?" He turned, voice rising as he confronted her. "Is it comforting to find me somehow less than what you knew? To judge me with your every breath?"

"Oh, gods," she whispered, breathless and shaking, a single choking sob escaping her as she covered her ears and shook her head in her hands. "No . . ."

Jinn stopped, her tears stabbing into his chest as he turned away, unwilling to witness what he had done. Quessahn's hope for a lost love sat bitterly in the pit of his stomach, crushed by his words and devoured by a petty rage that melted away as swiftly as it had come. He took hold of the ladder, his arm heavy and the climb to the surface seeming more difficult than before.

"I-I cannot be the man you once knew. My kind, no . . . I do not work that way," he managed, his voice softer as he climbed. "You should not have found me."

He slid the sewer covering away and rolled into the street, covering the entrance and staring blankly up at the gray sky, the damp cobbles soaking through his clothes. He listened for her voice, wondering if she might stop him to scream and curse his name. He imagined her again as he had in Tallus's tower, smiling and surrounded by an ocean of waving green, the faint memory of a bygone life reaching out to torment him.

Only silence kept him company on the cobbles of Seawind Alley, even the ghostly whisperers did not break the stillness that held him.

At length he stood and dashed into the streets, losing himself in the cold and racing against the harsh light of sunrise, bending his focus back to the hunt, to Sathariel, and to all the things that his immortal blood demanded of him, a fool of long-lost gods.

>——W——<

A swift wind swept through Pharra's Alley, its soft moan fading into a chorus of groaning voices that swirled together, a whirlwind of wails and roaring, green flames far below the wings of Sathariel. Empty eyes spun in slowly dying circles as the Nine gathered in their places, bobbing and regarding one another in silence. With as much emotion as fixed bone and lipless teeth could convey, they glowered at one another for several breaths, slowly turning round and round the place where they'd been bound, appearing as a tiny, green ring from the angel's place in the sky.

"We should have killed the deva," said one abruptly. "He is too close, too unpredictable. His witches are—"

"Be silent, Graius," another said. "The deva, while misguided, shall be our failsafe in the end. He has no choice."

"Then the angel shall kill him if we do not," Graius replied.

"Better that Sathariel is kept busy elsewhere, no?" the other responded as the rest of the circle nodded. "We have managed to evade the angel for centuries; no doubt we can fool him a few days more."

"One day, in fact," Sathariel added from above, his large wings beating as he descended into the alley. Out of the range of their green flames, he hovered between the buildings, capturing their attention in his cold eyes. He enjoyed the fear he inspired in them and wished nothing more than to fulfill their every nightmare, but he was powerless over them as of yet and attempted a note of diplomacy. "In one day Tallus will attempt to betray you and steal all that you have worked for."

"He lies!" Graius shouted. "He only speaks in traps and snares, much like his master."

"Why, angel?" another asked, the circle turning to accommodate the speaker known as Effram. "What does your lord gain from telling us this?"

"No, my old friends," Sathariel answered. "It is you who may gain, should you desire to survive what is to come. It is my understanding that survival is quite important to you, yes?"

"Do not listen, brothers," Graius grumbled. "Honeyed words and half truths, his tongue is silvered with deception."

"Indeed it is, dear Graius," the angel replied as he edged closer to the circle. "But not this night, not here. Now I speak of old words and ancient oaths. Your words, in fact. Contracts that you nine have yet to fulfill." A low growl passed through the skulls at the mention of their neglected obligations, the sins that had made them what they are. "I only offer you your own lies, and I offer you a chance to make amends. Give to me the souls that Tallus would steal, and my lord shall be lenient."

"Nonsense," Graius scoffed, an amused chuckle passing through the circle that threatened to destroy Sathariel's attempt at civility, the skulls' paranoia evident in their denial of anything that wasn't their idea first. The angel could not blame them.

"Asmodeus has certain . . . *interests* in the ritual to be performed," he continued, his voice rising above their derisive laughter. "He would offer you absolution for your parts in expediting these interests, a formal contract offered in good faith despite the betrayal you visited upon him in the centuries before his wondrous ascension."

"Absolution?" Effram asked.

"And flesh, my friends," Sathariel answered, the ice blue pinpoints within his black eyes flaring brighter. "Blood, bone, and all the carnal pleasures that go with them."

Effram turned to his eight brothers, all wizards and worshipers of fallen Mystra. Graius shook his head vehemently, yet they gathered and conferred, their emerald flames swirling together brightly like a rotting star as they argued and whispered. Sathariel held back, eyeing them carefully, wondering if for once their paranoia might break, allowing them to slip easily into his clutches.

"And death, I presume," Effram spoke as the skulls separated, their inscrutable, black stares returning to the angel.

"Pardon?" Sathariel asked.

"Death," Effram repeated. "I assume your lord's offer, however magnanimous, does not include eternity."

"There is a limit to Asmodeus's generosity," the angel responded sternly, wings spread across the alley as he clenched and unclenched his fists, his patience wearing thin. "But I assure you, there is no such limit upon his wrath."

"Then wrath!" Graius cried out. "Wrath before we sacrifice our chance at immortality!"

"You deny the contract?" Sathariel growled, ignoring the stubborn Graius and focusing on only Effram. Flames of shadow like ephemeral feathers writhed through his wings as the flameskull turned away, seemingly unimpressed with his fury.

"We do," Effram answered, adding slyly, "but fear not, lapdog, there are other contracts to be signed. Older contracts than ours, written in steel, I believe."

"The deva seeks to sign in your blood, or whatever passes for blood among your kind," Graius said. "And we believe that Asmodeus would be greater pleased with your sacrifice than our miserable souls. Our ritual, after all, is merely a parlor trick compared to the devil's plans."

"You have chosen," Sathariel said, ignoring their jibes as he rose higher, trails of shadow wavering in sheets beneath him. "Damnation, then. Only suffering for the nine souls you hide from my lord, may his mercy be as absent as my own!"

He ascended quickly, raging and spinning into the clouds until his wings disappeared against the night sky beyond, blotting out the stars. Arms crossed, he considered the tiny city far below, his mind racing, plotting through his options and finding only one source upon which to vent his fury.

"Tallus," he hissed, cursing the duplicitous wizard's impatience, but they were too close to the ritual's completion for him to simply slay the human. Asmodeus would likely not tolerate another delay, and Sathariel, like the skulls, clung to what life he had, unwilling to risk disappointing the devil-god on the cusp of such momentous events.

Fortunately the circle of skulls had one last ally, unstable and unreliable, but ambitious.

"Fine, then, one more betrayal," he muttered, clouds rolling beneath him as he contemplated gambling on yet another weak-willed human, but despite all he knew, he could count on the baser instincts of most of their short-lived race. He dived into the clouds, gliding in wide circles, whispering, "Let the archmage reap what he sows."

SIXTEEN

NIGHTAL 22, THE YEAR OF DEEP WATER DRIFTING (1480 DR)

Quessahn sat in silence as Maranyuss and Briarbones muttered and whispered over books and scrolls, lost in her own thoughts as the world revolved around her. Jinn had been right; she should never have sought him out, should never have hoped that what she'd had with Kehran could be resurrected, as Kehran had been, in Jinnaoth. All of that she knew and somehow had always known, in the deepest parts of herself, and yet Jinn had also been terribly wrong about one thing.

She had been obligated to try.

Rubbing her dry, reddened eyes, she placed it all behind her, feeling useless and self-absorbed as the others worked to solve the secrets of the murders and delve into the mysteries of the nine skulls. Dregg's body had been removed, taken away by Briar with his reluctant word given not to raise the rorden's body to serve as one of his macabre guards. The table he had lain upon had been cleaned and was strewn with pages and notes, as though Tallus's mind had been dissected and placed on display.

At length the strange pair stepped back, both still cloaked in the illusions that had become so much a part of them in Waterdeep; they wore their second faces like old clothes. Mara stared thoughtfully at the book, tapping her long fingers on the table, as Briar snatched up a single page, perusing it once more before setting it back down.

"The circle of skulls," Mara began slowly, as if choosing her words carefully, crossing her arms and pacing as she spoke. "Seeking to attain immortality, they began a ritual. They slew their bloodlines and made a deal with Asmodeus."

"Which they promptly broke," Briar added.

"And in the end they failed, were cursed, and lived as flameskulls. And for three centuries, they hid their souls from the archdevil," Mara continued, waving her hand at each point, ticking off the steps of the skulls' tale with a deft finger.

"During which time, Asmodeus became a god," Briar said as he absently twisted a length of dried flesh from the arm of one of his oblivious undead sentinels and began chewing on it. "Making what eternity they had managed to cling to even harder to hide."

"And now they mean to complete their old spell," Mara finished, "and spend the power they stole from the devil-god."

Quessahn shuddered in the contemplative silence that followed, wondering at the indomitable will that would gamble upon the wrath of a god, simply for the opportunity of immortality. Three hundred years of hiding their miserable souls, living as little more than magical oddities, the spellhaunt of the House of Wonders. When she had been but a child, the skulls had hidden in shadow for more than a century, a trivial topic for curious wizards as they schemed and plotted to take what they had lost.

"Nine immortal wizards with a century to adapt their Art to the effects of the Spellplague," she whispered in disbelief, having lived through the wave of blue fire following Mystra's death, but learning her magic well after the calamity that had swept the world.

"They are somewhat limited by their curse, only manifesting in Pharra's Alley and only dimly aware of events throughout the city in the time in between," Mara said, and she turned several pages in the book, near the end of Tallus's scribbled notes. "But the Nine are the least of our concerns."

"Sathariel?" Quessahn asked. "The angel?"

"Even he, whatever role he has to play, is nothing compared to the ritual itself," Briarbones said. "The birth of just one immortal, in this powerful release of old magic, could destroy a handful of city blocks."

"Then all nine at once . . . plus whoever is helping them . . . ," Quessahn whispered, her eyes widening at the implications.

"It could consume all of Sea Ward, at least," Mara said.

Quessahn shook her head, unable to imagine such destruction and looking to Briarbones. "Is this the prophecy you feared?" she asked.

The avolakia raised an eyebrow and leaned over the archmage's notes, his lips moving as he scanned several passages.

"I do not believe so, though Sathariel's interest in these killings makes me wonder," he replied. "The First Flensing, as it is called, is an ancient covenant, far older than the circle of skulls. It is a formal invitation, preparing a single front for battle, an outpost from which Asmodeus's influence in our world would become more direct. Before his ascension the prophecy was a frightening novelty, one of many such threats, and though dangerous, a manageable one, but now that he has attained true divinity . . . catastrophic."

"Likely angering the gods of good," Mara added. "And inspiring envy among those of evil."

"A war among the gods." Briar nodded. "With mortals caught in the middle."

Quessahn squeezed her eyes shut, rubbing her temples as the idea escalated. Her head ached, assaulted with far too much for one evening and wondering if the sleep she desired would be possible at all. She tried to banish the speculation of the others, but nagging details kept her from ignoring them completely. Jinn's words haunted her, his talk of the killings as a distraction, a show to obscure whatever Sathariel was truly working for—and she began to agree, finally seeing some of what he feared.

"I think," she said, "we must find the souls of the circle of skulls and protect them, keep them from the angel, just in case."

"And what of the other souls? Those of their slain bloodlines?" Mara asked. "Speculations of prophecy aside, the ritual of immortality being prepared is dangerous enough."

"How many do they have left to take?" Quessahn asked. "We must have time to find them."

"Less than a dozen remain," Briar answered. "All of them children, orphaned and displaced, living with other families. A well-kept secret of the Watch, but—"

"Not secret enough," Quessahn finished, cursing. "They saved the easiest for last. Gods above." She sighed. "And we need to rest, or we'll be useless to do anything."

"I do not sleep," Briarbones said, eyeing the list, his false face twitching as he waved her and Mara away. "Take what rest you need. I'll work on locating the children."

"Find them quickly; we need to keep them safe," the eladrin said, sitting in a dry corner and pulling her cloak tight.

"Yes, of course. Keep them safe, at least until we run out of options," Mara muttered as she took the opposite corner, her illusion fading as she curled within her long, tattered robes, crimson eyes glowing dimly in her hood.

There was no malice or feeling at all in the hag's words, though they sent a chill down Quessahn's spine. If they could not keep the children from the skulls, if all else failed, she wondered if she would have the conviction to kill them herself. The thought of it made her sick, but she could not deny the possibility of failure. It was some time before she could sleep, listening as Briar worked, wondering if all their study had been for naught.

It occurred to her that, if they were already too late, she might not wake up at all.

Thin, lacy threads of smoke drifted from the ashes of a hearth fire in a high-ceilinged drawing room. Chunks of charred wood tumbled and hissed, sending small sparks to fly and die through an ornate grating. They glowed, casting an eerie light on a fine-cushioned chair and low couch. The front doors stood open, unguarded and allowing the season's chill to race through the manse, though no one remained to clutch at warm covers or to investigate the source of the sudden cold.

Jinn stood before the glowing embers, sword drawn as he waited, listening and letting the settling noises of the Saerfynn house guide his senses. Drops of blood had pooled and dried near the cushioned chair. A large, woven carpet of simple design and bright thread dominated the center of the drawing room, its far edge stained by ashen boot prints. With Pharra's Alley a short walk from the front gates, he was not surprised to find evidence of something amiss in the mansion. What he could not understand was why it had been abandoned.

The quiet home remained uncooperative, giving no indication of anyone on the premises and keeping its secrets close. He strolled around the edge of the room, looking at the paintings of the Saerfynn family, of the absent parents and several children, most, he assumed, lost as well. Callak, he observed, bore the hawkish features of a cruel man even as a child, each depiction of him including a slight sneer. Those of Rilyana were plain and unassuming, though Jinn noticed that the two never appeared in any portrait together as the other children did.

He wandered the remainder of the house, swiftly and quietly examining each room, finding most well ordered but in need of dusting and two recently used. The one he presumed as Callak's was filthy and stank of sweat and stale spirits, the bed unmade for what appeared several days by the condition of the sheets. The other bore a large, four-poster bed veiled in lace with blood upon the pillow and the sheets.

It stained his fingertips, cold but still damp and sticky.

He turned to study the rest of the chamber when the sound of shattering glass echoed through the mansion, thunderous and startling as Jinn whirled, sword raised. His skin felt flush as he waited, muscles tensing and heart racing. Tingling arcs of energy stabbed through his limbs as he crept down the long halls and winding stairs back toward the drawing room. Trembling and anxious, he paused in the arching doorway, his eyes caught by the dangling shadow of a limp body high above.

A young woman, rope wrapped tightly about her torso, a gag in her mouth, hung from the rafters of the chamber, swinging slightly. Her eyes stared down, wide and silently screaming for help, but Jinn was drawn more to the other end of the rope. In the half light of the broken window, dark wings gently folded around Sathariel's armored body, the trailing ends of his angelic form folded like legs beneath a robe of shadow as the angel sat in the cushioned chair.

The stolen sword burned in Jinnaoth's grip as he stepped forward, unable to resist the strange energy flowing through his body, at one with the sharp intent of the blade.

"Do come forward, deva. I'm quite sure she won't mind," the angel purred, pulling on the rope so the young woman swung at its end, stiffening with a muffled gasp. "What is one life, after all, when compared to countless others, eh?"

Reluctantly, Jinn forced himself to stop, an action that tested his strength, the effort frightening and exciting all at once. He could not lower the strange sword, its point trained upon the angel's heart and urging him to follow through, as if every answer to his every question were but a few strides away, the whole of creation's mysteries hidden behind a veil of angelic flesh. He fought the desire, lowering the weapon a hand's width.

"What is this?" Sathariel asked, sitting forward, eyes bright with sparks of ice. "Why do you hesitate? Am I not what you have been seeking? Is this not the moment you have desired?"

Mastering himself, an eye on the girl dangling above them, Jinn took a single step backward but could retreat no farther. One step he demanded of himself, to be sure of his own will despite the hungry blade in his hand.

"Not this," he said at last, golden gaze absorbing every detail of the angel, dissecting his opponent into parts. "Face me on even ground; she is not a part of this."

"Isn't she?" Sathariel replied, glancing up to his captive. "She is young, innocent, and deliciously random. She is a world of souls contained in one supple body. Such as these will always be a part of this, they always have, since the beginning. They will always hang in the balance, so to speak."

"Your kind hangs them there like shields," Jinn muttered, holding his ground and mustering the patience to deal with Sathariel's overconfident preaching.

"Of course!" The angel laughed, a strange sound at odds with the blank face and flowing, mistlike hair. "It works so well! It has for eons. And your side, it is not always so righteous, no?"

"Say what you came for," Jinn said, feeling as though his resolve might slip at any moment, though he loathed the idea of proving the angel right. He tried not to think of Variel, tried not to imagine her in the angel's embrace, but his every effort only served to dredge up what he feared to recall.

"You are weary, deva," Sathariel replied, leaning back in the chair as he twisted and untwisted the rope around his wrist, causing the young woman to slowly spin back and forth. "There is a weight of time on your shoulders unlike others of your kind, pressing you down, grinding away at your spirit like a desert wind . . ."

"Where is Callak Saerfynn? Where is his sister?" Jinn asked, muscles tensed to leap across the room.

"He is with us," Sathariel answered. "And she is safe. Do you truly care?"

"I do," Jinn lied.

"I can give her back to you. It is within my power, a gift from me to you," the angel whispered, the simple words sliding into Jinn's mind like a cold razor, for there had truly only ever been one woman between him and Sathariel. He leaned back, sword shaking in his grip at the statement.

Absently Jinn shook his head, wide eyed at the very prospect, well aware of the twisted deals made with servants of the devil-god. They promised all one could wish for and generally held true to the letter of the contract—if not the spirit.

"In exchange for what?" he asked, the question slipping out before he could think.

"Very little. Take her and leave; live in peace. Live as she desired to, as you did once, but leave the souls of the Nine to me, they

have certainly earned the place that Variel currently resides in."
He placed a hand over his abdomen, stroking it softly as suffering
moans whispered from within him, wailing for release. "Surely
you cannot think to protect the circle of skulls for all that they
have done?"

"What all have they done?" Jinn asked, calming himself and
playing along, easily sensing the dark lie in Sathariel's offer, making
what truth he could glean shine all the brighter.

"The details are none of your concern, but consider, with their
plans and schemes ended, have you any idea how this city might
change? Who can know what all they have orchestrated in three
centuries?" the angel replied, rising from his seat to float just above
the floor. "In any case, they will trouble this city no more, and they
shall face a reckoning within the House of Thorne."

Jinn hid a smile and eased himself forward once again, sword
rising. Sathariel had shown his hand, using lies to tell the truth,
illusions of sincerity to display his true desires. Though Jinn saw
through the angel's double-speak, he would allow the deception
and use it to his advantage.

"Let me consider your offer. Just release the girl," he said evenly,
just desperate enough to sound genuine as he took a careful step
forward, his sword responding with renewed waves of fury that
banished all traces of hope of seeing Variel again.

"Of course, take your time, deva," Sathariel replied and let the
rope slide through his fingers.

Jinnaoth dashed across the room, leaping for the rope as his
blade cut a wide arc through where the angel had been. A blur of
wings and shadow streaked into the air, disappearing through the
window with a thunderous roar of beating wings. A step too late,
Jinn cursed, the rope slipping through his fingers. Unbalanced, he

tried to turn as the girl fell from the rafters, but could not reverse his momentum.

Her body made no sound as it struck the floor, and the rope faded into an insubstantial mist, leaving only a dirty dress, settling lightly, the angel's illusion revealed. The stolen blade fell still in Sathariel's absence, leaving Jinn light-headed and flushed. He leaned on the cushioned chair for long moments, staring at the place where Sathariel had sat, disgusted at how close he'd been but still heartened by the small measure of control he'd earned by the confrontation.

He knew the angel sought to use him. And Jinn decided that he would allow himself to be used. But the next time he encountered the angel, he planned to have his own stolen souls to barter with.

Commander Tavian strolled down Mendever Street amid long shadows stretched between shafts of yellow-gold morning light. Broadsheet criers ran excitedly through the streets, taking their corners for the midmorn rush, fresh broadsheets slung under their shoulders after selling through the early editions. The smell of baking bread, made sharp by the cold snap in the air, wafted everywhere, mingling with the familiar scents of the city.

Tavian drew his heavy cloak tight over his shoulders, suppressing a shiver and casting a withering glance at the nigh-ineffectual sun. He much preferred the spring and summer, never quite getting the knack for the winter patrol. He sneered as Swordcaptains Aeril and Naaris rounded a corner after him. Aeril drew in a long breath and rubbed his hands together, practically ignoring the warm cloak hanging loosely over his shoulder.

"Fine day, Comma—eh, Tavian," Aeril remarked as they avoided the thicker traffic of Mendever Street.

"Cold day, Aeril. Bitter, bright, and spiteful day," Tavian replied, keeping an eye peeled for more of the ward's Watch, hoping to catch a glimpse of Rorden Dregg in the press of bodies passing by. "I trust our other men have their orders?"

"Aye, sir—I mean, yes, they've been instructed to observe and report only," Naaris answered. "Though I have a feeling even if we were in full uniform, we might not be noticed . . ."

He gestured west, but Tavian was well ahead of the observant officer, noting the carriages lined up along two estate walls, some already laden with locked chests. Servants worked feverishly, hauling various items back and forth through the gates as hired guards stood by. Tavian had been told that once, well before the Spellplague, Sea Ward during winter was a veritable ghost town, nobles and the wealthy abandoning the area for homes elsewhere. The howling winter wind off the shoreline was not entirely unbearable, but those with enough gold had never had to bear what they could afford to avoid. In more recent times, the practice was mostly unheard of, especially among the newer families, not as loose with their coin as in times past.

Others with coin to spare seemed intent on staying put, their hired bodyguards reporting for duty and standing sentinel at ornate gates.

At the corners of the next intersection, two crowds had begun to gather, pausing to talk in low voices as the shouts of competing broadsheet criers echoed above the din of business as usual.

"Eighteen massacred in Sea Ward!" one cried.

"Wealthy blood on Sea Ward streets!" another added as customers crowded the lads, each vying to read the scandalous headlines first. Dozens were sold in a matter of breaths, the smiling boys stuffing coins into their satchels. Buyers stood by in small groups, poring over the tale and conferring with worried faces before racing away, lost in the tide of crowded streets.

"Torm's blessed fist!" Tavian swore quietly. He clapped Aeril on the shoulder. "Buy one of those broadsheets before they're all gone!" he said, backing out of the street. He crossed his arms as more full carriages rolled by, wealthy socialites riding with their valuables. "What in the Abyss is going on?"

At a second glance, as he absorbed the shouted headlines, he noted the lack of patrons in the eating establishments and the concerned looks of other shop owners as potential customers passed them by with barely a glance. Such was the frantic pace of it all that Tavian half expected to find similar scenes playing themselves out all across the city, business as usual forgotten in the mad dash to escape being the next victim or, he mused, the rush to gawk at the next body found.

Aeril returned, winding through the crowd, already reading the broadsheet.

"Two families slaughtered last evening, sir," he said, scanning the print for details. "The Loethes of Ivory Street and the Sedras Family off of Breezes Cut, along with six as of yet unidentified men in Watch uniforms. The bodies were marked up, but Watch commanders have made no comment yet on the details of the crimes or any possible suspects."

"So much for keeping this quiet," Tavian grumbled, absently tugging at the end of his beard. "Go. Get your uniforms and a sharp blade. Sea Ward is out at least one patrol; we can help with that. We'll gather the others at midday and have the Watchful Order in the ward by gateclose."

"Lucian Dregg appears to be missing, sir," Naaris said, reading over Aeril's shoulder. "He was last seen outside the Loethe manse, dueling an unusual man in the street."

"Well, it's not all bad news, then," Tavian replied under his breath. "Off you go. Meet back here within half a bell."

The swordcaptains joined the tide of bodies as Tavian lingered, carefully crossing the street, drawn by the sound of children. As worried parents oversaw the packing of their carriages, the children played in the street, turning in circles and singing within the imposing and jagged shadow of an older house, nearly overgrown by the creeping vines of a once-impressive garden.

Tavian shivered as they sang.

> *Roses in the garden, roses in the hall,*
> *Roses on the window, roses on the wall,*
> *Roses 'round your neck, nine stems shorn,*
> *Roses on the floor in the House of Thorne!*

SEVENTEEN

J inn awoke to the fading voices of the whisperers as they passed through Seawind Alley and away to unknown places. Unintelligible words drifted at the edges of a blurry dream, and he wondered for a moment what they had said to him, but the dream was gone, and only the stale scents of the sewer remained. Though Briarbones's lair sat at the top of an incline and remained fairly dry, the worst of the extensive maze of sewers flowed a mere short walk away. Jinn had no fear of his clothes becoming soiled, but he wondered if his nose would ever recover.

Quessahn slept in the corner opposite him, eyes darting beneath their lids as her breath came shallowly, her dreams not yet done with her. Mara snored lightly against the far wall, wrapped in her dark robes, barely a large smudge of shadow, more a stain than a slumbering hag.

Jinn started at the approach of something from the south, a dry, slithering sound echoing through the tunnel. Briar's multifaceted eyes broke through the faint light from the surface entrance first, turning on their stalks before withdrawing. Jinn could hear the avolakia changing in the dark and sat up from the wall.

"Do not cover yourself for my sake," he said, and the noises stopped. "I've lived with illusions long enough."

"I suppose you have," came the old man's voice, his face appearing in the light. "But I much prefer to speak like this, it seems more . . . *polite* than forcing words into someone's head."

The old man smiled and hobbled into the dry chamber, placing a small chapbook on the table and glancing at Quess and Mara before turning to Jinn.

"I have located the last of the bloodlines. They are safe now but not for long," he said, patting the chapbook lightly. "The Watch has almost tripled since this morning. The broadsheets were filled with tales of last night's murders, and the streets have become somewhat empty of most intelligent folk since. But the patrols can only do so much with what information they have, and if we attempt to tell them . . ."

"They'd take you in," Quessahn said, rubbing her eyes as she awoke. "They'd question you, lock you up, and by the time they realized you were telling the truth—"

"It would be all over," Mara supplied, the dark smudge of her body still against the wall though her crimson eyes glowed from beneath a tattered fold of her robe.

"Indeed," Briar said. "But whether we inform the Watch or not, their numbers will certainly stand in the way of anything we have planned. Speaking of . . . what *do* we have planned?"

Jinn stood and stretched, gathering his thoughts as everyone looked to him for an answer. For his own part, he knew what he needed to do; he'd mulled it over several times while trying to sleep in the uncomfortable lair of the avolakia. The grim surroundings and grave sentinels just beyond the pale shadows a few strides away had served only to cement his intention.

"What do you know of the House of Thorne?" he asked Briar.

The avolakia's face split into a curious grin. "Roses on the window, roses on the wall," Briar replied in the sing-song voice of a child and touched a gnarled finger to an old map upon the wall, the spot ominously smudged by his fingertip. "It once belonged to the Thorne family, and no one else for a full season in the three centuries or so since. Over two dozen bodies were found in the basement, the Thornes' included. They say that even after several paintings and remodelings, you can still see the old blood everywhere, as though the house were haunted by it."

"That's where he—I mean, they, will be," Jinn said.

"You are sure?" Mara asked as she unfolded from her dark corner.

"I am. It's likely they'll be there tonight, or if not, then I'll get to the house first," he answered.

"*We* will get there first," Quessahn added defiantly.

Jinn made as if to reply, but at sight of the determination in her eyes, he let the words die on his tongue, glad she was as willing as he to face the unknown but still troubled by the idea that she did so for the wrong reasons.

"I'll take care of the children," Mara stated, and Jinn nodded, sharing the worried look that flashed in Quess's eyes but having no time to question the hag's loyalty. Whatever Mara had in mind, the last of the skulls' bloodlines would be well out of their reach. He shut out the imagined details of what the hag was capable of and would curse himself for a fool later if need be. Better a handful of possible deaths than a ward full of bodies.

"We should at least wait for dark to—" Briarbones began then paused, his neck craning forward as he edged closer to the tunnel beyond the chamber. He sniffed the air and snarled, a screeching series of clicks and chirps escaping his open mouth. A dozen or so pairs of dead eyes turned to the avolakia, glittering in the dark before shuffling away. Briar turned, a feral look in his eye. "Something is coming. I don't know how many, but it's more than we need to deal with if we have more important things to do."

Jinn could hear them faintly, somewhere in the dark. Soft whimpers and moans echoed through the tunnels, accompanied by heavy, splashing steps.

"The ahimazzi," he muttered. "Quickly, we should get to the surface and lay low until nightfall. The soulless aren't bright, but they can overwhelm us with numbers."

The groans grew louder as the avolakia's zombies met the oncoming mob, the dull sound of fists smacking loudly in the tunnels accompanied by the scrape of curved knives on dry flesh and unfeeling bone. Jinn took the ladder swiftly, shoving the surface cover aside and helping the others out, keeping a careful watch for passing patrols as they escaped. The deva cursed quietly, wishing he'd had time to question Briarbones about the stolen sword at his belt and its strange hunger for Sathariel's blood.

The sounds of battle below were muffled as Briar slid the surface door back into place.

"They'll not stop," Jinn said. "They have no choice."

"Neither do we, apparently. That is if we, or anyone else for that matter, desire to draw breath tomorrow morning," Briar replied, appearing uncomfortable in the alley, nervous and fidgeting in the dim light of late afternoon.

"We'll split into pairs," Jinn said. He turned to Mara, the hag's face already hidden behind a smiling illusion, her arm gently but firmly within the elbow of Briarbones. "Find the children and guard them well, if not for their sakes, then—"

"For my own," Mara supplied mockingly and added with her knowing smile, "I am well aware of the consequences, deva, but as a self-serving creature of some taste, I am also aware of the rewards. I look forward to the dark souls you promised me."

"Very well. Good hunting," he replied reluctantly, far more trustful of the hag in the heat of battle than hidden away with the lives of children in her care. In the end he had only her greed to rely on.

"And to you," she replied and pulled Briar at her side, the pair whispering as they made their way out of the alley, to anyone else appearing as nothing more than a young woman escorting her elderly father.

Jinn turned to Quessahn, the previous night's confrontation hanging between them like a ghost, haunting the eladrin's eyes and inspiring the deva to keep moving. They exited the alley, racing against the sunset, Jinn's heart pounding in time with his boots, anxious for the battle to come.

Only a few candles were lit as darkness neared, scattered windows glowing dimly like faded stars as the destitute and soulless, the ahimazzi, were roused from their mindless wanderings. They shuffled shyly, hiding from the orange and purple twilight, averting their gazes from those few impoverished souls who rushed home and barred their doors.

A storm of whispers slithered through the streets, reaching the ears of bodies without reason, sparking their bestial minds to recall their duties. They followed, grasping at the whispers, their own voices, as if they would be reunited with what had been stolen. Souls upon souls wailed in their minds, spirits bound in the pit of Sathariel's gut, and the ahimazzi gathered to one another, all bound for the same destination.

A few of their number were called away, crawling into the

steaming sewers, blades bared and growling like animals. Others were roughly pulled aside and questioned by men in dark uniforms, weak eyes burned in green-tinted lantern light, tongues answerless to shouted questions and harsh commands. They were released at length, shoved to the walls, unable to speak of their misery or purpose, their faraway souls unwilling to give up on the hope for reunion—for the warmth of living flesh.

They scattered slowly as uniformed men attempted to follow them, fragmenting their numbers and wandering aimlessly until they could slip unnoticed into darkened alleys and answer their master's call.

Dark feathers only they could see teased them from above, half a wing fluttering over a steepled roof, a black claw clutching a tall spire, as the angel led them on ever faster, ever more determined to obey. Dim memories flickered in their brains as they drew close to something familiar, intangible flashes of power radiating outward in wide circles. They gasped and moaned as they drew closer, hands grasping at iron bars tipped with sharp, decorative blooms. Matted vines of dry thorns pulled at their robes and dug into their skin, an untended garden of dull greens and browns crawling over everything within the open gates. The ahimazzi wept without sorrow, dirty hands reaching for the dark walls of the small manse beyond the fence.

From somewhere beyond they could hear the faint *tap-tapping* of a gnarled, wooden staff and muffled chants underground. High above it all, their souls called to them in pain, promising an end, redemption for their failures. They turned their backs to the iron fence, crouching low, their rusty blades in hand. They waited in silence, the remnants of the Vigilant Order, to defend and to witness all that they were promised by the silvered tongue of an angel.

His black wings flapped slowly overhead, a single herald to a dark host their order had invited in ages long past. In the silent streets of Sea Ward, the roaring waves of the Sword Coast thundered like the armies they had once imagined, answering the call of the Flensing to come.

>———W———<

Jinn stared through a pane of glass dripping with rain, watching as the ahimazzi gathered within the circle of homes and businesses across the street, hiding outside the gates of the House of Thorne. Dark spires rose from the corners of its flat roof, gables along the sides, the windows blackened and stained by neglect. Amid the bright homes around it, it stood like an architectural cancer, fouling the order of an otherwise typical neighborhood.

The mansion Jinn stood within was empty, its owners packed and evacuated long before gateclose. A useless exodus, he reasoned, for the victims had been chosen long before their own births, taken—save for a precious few—all before the sun had risen, the slain bloodlines of nine men too greedy for life to die, too hungry for immortality to let blood relation stand in their way.

"They should have torn it down more than a century ago," Quessahn said from the shadows behind him.

"They couldn't. It was a fascination, a whispered story for their parties. Passed along like a secret," Jinn replied. "Besides, the skulls would have protected it, kept it safe until all was prepared for their working."

"Perhaps they might have hired a gardener, then," Quessahn muttered as she bent to her task, surrounding herself with spell components and an old scroll. She began to draw on the floor of the living room, the chalk giving off a bitter scent that mingled with that of dried petals and leaves as she prepared her ritual, the strange magic of a new age. "Do you trust her? Mara, I mean."

"I trust her to be what she is. I believe greed will keep her actions in line with ours, if not her intentions," Jinn answered as he waited for the last of the sunset to leave the ward in darkness. Quessahn did not reply, but he knew she wasn't convinced and he could not blame her, for he had his own doubts. "Do you trust the avolakia? Briarbones?"

"Until he grows bored, yes, I do," she said, the scrape of chalk on smooth stone accompanying her words. "He is very old and not afraid of death in the least. As long as there is something to interest him, to engage his voracious curiosity, he shouldn't feel the need to create something interesting. Luckily I think the whisperers of Seawind Alley should keep him occupied for decades at least."

"I doubt he will be easily bored tonight," Jinn said quietly.

"Do you really think Callak Saerfynn is involved in all of this?" she asked. "He has wealth, status—such as it is—and wants for nothing . . ."

"I imagine to some, the more gold one has, the less valuable it seems. To a few, immortality would be beyond value, even worth the life of a sister," he answered absently, musing as he studied the dark house and the dirtied host surrounding it.

"I guess those that don't have immortality—" Quessahn began then stopped abruptly, falling silent, her ghostly reflection in the window casting nervous glances at Jinn as she focused on the arcane circle drawn around her.

Jinn hesitated as he considered the door mere strides away, part of him already outside and retreating from the ghosts of his previous life, another part holding him still, waiting for her to speak again, to say things he had no right to ask of her.

He managed a single step, his hand rising to take the handle.

"I buried him," she said, her voice faltering slightly. "I . . . I don't know if that means anything to you, but you—I mean, Kehran—you both . . ." She sighed loudly and slumped, shaking her head as he turned to face her. "Gods above, but this is strange."

"Go on," Jinn said, unsure if he said it out of pity or just for himself, but he wanted to hear her, needed to hear her.

"He fought like you, endlessly. It was hard to keep him still most days," she said. "But for a time, he did stand still and we had a life together, deep in the High Forest. He had what, for him, passed for peace, like he had escaped something, and for almost a year, he was a different person." A brief smile crossed her face, disappearing as quickly as it had come. "But in the end, it called him back, his drive to fight, to chase down the memory of old causes and raise a standard against . . . Well, good and evil meant different things to him.

"We argued the last time I saw him alive, and I told him not to go, but . . ." Her voice broke and she breathed deeply, maintaining her composure. "I found his body the next day and buried him that evening."

Drops of rain tapped on the doorstep and on the grass outside, dripping from the trees outside as mist gathered in their branches and ran down the bark like tears. Jinn stared at the eladrin, her brief tale a unique experience for him, as though he'd witnessed his own funeral. He took the doorknob in his hand and turned it once.

"You're not really hunting Sathariel, are you," she said. It was a statement, almost an accusation, rather than a question. "He's just a means to an end, your connection to Asmodeus."

Jinn did not reply, for there was no need. He could not deny what was in his heart, what festered in the deepest parts of himself.

"Do you think to kill a god?" she asked quietly. "Or do you hope he has the power to kill you, to truly end you?"

"I don't know," he said, considering his answer carefully. "There is a reason, I suppose. For the cycles in the world, death and rebirth, over and again. They have a meaning, as if we are all being prepared for something, either glory or death or both." He shook his head and swore under his breath. "But damned if I'll ever understand it."

He opened the door and looked out across the street, silhouettes of the ahimazzi merging like the dark shape of a single crouched beast, their daggers its rusty teeth, their tattered robes its filthy mane.

"Be careful," he said to her as he stepped outside, leaving her to her ritual and praying that she would survive what she had planned.

"See you soon," she replied. He closed the door behind himself and made his way through the garden, sword drawn to challenge the many-eyed beast that awaited him—as they always did, time and again. He did not shout or flourish his sword in a duelist's manner, though his heart raced to meet them and to clip the wings of their dark master.

<hr />

Tavian's boots scuffed loudly in the empty streets, a patrol at his back as night settled into the alleys and dark avenues of Sea Ward. He had often wished to escape the bureaucracy of his command and put heels to the cobbles, but he'd never imagined he would regret that selfish desire. They carried their lanterns high along lines of dark street lamps, a casualty of the curfew and of the lamplighters' fear after the morning's news had spread to the other wards. Foolhardy gawkers and would-be adventurers were stopped and questioned before being sent away, though Tavian knew they would attempt to slip back in, to make a name for themselves or hire themselves out to nobles amassing armies of bodyguards.

The Watch commanders, fearing an increased lack of trust in their officers, had called for reinforcements to patrol until the ward's matters could be settled. Investigators had been summoned, and the details of the killings, such as they were, were under review. Already they had found odd notations and inconsistencies in the recent logs.

Primary among them was a sizable donation to the local Watch by the slain Loethe family, a donation recorded and signed for yet long since disappeared.

As much as he could, Tavian had defended Allek Marson to his superiors, proclaiming him to be a good man in unusual circumstances, but as evidence mounted and changed by the bell, he found he could no longer trust his own report of the man. He'd known Allek to be honest and trustworthy, an efficient officer if ever there was one, though he could not deny the growing sense that the fallen rorden had been manipulated and used. Worse still was the idea that Allek had allowed himself to be treated that way, pawn to a foul plot and seduced by something he could not turn down.

As rumors spread through the ranks, more and more patrols frequented the perimeter of the House of Wonder, suspicious of the magic-users within. Tavian imagined any sleeping wizards within would dream of armies on the march, such was the foot traffic outside their courtyard. The Watchful Order had been summoned to question the wizards, much to the discomfort of many of Sea Ward's regular officers, rumors of foul magic abounding in the tales of the murders. Tavian had never had much trouble with wizards, but somewhere in the ward, he smelled magic at work, as if it were on the air, worming itself into the cracks and gutters, making ready for some final act to unfold.

A shrill scream pierced the streets, echoing through the lofty spires. He stopped his men in their tracks, listening as it faded in the distance. Tavian held a gloved hand up, his breath steaming as they waited for the scream to repeat and give them a direction. His heart pounded and he wondered, after all the reports, what bloody scene might await them. The scream came again, and he dropped his fist, leading the patrol west and north to the disturbance.

Pale green light swung from one building to the next as the officers ran, breath steaming in puffs behind them as they turned a corner and found a woman, frantic and leaning out from a second-story window, wailing and pointing. Her face was white as a ghost, and masculine hands held her shoulders as she struggled, grasping for something unseen.

Half of Tavian's patrol entered the home as he directed the others to secure the entrances, confused bodyguards reluctantly making way, their eyes also on the rooftops. Signal horns blared short notes in quick succession at Tavian's back as he stood in the middle of the street, following the wild-eyed stare of the woman to the rooftops across the street. He saw nothing out of the ordinary. A single plume of smoke drifted from a lone chimney as drizzle swirled in the light of the Watch lanterns, but naught else caught his eye that might have caused such a stir.

He wandered down the street, following the roof line, squinting in the dark. The woman's cries quieted some as his officers reached her, though she remained at the window, speaking hysterically. At the end of the street, Tavian sighed and shook his head. Turning back, he paused, breath catching in his throat as a blot of shadow shifted him above him at the base of a cold chimney. He froze, staring at the spot for what seemed an eternity before two red eyes blinked open and glared at him from the dark. In that hellish light, he could make out long, gangly arms wrapped around a struggling bundle, held close in a cloud of wavering shadows.

Tavian's sword was halfway drawn, his signal horn barely from his belt, when the thing leaped into the air, tattered, black robes spread wide around it like the wings of a diseased crow. It landed on a wall across the street, flattening to the surface and crawling up like a spider as he loosed a strident call from his horn. The thing leaped again, almost gliding from one building to the next, nearly invisible against the sky.

"Mystra's bones!" he swore and stumbled back, waving his men on as they rushed to answer his call. "Eyes up high!" he shouted, pointing at the last place he'd seen the thing.

"A child, sir!" Aeril said, skidding to a stop at his side. "She says it took a child!"

"Bloody bones," he whispered, unblinking as he searched the northern skyline and waved Aeril to be silent.

"What is it, sir?" Aeril asked, catching his breath. "The woman said she caught just a glimpse before—"

"Hush, man!" Tavian demanded, listening, though only the wind could be heard for several breaths. Men shouted down the street, their boots echoing around the next corner, lanterns casting dancing shadows as they searched. Other horns echoed through the ward, other patrols seeking assistance, likely with the homeless vagabonds who'd wandered into the ward in mysterious numbers seemingly overnight. He cursed, sheathing his sword as the rest of the patrol caught up to him. He raised a hand to direct them north with the others, but the command was cut off by another scream, distant and pealing, from several blocks away. "There!" he said. "Move! Now!"

They ran west, signal horns calling to the other patrols though Tavian did not expect a swift answer, rushing through the cold night, chasing after shadows and screams.

EIGHTEEN

Jinnaoth crossed the street, his step quickening as the ahimazzi rose to face him. Their curved blades formed a jagged ring around the iron fence they guarded, a robed garden of rusty thorns to match the one at their backs. Several separated from the mob to meet his charge. He gripped his sword tightly, holding it low and back, a spark of primal bloodlust in his eyes as he swung and severed the first left hand that stabbed for him. He shoulder blocked another out of his way and kicked as he turned and slashed again, some part of his ancient soul taking over, directing his blade to the brute-force tactics of a battlefield rather than the finesse of single combat.

The soulless were quicker than normal, grunting and excited as they came for him, but there was no skill in their attacks, using only the press of numbers in their attempts to subdue him. He butchered the handful that rushed him, cutting them down like beasts and leaving them to flounder on the cobbles, clumsy daggers scraping weakly at his boots and tearing at his cloak. He cursed and swore at them in ancient languages, the tongues of the warrior spirits that surged through his veins, as gore covered his blade and splashed across his clothes.

His blood burned at the brief victory, eyes blazing as he turned to the dozens that remained, a stinking, unworthy host, an insult to the long road he had walked to face Sathariel. Pawns and fools of a cult that gave their lives no value, death was a blessing for the mindless existence they had earned. Their eyes regarded him blankly, thin lines of drool and froth dripping on their robes as their teeth gnashed and they growled like animals.

Whispering a prayer for their pitiful lives, he cleaved into the mass like a madman, cutting their throats and kicking them down as curved blades sought his flesh from all sides. He cleared a small circle in their midst, slowing as they pressed closer, roaring as the ground grew slick and uneven with blood and bodies. A dirty blade glanced along his collarbone, fingernails dug into his wrist and scratched at his scalp. They pulled painfully at his hair and tugged at the end of his cloak, but he kept cutting and stabbing, using the bodies of a few to trip up several more.

Losing himself in dull pains and bloodlust, the memories of more than a thousand battles raged in his mind. Each cut he suffered was echoed by grievous injuries from past lives, each wound he inflicted joined thousands more, and each life he took was added to the bloody path of his immortal soul. He whispered long-forgotten conversations as he pushed forward, arguing with dead generals and reciting eulogies from funeral rites no longer observed, in empires that no longer stood.

Flesh and bone split open like mouths at his blade's touch, spilling red secrets. Jinn stumbled forward and slashed instinctively, dried leaves and thorny vines falling to his feet. He whirled to see the open gate, finally at his back, and braced himself for the ahimazzi as they crowded the iron fence line. He spat at them, but they did not follow, their toes scarcely crossing the garden's edge before pulling away.

Lowering his sword, he spat again, the soulless either refusing to enter the garden or prevented from doing so. The evening grew quiet again save for the muffled groans and soft gurgles of the dying ahimazzi, their last breaths steaming around the soiled feet of the mob. Jinn stretched and caught his breath, wincing as little wounds and gouges stung with pain, none of them serious enough to warrant immediate attention but enough to itch beneath his clothes and leather armor. Exhaling, he released the savage spirit that had possessed him.

He wiped blood from his face and turned toward the house, slowing his racing pulse as he crossed the threshold of the open door. Every surface within was covered in patches of dark browns, moldy stains, and creeping vines that bristled with thorns. He proceeded cautiously at first, but as he prowled the dusty hallways and rooms of broken furniture, a sense of familiarity overcame him, as if the house had been waiting for him.

Shadows moved silently ahead of him, featureless silhouettes watching but not threatening as he searched for the basement doorway. Semitransparent, the ghosts, little more than persistent fetches, followed his progress, peering at him from darkened corners and long halls. He eyed them curiously, pitying them for the deaths that tied them to the property but wary of lingering too long in their presence lest he wake the reasonless anger of the dead.

The basement door had been left open, a black pit at the back of a small servants' kitchen. He descended the stairs, sword drawn. The musky scent of decay wafted up from the oddly warm chamber below. The walls were covered in dark handprints, all in pairs and all displaying only nine fingers.

At the base of the stairs, along the south wall, sat a dusty, old chair, and in it he spied a figure sprawled across its arms. A shock of blonde hair rested across the stained cushion. He crept across the room and knelt cautiously, reaching for the pale hand of Rilyana

Saerfynn. She stirred at his touch and moaned, rubbing her eyes as he stood and surveyed the large chamber. A single candle was set in a wall sconce on the north wall, but all else was cloaked in clinging darkness.

"Rilyana!" he whispered as loudly as he dared.

Her eyes fluttered open, finding him and appearing confused. She had several bruises on her arms, and dried blood covered the left side of her face.

"Wake up. You need to get out of here quickly!"

"Jinnaoth?" she mumbled and sat up, yawning lazily. "Haven't seen you since the fire at the tavern."

Jinn half spun at the sound of rough breathing in the dark, a rasping, hungry noise that set his nerves on edge. He grabbed Rilyana's arm and hauled her up, placing his sword between them and the thick shadows. He had no time to coddle privileged young women. He could feel the cloying presence of some dark power gathering in the basement.

"Get out of here!" he said, wide eyed as he searched the dark end of the chamber, trying to pierce the veil of shadows and wondering where Rilyana's brother would be hiding. "Now!"

"Oh, Jinn," she said, and she laid a hand upon his, her fingers soft on his skin. "No, I don't think so."

A shock of alarm ran through his body as he reversed his grip on the sword and turned half a breath too late. He felt a rush of hot breath on his cheek as she whispered an arcane syllable, her lips brushing against his ear as a sudden thrust of force slammed into his side. The candle became a blurry streak as he was hurled across the room and slammed against the far wall. The breath was knocked from his lungs, and he gasped like a landed fish, flopping onto his side and wincing at the pain he felt there. Candles bloomed to life across from him, haloed through the haze of fading pain as he coughed, slumped over in a dirty corner.

Silhouettes passed through the semicircle of light, one graceful and surefooted, the other hunched and leaning, the *tap-tap* of a wooden staff preceding each step. He shook his head and cursed, trying to sit up as the face of the archmage grew more distinct, the shadows curling away from him and Rilyana like thick smoke. As they did, Jinn noted the sprawled form on the floor before them, the battered and bruised body of Callak Saerfynn.

"We heard your battle outside, deva," Tallus said, his voice weak but mocking. "A glorious tribute of blood, I must admit, but surely you did not think to catch us unawares, eh?"

The wizard stood before a stone pedestal in the center of several concentric circles, similar to those in the archmage's tower, covered in overlapping symbols and glyphs that squirmed with power. Jinn merely glared at Tallus and rose to a crouch, pulling his sword behind him, prepared to make the wizard's once-apparent death a painful fact.

Rilyana drew close to Tallus, wrapping an arm around his waist and gently kissing his neck, her tongue darting close to his ear as she smiled cruelly at the deva.

"He doesn't seem particularly surprised to see you," she said, and she laid her head upon the archmage's shoulder.

Tallus grunted, grinning through his scraggly beard as he produced a wooden chest from beneath his robes and placed it upon the pedestal. "Only because he is a better actor than you, my dear. Had he known I was alive, he might not have wasted his time with that fool Dregg." The pedestal began to glow, the golden clasp and gilded edges of the chest flaring brightly even as the entire house groaned. "Though I must wonder, how did he find us here?"

"Perhaps you've been betrayed," Jinn muttered, lining the blade of his sword along the edge of his spine, leaning forward as he waited for Tallus to turn away once more. The wizard's confidence, though sickening, could serve Jinn's purpose.

"Oh, I've no doubt of that," the archmage replied and passed his hand over the wooden chest, chanting as the house seemed to lurch on its foundation, shaking violently. More dust fell and thorny vines crawled down through fresh cracks in the ceiling, writhing and spreading. The walls pulsed and undulated like flesh made of wood and stone, as though the entire structure were alive. "Too many would be more than willing to kill for my place in this ritual. Had I chosen to wait any longer, I might have ended up like the corpse you found in my tower."

"There's still time for that," Jinn said as the stone floor throbbed beneath his boots. An unholy energy seeped through the cracks that brought bile into Jinn's throat and twisted in his gut. The scents of the Nine Hells wafted through the room: sulfur, rot, and char.

Disoriented and nauseated, he choked and spat, sickened by the power the archmage was summoning, his heart pounding as his celestial nature was repelled by the ritual. Trying to focus on the wizard and his duplicitous lover, Jinn held on, waiting until Tallus finally turned. In a breath Jinn vaulted forward, sword drawn back as the archmage traced sigils on the chest, unaware of the impending doom at his back.

Quessahn stared out at the House of Thorne for several moments before drawing the curtains and returning to her ritual circle. A part of her feared for Jinn, just as another part wondered if she could trust his judgment, wondered if he were capable of sacrificing the lives of hundreds, possibly thousands, to satisfy his thirst for vengeance. She banished the thought, having her own work to complete. She sat, cross-legged, at the center of the design on the floor and shook her hands nervously then laid them gently upon her knees. Closing her eyes, she cleared her mind of all else but the spell prepared around her, mentally tracing each sigil and glyph, turning her mind through the arcane labyrinth of the ritual.

She whispered the runes of the outer circle, each symbol a listed name, all of them drawn from ancient texts and dark cults long dead. She called upon the power of stars and slumbering beings, many of whom were both, whose dreams were alive and whose nightmares fed upon the fabrics of the multiverse, infected by their creators' appetites for the flesh of reality itself. Invoking their essences, she worked to link the vast areas of space between one and the next, tracing her spell, her circle, in immeasurable symbols among the stars.

A dull ache settled in her bones as the pattern took shape, as if the raw magic she summoned had taken notice of her efforts and had begun to test the limits of her will. The names she uttered echoed through the outer circle, thrumming in powerful languages that were old when the world was yet young, naming themselves as she reigned in the power of the pattern. Sweat beaded on her forehead, and stars streaked through her field of vision as she shook, gritting her teeth and holding on to the magic. At length, mastering the power that flowed through and around her, she turned her attention to the inner circle.

The inner circle spun in her mind, the symbols turning as she spoke them, raising her hands and tracing them on the air. Her fingers clawed at ephemeral threads of energy, forcing them into the configurations she desired. Only one name was written within the inner circle, and she saved it for the last, holding it as it slid through her mind like a snake, its forked tongue flicking at her thoughts. It teased her and she trembled, fighting back the doubt that could destroy the spell. Infusing the ritual with her quiet fear, she turned her dread into bait for her target.

"Sathariel," she whispered, the word taking on a life of its own, drifting like smoke within the confines of the circles and tugging at her concentration, begging to be heard. It shouted itself in discordant echoes, over and over in rumbling waves that raised the hairs on her neck.

A quiet gasp escaped her as she fought to contain the power around her, the magic thrashing to be set free, loosed to her desired effect. At length the angel's name quieted in her mind, a cool calm settling among her thoughts, and she knew her spell had been answered.

The dark house grew darker, bereft of light save for the soft glow of the circles around her, a faerie fire to draw the angel in like a moth from the depths of the Nine Hells. Massive wings spoke in tones of thunder as he appeared, his very presence like a weakening of the heart. He drifted down from the tall ceiling, his body crafted of black flame, clothed in silvered armor shaped to resemble screaming faces. A long blade hung at his side, and a halo of flickering shadow curled around his featureless face, tiny, ice blue pinpoints glaring at her from within the twin pits of his eyes.

Is this your part to play, eladrin? his voice growled in her thoughts and shook the tenuous tethers of her spell. *To summon me here and somehow foil the dark ritual of the nine skulls? Or is it to save the courageous deva from my wrath?* Her mind filled with his laughter, a derisive storm that crashed against her resolve. *Your sacrifice is indeed noble but terribly misguided. I can almost taste your ignorance, a veritable feast of empty gestures that only delay the inevitable.*

"Y-you mock me. I court with beings far beyond the angelic lackeys of youngling gods," she said as the spell took on its final shape, binding itself to her as she bound herself to its purpose.

Indeed, a passing acquaintance, I am sure, with powers that defeated themselves in an age long before the rise of mortals, Sathariel replied. *Ah, but could they smell your weakness now, I daresay they might awaken again.*

"Until then . . . let us speak," she said, and she loosed the spell, sighing as it ran its course, flooding her body with tingling power.

A wave of green energy leaped from her palms at Sathariel as he drew and swung his heavy blade. The sword sparked at the edge of the circle, rebounding from the protective spell even as jade energy gripped his shadowlike body and mingled in its deep black like spilled ink.

What is this, witch? he shouted in her mind as his body shuddered and trembled, unable to escape the cloying power that coursed through him.

"A simple ward, a circle to keep you at arm's length, and this"—she held up her hands, flickering with a nimbus of green energy—"this will tell me a bit of your future, what those slumbering beings among the stars see in their dreams of things that are and things that could be."

Look well, then, elf, the angel replied, roaring in her thoughts as he crashed his blade against the outer circle, sparks showering around them both. *For you are a doomed voyeur, a witness to your own death . . . and the deva's!*

"Undoubtedly," she said, a familiar calm settling her racing heart, her mind's eye drifting to maps of the constellations. Her back arched painfully as power rushed between their bodies. Blinded by a flash of white light, she felt as though she were suddenly flying, the fate of an angel flooding her senses.

A swirl of colors swam on the insides of Jinn's eyelids. Breath, heavy and laborious, poured into his lungs like warm syrup, tasting of fire and things long dead. A grating noise, like boulders roughly dragged down a paved avenue, rumbled in his throat as sparks of consciousness hissed in his mind. He recalled a brief moment of savage fury, light on his heels, a sword in his hand as he leaped for the throat of Archmage Tallus.

All else was pain and rough stone floor on his back.

His skin felt burned as he turned on his side, leaning on one elbow and blinking the haze from his eyes. The edges of the wizard's ritual circle rippled lazily, waves flowing around and around the pair within the concentric rings of magic. Tallus glanced at him once, appearing amused but engrossed in his work as he carried out the instructions of the nine skulls. Rilyana's gaze did not falter, however, her face set in an excited, manic expression as Jinn sat up, grimacing as he took up his stolen blade.

"Do you feel better now?" the archmage asked, inscribing a deft sigil in the lid of the wooden chest on the pedestal. "I suspect your angel will make that attempt as well and gain much the same result."

"Your angel, I believe. I do not ally myself with lapdogs of Asmodeus," Jinn replied, sliding the edge of his blade along the perimeter of the ritual circle, air burning at the contact between magic and steel.

"Well, partnerships of convenience come and go so swiftly, do they not? And I believe you are the last one to be judging the dubious contacts of others, or have you and the night hag had a falling out?" Tallus sat back from the chest, grinning at his work.

Jinn ignored the human and shifted his weight, testing his legs before rising to a low crouch. He studied the chamber as he did so, looking for some crack, some weakness he might exploit to slow the progress of the skulls' ritual.

"Your kind are not welcome within this circle," Rilyana said, kneeling to catch Jinn's eye. "It has lain buried here for three centuries, waiting for this night to happen."

Jinn leaned close to the invisible barrier, a palpable charge around it tingling on his skin. He regarded the young woman who had seduced Allek Marson, Lucian Dregg, Archmage Tallus, and, if the rumors were to be believed, her own brother, who lay unconscious and bloodied barely a stride away.

"No, Mistress Saerfynn, it has been here far longer than that. This circle was a dream long before Waterdeep even had a name. The runes you hide behind owe more to prophecy than the villainy of greedy wizards," he said with a cruel smile, knowing the ambition that brought her to the brink of immortality would be the same that consigned her to the grim delights of a devil-god's court.

Rilyana leaned closer to him, her smile never faltering, her eyes bright and knowing. He could smell the heady scent of her perfume as she licked her lips and lowered her eyes demurely, smirking as she spoke.

"You and Sathariel *are* much alike, more than I'd expected," she said, adding mysteriously, "I can see why he likes you."

She withdrew swiftly to the archmage's side as Jinn leaned back, speechless as the wizard's voice rose to a shout, a profane chant that sent shivers through the deva's blood. The circle flared to brilliant life, energy spinning low over the carved symbols, raising sparks like the gears of a clockwork machine gone mad. The house shook, groaning again, and Jinn doubled over, sickened by a wave of unholy power as somehow, in the pit of his being, he felt a change in the air and knew what had happened.

The true ritual had just begun.

Hollow voices filled the chamber as Tallus fell silent and turned to the body of Callak, which stirred, writhing and convulsing on the floor.

"Tallus!" Callak cried, the name split among nine screeching tones, all of them furious.

Green flames burst from Callak's eyes, roaring high as shadows flooded from his wide mouth like thick smoke, curling and wrapping around his arms and legs, the misty strings of nine sorcerous puppeteers. He spasmed and lurched, rising on his hands as the darkness obscured his flesh, leaving only the flaming green eyes, which turned and glared at the archmage.

"Idiot! Fool! You have betrayed us!" they cried, voices cracking like a whip.

"Nonsense," Tallus replied calmly. "I have merely quickened the pace of our arrangement, though I suspected you would not be terribly pleased."

"We shall rip you limb from limb, knit you back together, make you a plaything for demons and a temple for maggots!" the Nine shouted.

"No, you won't," the archmage responded as Rilyana leaned upon his shoulder, "for there are a dozen souls left for you to prepare. Time is fleeting, but it has not yet left you behind. That is, provided you contribute your own souls to the ritual before the work is ruined . . ."

Jinnaoth listened to the exchange intently, quietly urging the souls to act upon their greed and reveal the location of their long-hidden souls. With that, he might draw out the angel, lure Sathariel with valuable secrets to within reach of his blade.

"Very well," the skulls growled at length, too close to the immortal flesh they so desired to resist its siren call. "Find them here . . ."

They drew a series of dark symbols upon the wooden chest, the characters matching the existing arcane designs as Jinn cursed under his breath, unable to read the language upon the box.

"Do not try us further, wizard. As it is, we shall have an interesting discussion when this business is concluded," they said, backing away from the pedestal, eyes flaring excitedly at sight of the wooden chest.

With an echoing whisper of magic, the nine skulls and the possessed body of Callak Saerfynn were gone. Taking their secrets with them, they left Jinn, bereft of all that he'd come for, alone and barred from the hellish circle where Tallus orchestrated a symphony of immortality for himself—and death for every soul within the reach of the foul ritual.

NINETEEN

I am sorry about your brother, dear Rilyana," Tallus muttered absently as he worked the clasps on the wooden chest, tracing a sigil upon each with the tip of his finger. "Callak's death will be slow and painful, but it will pave the way for you to join me . . . forever."

She smiled, her hand sliding from his right shoulder to around his waist, kissing him roughly and pressing her body close. Jinn turned away from the spectacle, collecting his scattered thoughts toward some other plan, some way to foil Tallus and draw Sathariel out of hiding.

"Never worry, my love. I mourn no lost brother," Rilyana purred, and something in her voice caught Jinn's attention, her words reverberating like a slipped secret plucked from the air on a crowded street. He glanced up, curious, his thoughts racing back to Rilyana's mansion and the paintings upon the walls of the drawing room. Rilyana's tongue traced the lobe of Tallus's ear as she continued, looking sidelong at the dawning realization on the deva's face. A flash of curved steel appeared in her left hand, hidden at her side, as she added in a husky whisper, "I was adopted, my dear uncle."

Tallus's eyes widened in horror half a breath before Rilyana's blade plunged into his chest. The archmage gasped once, waving his hands as he tried to push away from the young woman, but she held on, wrestling his arms down and covering his mouth, foiling his attempts to save himself with magic. His next breaths gurgled in his throat as his face turned red, eyes burning into Rilyana's as she bore him to the floor, her white gown stained with his blood. She held him tightly, as though squeezing the last dregs of life from his body before rising to survey her work.

Her fingers dripping with blood, she traced a symbol upon the last clasp of the chest, and the house shuddered as the box slowly opened. A column of blue-white light erupted from the pedestal, giving Jinn a brief glimpse at the chest's contents before he was forced to turn away. He was not surprised at the sight of dried blood on gold satin, of yellowed bone and gray flesh—the collected fingers of the skulls' victims, vessels for their souls, to burn on the pyre of immortality.

Rilyana smiled, chanting over the box's contents, spatters of Tallus's blood dripping onto the circle as she took up the ritual chant. The energy over the runes spun ever faster, blurring into a disk of flickering yellow flames before she fell silent and knelt over the body of the archmage. She ripped open the front of his robes, her blade poised over his chest as she prepared his body for the rite, one more soul for the fire and a tenth family, the Saerfynns, added to the list of would-be immortals.

>=====W=<

A blanket of white clouds rolled slowly eastward beneath Quessahn as a sky full of stars wheeled overhead. Somewhere below the clouds, locked in the throes of magic, she could faintly feel the pressure of her body, the tightness of her skin and the cold sweat running down her neck, but it was as a dream, something outside of herself and bordering on the unreal. Close by she could feel the presence of Sathariel, caught in her spell, his future and fragments of his past feeding the magic as he struggled to free himself. Little tremors of pain danced in her distant wrists, traveling up her arms as she fought to hold him for just a few breaths more.

Weightless, she soared through the air, borne on the currents of time past and yet to be, spinning in the occasional whirlpools of random events until that which she sought came surging from the depths, showing her visions of the angel's future.

The stars flashed and her entire being shuddered as she plunged through the clouds, hurtling forward—or possibly backward, she couldn't tell which. Waterdeep stretched out beneath her, the streets a blur of activity and changing shadows as day and night turned over one another more than a dozen times in the space of a breath. Turning toward Sea Ward, she descended over its many-spired homes and grandiose temples as the moon took dominance over the sun. All across the city, streetlamps were lit, tracing a maze of light through main streets and winding avenues alike, though in Sea Ward the streets remained dark and foreboding.

Watch patrols rushed from block to block, like ants running in inexplicable patterns, chasing screams and shadows. Windows were lit in the House of Wonder as sleeping wizards awoke, responding to some commotion or another outside. The Watchful Order had roused the mages, separating and questioning them, keeping them from leaving the house. Instinct made her want to call out, to warn them that something was coming, but the course of the spell carried her quietly by, heading south, where a dark and dilapidated house awaited her.

The House of Thorne throbbed with energy as she neared, light pouring from dirty windows and exciting the once-dead gardens to life. Vines thrashed and writhed against brick and iron as thunder rumbled through the sky, orange flames erupting within the clouds as tiny motes of blue light drifted from the house and swirled around her. The motes whispered as they passed, their somber light guttering as they were drawn together to a single place. She saw the angel then, rising above the house, black wings outstretched, the tips of his clawlike hands close enough to touch. He was beautiful and horrifying all at once, bathed in a shaft of crimson light that crackled and hummed as he began to speak.

"Let it be done," he said, cold eyes rising to the sky. "The invitation has been given."

The roof below him exploded in a shower of wild energy, engulfing them as the ground quaked. Homes and businesses shifted on their foundations, and shards of glass rained down to the streets. Several spires shook from their places and crashed to the cobbles as Quessahn gaped in disbelief, unable to breathe.

She flinched as the screams began.

Those nobles and wealthy who had remained in the ward ran from their homes, filling the nearly empty avenues with renewed life; suddenly another day to live had become more valuable than the gold they left behind. Bodyguards and servants abandoned their frightened masters, shoving them aside in their haste to escape. The Watch marshaled their scattered forces, converging on the House of Thorne with strident horns and swinging lanterns. The House of Wonder erupted with flashes of magic as several wizards teleported away, leaving the rest to rush outside, gaping at the spectacle in the sky as the Watchful Order abandoned their interrogations.

Quessahn felt other eyes across the city, powerful eyes, finally turn their attentions to Sea Ward.

Sathariel's voice thundered around her in a language of pure pain that wracked her spirit, the words unknown save for a couple, which Briarbones had muttered during his study of hellish prophecies—*first* and *flensing*.

The words echoed, over and over, in the angel's chant as cracks spread through the streets, each glowing with a pulsing, fiery light.

The ahimazzi gathered below fell to their knees, hands upraised, bloody tears streaming down their cheeks. Their eyes flickered with reflected fire from the clouds, and they smiled mad grins, their souls returned, zealous witnesses to the breaking of the city.

Quessahn fought against the vision, straining to escape, to find what had come before to cause the angel's victory, but the vision persisted, holding her tightly. Watchmen and the City Guard encircled the property, their crossbow bolts falling short of Sathariel as he ascended higher, chanting to the sky. The Watchful Order and other wizards arrived, stopping short in their tracks, dumbfounded, reflected flames flickering in the spectacles of several, though others raised glowing staffs and shouted words of power.

More spires crumbled, crushing those too slow to escape. The ocean roared beyond the west wall, giant waves crashing and breaking through the gates, steaming as they poured into the glowing vents in the streets. The city turned beneath her as she was drawn inexorably to the sky, Sathariel reaching up as the clouds parted, revealing a fiery vortex dotted with a host of descending figures. Screams echoed throughout the ward, and crowds pressed away from the spectacle, smothering each other in their haste to escape.

"Let the first bastion be sealed," Sathariel said.

"Oh, gods no," Quessahn muttered as the vortex widened, revealing a fire-blasted landscape beyond, a world upside down, with massive cities of glowing iron and lakes of ash and smoke. Flaming spires dipped downward, as if reaching for the lofty heights of the greatest mansions and wizards' towers. She paled at the sight of it, shaken to her core and infected by the waves of fear that rose from the streets. Fire rained down from the sky as spells were hurled from the ground, powerful wizards fighting back, flinging magic at what, she realized, had become inevitable.

Gritting her teeth and closing her eyes, Quessahn strained against the spell of seeing, banishing the vision and commanding it to carry her back, to show her the cause and the moment that the future she'd witnessed had been born.

In a blink the terrible battle was gone, leaving her in a silent, oppressive darkness. She gasped, fearing she had ended the spell prematurely until a familiar brick wall materialized nearby. Turning, she found the gates of the House of Wonder, its windows still dark, the doors closed and barred for the evening. In a rush of shadowy feathers, Sathariel appeared again, drifting low to the ground and kneeling on the cobbles, his form and Pharra's Alley wavering as she felt her hold on the angel begin to slip.

She struggled a breath longer, her distant pulse racing, to watch as the angel plunged his fist into the ground, his arm shoulder deep beneath the cobbles. The image flickered as he dragged his fist from the ground, nine tendrils of green flame licking through his fingers, each wailing in pain as he held them aloft with an unholy roar of triumph.

"The circle of skulls . . . the nine souls," she whispered.

The words felt suddenly closer, more intimate, as she felt the last of the spell fade from her control. She slumped into her body, wincing at the aches and pains that greeted her upon return. Her eyes felt heavy and ponderous, blinking with lids that seemed alien to her. She flexed her fingers, the final remnants of an emerald flame dissipating from her fingertips, and the inner circle of her ritual fell quiet, little more than a smoking stain on the cold, stone floor. Sathariel hung on the air like a puppet, green energy racing through his wings and evaporating slowly, his black-pit eyes still dark.

"The circle of skulls," she said, eyes widening as the vision hit her all at once. "How did he find them? Who could have known—?"

The question caught in her throat, and she stared at her hands, the stench of charred stone stinging her nostrils. A shiver ran down her spine.

"I know," she said breathlessly, trembling and trying to stand. Sathariel's wings twitched and his body shook as she nudged a toe close to the edge of the protective outer circle, cursing herself. "I know where the skulls hid their souls and he could . . . No!"

She bolted for the door, her body's pain forgotten as unimaginable fear flooded through her, twisting in her gut like a serpent—the potential doom of hundreds weighing heavily on her shoulders. The angel stirred as she passed, his voice growling in her head, unintelligible as he awoke, unharmed by her magic. She opened the door, and the cold lights in Sathariel's eyes glimmered to life.

"Eladrin . . ." he rumbled hungrily, the word spurring her to greater speed.

She crossed the garden in a few breaths, her heart pounding in her ears as she entered the street. The ground shook as she ran, and a bellowing roar followed her, shattering windows as the angel found his strength. Wood and stone cracked loudly, exploding outward in a shower of debris that skittered along the cobbles at her heels. Quessahn struggled to work a spell, her thoughts slippery and jumbled.

Ahead of her the ahimazzi turned, moaning softly with raised knives as she rushed toward them and choked back the doubt that threatened to paralyze her. She chanted and ran, each action speeding the other, words tumbling across her tongue, shoved out by quick breaths and heart-stopping fear. The dry branches of bare trees clacked and snapped as the angel stormed through the mansion garden, charging after her.

A brief spark of magic tingled around her as she ran headlong toward the curved daggers of the ahimazzi, having no recourse if her spell failed but to be slain by the soulless men and women, taking knowledge of the circle of skulls' souls with her to a bloody end. As the stink of their bodies struck her nose, she forced out the last of the spell, a wave of nausea caused her to stumble forward into a widening pit of swirling shadow.

Plunging into the limitless dark of the spell, a hideous howling followed her as she fell and fell, tumbling into a vast and silent void.

"Sathariel will devour you," Jinn said, pacing the edge of the ritual circle, his blade hissing as he traced it over and over, watching Rilyana and waiting for just one slip, one misspoken rune to foul the protective barrier and allow him entrance.

"He already has devoured me. He won me over, heart and soul. I was only ten years old when he found me. He was ancient . . . and beautiful," Rilyana replied absently, paying him no attention as she focused on her work, preparing the wooden chest and the pedestal it sat upon for the spell's last enchantment.

"He groomed you for this moment. I assume he arranged your adoption? Gave you a good life? And education? All just to get you to this place, to get what he wants and then leave you to die," Jinn said, trying not to imagine the angel's hands upon an innocent child.

"Perhaps," she answered. "But would you not also die for someone you loved?"

"Not like this," he answered, stopping short as she turned to face him, hands raised. Her bright hazel eyes narrowed as she approached the edge of the circle, and he stepped back, sword drawn back to strike. "But unless I am mistaken, you do not intend to die at all. Ever, in fact."

"Enough, deva," she said coldly. "Did you know that Sathariel told me to let you live? Back at the Storm's Front, I could have easily made you the puppet of the nine skulls, but Sathariel stopped me. And do you know why?"

Jinn shook his head slowly, watching her every move as she drew closer. The curved blade she killed Tallus with lay discarded next to the wizard's body, but he could feel the magic she might wield against him. He quietly cursed the barrier between them, preparing himself for the worst.

"Choice," she said, spitting the word with a brief sneer. "He told me that that there were rules among his kind, ancient laws that even the gods were bound by, and that they required a choice, a balance between this world and theirs."

"What choice?" Jinn asked. "Who chooses?"

"It doesn't matter now," she said with a grin, "because, unlike him, *I* am not bound by laws or balance." Bright energy crackled across her fingertips, arcing down her wrist as she whispered an arcane phrase. "And I will not give you the chance to hurt him!"

"What—?" Jinn began, mystified, and he leaped to the side as white bolts of electricity flew from her palms. He rolled to the floor, blinded as the stone wall behind him erupted in a shower of sparks. She chanted again and his sword was ripped from his hand and flung to the far corner. Her eyes and fists blazed with red fire.

"Sathariel said I couldn't kill you," she growled. "He said it was impossible!"

Jinn swore and covered his head. Unable to strike back or escape, he hoped merely to survive. Heat filled the room and Rilyana screamed. Jinn braced himself for the fire, but it never came. He heard a loud crash followed by a silence broken only by a heavy breathing and the constant hum of the ritual circle. Raising his head cautiously, he saw Rilyana slumped against the wall, groaning and swearing as she tried to stand.

On the stairs, leaning on one elbow, her hand still steaming from a well-placed spell, Quessahn sat, glaring at the human. Teeth clenched and grunting in pain, the eladrin stood and brushed her hands off on her robes, muttering angrily.

"Sathariel was right."

Cold wind whistled through the borrowed ears of the nine skulls. Branches snagged at their clothes, snapped, and fell around them as they landed in a low crouch on damp grass and hard soil. They tore through the garden, boots crunching on deadfall, their nose lifted high, sniffing like an animal. Callak's body was weak, softened by a life of luxury, but their power made it strong, despite its physical limitations. Broken bones shifted in their right leg, and they could feel a torn hamstring worming its way up their right calf, loosed from its moorings.

Several of the nine skulls were amused by the sensation of pain, as with all they had nearly forgotten about the trappings of warm flesh. Pausing alongside the mansion, they grinned and tried to peer within the tall windows of the house, catching a familiar scent, one of family and connection.

"This one," Effram said as they slid along the wall and pressed their hands against the front doors. "All of them, I think."

"Gathered together? A gift or a ruse?" Graius asked.

The others, desperate and feeling time slip from their grasp, pressed Callak's hands against the hard wood, the oak feeling soft and pliable to their collected strength. They pushed. "Whatever it is, let us be quiet, swift, and watchful," he said as the door began to buckle. "Above all, be swift. If we hadn't written this last possession into the ritual, Tallus would have abandoned us completely. I doubt he will waste time waiting for us."

"Fortunately he is more buffoon than wizard," Graius added. "But be aware, the deva's witches are unaccounted for, and at least one of them has some real power."

"Duly noted," Effram said as the doors gave way, ripping away from their hinges and splitting like soft pine.

They prowled, well hidden in the dark by the shroud of shadow that clung to Callak's body, appearing as little more than a pair of emerald flames, floating through hallways and empty chambers. The scent grew stronger, smelling of fearful children and hushed breaths, puffing in time with fluttering hearts. An aura of heat drew them to a large drawing room.

A chorus of quiet whimpers greeted the skulls as they slunk forward, drawn by the stink of primal fear and . . . something else, something older. Bright eyes huddled together, their bodies dressed in nightclothes, as if they'd been stolen from their beds. They shivered and the skulls forgot their caution, but Effram remained troubled.

"Who brought them here?" he whispered as a shudder passed through Callak's body, a pang of curious weakness that gave the skulls pause. It grew to an odd ache, a pain they could not ignore. "What is this?"

"The witch!" Graius growled and pointed as a figure hobbled from the shadows. The skulls attempted to react, fighting inside Callak's head for consensus, centuries of magical knowledge cluttering their ability to cast even one spell at a moment's notice.

The figure drew closer and stood between them and the children, revealing itself to be an unfamiliar old man, a broad smile stretched unnaturally across his wrinkled face as he addressed them.

"Not who you were expecting, eh?"

Mara turned a wide circle in the alley, slow and deliberate, enjoying the drizzle and cold. She sprinkled fistfuls of salt on the cobbles of Pharra's Alley, sparing a disdainful glance at the House of Wonder, voices raised beyond the wall as the Watchful Order attempted to question the wizards within. She'd been compelled to wait until they had forced the gates open. An ancient scroll, drawn from her vast collection, had served well to mask the alley in illusion and hide her actions from those within the courtyard, but time was growing short, and she risked drawing the Watchful Order's attention, something she had managed to avoid for several years. Despite her hunger for the souls of the skulls, she had no wish to involve the authorities in her life any more than was necessary.

She focused on the circle of salt, whispering incantations and taking pleasure as the enchanted grains hissed on and between the cobbles.

"You can't be killed, can't be harmed, and you flaunt a long-avoided grave. You know and do far more than you should be able, considering your pathetic condition," she muttered, hoping that the nine skulls might hear her. "Yet this pitiful alley is your place. You return here time and again." The last grains of salt slipped through her fingers. "And I bid you return now!"

The salt sizzled and burned, white smoke gathering in streams that spun around the circle. It was an old and crude form of summoning, the enchanted salt a gift to her from an amorous and ambitious archfey whose name she could not recall, but for her purposes it was effective. More so as she knelt and pressed a stained strip of cloth to the cobbles, a torn shred of discarded dress soaked in the blood of the Loethe family.

The circle flared to a bright glow, tendrils of green rising into the spinning smoke as tiny arcs of energy lanced through the wide column. A distant murmur rose from the center of the circle, soft and muffled, growing louder by the breath until it became an angry cursing. Four spherical objects manifested, wreathed in green flame, swearing madly as they took shape, their empty sockets glaring at the hag.

"You face us alone, witch?" one said.

"Indeed I do," she replied with a grin, hearing the desperation in its voice and stretching her long fingers, a spell readied at the forefront of her mind. "And I intend to summon your brothers as well."

"You summon your own death!" it responded. "Leave us and we shall not hunt you down for this offense!"

"I was banished to this world and survived the wrath of Asmodeus himself," she said. "Pray pardon if I choose to decline your generous offer. Now come!"

Bolts of blue energy flew from her hands as she leaped, narrowly dodging four streams of green flame from the enraged skulls. She laughed at their efforts, inciting their fury to greater heights as she danced around their circle, hurtling spell after spell at the indestructible skulls. They spat more fire and chanted spells of their own, though with each they found their power weakening, the magic leeched bit by bit into the ensorcelled salt beneath them.

Within moments they grew more cautious, more conservative with their spells, and Mara pressed them further, forcing the circle of nine to divide their attentions between the alley they were bound to and the body they had possessed. Hungrily she accepted the minor pain of their fire or a well-aimed bolt of acid, still smelling the precious scent of their souls as she wore them down.

TWENTY

Wild eyed and breathless, Quessahn descended the stairs slowly, her gaze fixed on the spinning energies of the ritual, unable to look away. She flinched as Jinn reached for her arm, shying away from his touch. The wooden chest at the center of the spell glowed with a brilliant blue light and she imagined she could hear voices calling from within, emanating through the dried flesh and bloodstained fingernails of the collected fingers.

The walls hummed with power and she shivered.

"It's gone too far . . . ," she said, the terrible light dancing in her eyes as she drew away from the circle, visions of destruction still flashing through her mind as Jinn took her by the shoulders.

"Quess," he said quietly, holding her tight. "There isn't much time."

"Don't," she said. "Don't ask it. It's not safe—"

"Did the spell work? Do you know?" he asked, glancing at Rilyana as the human slumped forward on her hands, slowly recovering from the eladrin's attack.

Quessahn lowered her eyes and turned away.

"I saw it all," she answered quietly. "Like the beginning of the end."

"Where are they?" he pressed. "Where are the souls of the skulls?"

"No . . . ," Rilyana muttered. "Say nothing. He doesn't care about you or anyone . . ."

Quess glared at the human for several breaths, unsurprised to find Rilyana Saerfynn alive with Archmage Tallus dead at her feet. She drew her runic dagger as Rilyana stood, grinning slyly, her hands smeared with blood. Quessahn felt trapped between the skulls' ritual and the angel's prophecy, either condemning hundreds, possibly thousands, to horrible deaths. Jinn placed a hand on her shoulder, and for a moment she gripped the handle of the dagger tightly, but the ritual had begun and the prophecy would stand as long as Sathariel lived.

"Pharra's Alley—," she began, the words catching in her throat as the floor buckled and the walls shook. Dust rained down around them, accompanied by a hideous, droning chant from within the ritual circle.

"Silence!" Rilyana shouted, her hands clasped on either side of the wooden chest as a howling chant growled from within her. Vines curled through the walls, slithering like thorn-covered snakes and thrashing as they surrounded Quessahn and the deva.

They took on beastly shapes as they neared, forcing Quess away from Jinn and blocking the remote escape of the basement stairway. Thorns hissed against one another, dry leaves on the vines shuddering like ghastly whispers. Jinn took up his sword, slashing madly as they closed in upon him, though for each vine he cut, several more curled into being. They whipped at his face and arms, drawing tiny lines of blood on his pale skin.

Quessahn felt a tug on her ankle as arcane phrases spilled from her lips. Thorns pierced her boots as the vines tightened. The spell rushed through her arms and burned across her skin, gripping the thorns in a tight embrace. Dark patches of living metal spread over her flesh, encasing her and repelling the vines as she raised her dagger. Kissing the blade, she whispered a forgotten star's name across the steel. Flames leaped from the dagger, white hot and roaring, as she directed them to the vines.

She strode through the thorns as they blackened and withered, crumbling embers surrounding her in a sparkling cloud. Spreading fires at her whim, she freed Jinn in a shower of orange light and smoke before facing the ritual circle, its light reflecting off her black steel skin, tendrils of smoke rising from her shoulders as she regarded the furious Rilyana.

"You doom us all, eladrin!" the human shouted.

"Is she right, Jinn?" Quessahn asked. "You'll be giving Sathariel what he wants."

"No, I will *have* what he wants," Jinn replied. "There is a difference. I have a choice."

"You choose death, deva! Death, over and over again . . . but this time, you take thousands with you!" Rilyana shouted and chuckled low in her throat, though she appeared tired and drained, leaning on the pedestal as the house shook around them.

Quessahn turned to Jinn, looking deep into his golden eyes.

"Whom shall you trust?" he asked. "That is *your* choice."

She stared at him a moment longer, glancing once at the blood-covered Rilyana. She knew that either way, if Jinn or the angel failed, that thousands could die, souls fed to angels and gods that cared little for mortal choice. With a final burst of flame, she seared the wall of thorns blocking the stairway, reducing them to little more than ash and tumbling char.

"Pharra's Alley, buried deep beneath where the skulls gather," she said, the words cold and haunting as she said them, one burden lifted though it was quickly replaced by another. Rilyana's face twisted in fury, haloed by the eldritch light of the ritual. Quess took a defensive stance, raising her dagger as spells welled within her mind. "Go now. Kill the angel . . . I shall take care of his whore."

She wondered briefly if Jinn would hesitate, spare her a glance or a word before disappearing up the stairs and into the dark beyond, but his step was whisper quiet, and wordlessly, he was gone before even the ash had settled upon the stairs.

"He is a fool," Rilyana growled, mirroring Quess's stance, hands poised and standing in front of the wooden chest defensively.

"No, he is a single-minded bastard with little thought for anyone or anything that gets in his way," Quessahn replied, a cruel grin crawling across her steel-skinned lips as she kissed her blade again, invoking the names of ancient and powerful beings, terrible stars that streaked through her mind's eye like burning titans hurled from the heavens. "But he means well."

Quessahn stumbled back as the ritual circle flared with scarlet light, blinding her as the howling energy spun ever faster. More tremors shook the house, and she shielded her eyes, searching for Rilyana in the brilliant glare. She heard laughter within the circle, saw a pale silhouette with arms upraised, and Quess began to chant, tiny stars gathering along the length of her dagger.

The stars streaked toward the human, spinning around her and stabbing her with shafts of burning light. Rilyana screamed and writhed, batting at the stars even as she shouted her own spell. Force coalesced in the air between them and rushed from Rilyana's outstretched hand, slamming hard into Quessahn's chest. The eladrin crashed into the basement wall, the coppery taste of blood filling her mouth. She snarled, biting her tongue for more blood as she worked her next spell, speaking the words as the magic's red component stained her lips.

She traded burning shadows for numbing ice, foul curses for

searing acid as they fought, neither gaining ground. The ritual pulsed onward, possessed of its own life. The steel skin she had summoned smoked from the human's last spell, hissing as the last remnants of a blast of acid ate through her enchanted flesh and drew blood through the arcane steel. Her legs ached with exhaustion, and her mind burned with each spell she cast, but she still stood.

"This is futile, elf," Rilyana cried. "You cannot stop this. All you do is earn yourself an early death."

Quessahn's heart pounded and her legs felt heavy, every step seeming prelude to a fall that never came. Arcane patterns and constellations wheeled through her thoughts ponderously, pulsing with power in tune to the blood in her veins.

"Keep your condemnations," she said. "Unless I'm mistaken, your ritual is not yet complete, and death still hangs over your head as well."

"Momentarily, I assure you," the human replied. "Once Sathariel takes the souls of the Nine, you shall see more clearly, and your deva will die . . . again."

"You're scared. You tried to kill Jinnaoth despite Sathariel's warning. If he is to deliver the circle of skulls to the angel, why would you try to stop him?" Quessahn said as she stepped closer to the crimson light of the circle, seeing the fear hiding in Rilyana's eyes.

"Be quiet," Rilyana growled, her hands steaming with magic.

"Afraid the angel might forget about you, eh?" Quessahn asked.

"Be quiet!" the human shouted, spheres of burning ice erupting from her palms.

Quessahn threw herself to the side, dodging the worst of the spell but caught by stinging shards of frost as the spheres exploded behind her. Ice rattled against her metal skin, testing the remaining strength of the protective spell and cutting her where it had become weak. She rolled forward into the crimson light, chanting as she turned and uttered a fiendish name to complete her spell. Sparks leaped from her runic dagger, fluttering on the air and growing. Batlike wings sprung from small, burning bodies, and the fiery imps screeched, instantly turning on Rilyana and surrounding her.

They scorched her with tiny claws and bit at her flesh as she swatted at them and fell back, stumbling over the body of Archmage Tallus as she fought to escape them. Quessahn scrambled to her feet and approached the chest. Pale, desiccated fingers filled the container, each surrounded by a soft blue glow. A single bloody digit on top still bore fresh blood, the finger of the archmage, she surmised. Ancient runes covered the chest, mysterious yet familiar, in patterns more akin to the old magic of more than a century gone.

"This can't be," she said in disbelief. "Mystra's Weave is gone, the ritual would never work! The magic must be here, in this house. It's been waiting for this!"

"Clever." Rilyana muttered an incantation.

Quessahn felt her body grow lighter. The black steel on her hands melted away, revealing bruised skin and bloodied knuckles beneath. A wave of nausea left her dazed as the magic steel was dispelled, and she shivered as cold air hit her naked skin. She leaned on the pedestal and the chest, sickened further by the feel of cold flesh beneath her hands. Rilyana rushed forward and punched Quessahn, sending her sprawling to the floor. The spinning energies of the ritual streamed around her body as she gasped for air, shaking her head and rubbing her jaw.

"The skulls were once priests of Mystra, but they betrayed her, called upon Asmodeus, and promised their souls to him. He gave them a part of his power, an exchange that they betrayed in the end, though ultimately they failed. The immortality they sought became undeath, a curse. But they still had the archdevil's power, and their spell, their grand ritual, was left here, carved into a forgotten basement floor, waiting for their return," Rilyana said, studying the wooden chest, as if making sure the eladrin had not somehow fouled the magic.

"In exchange for what? What did the skulls offer Asmodeus?" Quess asked, crawling onto her side and spitting blood. She knew the answer, having made her own dark pacts in recent years, but she wanted to keep the human talking and confident.

"Their souls, obviously, but also an invitation, one that they had no intention of fulfilling, but an invitation nonetheless. One that Asmodeus now wishes to answer," Rilyana answered, kneeling before the injured eladrin.

"The prophecy . . . ," Quess whispered, one fist clenched around something cold and soft.

"Clever again," Rilyana replied, returning to the pedestal. "The skulls receive the damnation they deserve, Sathariel completes the prophecy, and I finish the ritual, joining him in immortality."

Quessahn crawled out of the ritual circle and rose on her hands, panting from the effort. She clutched one fist to her stomach as if in pain. Rilyana did not follow, hurled no more spells, and seemed to pay her no mind as she attended to the ritual's progress.

"Why are you telling me this?" Quessahn asked nervously, drawing the human's attention away from the chest.

"Isn't that how this all works?" Rilyana asked, smiling. "First I break your body; then I break your spirit. Besides, what fun is all this work without an audience?"

"I can still fight you," Quessahn replied angrily.

"Indeed you could," the human said, "but to what end?"

Quessahn stared at the woman for a breath before lowering her gaze. Pain wracked her limbs, and she felt brittle, like the bed of a dried river, wasted by floods of magic without rest. Stealthily she turned her hand up in her lap and opened her fist slowly to see the severed finger she'd stolen from the chest. Its blue glow gone, congealed blood stained her palm as she looked up, noting sluggish movement near Rilyana's foot.

"A bloody end," she replied at length and steeled herself to open the dam again, willing the first trickles of magic to well agonizingly in her mind.

>———W———<

Pain flowed through the skulls as they struggled to stand, Callak's legs failing as his suppressed mind grew stronger with every breath. They cursed in unison as the avolakia slithered out of the illusory skin of the old man, its alien form half hidden in shadow, tentacles writhing with a hideous grace. Green light glowed from its circular maw of hooks and tiny teeth, belching forth a wave of hissing liquid that flooded toward the skulls, spattering and popping across Callak's body.

Arguing among themselves, the five skulls remaining in the man's body managed to roll Callak's body beyond the widening pool of acid, one arm flailing madly as their legs twitched. The scent of burning flesh stung their sensitive nostrils, and bile rose in Callak's throat, an unfamiliar sense of nausea twisting in the body's gut.

Effram fumed as the others succumbed to mortal pain, howling as acid chewed through muscle and soft tissue, tendrils of foul smoke rising from the wounds. He could see the huddled children, pressed into a far corner of the room, staring at him with wide eyes beneath a painting of Callak Saerfynn as a young man. Taking control, Effram issued a swift chant and raised Callak's arm as silvery bolts of force ripped into the avolakia's body, leaving gaping wounds that wept with sickly yellow fluid.

But the beast merely twisted, undulating its quivering, bone-less body until the bleeding stopped, its tentacled maw already screeching an arcane counterspell. Effram responded quickly, but the other skulls panicked, attempting to wrest away his control of Callak's body even as waves of mortal fear rose from the recesses of the man's mind. Effram's efforts faltered, his spell ruined in a stream of spewing gibberish, Callak's tongue useless as their coop-eration fell apart. He could only watch as sheets of black flame rushed toward them.

They screamed together, the dark energy searing flesh and spirit alike as they were hurled against the wall, paralyzed and fighting to keep Callak's emotions at bay. His body twitched and thrashed against the wall, a broken puppet. The avolakia slithered nearer, multifaceted eyes turning among his many tentacles as he addressed them. His voice thundered through the space they occupied in Callak's mind, his tone soft and sinuous.

Hold still. This will only hurt for a moment.

"What do you want?" Effram shouted desperately as the others cursed, screaming in fury, everything they had worked for within sight, within reach, just a simple blood-letting away from their grasp, but still so far away, like a nightmare. "Tell us and it is yours! Anything!"

"Anything?"

Maranyuss grinned as she circled around the four skulls, limping and exhausted as thick smoke drifted through the scorched alley. Her hands flinched reflexively as the skulls withdrew from the edges of their circle, gathering together. She narrowed her crimson eyes and held her breath, suspecting a trick, but heard nothing but the wind whistling through the long alley, fluttering the tattered ends of her dark robes. She cast a furtive glance toward the House of Wonder, eyeing the courtyard through the gates and expecting her illusion to fall at any moment, exposing the battle and summoning the Watchful Order.

"Anything," they repeated in unison, their hollow voices small and desperate, dripping with a sickening weakness that Mara could almost taste. Her stomach growled and she bared her lionlike teeth, whipping stringy, black hair from her dark-skinned brow.

"Let me think," she replied slyly as a strange, distant wailing echoed from the ground.

The green flames of the circle flared brightly, roaring into an emerald pyre and turning the night into a pale, glowing day. Curses and shouts filled the circle as the remaining five manifested, spitting and burning with unparalleled fury. Mara backed away, smiling as they spun on one another, three hundred years of ruined work seeming to drive them entirely mad. She bowed mockingly as she retreated into the shadows but paused as an ominous tremor rumbled through the streets.

Her smile faded as thunder growled overhead in clouds that spun in slow, unnatural circles. Flashes of muted, orange flame hid behind the strange storm, and despite all, Mara sighed in brief contentment, recalling the tempests that would roar over the landscapes she'd once walked centuries ago. Strident horns echoed through the deserted avenues of Sea Ward as the Watch responded, booted feet on the march and drawing near as the circle of skulls fell eerily silent.

Their empty eyes fell on her, green fires flickering, mirroring the swinging lanterns of the Watch patrols.

"Enjoy this moment while you can, hag," they grumbled. "You have written the beginning of the end. The angel's prophecy will come. Our wrath is nothing next to what awaits you now."

Mara regarded them curiously then turned south, shivering despite herself as she imagined Jinnaoth facing down Sathariel. A thin column of pale crimson light, barely more than a staining mist, rose into the sky above the city. Another tremor rumbled beneath her feet, and shadowy figures turned a corner nearby, heading in her direction with lanterns blazing. Shouts echoed from within the House of Wonder as her illusion faded away. Robed figures streamed into the House's courtyard, drawn to the green flames of the skulls.

She twisted the silver ring on her hand, hiding herself in perfect illusion, and grinned at the circle of skulls, her arms crossed as they faded from sight, their green flames swirling into the cobbles. Fingering a large, ruby pendant around her neck, she eyed the last of the Nine's jade fire hungrily, eager to claim their souls.

"No, my friends. The angel has not claimed his prize. Not just yet," she whispered as she quickly melted into the alley's shadows.

Watchmen raced down Flint Street, pointing to the sky and blowing their horns as wizards gathered in the courtyard of the House of Wonder, their eyes fixed on the clouds, mouths agape in mystified awe.

Jinn's heart pounded in time with the thunder, impatience trembling in his blood. Raindrops slid down the length of his stolen sword as pale red light emanated from the edges of the roof, rising toward the sky. He stood upon the House of Thorne as though he'd been there for millennia, waiting for Sathariel to scent the knowledge he carried, to answer a call to battle issued years ago, shouted over the corpse of the woman Jinn loved.

Four steepled spires rose from the corners of the wide, flat roof, the remnants of a long-forgotten garden staining the wood and stone beneath his boots. Fragments of centuries-old pottery littered the edges of an iron railing that was loosely strung with wispy, abandoned webs. He eyed the dried, silk-wrapped husks of flies and mosquitoes, his thoughts drifting to ancient fields of war as the streets below shook with tremors.

A familiar warmth throbbed from the grip of his sword, rising through the steel and worming into his flesh like a living thing. Spikes of brief pain arced though his limbs as the steel vibrated in his grasp, a burning sensation that flooded into his mind with bloody thoughts and terrible hatred. The blade glimmered as he turned it over, studying the tiny, sparkling runes along the edge, their strange shapes and designs reaching for some lost piece of his soul. Though he could not read them or determine their origins, they flashed through his mind, burned into his memory like the script of a hallowed scroll.

The sword tugged at his wrist, and he turned, already picking out the regular beat of powerful wings through the whistling wind. Silvered armor glinted in the orange light of the fire curling through the clouds. Sathariel approached and Jinn clenched his jaw, holding the strange energy that boiled through his spirit at bay, bargaining with the stolen blade and promising blood in exchange for patience. Threads of gleaming silver in a mass of shadow distinguished themselves between the spires at the far end of the roof as the angel drew closer, wispy feathers like flames in silhouette at the edges of his wings. He held a long, curved blade of serrated steel at his side as he hovered between the spires, his cold, black eyes fixed on the deva.

"I know, Sathariel. I know where they are," Jinn said, holding his ground though every fiber of his being screamed to be loosed upon the angel.

"I suspected as much," Sathariel replied. "And my offer? You have come to accept it?"

"You know better than that," Jinn answered. "I followed your trail of bread crumbs, found this house, Archmage Tallus, Rilyana Saerfynn. I did all that you expected me to do, just to summon you here, to have this moment."

"And Variel?" the angel asked. "What of her soul? Shall she die with me on the point of your sword?"

"She made a choice," Jinn said coldly. "It was the wrong one."

"Indeed. I could rip the secret from your mind, deva. Leave you here to watch, helpless," Sathariel responded, pinpoints of blue light flashing in his black eyes.

"Then I pray you be quick about it. I have been waiting far too long," Jinn growled, raising his sword. The steel hummed, pulsing like a second heart.

"An eternity," the angel replied.

Sathariel charged, his eyes little more than streaks of blue light, twin stars falling toward Jinn's eager sword.

TWENTY-ONE

NIGHTAL 22, THE YEAR OF DEEP WATER DRIFTING (1480 DR)

Jinn fell back, circling the rooftop as Sathariel whirled around him, a blur of black wings and flashing silver. Each strike of the angel's blade against his own resonated like a thunderclap, threatening to break his bones. Centuries of endless battle echoed through him, every identity he'd ever lived fought with him, making him quick and strong. Four thousand years of experience directed his blade, but it was not enough.

Pain shot through his right elbow as Sathariel pounded on his blade, steel grating loudly as their swords met, squealing as they parted. Jinn spun from the slash, whirling to deflect the next, searching for an opening, but the angel turned as well, thrusting from his side. Leaning back from the blow, Jinn caught the edge of the roof and glanced down upon the street below and the battle lines being drawn between the Watch and the ahimazzi. The iron railing stopped his fall but kept him still as the angel's blade cut a thin line across his chest. Blood blossomed on his tunic as he rolled away, his blade raised to meet Sathariel's charge, but the angel was gone.

He winced at the stinging pain in his chest, turning slowly and listening. The stolen sword writhed in his grip, turning with him as if it conducted its own hunt. Instinct told him to hurl the weapon away, somehow repulsed by its mysterious power, but he had no other options, preferring a potentially cursed blade to the suicidal prospect of fighting the angel barehanded.

The air *thumped* behind him, and he spun, immediately deflecting the long, silver blade aimed for his stomach but thrown off balance. Sathariel's fist crashed into his face, and stars exploded behind his eyes. His sword licked out, slashing at where the angel had been then reversing its course, chasing the feathery wisps of shadow in Sathariel's wake. Blood streaming from his nose, he turned, cutting at anything that moved, trying to focus his eyes as he regained his balance.

"You were tricked into coming here, deva," Sathariel said, his voice thundering from all directions. "Led here, step by step, as you fought through the ranks of the Vigilant Order, seeking vengeance even as you grew ever colder to the lost love that began this journey. I knew you would succeed where others had failed. I knew you would bring me the circle of skulls."

"Never!" Jinn screamed, spitting blood. "I will never give them to you! I baited you here with them! I used you!"

"A delusion, Jinnaoth," the angel replied. "Your single-minded pursuit blinded you, made you see what I wanted you to see. My trail of bread crumbs, as you called it. And here you are, bleeding, flailing about, and well out of your depth."

"No," Jinn muttered under his breath.

"My offer still stands. You may take Variel, perhaps even your elf, and leave this place, a fair exchange," Sathariel said, the beating of his wings somewhere close by.

"And leave Waterdeep to you? To drag the Hells' influence into the streets?" Jinn asked. "I think not."

"Think at what you might gain, deva. One small sacrifice, one section of this city devoted to Asmodeus, could begin the war you've always wanted. Think of it! A final war. An end to thousands of years of searching, battle after battle without an end in sight," the angel said, appearing at the northern end of the roof, wings outstretched between the spires, bright sword held low.

Nausea gripped Jinnaoth as he considered the idea, attracted to the thought of a last war, being a soldier, knowing that every kill and little victory would stand and last. Then shame flooded through him, and he banished the thought, his very soul shaken by the prospect of dealing with a minion of Asmodeus.

"This is the final war."

"I assure you, it is not." Sathariel chuckled. "This is one man's pathetic last stand—"

"Every day!" Jinn shouted, raising his blade, his golden eyes blazing with fury. "Every day for thousands of years, every fight, every stolen crust of bread, every murderer brought to justice, every innocent slain! *This* is the final war. It rages through time and needs no arrogant god or even his silver-tongued angel to set boundaries upon when it ends, least of all a simple soldier like myself!"

"You are beaten. I spoke true when I said I would rip the information from your mind!" The angel growled and charged, crossing the distance between them in a half a breath. Their blades clashed twice, then locked, steel grinding on steel, as Sathariel pressed his strength against Jinn's. The angel's wings beat furiously as he pushed Jinn's back to a crumbling spire. His free hand rose and clutched the deva's head.

Icy tendrils wormed across Jinn's scalp as he struggled to push the angel away, the stolen blade squirming in his hand, shaking like a caged beast begging to be set free. Power flowed from the weapon into his arm, and he felt some strength returning, but he could not contest the angel's power. With a gasp of horror, he felt a single cold tendril slip into his thoughts and drag the location of the skulls' souls from his mind.

The house shook as the tendril withdrew. Red light flared through the sky as the angel's icy eyes gleamed in victory—the last component of the terrible prophecy within his grasp.

"You played your part well, deva," Sathariel whispered as he pulled his hand away from Jinnaoth's scalp. "I will let you live, a reward for your fine service."

Jinn pushed on the silver blade of the angel, breathless and enraged. A curious glow rose between them, and the angel's wings slowed their pressing beat. Tiny sigils flared on the edge of Jinn's stolen blade, throbbing as the angel prepared to leave, angling his body to take flight even as he held Jinn against the spire. As soon as the silver blade's pressure lessened, Jinn shoved, bursting with speed as the black wings turned and twisted.

The glowing sword became a blur as he chased the angel backward, sparks flying as they dueled, Sathariel just one misstep away from escaping. Jinn roared as he fought, heartbeats slipping by faster and faster, everything he'd ever battled for sliding away from him. Unnatural swiftness infected his blade and rushed down his arm. He didn't care where the sword had come from, why the Vigilant Order had guarded it, or even why he had chosen to steal it from them in the first place. It had shed the blood of the order well, and he was determined to sheath it in the heart of the angel.

With a deft twist of his body, Sathariel slid to the side, and Jinn stumbled forward, though he managed one last arcing slash, quick as a striking snake, before the angel could get away. Sathariel howled in pain as he ascended into the sky.

For half a breath, Jinn felt overwhelming despair crush him to his knees, defeated and used as the angel escaped. But before he could draw breath or curse all the gods he could name, a peculiar rush of alien power overcame him and left him gasping for air. Strange energy flowed through him, burning from the sword in his hand. Warm and quiet, it soothed his rage into a tranquil calm, the likes of which he had not experienced for many years.

He raised the sword, eyeing the smear of crimson on the steel as it dripped and fell, dissipating before it touched the rooftop—the ethereal flesh and blood of an angel.

He stood as the sword brightened, nearly invisible sigils along its length gleaming in the scarlet column of light. Blue spheres whispered around him as they rose from the house, reflected on the edge of the sword. As Sathariel's blood flowed down the edge, strange patterns were revealed, sigils that burned themselves into his mind. Somewhere, in the eldest of his forgotten memories, a fragment of his soul read the language on the blade and felt its ancient power.

Images of the Astral Sea flashed through his thoughts, and he recalled a time long before flesh and blood, when powerful laws were spoken to those angelic beings serving at the pleasure of the gods.

"Sathariel," he shouted, his voice full of command. He raised the glowing blade, speaking the divine words written in flowing script on the guard as if he had spoken them a hundred times. "By Zaphkiel the Watcher and Dumariel of the Eleventh Hour, and by all the lost gods of Mulhorand, I bind thee, dark spirit! And I command you . . . to stand!"

The angel, little more than a distant blot against the clouds, paused and turned.

"You do not want this, deva," the angel replied, speaking as though next to Jinn, growling in his ear. "You would be better served dying or running for your life, but this—"

"Silence!" Jinn roared and held the blade higher, its light shining on Sathariel's silvered armor and sword.

"You do not know what you do, nor do you have any idea what you wield. Drop that blade and leave this place, and I shall forgive this sickening offense. You cannot survive this," the angel said, an edge of anger creeping into his thunderous words.

"I have outlived gods, Sathariel. I intend to outlive yours, and by all the souls in the Astral Sea, I shall outlive you!" Jinn cried. His sword blazed in his hand, and his golden eyes shone with the terrible brilliance of the angel he once was. "Now stand!"

"This is your choice, deva? You make it freely, then?" Sathariel asked, drifting closer, returning to the rooftop, bound by ancient laws and mortal magic.

"It is and I do," Jinn replied.

"The choice is made. Let the contract be decided," the angel intoned, his voice ominous and formal.

Sathariel charged, eerily silent as Jinn rushed to meet him.

Rilyana raised her hands, exultant as the ritual circle brightened, long arcs of magic flashing through the runes in the floor. Quessahn shielded her eyes and backed away from the circle, watching in horror as power flowed through the room and spun around the small pedestal at its center. The ground quaked as blue motes of bright light ascended from the wooden chest, each one whispering or moaning as they turned in languid circles. The remnants of dead vines at the room's perimeter twisted and turned green, sprouting dark red roses.

"Now!" Rilyana cried. "The deva is dead, and I shall never die!"

She paced around the pedestal, crimson energy eddying around her ankles, blue lights spinning from the grisly box, but Rilyana appeared no different than before.

She turned on the pedestal, eyes narrowed, lips trembling in anger as she searched for something. Her hands shook as she ground her teeth, seething as she waited, staring at the burns on her arms, feeling the bruises on her face. She traced the sigils upon the chest and scratched at her wrist, drawing thin lines of blood that she stared at in horror.

"Mortal . . . ?" she said. "Nothing! What is this?"

"Something wrong?" Quessahn asked, rising to one knee and wincing at the effort.

"What did you do?" Rilyana growled.

"I studied the notes of Archmage Tallus. And I'm fairly certain you need this," Quessahn said and produced the bloodstained finger of the wizard in her palm.

"Thieving whore!" the human shouted and rushed at the eladrin.

Quessahn allowed Rilyana two strides before lifting her dagger and willing the spell within it to be freed. A curling stream of darkness shot from the end of the blade, eel-like and screeching as it connected with Rilyana's chest. The human's eyes widened as she fell back, crimson stains blossoming around the tentacle as it drained the blood from her body. She wrestled with the black eel, screaming as it pressed her to the ground.

The taste of blood, salty and metallic, filled Quessahn's mouth as she held on to the dagger and the writhing ebony rope. Several cuts on her arms disappeared, bruises faded, and her breath came easily as the spell fed upon Rilyana's pulse, passing the energy back through the eladrin's blade. Stronger, she stepped into the ritual circle as the shadowy eel faded, leaving the human pale and tired.

"You've taken more lives than I care to count. I thought it was about time you gave a little life back," Quess said.

"Parlor tricks, elf," Rilyana grumbled as she tried to stand. "I have studied magic since I was eleven years old. I will show you real power!"

"When you were eleven, I was one hundred and fifty. Yet it seems I learned all I needed to defeat you within the last two days," Quessahn countered, squeezing tightly the cold finger of the archmage, her thoughts whispering his name as Rilyana rose to a low crouch.

The human gasped as a hand wrapped around her ankle and pulled. She fell forward, scrambling to free herself, kicking and screaming as the body of Tallus crawled on top of her legs and pulled himself onto her back. Quessahn stepped back from the spectacle as nine bloody fingers wrapped around Rilyana's throat and tightened in a murderous embrace.

"You should have studied more," Quess said as the human's face turned dark red, straining for air and scratching at the stone floor. The eladrin held up the severed finger, recalling the words of Maranyuss from the candlelit gloom of the Pages Curious bookshop. "The souls are bound in the left ring finger, and the bodies are either abandoned . . . or controlled."

A hideous croak escaped Rilyana's lips as the last bit of precious air she could manage left her. Her eyes bulged unnaturally, her face contorted in desperate rage for a moment before her eyelids went slack. Her throat bent forward with a sickening, muffled crunch that sent shivers down Quessahn's spine. She dropped the archmage's finger, letting his body fall limp on top of Rilyana's.

She stared at the wooden chest and the pedestal for long moments, a brief hope fading as the ritual continued to spin and growl with power. Lashing out, she shoved the wooden chest from the pedestal. It crashed to the stone floor, scattering its morbid contents across the rune-carved circles, yet the ritual continued. Her thoughts raced, searching the room for something, anything that might end the spell before it was too late.

"Perhaps *I* should have studied more," she muttered, cursing as another tremor flowed outward from the pedestal. As dust fell from the ceiling, she looked up, and the turning blue motes of light, each a stolen soul, continued to rise into the floor above, to join the crimson column of light that had haunted her vision. "I can't stop it now."

Abandoning the ritual, she ran up the stairs, fresh strength flowing through her body as she made her way through the House of Thorne, vibrant red roses leading the way.

She dashed out of the shaking house and into a garden full of unseasonable green and deep red blooms. Skidding to a stop before the gate, she drew her dagger at the sounds of battle erupting in the streets. The Watch had engaged the ahimazzi mob, the Watchful Order at their backs, each trying to get closer to the glowing House of Thorne.

Above her the brilliant column of crimson light pulsed, the star-like souls drifting below the clouds. Flames erupted in the spinning, unnatural storm, though fire did not rain from the sky as in her vision. She flinched as a black wing appeared over the side of the roof and stumbled back, steel ringing through the air.

"Jinn is still alive," she said. "But if Sathariel knows where the skulls' souls are hidden . . ."

The ahimazzi numbers pressed hard against the Watch, pushing to escape the closed circle of homes in the direction of Feather Street—roughly three blocks away from Pharra's Alley and the nine souls Sathariel so desperately hunted.

Shouts erupted from the shadows of the far street as more lights appeared around the corner, bright lanterns shining green through tinted glass. The officers engaged the ahimazzi in strict lines, spreading out to fight the shambling men and women. Horns blared through the night air, calling for reinforcements as the Watchful Order hurled spells into the soulless crowd.

Quessahn cursed despite the Watch's efforts, knowing that there were other soulless in Sea Ward and fearing they might be caught too late. She ran toward the battle, following the sound of an authoritative voice from among the ranks of the Watch. Incantations slithered across her body as she ran, an inky darkness manifesting around her, cloaking her from sight and muffling her footsteps. She slipped through the soulless, slashing indiscriminately as she made her way through the press of stinking bodies, not stopping until she had breached the edge of the fight.

Dismissing the spell, she approached an aging Watchman.

"Officer! Good sir!" she panted, getting his attention before drawing too close.

"What—?" the Watchman turned, sword in hand, a tall, lean man with gray streaking his dark brown hair and peppering his thick mustache. He lowered the blade slightly, glancing at the fight. "Good gods, lass! Get out of here before you get skewered. I nearly gutted you myself! Can't you see we're a bit engaged at the moment?"

"Indeed, sir," she replied. "But I need your help! I can't explain right now, but unless you want this night to get any worse, we need to protect Pharra's Alley!"

"What do you know about 'this night,' eh?" he asked, blowing his horn again and grinning as another patrol arrived. "I've half a mind to have you taken in for questioning. Unless you want to spend the night in a cell, I suggest you let us work!"

Quessahn swore under her breath, having no time to explain herself.

"I was a friend to Rorden Allek Marson," she called over the din of shouts and clashing blades. "And if you have any respect for his memory at all, you will—"

"I patrolled with Allek Marson for five years!" he growled, fire in his sharp eyes. "And I'll not have some fey lass with a fancy dagger in her belt question my loyalty to the man, gods rest his poor soul!"

"Good! Then follow me and keep the bastards responsible for his death from killing anyone else!" she countered angrily, matching his stare.

He bristled for a breath, glancing between her and the battle behind them, then nodded reluctantly.

"Aeril!" he shouted, turning a startled young officer around. "Grab one of those patrols and follow me." The man saluted and ran ahead of the arriving patrol, waving them to a stop. "Naaris, hold this line! Warden Tallmantle has more patrols en route from North Ward. And take one of these rabid derelicts alive if possible!"

"Now, lass," he said, turning back to Quessahn and striding north. "Commander Gravus Tavian at your service, at least until I find out what's going on, then I'm likely to have you arrested by morning. Sound fair?"

"Quessahn Uthraebor," she replied, "not 'lass,' and if we are alive by morning, I will count myself lucky to sleep for several days in one of your cells!"

Jinn felt a new strength flowing through his arms as he bashed Sathariel's sword aside and ripped a burning gash through the angel's breastplate. Sathariel roared in pain and drove the deva back, scoring a jagged cut on his arm. Jinn ignored the wound. Sathariel seemed weakened. Perhaps the stolen sword had evened the ground between them. He tumbled out of the path of the angel's blade and into a defensive crouch.

His body tensed like a spring as he jumped again, clashing with the angel in midair. He remembered things, envisioning the battles he had fought in the palaces of demon princes and on the scorched fields of lost Mulhorand. His thirst for vengeance was gone, and he embraced that quiet part of his heritage that had always urged him to fight, to the exclusion of all else, as a mortal angel drenched in the bloody business of a greater good. He had forgotten much of that, caught up in the daily lives and trials of mortals, and it had taken a mysterious blade stolen from his enemy to remind him.

It crashed against Sathariel's vambrace, leaving scorch marks where it touched the silver armor and drawing wispy streams of ethereal blood in its wake. Though he exulted in the blade's power, a lingering suspicion of the blade made the steel feel strange in his hand. Though he felt he had stolen it of his own free will, he feared other forces were at work.

"Fool of dead gods," Sathariel rumbled as they traded blows relentlessly. "You have no idea what you have involved yourself in!"

The silver blade whistled by Jinn's ear, drawing sparks on the iron railing as he ducked and thrust at the angel's arm. Sathariel's quick blade slapped his strike aside.

"I've always been here. It was never my place to understand or question the desires of the gods," he replied, rolling away from the edge of the roof.

A silver blur followed him as Sathariel whirled, slashing in a wide arc. Jinn stopped and braced himself, sword raised to block the angel's blow and wincing at the force behind it.

"Then you are ignorant as well as a fool," the angel thundered, "and that blade you wield has suffered many such fools. They died well before drawing my blood, and they died gladly, I assure you."

Jinn glanced at the shining sword then cursed as Sathariel took advantage of his distraction, opening a deep cut in his side and reopening the wound he'd suffered from Lucian Dregg. The pain was fleeting, overcome by the stolen sword's curious hunger and old power. He pressed back, parrying the angel's blade and opening a sister wound in Sathariel, dragging the length of his sword through the angel's side. Steel crashed between them, but neither called out in pain, unwilling to give the other the satisfaction.

The sky was alive with dancing lights and rolling fire. Whispers and wails surrounded them even as the streets below echoed with battle. Dark clouds roiled in wide circles, thundering though the rain had stopped. Tremors rumbled from the abandoned house. Though he battled relentlessly, the stolen sword fought with a passion of its own. It squirmed in his grip, the sensation sickening, but he could not release it, did not dare try. He clung to the steel and prayed he had made the right decision, prayed for his very soul.

Striking low and spinning to his right, Jinn nimbly avoided a killing blow, but Sathariel rushed forward, slamming into the deva with his armored shoulder. Jinn stumbled back, deflecting another fatal slash but taking a deep cut across the back of his leg in return. He fell to one knee, gritting his teeth against the pain, and tried to rise but faltered, pain shooting up the side of his body like fire.

He watched helplessly as the angel drew close and stared at the blade as though it had betrayed him. Heart pounding in his chest, Jinn raised the sword, determined to fight from the ground if he had to, though the hopelessness of his resolve sat bitterly in his thoughts. He had experienced a thousand deaths, both spectacular and mundane, but as he looked into the twinkling blue lights of the angel's pitted eyes, he saw something different. His rage battled with a faint hope as he spoke.

"This sword . . . this choice I've made," Jinn said, gasping. "Will I die? Truly die?"

"None can know, deva. The contract has never been answered before," Sathariel replied, his sword rising.

"Contract?" Jinn asked, his eyes fixed on the silver blade over the angel's shoulder, his thoughts racing as a hundred battles came to mind, a hundred deaths flashing through his soul, each life fading with the same wish, for one more chance to relive the moment.

"No time for that now. Farewell, Jinnaoth. You should never have come to this world," Sathariel replied, his voice ominously gentle.

The silver sword fell, its arc mirroring that of a hundred others, an executioner's strike, clean and perfect.

TWENTY-TWO

The stolen blade shivered in his hand as he followed the stroke of the angel's sword, his death written on its edge. Though he had faced his ending a thousand times, instinct would not let him rest again so soon. The motions were reflex, written in hopeless thoughts on a battlefield whose name he could not recall. He had died that day with a glimmer of regret burned into his thoughts, a regret that moved his good leg and placed strength in his arm.

He hacked at Sathariel's blade, battering it aside as he lunged within the angel's guard and drove the steel of his stolen blade deep into Sathariel's chest. The shining sword screamed through the silvered armor. It burned and hissed through the angel as ethereal blood streamed from the injury.

Sathariel's sword clattered to the ground, and he gripped Jinn's shoulders, wings beating furiously in a panic to escape. The deva held on tightly, keeping the angel close as Sathariel howled in his ear, pulling him toward the iron railing. Glowing light poured from the wound as the angel's struggles slowed and grew sluggish. With a final beat of his massive wings, Sathariel fell.

Jinn collapsed at the edge of the roof, gripping the deep cut in his leg as the angel slumped upon the iron railing, his armor caught on rusted spikes, his wings stretched out, twitching as his life bled away. The deva held on to the hungry blade, clutching it fast and bearing witness to the long-sought death of his enemy.

"I do not envy you . . . deva," Sathariel rasped as ribbons of shadow bled from his body, drawn into the shining blade in his chest. "In victory I was to be rewarded . . . finished . . . a powerful vassal of a pleased god . . . but you . . . you must now go on . . ."

Jinn pulled close as the angel's voice grew weak, sparks of warm power racing through his sword arm.

"Why? What do you mean?" he asked.

"The contract . . . lies in your hand . . . ," Sathariel replied, chuckling softly. "Forged when the world was young . . . a contract of steel . . . a bargain made between the forces of darkness and light . . . an invitation to Asmodeus . . ."

Jinn stared at the blade as it drank the angel's shadowy essence, devouring the darkness in his wings. It drew rivers of ethereal blood from the black pits of Sathariel's eyes. It glowed brighter with every strip of angelic flesh. Jinn released it and fell back, the horrid power still pulsing through his blood.

"You are now a balance . . . fulcrum between this world and a god's wrath . . ." Sathariel laughed again, writhing in pain. "Devils and angels will seek you out, deva! Your wars will never end! And every time . . . you must choose . . ."

The angel shook as he chuckled, weaker and weaker, his mighty wings shrinking to little more than feathered stumps of shadow. Jinnaoth felt the pain in his leg subside, the wound nearly closed by the sword's power, and a sickening hollow formed in his gut. Nauseated, he looked away, staring into the crimson column of light and the burning clouds overhead, their fires already lessening as the angel died.

"Why do you tell me this?" he asked.

"Because . . . it pleases me to do so . . . ," Sathariel answered. Then he shuddered violently, falling silent as his body fell apart, the remnants taken up by the wind in a cloud of ash, embers, and dissipating feathers.

The sword remained lodged in the silvered breastplate, and Jinn stared at it with a mixture of awe and terror. He touched its pommel once, and his mind was assaulted with a flash of power. It showed him images of the Astral Sea and a burning ocean of fire, veils of energy rippling across a spinning sphere of brilliant blues; rough browns; and drifting, white clouds—the very moment he had chosen to follow his gods into a world of flesh and blood.

He snatched his hand away from the sword, his wrist burning from the contact as he stood and limped away from the weapon. He clutched his arm close, cradling it as he retreated, leaving the sword behind and slowly descending a narrow stairway into the House of Thorne.

>———W———<

Shattered glass crunched beneath their boots as Quessahn and Tavian ran up the length of Flint Street, slowing as they neared the House of Wonder and stopping short at the grisly scene that awaited them. Smaller tremors rumbled through the cobbles as they edged closer to the scattered bodies sprawled across the avenue, several grouped together near the mouth of Pharra's Alley. Quessahn counted almost two dozen, all of them in the dingy, stinking robes of the ahimazzi, their curved blades rattling on the ground as the street vibrated slightly then quickly ceased.

A peaceful silence once again fell over the darkened ward. Steam rose from the slowly cooling bodies as Quessahn stepped through and over them to peer into the alley.

"What in blazes is this? Did someone beat us to the punch?"

Tavian grumbled, covering his nose and mouth, the stench of the soulless even more pungent in death.

"I don't think so," Quessahn replied as she glanced to the southern sky and pointed. The column of crimson light had disappeared, leaving only a sparkling cloud of blue, drifting in the wind as the roiling clouds fell apart and returned to their normal courses. The fires in the sky were gone, and the chilling mist returned, setting Quess to shivering even as a glimmer of hope warmed in her heart. "He must have done it," she whispered. "It must have been Sathariel himself . . . tied to the ritual somehow. The angel died and—"

"What in Torm's name are you babbling on about, lass?" Tavian asked and grasped her shoulder, shaking the daze from her eyes. "An angel? Rituals? You're not making any sense!"

"No, she is not," a voice added from the alley as a figure approached, two faintly glowing eyes accompanied by the tapping of a wooden staff. Quess flinched for a moment but calmed as the familiar wizard came into view, dark robes covered in ancient, barbaric runes and accented by guards of leather. Long braids covered his shoulders and he wore a strange, wavy-bladed sword at his side. His eyes, blue orbs of glowing ice set in a too-pale face, regarded Quessahn curiously. "However, I am eager to hear the tale of this night if you are willing to spare her for a moment or two, Commander."

"Master Bastun, I wasn't aware that you had returned from Shadowdale," Quess said, inclining her head slightly.

"Apparently not," Bastun replied.

"I'll do better than spare her for a moment," Tavian said, sheathing his sword. "I'll join you for a bit of a chat. Warden Tallmantle will want a full report, and my own curiosity will not easily be put to rest until the tale is told . . . well, at least this young woman's version of it, that is." The last he added with a narrowed glance at the eladrin before extending his hand to the wizard. "Well met, Master Bastun, was it?"

"It was—I mean, it is," Quessahn stammered, her tongue caught between her racing thoughts and her racing heart, keeping the southern sky in sight as she introduced the officer. "This is Commander Gravus Tavian. He was escorting me, that is, I was leading him—"

"Calm, child. There is time. Shall we go inside and warm ourselves?" Bastun said, placing an unnaturally cold hand upon her arm as he directed the officer toward the house gate.

"You read my mind, Master Bastun," Tavian replied. He shouted over his shoulder as they strode toward the gate, "Aeril! You enjoy the cold so much, keep this alley secure until I return."

Quessahn walked with them slowly, distracted as she stared at the sky in wonder, looking for Jinnaoth until Flint Street was out of sight. Even as she tried to arrange her thoughts, placing her experiences of the past two days in some kind of understandable order, she kept thinking of the deva.

For all that had passed between them, she longed to see him alive and well—and, almost shamefully, she hoped he felt the same.

Maranyuss spied upon the eladrin as she walked through the gate of the House of Wonder. Wizards filled the alley, pointing to the sky and discussing wild theories on what had just occurred in hushed voices. Officers of the Watchful Order began gathering the magic-users in groups, questioning them as the Watch set out to return order to the ward.

The night hag stroked the ruby pendant around her neck, calming her greedy hunger for the skulls' souls, patient enough to wait until the excitement wore down. She smiled, despite herself, at the little victory they had achieved, though she would never admit such a thing to her strange allies.

"Interesting evening, eh?" Briarbones remarked as he shuffled up to her, leaning on a branch that served as a makeshift walking stick. "It is nice to be surprised every century or two."

"Surprised?" Mara asked.

"Well, it's not every day that a gruesome series of mass murders results in what some might construe as good news. Most end quite tragically, that is, if anyone survives to tell the tale at all," he answered. "Though, I must say I am curious to hear Jinnaoth's version of events."

"I'm sure you are. You knew about that sword he carried, didn't you?" Mara asked, her eyes flashing crimson through the illusory gaze she wore.

"I suspect I knew just as much as you did." Briar grinned slyly. "Much more than him, at any rate. I honestly thought it was just a myth, a bedtime tale for good little devils to hear upon their fiery pillows at night . . . but the deva would have thrown it away if we had told him."

"And we would all be dead," Mara added casually, not feeling too strongly one way or another about the prospect, but not disappointed at being counted among the living. "Do you suppose we were nobly withholding a secret? Or do we merely value our lives more than we do his?"

"Well, one doesn't grow as old as I am by acting overly noble," Briarbones replied. "Make of that what you will."

"I shall," she said, slipping her hand into the crook of his good arm as they strolled away from the suddenly crowded alleyway. Mara was somewhat troubled, considering the deva as a strange emotion flickered in her fickle heart, and she wondered at it, musing it to be some kind of caring or perhaps a less disdainful form of apathy. She marveled at the curiosity a breath before scowling. "I have spent far too much time among mortals."

"Yes," Briar agreed, hissing. "They tend to get under the skin after a few centuries, don't they?"

"Disgusting," she added.

"Is it the struggle, do you think?" the avolakia asked. "Watching them fight and scratch, clawing at one another and praying to any god that will listen, always crying for something better?"

"No, I think it's the hope," Maranyuss answered. "It's rather unique among them. Where I'm from there's precious little of it."

"There is a certain appeal to that as well," Briar added. "I'll never get used to the smell of them, though."

EPILOGUE

The street below Pages Curious was as busy as ever as Jinnaoth stood by his window, staring out through the narrowed curtains. A blur of people rushed by beneath his golden gaze, though, day by day, he found himself looking for only one among the crowds. Since returning he had slept little and eaten less, troubled each day he walked the city streets, wondering when the moment he both feared and desired would come—and receiving his answer early in the morning, when the broadcriers began hawking stories of angels and bloody murders.

As the sun set and shadows lengthened, he saw her face in the crowd, pushing her way through the heavy traffic before gateclose. A large bag was slung over Quessahn's shoulder as she approached the bookshop, sliding along the edges of the street before attempting to cross. Jinn suspected she had chosen to leave the House of Wonder, having learned all that she could in her time there, and he had wondered if she would make for the High Forest again, a return to her people.

She stopped suddenly in the street, tilting her head as he caught her eye through the window. Her hair blew in the cold breeze, dancing across her shoulders, and as bodies passed her by, a lone still figure among the throngs, she smiled at him. In a blink he saw her again as he had in the tower of Archmage Tallus, the faint memory of her looking at him, surrounded by a field of green and smiling, a vision of a forgotten love in the deep forest. He smiled back at her as she continued toward the shop, but his grin faded as she disappeared below his view.

He looked down as he drew the curtains closed, raising his left arm, brow furrowed as he pulled his sleeve back to stare at the pale skin of his wrist. Every day since he had slain Sathariel, he had studied the strange scar that had been burned into his flesh, a divine sigil, some kind of angelic script that tugged at his memory and gave him only fleeting visions of the Astral Sea, flashing images of the bright and powerful gods he had once followed. They looked upon him in the visions, cold and uncaring, speaking to him though he could not hear what they said.

The bell on the front door rang downstairs, drawing his attention away from the scar, listening as footsteps crossed the bookshop floor and took the first few steps leading to his small room. They climbed the stairs slowly, as if dreading what they might find or the reaction they might garner.

Jinnaoth looked from the closed door to the foot of his bed, finding the sister symbol to the scar on his wrist glowing on the blade he had stolen from the Vigilant Order and had left embedded in the smoking armor of Sathariel atop the House of Thorne. Since then he had thrown it away dozens of times and seen it destroyed by a skilled blacksmith who was well paid for the effort.

But each time it returned to him, appearing someplace close by, occasionally returning to his hand or slipped beneath his belt, hanging ominously at his side. He had thrown it away again that morning, casting it into the sea after hearing the broadcriers at dawn, selling tales of his last night in Sea Ward, his name and description curiously absent from the printed text.

As Quessahn lightly knocked on his door, Jinn felt he was ready to accept the responsibility of the sword, though he wondered—and feared—if the eladrin would accept him along with it. He crossed the room and reached for the door, letting his actions be guided, for once, by hope.

An excerpt from

ELMINSTER
MUST DIE

ED GREENWOOD

PROLOGUE

The wardrobe was a cursedly tight fit.

Even for one of the most handsome, suave, lithely athletic, and debonair nobles currently inhaling the sweet air of the Forest Kingdom of Cormyr.

Even a sneering rival would have had to grant that Lord Arclath Argustagus Delcastle was all of those things in the judgment of many a lass, not just his own.

Yet, despite all of those splendid qualities, the heir of House Delcastle could *just* squeeze himself inside the massive oak wardrobe. To keep company with old mildew and older dust. Whose familiar reek reassured him that this was the palace, all right.

Left knee above his left ear and fingers braced like claws to keep his cramped body from slipping and making the slightest sound, Arclath stared into the darkness wrought by the closed door right in front of his nose, and prayed fervently that Ganrahast and Vainrence would be in a hurry and keep their secret meeting brief.

So it would end, for instance, before he happened to need to sneeze.

No one ever came to this dusty, long-disused bedchamber high in the north turret—or so Arclath had once thought. He'd found the place after a feast some years ago, while wandering the palace to walk off the effects of far too much firewine before he braved the dark night streets homeward, and had employed it thereafter to enjoy the charms of a certain palace maid in private—a sleek delight since sadly gone off to Neverwinter in the employ of a wealthy merchant—and then as a retreat to sit alone and think, when that need came upon him.

It had come as a less than pleasant surprise, moments ago, to learn that the Royal Magician of Cormyr, the widely feared Ganrahast, and his calmly ruthless second-in-command, "Foedoom" Vainrence, favored this same north turret bedchamber for private parleys.

Arclath hadn't had time to try to dodge into the little space behind the wardrobe, which stood straight and square where the bedchamber wall behind curved. He'd only just had time enough to scramble into the closet, drag its door closed, and compose himself into cramped but silent immobility before the two powerful wizards had come striding into the room, muttering grimly.

They were more than muttering now.

Arclath felt an itch starting, and set his teeth in exasperation. He should have known *someone* came here to discuss confidential and sensitive matters, given the warding spells that always made his skin tingle and prickle on the stair ascending to this uppermost room.

A moment later, a glow kindled in the darkness right beside Arclath's head, startling him almost into gasping aloud.

He managed—*just*—not to do that.

Instead, he froze, chilled and helpless, as an old spell flared into life right beside him.

A radiance that slowly became a silent, floating scene of a nearby spot he recognized. That same stretch of stair where the wards tingled, looking down from the turret room.

A scene where someone stood silently, hands raised to claw at the wards that were keeping her at bay, eyes blazing in frustrated fury. It was someone who'd been dead for years, a ghost Arclath had seen once from afar.

The Princess Alusair, the ruling Steel Regent of the realm almost a century ago; familiar and unmistakable from all the portraits and tapestries in nigh every high house of Cormyr, her long hair flowing free and face set in anger—and her eyes seemingly fixed on him.

Arclath swallowed. He could see right through her, armor and long sword at her hip and all, and by the way she peered and turned her head from time to time, it was apparent she could hear but not quite see the two wizards as they stood talking, just outside his wardrobe.

"Grave enough," the Royal Magician was saying, "but hardly a surprise. You didn't call me here just to tell me *that*. What else?"

"The Royal Gorget of Battle is missing from its case," Vainrence replied flatly. "Which stands otherwise undisturbed, all its spells intact. And it was there an hour ago; I happened to walk past, and saw it myself."

Arclath raised an eyebrow. The gorget was *old*. An Obarskyr treasure that had lain in its case, proudly displayed in the Warhorn Room, for as long as he'd been old enough to remember what was where in the palace.

"Elminster again." Ganrahast sighed, slamming a fist against the wardrobe doors in exasperation.

One of them shuddered a little open, freezing Arclath's heart again. However, its movement caused the spell to wink out, restoring darkness and snatching away the furiously staring ghost.

Neither of the wizards seemed to notice either the door or that momentarily visible glow. They *must* be upset.

Through the gap, the young noble saw Vainrence nod and say eagerly, "However, *this* time we've got him. I thought he'd go for the gorget—he seems to prefer the older magics—so it's one of the twoscore I've cast tracers on. We can teleport as near as we choose to wherever he's taken it, just a breath or two after you give the order; the team is ready. Right now, Elminster's in the wildest part of the Hullack, and not moving. No doubt sitting around a campfire with his bedmate the crazed Witch-Queen, as they melt down the gorget together and feed on its power. Therlon reported in an hour ago; she blasted another steading to ashes, three nights back."

Ganrahast sighed again. "You're right. It's time we dealt with them both. Send in Kelgantor and his wolves. And may the gods be with them."

"Done, just as fast as I can muster them in the Hall of Spurs! They're more than ready for battle—and, mark you, Elminster and the Witch-Queen may once have been formidable, but they're a lot less than that now."

Ganrahast spread his hands. "So others have said, down the centuries. Yet those two are still with us, and the claimants are all gone to dust."

Vainrence waved a dismissive hand. "Aye, but she's now a gibbering madwoman and he's little more than an old dodderer, not the realm-shaking spell lion of legend!"

Ganrahast wagged a reproving finger. "Aye, I know legend has a way of making us all greater lions than we are . . . yet its glory must cling to *something*. Be sure Kelgantor's ready for the worst spell-brawl of his life."

"He is, and I'm sending a dozen highknights with him, if blades and quarrels are needed where spells fail. This time the old lion and his mad bitch are going down. While we still have an enchanted treasure or two *left* in the palace."

CHAPTER ONE

DARK DECISIONS

A little deeper into the wild heart of Hullack Forest than they remembered it being, the gaunt, bearded old man in dark rags and the tall, striking, silver-haired woman in leather armor came at last to a certain high rock in the forest.

"This is it," Elminster murmured grimly, looking at the upthrust slab of stone. Once it had been the base of the tallest tower of Tethgard, but all trace of the ruins were overgrown or swept away. Yet despite its innocuous appearance, he'd seen it more times than he cared to remember, in recent seasons, and knew this was the place. "Cast the spell."

Storm Silverhand nodded and stepped past him to find stable footing, as birds called and whirred around them, and the light of late day lanced low through the leaves.

Before them the rock thrust its small balcony out of the trees, spattered with bird droppings, but deserted. On its far side, a flight of stone steps descended into a tangle of wild thorns, stairs from nowhere to nowhere. Storm stared at the stony height for a long moment, like an archer studying a target, then tossed her head to send her long silver hair out of the way, and set about working her spell with slow, quiet care.

She looked as if a bare twenty summers had shaped her sleek curves and brought color to her cheeks. The Spellplague had done that, making her seem young even as it stole much of her magic, a jest as cruel as it was inexplicable. Only when looking into her eyes, and meeting the weary wisdom of some seven hundred years gazing back, did the world see something of her true age.

As she worked, an illusion of the man beside her slowly faded into view atop the rock, shifting from smokelike shadows to recognizable solidity. Not the gaunt Elminster at her elbow, but the Old Mage in his prime: burlier, sharp-eyed above a long pepper-and-salt beard, staff in hand, robes flowing, and arms flung wide in spellcasting.

Atop the rock this brighter Elminster stood, glowing vividly as it looked to the sky and spoke silent words, arms and hands moving in grand gestures of the Art . . . and nothing else happened.

A gentle breeze rose and trailed past them, rustling a few leaves, then faded again. The Realms around them was otherwise silent.

A silence that started to stretch.

"And now?" Storm asked.

"We wait," El said wearily. "What else?"

They retreated to the welcoming trunk of an old duskwood and sat together in the shade, staring up at the empty skies above, for what seemed a very long time before the wizard glanced sideways at his companion—and saw tears trickling quietly down her face.

"All right, lass?" he asked gruffly, reaching out a long arm to drag her against him, knowing how paltry the measure of comfort he could lend was.

She shook her head. "These shapings are the only magic I have left." Her whisper was mournful. "What have we become? Oh, El, what have we become?"

They both knew the answer. Though mirrors didn't shout it at them, silent reflections could still speak. They didn't go near mirrors often.

They were aging husks: Storm shapely and young-seeming, yet with her rich singing voice gone and almost all of her magic with it, and Elminster still powerful in Art but hardly daring to use his spells, because sanity fled with each casting. More times since the Year of Blue Fire than they cared to remember—perhaps more than either of them *could* remember—Storm had guided and cared for her onetime teacher after he'd seen this or that desperate need to hurl spells . . . and ended up insane for long seasons.

And he possessed a hunger.

A gnawing, desperate hunger for life and youth. Thanks to a crumbling cache that had once belonged to Azuth, he knew how to take over the bodies of the young and strong. By all the vanished gods, the spell was so *simple!*

So he was endlessly tempted. To snatch new bodies, and build new lives . . . or to die.

It was time and past time for oblivion, and they were so *tired* of the burdens of the Chosen, but somehow just couldn't give in to the last, cold embrace. Not yet.

Not after they'd hung on for so long, working here, there, and everywhere to set things right in the Realms. An unending task, to be sure, but there was *so* much more to do.

And there was no one else they could trust to do it. No one.

Every last entity they'd met since the blue fire cared only for his- or herself, or couldn't even see what needed doing.

So Storm and Elminster, agents of the mightiest goddess in the world no longer, went on doing what little they still could—a rumor started here, a rescue or a slaying there . . . still at the tiller, still steering . . . the work that had kept them alive this last century.

Someone had to save the Realms.

Why? And who were they to dare such meddlings?

They were the old guard, the paltry handful who still saw needs and cared. More than that . . . even with Mystra and Azuth both gone, *someone* still whispered in their dreams, telling them to go on sharing their magic among the poor and powerless, and working against evil rulers and all who used magic to harm and oppress.

Yet there was no denying they were growing ever weaker and more weary. This was the fourth time so far this year they'd come here, and it was only—what?—the fifth of Mirtul. A warm and early spring, aye, but still—

A hawk stooped suddenly out of the sky, hurtling down at the illusory Elminster.

"Well, at least she's not a stinking vulture this time," Storm murmured, finding her feet with her usual swift and long-limbed grace, and ducking hastily away into the trees. "I'll be back when you light the fire."

She still moved as quickly as ever; El found himself turning to answer only dancing branches.

So he swallowed his words and shrugged instead. 'Twas as well she'd taken herself so swiftly into hiding; these last few trips, the very sight of Storm had driven her sister wild.

The false Elminster vanished in an instant as talons tore through it.

Then the startled hawk flapped to an awkward landing and stood on the rock blinking, looking a little lost.

The real Elminster swallowed a sigh, pulled the stolen glowing dagger he'd brought with him out of its sheath in the breast of his robes, and crawled out onto the rock holding it out in offering. The feel of the magic would conquer her utterly.

A little meal first, to banish her wildness. When she was herself again, there would time enough to feed her the gorget and do her longer-lasting good.

A dreadful hunger kindled in the hawk's golden eyes, and she sprang at him, shrieking as her wings clapped the air.

As her beak closed on the blade of the dagger, the hawk melted and *flowed*, an eerie swirling of flesh that spun into a filthy, naked crone, wild-eyed and wild-haired, a bony old woman sucking on the weapon like a babe single-mindedly worrying a mother's teat.

There was a glow in her mouth as she sucked, heedless of the sharp steel—and the dagger melted away. Just as the magic he brought her always did.

She crouched on the rock like a panther, greedy mouth fighting to draw in the hilt, now, her body becoming larger, stronger, and more curvaceous. Her hair shone, she looked younger . . .

As she always did. For a little while.

For too many years now, his Alassra—The Simbul, the once proud Witch-Queen of Aglarond and the singlehanded scourge of Thay, the slave empire ruled by Red Wizards beyond counting—had been a frail husk of her former self. Dwelling alone and wild in the Dales, the Thunder Peaks, and the Hullack, shapechanging into endless guises, usually the shapes of raptors as she lapsed in and out of madness.

Magic always made her intellect and control brighten for a time, so for many seasons Elminster had been making these visits to the lady he loved. Or what was left of her.

Stealing, seizing, and digging out of ruins an endless stream of magic items, he had brought them here to this rock, for her to subsume and regain fleeting control over her decaying wits.

The Spellplague had not been a kind thing.

The dagger was gone, its pommel a brief pearl on her tongue that died with the last of the glow. Then her eyes were upon him and she was in his arms, weeping.

"El, oh, *El*," was all she could say, between her foul kisses. Her stink almost overwhelmed Elminster as she clung to him, wrapping her limbs around him, running her long fingers over all of him she could reach and clawing at his worn and patched robes to try to reach more of him.

"So lonely!" she gasped, when at last she had to free his mouth so she could breathe. "Thank you, thank you, *thank* you!"

She buried her face against his neck as the tears came, managing to gasp, "My love!" through their flood.

Elminster held her both tightly and with great care, as if cradling something very precious and fragile. As she clung to him and writhed against him and tried to bury herself *inside* him.

"My love," he murmured tenderly, as she started to really sob, her body shaking. It was always thus, and he smiled in anticipation of what she'd say next, knowing she'd not disappoint him.

"Oh, my *Elminster*," she hissed fiercely, when she had mastered her tears. "I've been so *lonely*!"

"So have I," he muttered, brushing the silver-haired crown of her head with his lips, "without ye."

That brought fresh sobs, but they were soon conquered; when her wits were her own, Alassra Silverhand was acutely aware of how precious every moment was. "What . . . what year is it, and what month?"

"The fifth of Mirtul, of the Ageless One," Elminster told her gently, knowing her next question before she asked it.

"What's been happening, while I've been . . . wandering?"

El murmured replies and comforting words of love as he held her in one arm, feeling among his pouches with the other. He fed her some rather squashed grapes from one, then strong and crumbling Aereld cheese from another, and finally the ruined remnants of some utterly crushed little raisin tarts.

"Ahhh, I've missed those," she said, savoring every crumb. Then a look of disgust passed over her face, and she peered around at the droppings and tiny bones strewn all over the rock. "What," she whispered, "have I been eating?"

"The usual," El told her soothingly. "Never mind that, my lady. We do what we must."

She shuddered, but that shudder became a nod. She let out a deep sigh and clung to him, arms tightening. "Oh, I've missed you, El. Don't leave me again."

"I've missed ye, too. Don't leave *me* again, lady mine."

The slayer of hundreds of Red Wizards smiled thinly through fresh, glimmering tears. "I'm through making promises I can't keep," she hissed. Her fingers clawed at him, at his tattered clothing.

Elminster's chuckle, as he drew her back from the rock into the little hollow cloaked in moss, was soft and teasing. He almost managed to keep the sadness out of it.

As night came down over the Hullack Forest, Storm turned back into the trees to make another stealthy circle around the stones of Tethgard, one more patrol guarding the couple now abed in the moss. As she slipped between the dark trunks like a watchful shadow, she let her face go wry for just a moment.

Alassra had always been the hardest of her sisters to love, though she'd worked hard to keep things trusting and not too distant between them. And as long as his beloved Witch-Queen lived, Elminster would see Storm only as a friend.

She wanted so much more, but neither El nor Alassra would learn that from her. Ever.

She held some measure of power over both of them, if she'd been the sort of worm to seek to wield it. The Simbul had been torn witless by the Spellplague, magic ravaging her mind; now, only magic made her sane.

Magic she'd accept only from Elminster. Magic he could only give her by letting the fires within her consume the frozen fires of enchanted items he brought her—because the Spellplague had marred *him*, too. Casting spells now plunged him into barking, drooling madness on the spot.

Unless one person—just one, in all Faerûn, for all she or he knew—healed him, with almost the only magic the Spellplague had left her. Storm Silverhand, the Bard of Shadowdale no longer. Now she was Elminster's healer, though they'd taken great care the Realms never learned that. By touch and will she could heal his mind, pouring her vitality into him shaped by the paltry Art left to her, to bring him back to sanity almost as fast as he lost it, if she stood with him. Time and again she had done so.

So the feared Witch-Queen needed magic to regain sanity for fleeting times, magic she trusted only Elminster to give her, and Elminster needed Storm if he was to work magic at all.

The very sight of Storm enraged Alassra whenever she was less than lucid, and El, damn him, trusted Storm as a friend, road-companion, and fellow warrior. Not as his lady.

"I am Storm Silverhand," she told the nearest tree in a fierce but almost soundless whisper. "And I want more. So much more."

They had lain together in each other's arms and watched the dusking sky above them . . . as one by one, the stars had come out.

She was asleep now, and dreaming. Moving against him, clinging to him for comfort, murmuring and caressing. Alassra was dreaming of making love to him again.

As still as he could keep himself, his arms going numb around her, Elminster lay awake, staring grimly up at the coldly twinkling stars.

A wolf howled, far off to the north, and there had been nearer hootings and rustlings from time to time, but El feared no foraging beasts; Storm was somewhere near, standing sentinel. She'd stolen out of the trees to stand silently looking at them both a little while ago, tears glimmering in her eyes as she stared down at her sister—but had gone again, a softly hastening shadow, when Alassra had stirred.

Leaving Elminster alone with his brooding.

How long would she stay herself this time? He needed to find more powerful magic, and have done with this business once and for all.

He was *tired* of feeding her little oddments of Art to win her a mere handful of days and nights of sanity, then do it all again for another paltry handful a few months hence. If he could lay hands on something *truly* powerful, that hadn't been twisted too wild by the Spellplague, he might be able to make The Simbul whole and sane again. There was risk, but he knew how.

The gorget he'd brought with him wasn't enough. It should buy her days, perhaps a month or more, and when she sank into deeper dreaming he'd feed it to her. When she'd have some time asleep for it to work its way through her.

Aye, he needed mightier magic. Not that he didn't need powerful enchanted items—whose wielding, unlike the casting of a spell, wouldn't plunge him into madness—for other uses. Such as destroying or at least blunting some of the more pressing dangers of the Realms.

Foes he once would have been able to blast at will, or misdirect into doing good they did not intend. Back when he dared use magic, back when he still had a body that would obey him.

Back when he was still someone.

Now Elminster of Shadowdale might not be much more than a shell, a husk of someone the Realms still needed, but no longer had. Was his Art fading? Or was his body failing him in more and more little ways, until it reached the edge of a cliff that would end in sudden, catastrophic collapse?

The worst of it was that he knew where so much powerful magic was . . . or had been. Yet the greater part of it was now lost, or buried, or walled away beyond his failing strength, or hidden from his fading senses. The mighty Elminster couldn't steal much more deftly than a good thief, these days; he was reduced to picking up fallen battle-spoils, or plucking whatever was left unguarded. Or swooping in after someone else did the finding for him.

Someone like that young fool Marlin Stormserpent back in Cormyr, who even now was seeking the nine ghosts he thought would swiftly slay all the war wizards and loyal Purple Dragons and rival traitor nobles alike, and deliver the Dragon Throne into his idle lap.

Lovely Laeral was gone, so there weren't nine deadly ghosts to be had. Yet there were still six, possibly seven—and if a certain Elminster commanded them, he could hurl back the shadows in Sembia and make the Forest Kingdom bright and strong again, a bastion for Harpers and those who had a talent for the Art but lacked training. A land where he could make mages trusted and respected again, and from which he could send them forth to deliver the rest of Faerûn from so much of its lawless, bloody chaos. New guardians, to take up the burden of defending the Realms from all who'd cheerfully destroy it while conquering it.

Or he could let Alassra consume them, and be restored.

That much power and that many memories would be enough to make her whole again, the twisting taint burned right out of her, to stand strong at his side, his lady love once more bright in all her power and fury. Together they could tame the Realms, and set it to rights.

So, the Crown . . . or the Mad Queen?

Ah, dark decisions . . .

Easily made, this time.

His Alassra.

Soft lips found his throat in the dark, just above his collarbone. She was still asleep, loving him in her dreams.

El smiled thinly. He loved the Obarskyrs and the Land of the Purple Dragon dearly, but it could all be swept away in scouring fire in an instant if that was what it would take to make his Simbul herself again.

To have his Alassra back, he would do anything.

Anything.

CHAPTER TWO

ANOTHER BOLD NIGHT IN BRAVE CORMYR

H*old!* What was that?"

The hoarse whisper came out of the night not much more than twice her arm's reach in front of her, where a cluster of duskwoods stood dark and tall. Storm Silverhand froze.

"Some scuttling furry thing. What else'd be creeping around the heart of Hullack at *this* time of night?" This second voice was thinner and sharper. It was also higher up, coming from somewhere in one of the trees in front of her.

"Elminster and The Simbul?"

"*Very* funny." Storm heard a faint scuffling as the second speaker clambered down to the ground before adding, "Well, I can't trace a thing. We're too close to the ruin. What's left of the tower's wardings won't keep a mouse at bay, but their decay is like a great seething hearth-cauldron in front of us, roiling and echoing. It may be silent and unseen, but it's all too damned effective at foiling my scrying magic. Trying to find those two with spells, if they're anywhere in front of us, is impossible." There followed a gusty sigh, then, "Heard anything more?"

Storm stood right where she was, thankful it was dark enough in the hollow that it was easier for the men to move by feel than by sight.

"No," said the first whisperer, a little doubtfully.

"Well, *I'm* not telling Kelgantor we heard a little rustling we can't identify, just once, and only for a moment."

Kelgantor. These were war wizards. Storm kept very still.

"What ruin?" the first whisperer hissed. "What sort of fool would build in the heart of the Hullack?"

"A long-ago fool, that's who. Your older colleagues tell me it was called Tethgard. Some fallen fortress from the bygone days of the realm, back when this Elminster—if he really *is* as old as all the legends say he is—was young. *You* know; when gods walked the earth, and Anauroch was all empty desert, and a dragon laired on every hilltop."

Ah. War wizards paired with highknights. Far more of them than just this pair, and probably led by Kelgantor, because that was what the battlemage Kelgantor did. All of them out here in the deep forest, creeping through the night, seeking Elminster and The Simbul. *Knowing* El and Lass were here.

There came the faintest of rustlings from the far side of the duskwoods.

"That *was* someone, to be sure," the second voice snapped. "When I—"

"Aye," a third voice growled disgustedly. "T'was *me*. Can't you two move through the Hullack without hissing like a pair of chambermaids hard at their gossip? Merlar, I know wizards of war can't take six steps without talking about it, but I expect better of you. I trained you."

"Sorry," the first whisperer muttered, so close to Storm that she could have reached out and slapped him without fully straightening her arm.

"Come," the third voice breathed, soft and deep, and Storm heard the faintest of footfalls on damp dead leaves underfoot. The newcomer was advancing straight toward Tethgard.

Straight toward El and Lass.

Merlar and the mage who'd been up in the tree moved to follow, and Storm moved with them, hidden amid their noise.

"Who's that?" another voice hissed out of the darkness on the other side of the three Cormyreans from Storm.

"Nordroun," the third voice replied flatly, "and who are you to be issuing challenges, Shuldroon? As I recall, you're supposed to be over on our other flank, with Kelgantor between us."

"I *am* between," came a new voice, cold and level. "The land rises, to our east, and its slope seems to have brought Shuldroon and his three straying back this way, bringing us all together. So halt, everyone, before someone's blundering ends in a blade finding friendly flesh in the dark. Sir Nordroun, call your roll."

"Merlar?" came the prompt whisper.

"Here," that highknight replied, from right in front of Storm. "Therlon is with me, and Starbridge our rearguard." Two nearby murmurs came out of the night as those men confirmed their presence.

"And I," Nordroun continued, "stand near enough to touch Merlar. My mage is Hondryn—"

"Here," a thin and unfriendly voice put in.

"—and Danthalus is my rearguard." Another murmur.

"Rorsorn?" Nordroun asked.

"I'm here, accompanying ranking Wizard of War Kelgantor and the mages Tethlor and Mreldrake. Jusprar's our rearguard."

Kelgantor gave his name with prompt, cold clarity, and the other three muttered theirs dutifully in his wake.

Shuldroon did not wait for Nordroun, highest ranking of all highknights in the realm notwithstanding. His tone of voice made it clear that he considered all highknights lackeys whose proper place was behind and beneath every wizard of war—and the sooner they all learned that, the better. "I am here, the knight Athlar is with me, and the knight Rondrand follows behind us." He was echoed by the two highknights confirming their presence.

"Anyone else?" Kelgantor asked, and a little silence fell.

"Good, we don't seem to have acquired any eavesdroppers," the leader of the force announced a few breaths later, his voice too flat and cold for anyone to dare to laugh. "Therlon, report."

"My spells can't detect the two we seek—or anyone else—ahead of us. The warding spells around Tethgard have decayed into an utter chaos of moving, ever-changing Art that foils all scrying magic. In both directions, I'd judge."

"I am less than surprised," Kelgantor replied. "Tethlor reported the same conditions. Enough delay. Rearguards, maintain your positions; all other knights, advance three paces, forming a front line as well as you can in this murk. We wizards will follow behind you. Rearguards, when you hear us start to move, follow on. No need for delay and little enough for caution, I'd say. Parley if it is offered, but strike back to slay without hesitation if magic is sent against us. Any queries?"

"Kelgantor," Tethlor said quietly, "Ganrahast warned us to be very careful. 'Beware Elminster,' he said. 'He's more formidable than he seems.' "

Kelgantor's voice came back a shade colder. "I've not forgotten that advice. Yet heading up the wizards of war does something regrettable but inescapable to every mage who's tried it; every Royal Magician I've known or read about has come to see lurking shadows behind every door, and whispering conspirators beneath every bed in the realm. Let me remind you that no lone wizard—no matter how old, crazed, or infamous—can hope to match us in battle."

"For my part," Shuldroon put in, "I don't think this Elminster is the one in the legends at all. *I* think a series of old men, down the passing years, have used the fell name of a long-dead mage to cloak their own lesser wizardries. And this self-styled Elminster who thieves magic from us now is the least of them all; an old hedge wizard who avoids casting every spell he can, bluffing his way into getting what he wants through fear of what the mighty Elminster of old might do if roused. I've heard he dare not cast the simplest spell, because he goes mad."

"We've all heard that," Nordroun said heavily. "I hope it's true."

Storm listened as they all started to speak. Kelgantor was the calm, level-headed, coldly ruthless commander of this force, a veteran war wizard, smart and decisive. Tethlor was competent, wary and loyal. Therlon she knew well; a good sort, along for his local knowledge, far less of a spellhurler than the others. Shuldroon was a zealous, overconfident killer, a youngling out to make his mark, with Hondryn his echo and crony. Mreldrake was a pompous, cowardly ass, a measure of how far the wizards of war had fallen these latter decades.

Aside from Eskrel Starbridge, whom she respected, the high-knights she knew less well. Nordroun was head of them all, and well regarded; Merlar was an able, amiable youngling, widely liked . . . and the rest were just names to her.

"Well, *I* think we'd best curl our line forward at both ends like a fork," Shuldroon was saying now, "to surround the ruins, or we'll end up huffing and puffing through these trees until dawn, with the two we seek fleeing just ahead of us. Or they'll climb trees or hide amongst the trunks, and we'll blunder right past, and—"

He broke off, then, as the air around them all seemed to smite the ears with a heavy blow that was felt more than heard, a surge of flaring unseen force that came charging soundlessly out of the trees to wash over them and race on, away through the forest behind them, trees creaking here and there as if bent in a gale, though no leaves stirred.

Wizards cursed. "Strong magic!" Hondryn snarled. "Flaring as if uncontrolled, just unleashed . . ."

"I felt it," Kelgantor snapped. "The old man has unbound an enchanted item. Forward! Quick, before he destroys another!"

Storm moved with them, knowing what that flare of magic had been. Elminster had just destroyed the gorget.

Its magic was flowing into someone right now, either the Old Mage or The Simbul . . . but if 'twas Lass, that flood had been so smooth and quiet, with the darkness unbroken ahead, that she must be asleep or unconscious, not her raving, seething, exulting self.

"No doubt he's stealing magic for himself," the war wizard commander added, as they hastened on, heedless of the din of snapping branches and rustling footfalls. "Know this secret of the realm, all of you: Elminster does indeed need magic to recover after every casting, or he goes a little mad for awhile. Not mere rumor, but observed and confirmed truth. He always heals himself in the end—but each time he works a spell, he goes erratic if it's a minor magic and barking madwits if he's unleashed something mightier. So all we need do is survive his first spell, and our foe will be a staggering madman, far too gone to work a second magic on us. So when you hear my owl-hoot in your minds—not with your ears; anything you hear will be a real owl—spread out and advance *very* quietly. We can't be far from him now."

"What if that was the gorget?" Merlar asked hesitantly. "Being destroyed, I mean?"

"Then their lives are forfeit," Kelgantor said flatly. "Slay them at all costs and by any means, no matter what they threaten or offer. *Move*."

The Cormyreans hastened, crashing through leaves and branches. Someone rather tunelessly chanted, "Another bold night in brave Cormyr," a line from the old ballad popular with the soldiers of the realm. Smiling at that, Storm faded back, seeking to drop behind them all and get clear.

"Not *now*," a highknight muttered beside her ear in the now-impenetrable darkness, mistaking her for one of the war wizards. "You should have emptied your bladder two ridges back, when Kelgantor gave the order. If we—"

Storm knew that cautious growl, and allowed herself a thin smile. Eskrel Starbridge was a grizzled old veteran . . . and one of the few current highknights she'd trust to defend Cormyr. Or do much of anything, for that matter.

So she turned and struck him cold almost gently.

Catching him in her arms before he could thud heavily to the damp leaves underfoot, she thrust the forefinger she'd dipped in her longsleep herb mix up Starbridge's nose to keep him down and slumbrous. Stretching him out gently on the sodden forest floor made no more noise than the boots of his nearest oblivious fellows ahead of them . . . and passed unnoticed.

As silently as she knew how, Storm set off through the trees in a wide, swift circle. She *had* to get to Elminster and Alassra before the Cormyreans did.

>———W———<

The gorget flickered feebly once as Elminster whispered the last word of the incantation. Then it tingled, dark once more, and started to sink into nothingness under his fingertips, melting amid a few wisps of smoke as its ancient magics flowed into Alassra.

She stirred in her sleep, frowning, probably dreaming of someone throttling her as the tips of El's fingers touched her throat through the fading metal . . . then smiled, her body seeming to grow more lush and strong under him, as the magic fed her.

Her eyelids flickered, and she purred like a satisfied cat, stretching and arching under him, ere murmuring, "Tremble, all, for the Witch-Queen is truly back . . ."

Her eyes opened, and her arms reached up to encircle him. "Oh, my Aumar," she said delightedly. "You've—"

The spell that struck them then flung them a few feet, wreathed in snarling flames that clawed at them but could not scorch. It tore them apart, to tumble away side by side, unharmed but furious. As if heeding a cue, the moon burst through the scudding clouds and flooded the tumbled rocks of Tethgard all around with cold, clear light.

Elminster cursed as he felt the soundless burst of sparks that meant the enspelled badge he'd recovered from a Sembian burial vault had just been destroyed, consumed in shielding Lass and himself from the attack. Which meant he had just one enchanted item left.

Without Storm's aid, he could withstand only one more hostile magic. Or hurl just one spell.

For her part, The Simbul was on her feet and glaring into the trees whence the attack had come, eyes afire. "Who *dares*—?"

"*We* dare, witch!" came the cold reply, as a dozen men strode just clear of the trees, some in dark war-leathers and bearing drawn swords. "You stand in Cormyr, and are subject to the king's justice! In his name we call on you to surrender, working no magic and offering no defiance, and submit to our will!"

"Submit to your will? Nay, I choose my own lovers," The Simbul told them coldly. "I do not submit to armed men who threaten me in the forest. You strike me as brigands, not men of the Crown. Those who uphold justice call polite parley from a distance, rather than hurling spells without warning at couples they espy in the night."

"You are the mages Elminster and The Simbul, and we have orders to arrest you and obtain from you the Royal Gorget of Battle, stolen from the Crown of Cormyr. We are wizards of war and highknights of the realm, not brigands, and we call again upon you to surrender! Lay down all weapons and work no spells, and you will be dealt with accordingly."

The men were moving again now, spreading out and advancing more swiftly at either end of their line, as if to encircle the couple amid the rocks.

"Where's Starbridge?" one of them muttered, looking suddenly to right and left along the line, but the man beside him—the one who'd called out to Elminster and The Simbul—waved a silencing hand, swiftly and imperiously.

"Leave us be," Elminster warned the Cormyreans, then cast a swift glance over his shoulder at a faint sound behind him. Storm was hastening up through the rocks to join them, crawling like a swift jungle cat. Heartened, he went to stand beside his lady, facing into the closing ring of men with her.

Seeing no signs of his quarry fleeing, the Cormyrean commander waved a hand, and two men strode forward from the closing ring. El recognized one almost immediately: Sir Ilvellund Nordroun, the head highknight of Cormyr. The other was a young war wizard he'd seen striding haughtily around the palace, whose name he didn't know.

"A parley, or are these two sent to wrestle us down?" Alassra mused calmly.

Elminster shrugged. "Perhaps thy reminder of proper courtesy stung them into this gesture. I've no doubt this will end in violence."

"I find myself less than surprised," The Simbul replied dryly, as the highknight and the mage came to a halt a careful four paces away.

"Yield the gorget," the young war wizard demanded. "Now."

"Youngling," Elminster said gravely, "ye stand in the presence of a queen. Can ye not manage a trifling minimum of courtesy?"

"This *is* courtesy," the mage flung back. "We could have just blasted you down."

"You could have tried," The Simbul replied almost gently, meeting his sneer with a look of disdain that made him flush and look away.

"You've heard our orders to you," he told them almost sullenly. "Obey, or face our lawful wrath—and your doom."

"Doom," Elminster murmured. "Villains always seem to love that word. I wonder why?"

"Villains? *You're* the villains here! *We* are lawkeepers of Cormyr, and stand for justice and good!"

The Old Mage sighed. "Are ye still such a child as to divide all the folk ye meet into 'good' and 'bad'? Lad, lad, there are no good people and bad people—there are just *people*, doing things others deem good or bad. If ye serve most of the gods well, ye should end up doing more good than bad. I try to do good things. Do ye?"

"I'm not here to bandy words with you, old man. Give us the gorget, and surrender yourselves into our custody. I warn you, we'll have it from you peacefully—or the other way."

Elminster and his lady traded calm looks, then faced the young war wizard together and said in unison, "No."

Shuldroon looked almost gleeful. "You seek to defy all of us? I remind you that you are overmatched six-fold by we wizards of war, and again by the highknights, the best warriors of the realm. See sense, man, and surrender."

Elminster scratched at his beard, looking almost bored. "So ye can slay me without a battle, is that it? Nay, loud-tongue, I've not lived so long by abandoning all my principles. Here's one ye younglings would do well to live by: if ye've done the right thing, stand thy ground."

"Sir Nordroun," the wizard commanded, "take and bind the woman. We'll see then if the old man wags his tongue quite so defiantly."

The highknight sighed. "That is less than wise, Shuldroon. I will take orders from Kelgantor, but not from you."

The young war wizard turned in swift rage. "Are my ears actually hearing—"

"They are," Storm Silverhand said in a level voice, rising up between Elminster and The Simbul with her sword in her hand. "And you should heed Sir Nordroun's wisdom, Wizard of War Shuldroon, and abandon any schemes of taking and binding anyone. A few loyal guardians of Cormyr might live longer, that way."

"And just *who* are *you*?"

"Storm Silverhand is my name."

"*Another* liar using a name out of legend?" Shaking his head and sneering anew, Shuldroon put one hand behind his back and gestured.

Behind him, the ring of Cormyreans around the three standing amid the rocks started to tighten. All save one man. Wizard of War Kelgantor, it seemed, had decided to hang back and watch, wands in both of his hands, ready to unleash magic when necessary.

Storm shook her head. "So it's to be another bold night in brave Cormyr," she murmured. She laid a hand on her sister's shoulder, finding it a-tremble with rage, and added, "Don't blast them just yet, Lass. We should warn them once more; give them another chance."

The Simbul's answer was a low, feline growl.

"We know you're scared to use your paltry magic," Shuldroon told Elminster. "And that you have taken to not using it in favor of menacing folk and trading on your fearsome—and borrowed— reputation. Unfortunately for you, old charlatan, we don't scare."

He took a step forward and struck a defiant pose, his shoulders squared and his hands on his hips, to add, "I'm not scared."

Elminster replied dryly, "Ye should be."

Read the rest of Elminster's adventures in

ELMINSTER MUST DIE

due out August 2010!

RICHARD LEE BYERS

BROTHERHOOD OF THE GRIFFON

NOBODY DARED TO CROSS CHESSENTA...

BOOK I
THE CAPTIVE FLAME
APRIL 2010

BOOK II
WHISPER OF VENOM
FEBRUARY 2011

BOOK III
THE SPECTRAL BLAZE
FEBRUARY 2012

...WHEN THE RED DRAGON WAS KING.

"This is Thay as it's never been shown before . . . Dark, sinister,
foreboding and downright disturbing!"
—Alaundo, Candlekeep.com on Richard Byers's *Unclean*

ALSO AVAILABLE AS E-BOOKS!

DUNGEONS & DRAGONS

FROM THE RUINS OF FALLEN EMPIRES, A NEW AGE OF HEROES ARISES

It is a time of magic and monsters, a time when the world struggles against a rising tide of shadow. Only a few scattered points of light glow with stubborn determination in the deepening darkness.

It is a time where everything is new in an ancient and mysterious world.

BE THERE AS THE FIRST ADVENTURES UNFOLD.

THE MARK OF NERATH
Bill Slavicsek
August 2010

THE SEAL OF KARGA KUL
Alex Irvine
December 2010

The first two novels in a new line set in the evolving world of the DUNGEONS & DRAGONS® game setting. If you haven't played . . . or read D&D® in a while, your reintroduction starts in August!

ALSO AVAILABLE AS E-BOOKS!